THE FRAUD

By the same author

THE FRAUD

Zadie Smith

PENGUIN PRESS

NEW YORK

2023

PENGUIN PRESS

An imprint of Penguin Random House LLC

penguinrandomhouse.com

ISBN 9780525558965 (hardcover)
ISBN 9780525558972 (ebook)

Printed in the United States of America
1st Printing

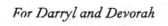

For Darryl and Devorah

VOLUME ONE

I've seen this great city of London pulled down, and built up again — if that's anything. I've seen it grow, and grow, till it has reached its present size. You'll scarcely believe me, when I tell you, that I recollect this Rookery of ours — this foul vagabond neighbourhood — an open country field, with hedges round it, and trees. And a lovely spot it was.

WILLIAM HARRISON AINSWORTH

I.

A Very Large Hole

A filthy boy stood on the doorstep. He might be scrubbed of all that dirt, eventually — but not of so many orange freckles. No more than fourteen, with skinny, unstable legs like a marionette, he kept pitching forward, shifting soot into the hall. Still, the woman who'd opened the door — easily amused, susceptible to beauty — found she couldn't despise him.

'You're from Tobin's?'

'Yes, missus. Here about the ceiling. Fell in, didn't it?'

'But two men were requested!'

'All up in London, missus. Tiling. Fearsome amount of tiling needs doing in London, madam . . .'

He saw of course that she was an old woman, but she didn't move or speak like one. A high bosom, handsome, her face had few wrinkles and her hair was black. Above her chin, a half-moon line, turned upside down. Such ambiguities were more than the boy could unravel. He deferred to the paper in his hand, reading slowly:

'Number One, St James-es Villas, St James-es Road, Tunbridge Wells. The name's Touch-it, ain't it?'

From inside the house came a full-throated *Ha!* The woman didn't flinch. She struck the boy as both canny and hard, like most Scots.

'All pronunciations of my late husband's name are absurd. I choose to err on the side of France.'

Now a bearded, well-padded man emerged behind her in the hall. In a dressing gown and slippers, with grey through his whiskers and a newspaper in hand, he walked with purpose towards a bright conservatory. Two King Charles spaniels followed, barking madly. He spoke over his shoulder – 'Cousin, I see you are bored and dangerous this morning!' – and was gone.

The woman addressed her visitor with fresh energy: 'This is Mr Ainsworth's house. I am his housekeeper, Mrs Eliza Touchet. We have a very large hole on the second floor – a crater. The structural integrity of the second floor is in question. But it is a job for two men, at the very least, as I explained in my note.'

The boy blinked stupidly. Could it really be on account of so many books?

'Never you mind what it was on account of. Child, have you recently been up a chimney?'

The visitor took exception to 'child'. Tobin's was a respectable firm: he'd done skirting boards in Knightsbridge, if it came to that. 'We was told it was an emergency, and not to dawdle. Tradesmen's entrance there is, usually.'

Cheek, but Mrs Touchet was amused. She thought of happier days in grand old Kensal Rise. Then of smaller, charming Brighton. Then of this present situation in which no window quite fit its frame. She thought of decline and the fact that she was tied to it. She stopped smiling.

'When entering a respectable home,' she remarked, lifting her skirts from the step to avoid the dirt he had deposited there, 'it is wise to prepare for all eventualities.'

The boy pulled off his cap. It was a hot September day, hard to think through. Shame to have to move a finger on such a day! But cunts like this were sent to try you, and September meant work, only work.

'I'll come in or I won't come in?' he muttered, into his cap.

2.

A Late Ainsworth

She walked swiftly across the black and white diamonds of the hall, taking the stairs two at a time without touching the banister.

'Name?'

'Joseph, ma'am.'

'It's narrow here – mind the pictures.'

Books lined the landing like a second wall. The pictures were of Venice, a place he'd always found hard to credit, but then you saw these dusty old prints in people's houses so you had to believe. He felt sorry for Italian boys. How do you go about tiling a doorstep with water coming right up to it? What kind of plumbing can be managed if there's no basement to take the pipes?

They arrived at the library disaster. The little dogs – stupid as they looked – skittered right to the edge but no further. Joseph tried standing as Tobin himself would, legs wide, arms folded, nodding sadly at the sight of this hole, as you might before a fallen woman or an open sewer.

'So many books. What's he need with them all?'

'Mr Ainsworth is a writer.'

'What – so he writ them all?'

'A surprising amount of them.'

The boy stepped forward to peer into the crater, as over the lip of a volcano. She joined him. These shelves had held histories three volumes deep: the kings, queens, clothes, foods, castles, plagues and wars of bygone days. But it was the Battle of Culloden that had pushed things over the edge. Anything referring to Bonnie Prince Charlie was now in the downstairs parlour, covered in plaster, or else caught in the embrace of the library's Persian rug, which sagged through the hole in the floor, creating a huge, suspended, pendulous shape like an upturned hot air balloon.

'Well, now you see, madam, and if you don't mind me saying' — he picked up a dusty book and turned it over in his hand with a prosecutorial look on his face — 'the sheer weight of literature you've got here, well, that will put a terrible strain on a house, Mrs Touchet. Terrible strain.'

'You are exactly right.'

Was she laughing at him? Perhaps 'literature' was the wrong word. Perhaps he had pronounced it wrong. He dropped the book, discouraged, knelt down, and took out his yardstick to measure the hole.

Just as he was straightening up, a young child ran in, slid on what was left of the parquet and overturned an Indian fern. She was pursued by a nice-looking, bosomy sort in an apron, who managed to catch the child moments before she fell through the house. 'Clara Rose! I *told* you — you ain't allowed. Sorry about that, Eliza.' This was said to the prickly Scot, who replied: 'That's quite all right, Sarah, but perhaps it's time for Clara's nap . . .' The little Clara person, in response to being held so tight at the waist, cried: 'No, Mama, *NO!*' — yet seemed to be addressing the maid. The boy from Tobin's gave up all hope of understanding this peculiar household. He watched the maid grasp the child, too hard, by the wrist, as mothers did round his way. Off they went. 'A late Ainsworth,' explained the housekeeper, righting the fern.

3.

A New Spirit of the Age

Downstairs, the *Morning Post* lay discarded by an uneaten break-fast. William sat brooding, his chair facing the window. There was a brown paper package in his lap. He started at the sound of the door. Was she not meant to see him in his sadness?

'Eliza! Miladies! There you are. I thought you'd abandoned me . . .'

The dogs arrived panting at his feet. He didn't look down or stroke them.

'Well, I'm afraid it'll be a week at least, William.'

'Hmmm?'

'The ceiling. Tobin only sent one boy.'

'Ah.' As she reached for his breakfast things he put a hand out to stop her: 'Leave that. Sarah will take that.' Then stood up, and seemed to glide away in his slippers, silent as a shade.

Something was wrong. Her first instinct was to check the news-paper. She read the front page and scanned the rest. No friends suddenly dead or disturbingly successful. No unusual or uniquely depressing news. More working men were to be allowed to vote. Criminals were no longer to be transported. The Claimant had been found not to speak a word of French, although the real Roger Tichborne grew up speak-ing it. She put everything back on the tray. As she understood it, Sarah's opinion was that breakfast trays were now beneath her dignity. Yet no maid had been hired to replace her, and so it fell to Mrs Touchet.

Turning to leave, she tripped on something – the package. It was a book, unwrapped only so far as to reveal the title: *A New Spirit of the*

Age, by R. H. Horne. It was a long time since she'd seen that book. Not quite long enough to forget it. She picked it up and looked furtively around the room – she hardly knew why. Opening it, she hoped she would be mistaken, or that possibly it was a new edition. But it was the very same volume of literary critiques, and with the same short, damning entry on her poor cousin, towards the back.

Twenty years ago, the publication of this book had merely darkly clouded one dinner party and mildly spoiled the morning after. Back then William was not so easily deflated. She brought the two sides of the torn brown paper together. No postmark. But it was addressed in a clear hand to the man whose life's work was summarized within as *'generally dull, except when it is revolting'*.

4.

The Lady of the House

A misfortune of the Tunbridge house: everything could be heard, room to room, top to bottom. But William walked the dogs each morning around eleven. As soon as the front door closed, Mrs Touchet moved to intercept Sarah. She found her kneeling in the downstairs parlour with her child, surrounded by splayed books with broken spines. Three stacks were being organized, evidently according to size. Mrs Touchet wondered if she might be of any assistance.

'No, we're getting on very well, thanking you, Eliza, I mean to say, very well without you . . . And you'll have lunch to be getting on with, naturally.' Lunch, too, now fell to Mrs Touchet. 'Hoo, Clara! Look at these! These'd be your dad's! Ainsworth, Ainsworth, Ainsworth, Ainsworth, Ainsworth.' This much, at least, the poor woman could read. Her face shone with pride. Eliza despised the part of herself that felt duty-bound to make a correction:

'But those are periodicals, Sarah, not novels. They will need to go over here with the *Bentley's* and the *Fraser's* . . . That's *Ainsworth's Magazine* — it had many contributors. But William began it and was the Conductor for some years. That is, the man who chooses the pieces and edits them. Now in fact he edits *Bentley's*, though for how much long—'

'Conductor! That's a manager, Clara. Nothing higher than Conductor!' Kneeling together, they seemed two daughters, side by side. 'Ooh, and look at him there!' Little Clara had picked up the July '34 issue of *Fraser's* magazine, issue number fifty, which promptly fell open to a handsome portrait of William as a young dandy. 'And all this writ underneath! Look!' Mother and daughter looked at it. Nothing followed, or could be expected to follow. Mrs Touchet sighed, stepped forward, and read the piece of puffery aloud to the both of them. Sarah listened intently and, when it was finished, clapped her hands in satisfaction.

'Ha! And he should have been well flattered by all that, naturally!' – said with great condescension, as if she'd written it herself. 'Clever girl you are, Clara Rose, to find your daddy's picture like that – and so handsome as he was in them days, and all them nice things said about him! That's luck, eh?'

But Mrs Touchet did not doubt they could find something similar in many of the magazines that lay before them. No one had ever accused William of being backward about putting himself forward.

'Imagine there's that many words writ about you and *by* you so that the floor caves in under the weight of it! Ha! Ha! Ha!'

'Sarah, may I ask something of you?'

'Naturally, you can' – stubby little fingers folded placidly in her lap, like the Queen herself – 'speak your mind.'

'Well, there was a package this morning—'

'So there was.'

'You didn't see who left it, by any chance?'

'It was on the doorstep. I pick it up and give it him, as anybody would, naturally.' Somewhere Sarah had got the idea that 'naturally' was the mark of a distinguished speaker.

'Well, I must ask, Sarah, that you alert me to the arrival of anything in the post – letters or books or packages that may come to the house – *before* you deliver them to William.'

'And it was him what asked this, was it?'

Eliza blushed, more in fury than embarrassment.

Sarah pressed her advantage: 'Cos I wouldn't imagine a housekeeper and the lady of the house would be having secrets between them two only that the gentleman did not know himself' – declared with great solemnity and with only one 'h' successfully sounded, at the beginning of 'only' — 'that don't seem right *nor* natural. And as I recall, when we first moved establishments, it was you what suggested that the big painting of him when he was young — it was *you* said that it mustn't be hung again, because he wouldn't like it no more, being old, *you* said — and then first time he walks in here he cries *"Where's my old Maclise!"* — meaning his portrait, because it was a fellow called Maclise what painted it — and naturally he weren't pleased, as he likes that picture of himself particularly as it turns out, so naturally I'd be asking him his own views on the post, I think, Mrs Touchet, if you don't mind.'

'Naturally.'

On her way out, Eliza passed under the lively eye of the old portrait by Maclise. Lively eye, lively sideburns, lively curls — none of it inaccurate at the moment of composition. Pretty like a woman, florid-cheeked like a baby. This, too, had been William.

5.

Liking William

Out in the hall, she had to sit on the stairs and take long, deep breaths. It was in this state that her cousin came upon her. He was sweating from the unseasonable heat and talking to himself about talking to himself.

'I said to myself: "*I'll think of my old Manchester stomping grounds; I shall use my memories of the old town and apply them to the Jacobite rebellion. I'll outline it all in my head between here and the train station and then go straight to my desk and begin.*" But – nothing. For some reason, Eliza, today I . . .'

Eliza knew the reason. She knew, too, that it was unspeakable between them. She stood up and followed him into the study. He sat at his desk, slapped the baize, groaned.

'Well, William, maybe the topic itself . . . You've written so much about the distant past.'

'You disapprove of the subject?'

On the contrary: 1745 was a subject close to Mrs Touchet's heart. Her mother was a passionate Jacobite – the family porridge bowls had the Stuarts' seal stamped on the bottom – and as a boy her father had been taken to Edinburgh, to witness Bonnie Prince Charlie entering Holyrood. But she could not pretend she considered the Lost Cause a good topic for William, for whom a little history went a long, long way. Looking into her future she saw herself very clearly, six months from now, seated at a desk, struggling through dense descriptions of the various types of dwellings to be found in the Outer Hebrides, perhaps, or an exhaustive list of the various kilts worn by the Royal Company of Archers—

'I see it in your face. You're grimacing. You disapprove.'

'Well, it might be that a more contemporary or personal theme . . .'

Wincing: '*Clitheroe* was not a success.'

'But that was a book about childhood.'

Sighing: '*They are in vogue.*' It was a quotation, and Mrs Touchet truly regretted ever saying it – ever suggesting it. Reading *Mervyn Clitheroe* had turned out to be nothing at all like reading *Jane Eyre*. Finishing it had left her with the odd impression that William had never been a child nor ever met one.

'I'm thinking now of your adult life.'

'Eliza, my adult life has been spent exactly so.' He picked up a pen, but halfway through his mime put it down, distraught. That handsome young buck of the '30s, hair slick with Macassar oil, had somehow become this whiskery, jowly, dejected, old man.

'But all those interesting dinners!'

His mouth turned down sadly as if to say: *I have lost my taste for them.*

'The truth is, William, fiction is made of fascinating characters and you have been surrounded by fascinating characters all your life.'

'Hmmm. You didn't think so at the time.'

'I always thought so! I was only annoyed at endlessly refilling port bottles.'

'Hmmm.'

'William, if you are implying that I'm one of these fools who let the present fame of certain people distort my own memories, I can tell you I took the measure of you and all your clever friends long ago, and my measure hasn't changed.'

But even as she spoke, she thought, disloyally, of *A New Spirit of the Age* – presently burning on a pile of splintered floorboards in the garden. There they all were, those spirits of an earlier age, for whom she had once poured drinks and roasted chickens. Quantified, described, flattered, critiqued, measured. William's entry the shortest by far. A fact the editor, in his chapter on her cousin, had made clear he considered a mercy to a man *usually spared in public, because so much esteemed and regarded in private.* She remembered Richard Horne: he was one of the clever young men she had regularly fed and watered, back in the Kensal Rise days, and it was her memory that he, in common with everyone else around that dinner table, had liked William very much. But liking William and reading him had long been vastly different matters. Which reminded Eliza that what she had said was true – within very narrow confines. She had taken the measure of William and his friends long ago, had always known who had talent and who did not, and as long as her cousin asked no further questions, her discreet, ironic and yet absolute God would wink at it.

6.

The Mystery of Pain

All autumn, Mrs Touchet kept a close eye on the post. But William never mentioned the package and nothing similar arrived. By late November she had forgotten all about it. Larger matters occupied her. Tunbridge was a failure: the garden was small and shaded and from his desk he could hear the train. They would move again in the spring. But what was, for William, only a matter of speaking a sentence aloud, would entail, for his cousin, many months of planning and organization. At night, dreams of trunks plagued her. They were the same trunks from last year except they were full, and pointing this out to blank-faced cartmen, over and over, constituted the dream. She was irritable with everybody. She could not keep her temper with Sarah, the child, the dogs, or even with *To Whom It May Concern* at the county office of Births, Marriages and Deaths:

You misunderstand my previous letter. In this case it is expressly desired that the wedding, though conducted in a church, be effected by private licence, with no banns read.

The licence arrived in February. The groom was too busy for paperwork. Having recently given up the subject of the Manchester Rebellion – 'for the time being' – he was instead embarking on a novel 'set partially in Jamaica', an island upon which he had never set foot. ('Yes, but Eliza, neither have I lived through the Restoration, or been a highwayman, or met Guy Fawkes.') The bride, for her part, was unable to mark anything on paper aside from an X. It fell to Mrs Touchet to provide the particulars. Writing the basic facts gave her a light-headed feeling:

Sarah Wells, aged 26, of Stepney; maid.
William Harrison Ainsworth, aged 63, of Manchester; widower.

Maid! In one sense only. Further down the licence, out of brutal expedience, she killed off Sarah's parents with a stroke of her pen, unwilling to put 'Boot-black' and 'Prostitute' under their respective professions. As she was not asked about any child she did not mention one. Contrasting with these painful omissions, it was a pleasant, melancholy thing to write out the name of dear, decent Thomas Ainsworth, solicitor, of Manchester, long dead, and his sweet though dim-witted wife, Ann, also dead. For almost three years she had been married to their nephew. These good people had made generous appearances at her wedding, her son's baptism, and the joint funeral of her little family, felled by scarlet fever, five days apart. She remembered Ann at the wake, her kindly hedgehog face framed by a quantity of black crêpe, attempting to bring comfort:

'Pain is a mystery. Who knows why it is visited upon us! We can only bear it.'

'But I know why.'

'Oh, poor Eliza! You don't imagine any meaning may be drawn from this tragedy! It is mystery, only.'

'No. It is a punishment.'

Ann's hazy, muddle-headed vision of ultimate reality had been, in Eliza's view, the unavoidable consequence of being brought up in the wrong church, the only child of a Unitarian minister.

7.

The Flitch of Bacon

On a bitter afternoon in March, Eliza took a pew beside William's three
middle-aged daughters, while the fourth and youngest squirmed in her
arms. In front of her sat William's unfortunate brother, Gilbert, making
strange noises and wagging his head. If either the noises or the wagging
became excessive she had been instructed to put a hand to his shoulder
and lead him out. The groom, the bride and the vicar made up the rest
of the 'wedding party'. Christ Church. Only a dozen years old, yet the
front looked like a medieval Italian monastery, the back a Domesday
vicarage. Still, the one, true Roman Catholic sun was filtering through
the dour and narrow Protestant windows, and this lent the space something holy, despite everything. In this light she now tried to lose herself.
Away to a happier ceremony, one wet July day, over a decade ago. The
little village of Dunmow. At the very moment when the rain – which
had threatened to ruin everything – suddenly cleared, and the sun burst
through and bathed in buttery light two couples dressed for a country
wedding. One couple was young, beautiful, from the village itself; the
other middle-aged, handsome, German – old friends of William's. All
four were held aloft on wicker chairs and trailed by villagers through the
country lanes – women with flowers in their hair, men in their best
suits – until they reached Dunmow Town Hall, itself bedecked in pop-
pies and loosestrife. There William had sat in a throne on a raised dais
and given an interminable speech, just like a vicar, although, in Eliza's
memory, this speech could be mercifully and radically truncated:

'We are gathered here today to revive an ancient tradition of this place, that is, the contest for the *"Dunmow Flitch"* ' – cheers from crowd, posies of flowers waved – 'a custom which, though so ancient we find it in Chaucer, has not been celebrated here these past hundred years, for it has, like so many traditions of our impoverished island, been lost to that relentless machine "progress" ' – unconvincing boos – 'but which it is my delight to remember and preserve, as my novel *The Flitch of Bacon, or The Custom of Dunmow* makes evident, and upon the popularity of which I dare to presume I have been invited here today!' Confusion from villagers, enthusiastic nod from Mayor . . .

A side of bacon was to be awarded to the couple who could prove, before a 'jury of their peers', that they had been blissfully married for a year, with no cross words spoken in the preceding twelve months. Mrs Touchet, the Mayor and William formed the jury. It was all very jolly, and in the end William – constitutionally unable to disappoint anybody – had awarded a flitch to both happy couples. Several London reporters were in attendance, so no one was happier than William. Then out they all bustled into the sun for a parade. Someone had taken the lyric from the novel and set it to music:

> *You shall swear by Custom of Confession,*
> *That you ne'er made nuptial transgression;*
> *Nor since you were married man and wife*
> *By household brawls or contentious strife,*
> *Or otherwise at bed or at board*
> *Offended each other in deed or word:*
> *Or since the parish clerk said Amen*
> *Wished yourselves unmarried again:*
> *Or in a Twelvemonth and a Day*
> *Repented not in thought any way.*

William's lyrics were the best of him. The parade route ended at a daisy-flecked field, where the couples knelt on stones – per the custom — and accepted their bacons. Merriment ensued. Too much merriment: on the train back to London, Eliza pretended to sleep to hide the effects of an excess of cider. And this absurd custom had continued each year since, or so she'd heard: they'd never been back. The only force comparable to an Ainsworth enthusiasm was the speed with which it passed. But how happy he had seemed that day compared to this!

William and Sarah walked up the silent aisle. 'Mother's dress!' whispered Fanny — the oldest and severest of the daughters — to practical Emily, and ever-wounded Anne-Blanche, who began quietly weeping. Upon their mother's death, one of Mrs Touchet's first duties — after moving permanently into the Ainsworth household — was to pack all Mrs Ainsworth's dresses carefully in tissue paper, so that they might be preserved for her daughters to wear, one day. When a woman dies so young — at only thirty-three — her dresses will be well preserved anyway. They will not need much alteration to remain in fashion, thirty years later. But no one ever wore them like Frances. The first Mrs Ainsworth had been slight, fair-haired. Elegant. In this dress. In all dresses. And it was only by thinking of that original, beloved, long-dead woman — to whom no flitch could ever have been awarded — that Eliza was able to produce the tears appropriate to the occasion.

8.

The Ainsworth Sisters

Back at the house, the bride went to put Clara down for a nap. The vision of a wake returned. Such was the grim silence in the parlour, broken only by Gilbert's wagging and wailing. Eliza struggled with a feeling of exasperation. She had practically raised these girls: she was fond of them. But why couldn't they be married? It was all that had ever been asked of them. Only the youngest, Anne-Blanche, had managed it, and only recently, at the grand old age of thirty-seven, and to a man with no real money. Fanny and Emily lived with and looked after Gilbert in Reigate. Yet they had all been beauties, once, and much admired. Something had gone wrong somewhere.

Anne-Blanche wept. Emily brewed tea. Fanny finally managed to ask a series of pointed questions that made no pretence of disguising their financial motive. What, in the end, had been decided about their grandparents' Manchester home? Sold – at a loss. William had also been forced to sell Beech Hill, their country place, six months prior. *Bentley's Miscellany* he had just sold back to Bentley. In fact, truth be told, they could not really afford London any more.

'But I see there's a new serial?' tried Emily, valiantly. '*On the South Seas*?'

The novel in question, his twenty-sixth, was called *The South-Sea Bubble, A Tale of the Year 1720*. It was serialized in a weekly rag called *Bow Bells*, but no one in the year 1868 was buying or reading it, not even Eliza, who had the manuscript at her disposal.

'Agaaryyyuu,' moaned Gilbert, and wagged his head. 'GUGGA-AWOO.'

'Shhh . . . It's all right.' William put a tender hand to the old man's cheek. 'No one's angry, dear brother. We're only discussing what's best for everyone.'

It was not best for Mrs Touchet that Fanny and Emily be invited to move with them to West Sussex, but she now understood this inevitability to be mere moments away. As if to forestall it, Sarah ran in wearing an old house dress, a little coal dust on her nose, her mighty bosom freed from the constraints of her predecessor's gown.

'Hip, you'll never guess what the coal-boy just told me! That Tichborne fella's mum's only gone and bloody died! It's all over the papers. Well, someone please tell me: who'll believe the fat bastard now?'

9.

'I'm a writer'

The first time Mrs Touchet was called upon to rescue the Ainsworth girls they were too small to know it. Fanny was three, Emily only a year, Anne-Blanche a babe in arms. Their young mother, never robust – and overwhelmed by three children in so many years – wrote to Eliza for help. Her young husband had gone to Italy. Why had he gone to Italy?

> *I cannot tell you exactly why; I am not literary and do not understand his explanations, which tend to be literary. It was hoped he would follow his father into the law – he is a qualified solicitor. My own father tried to establish him as a bookseller and publisher, but as you know William has no head for business. Last month, after losses on all sides, he gave it up. It was my understanding he would return to the law. Now he has surprised us all and gone to Italy. He says he is almost 25 and must see beauty and write.*
>
> *I enclose his last letter from Venice which has many descriptions of the landscape. As someone who has known such intimate difficulty in her life, I hope I am not mistaken in the hope that you might accompany and advise me in mine,*
> *Yours with great affection,*
> *Anne Frances*
> *Elm Lodge, Kilburn*
> *March 12th, 1830*

On the crowded coach down from Chesterfield, Eliza had tried to puzzle out the situation. Regarding William, what surprised her was that anyone could be surprised. She did not claim to know him well, but the first thing he ever said to her was: *I'm a writer and I've no intention of being anything else.* A sentence that stuck in her mind: he was fifteen years old at the time. She herself was then twenty-one, and recently married to his Derbyshire cousin James Touchet. Invited to dinner with the Manchester Ainsworths, she was glad to find the extended family cheery, uncomplicated, undramatic people, with none of the fiery or melancholic tendencies she had begun to notice in her husband. But drama there was: after pudding, the newly-weds were handed a home-made playbill (*Ghiotto: The Fatal Revenge. Being a new Melodramatic Spectacle By William Harrison Ainsworth*) and ushered into the basement to watch a one-act play, performed by the Ainsworth brothers. Poignant to remember that Gilbert had been the more dashing of the two, and the better actor. Though who could do much with this dialogue? *Rave on, ye elements! Ye thunders roll! Flash on, strange fire, ethereal visitant!* Even as an adolescent, William fatally overestimated the literary significance of weather. His play was ghastly – and long. Afterwards, he bounded up and paid her special attention, as if he had somehow guessed at her marital misery. He had long eyelashes, a lovely face like a doe. He flirted like a grown man. Her impression was of an exceptionally forward, driven boy, with ambitions far outstripping his ability.

And yet! A few weeks later, at Chesterfield, a copy of *Arliss's Pocket Magazine* arrived, with *Ghiotto* in its pages. He even had a pen name: T. Hall. More issues followed, with ingenuous, self-flattering notes attached:

Dear Mrs Touchet,
    This month I have the very great pleasure of sending you a literary pastiche by our 'Mr Hall', in which he purports to have

discovered the previously forgotten work of the seventeenth-century dramatist 'William Aynesworthe' – and quotes from him extensively ha ha – which bold act of fraud I dare to hope will delight and fool the reading public, and bring you, especially, as much pleasure as its humble author had in the writing of it,

    Most sincerely yours,

        W. Harrison Ainsworth

Not long after came a first book, under a new pseudonym: *Poems by Cheviot Ticheburne*. It was dedicated to Charles Lamb, whom this ambitious young man had somehow already befriended. Mrs Touchet could not get on with these poems: they were infused with romantic regret for 'our long lost youth in the fields' and those 'dear playground days that fadeth too, too fast', although she happened to know the poet had left school only a month ago and was now apprenticed at his father's law firm. Law briefly impeded the torrent of words. The only letter she received from William that autumn brought the sad news of his brother's head-first fall from a horse, an accident from which it was then imagined Gilbert would 'soon recover'.

IO.

'My prime of youth is but a frost of cares'

Aged eighteen, he sent his first book of stories. There was no way he could have known it, but *December Tales* arrived on a day of utter desperation and misery for Eliza – in fact, she planned for it to be her last. For an epigraph, William had chosen the famed verse by Sir Chidiock Tichborne, that failed assassin of the Virgin Queen, that poor, misguided martyr to the true faith . . . Like any good convent girl, Eliza had read these lines many times over the years. Never before had she been unsure as to whether or not she would survive them:

> *My prime of youth is but a frost of cares,*
> *My feast of joy is but a dish of pain;*
> *My crop of corn is but a field of tares,*
> *And all my good is but vain hope of gain:*
> *The day is fled – and yet I saw no sun,*
> *And now I live – and now my life is done!*

She survived. With shaking hands she took the cord she had been considering for length and strength and threaded it back through her husband's dressing gown. If old Tichborne could be hung, drawn, quartered, have his guts dragged through the streets of Elizabethan London, and still keep his eternal soul, so might Mrs Touchet keep hers, despite all her suffering.

It was a long time before she read the book itself. But she preferred stories to poems, and when she did get to it, she read it all the way through. Not much had changed. Lightning continued to *blaze from the sky in vivid sheets*, preposterous murders happened for no earthly reason, graves opened, ghosts walked, nobody said or did anything sensible, all the women seemed utterly out of their wits, clothes and furniture were minutely described, and blood was either 'running cold' or spurting continually. But! Broken herself, desperate for any world beyond her own, she fell into its pages. And found herself smiling for the first time in many months at the description of one Eliza, a black-haired mystery woman, whom the bigamist narrator of 'Mary Stukely' feels compelled to marry, although he is already married to 'fair Mary':

> *She was above the middle size, of a commanding appearance, and the most expressive countenance I think I ever beheld. She was not, perhaps, what many might call beautiful, but I never knew any one who possessed so much the power of interesting at a first look. There was perceivable too a lurking trace of the darker passions . . .*

She was then twenty-four. For three years she had been married. In the first year she learned she could not be a wife. In the second, that she could be a mother – that she was one. In the third she came to understand that no matter what she thought she was, a mother had no more rights over her child than a slave has over his life. Wherever James Touchet had now absconded with her dear Toby she had no means of discovering it, no recourse to the law, and therefore no hope of the child's return. But even if she had possessed the legal right she knew she had no moral one. If her husband was a drunk, well, hadn't she driven him to it? If he had left her in the middle of the night, fleeing with the child, wasn't it because he knew what she really was? How he knew, she couldn't make out. But some knowledge is beyond language.

11.

A Hundred Pounds a Year

Her husband and child were gone. To whom could she turn? Who
would intercede on her behalf? Her father was dead; she had no brother.
She remembered her husband's young literary cousin, presently training in law. She wrote a humiliating letter. He appeared on her doorstep
the next day, almost by return of post, looking even younger than she
remembered, and dandified as the Count d'Orsay. Ridiculous curls
about the face, a pristine blue tailcoat with brass buttons, shiny boots
you could see your face in, an elaborately tied yellow cravat. But he
was her only hope, and proved discreet and kind. He asked for no
details, only enquiring after the names of any acquaintances James
might have in London. Within a week he had a lead, and then an
address in Regent's Park. He wrote to Eliza asking permission to 'patch
this silly lovers' quarrel'. He promised to bring his cousin back to his
senses. Mrs Touchet did not expect nor wish for reconciliation: she only
wanted her child. She had never known a man to take care of a baby.
She had no faith in the possibility. All her prayers were therefore with
the nursemaid, Jenny, who had disappeared with them. But even this
prayer turned out to be poison. It was Jenny who brought them the
fever.

The news of their deaths William delivered himself, not by letter but
in person, and so he was there when she fell to the flagstones in the hall.
He caught her. He lay her down. He called the doctor. He instructed
the maid in her care. He dealt with all the particulars with a tact she
considered remarkable in one so young. And when the will was

discovered, and the time came to consider her future, she was implored to leave 'everything to the capable gentlemen of law in my father's office'. But it turned out to be the professional opinion of these men that the will of Mr James Touchet was hastily composed, 'shameful and ill-written' and could not possibly be read aloud to any respectable woman. It had been written in the 'throes of fever, which is known to affect the brain' and was 'unworthy of any decent Christian'. It left Eliza no provision whatsoever. Aside from this salient detail, William revealed nothing more about its particulars, and she did not press him, not at the time nor ever after. It was enough to know that her young cousin – though he had surely read the ugly accusations she presumed the will contained – did not seem to revile her. On the contrary, he declared himself 'devoted' to her protection, and determined to secure her an annuity. 'Be assured: we will wheedle that side of the family out of a small portion of their Jamaican fortune. Everyone knows Samuel Touchet died a bankrupt, but the Touchets themselves were never as poor as they pretended, including your James . . . plenty was squirreled away before our notorious ancestor strung himself up from the bedposts!' This much he managed. A hundred pounds a year. If she lived quietly it was enough.

Now she was thirty-one. The pain had not gone though it had settled: it was the foundations of the house of herself. But if she was different from the other people squeezed into that crowded coach, heading to London, she didn't think it visible. She felt certain she looked like any other woman of her class. Self-contained and sensible, clutching a reticule, a satchel and a carpet bag, for unlike the gentry and the poor, drastic changes in one's situation were always possible, and it was best to be prepared. And this was the second puzzle of Anne Frances' letter: what was Eliza Touchet's role, now, in life? She understood that she was the bereaved. That she had suffered. But didn't everybody suffer? Perhaps she was the one to whom suffering had come relatively early, bestowing upon her special insight. She was that poor young widow who had known 'intimate difficulty'. She was the mother whose child had died of scarlet fever, far from home, in a strange city, in an Irish nursemaid's arms. She was one to whom the worst has occurred. And what did this mean to people? That she could help? Why did they think that?

12.

Visiting Elm Lodge, Spring 1830

It was no doubt a mark of bad character but she did not like the countryside. She lived in it but she did not like it. Edinburgh was in her bones. Cities were in her bones. Her fellow passengers could complain of smuts and smells, of the incredible chaos of carriages and wagons, but Eliza enjoyed her glimpses of a Mayfair wedding, a woman hitting another woman with a broom on the Charing Cross Road and a band of Ethiopian minstrels outside Westminster. Too soon the fascinating *mêlée* of Oxford Street came to an end. As they rounded Tyburn Tree, she discreetly prayed for the souls of the martyred before settling into the long rural boredom of the Edgware Road. Fields as far as the eye could see.

At the Red Lion the horses were changed. Eliza decided to walk the final half-mile through pretty Kilburn as a penance. Look at the lamb that springeth through the bluebells, she told herself, but in all honesty the lamb didst bore her. Instead she took mental note of the order of inns – the Cock Tavern, the Old Bell, the Black Lion – and of the distance to Kilburn Wells, where a young mother could take the waters and Mrs Touchet might get a good pot of shrimp. *I'll stay three weeks – at the most a month. I'll make it very clear from the beginning. I have my own course in life and – thank God – my own annuity, and I do not need anyone or anything. This I will make very clear.* No one passed Mrs Touchet on the road except a toothless farmer driving a crowd of pigs with a stick, but she felt even he could see that this tall, resolute woman, carrying three bags without help, needed no one and nothing.

She hadn't counted on the pleasure of being needed.

'Eliza! But you're so much taller than I imagined!'

Anne Frances Ainsworth stood in the doorway of Elm Lodge, a plain square house covered in climbing roses and surrounded by elms. Her yellow hair hung loose at her shoulders. Eliza thought her features finer than her picture. She had a look of pure simplicity on her face – as if it had never occurred to her to say anything but exactly what she was thinking – and she was crawling with children – they clung to her legs and hung from her arms. Practical Eliza put her bags down where she stood, under an apple tree, and stepped forward to take the baby. Toby weight. Toby smell.

'You must call me "Annie" – William does, everybody does.'

But Eliza already sensed that she herself wanted to be, in the mind of this Anne Frances, separate and distinct from 'everybody'. She would call her Frances.

'It's so good of you to come. So good. Yesterday I learned we're to lose our Ethel: she means to marry a Willesden boy from Mapesbury Farm! It's a poor match but there you are. Which will leave only Eleanor, and she has her hands full with the kitchen. Oh, but you are good to come!'

The strange thing about good people, Eliza had noticed, was the manner in which they saw that same quality everywhere and in everyone, when in truth it is vanishingly rare.

13.

Taking the Waters at Kilburn Wells

She had arrived at Elm Lodge on the twenty-third of April, 1830. Ever after she marked the day in her heart. No language attended it. No conscious ritual. If asked what the date meant to her she would have spoken the truth and called it St George's Day and denied attaching any personal significance to it. But somewhere deeper, past language, it was marked. A cluster of sensations. The climbing rose. Frances in the doorway. That first, unmistakeable, impression of her goodness. The feeling of walking down grassy Willesden Lane, early in the morning, plucking wildflowers out of the hedgerows and trying to appreciate them. The happiness of knowing she would soon turn round and walk back to a house of steamed rags and strung-up rabbits, drying linens and chubby baby ankles, small hands with food on them, the smell of bacon, fruit cakes wrapped in cloth, the swampy whiff of pea soup, and the simplest chords of Bach played clumsily but with good humour. All of this warm human sacred business she had almost forgotten existed.

In her conscious record of that period she knew that three weeks passed like the mayfly. Everyone was glad she had come. She proved extremely competent, both with the children and the household. She was 'a godsend'. And given the housemaid's sudden absence, and the fact that the two oldest girls, Fanny and Emily, kept waking each other up – while Cook Eleanor, tired of sleeping on the kitchen floor, coveted the maid's old room – given all this, it simply made sense that Fanny and Emily be separated, and Eliza give up her room and share a bed with Mrs Ainsworth.

On the day she'd marked as her latest possible departure, she found herself instead walking to Kilburn Wells with Mrs Ainsworth, arms linked.

'It's silly, but I think Kilburn sunsets are prettier than anywhere.'

'That *is* silly.'

'But you'll admit it is a beautiful sky? Yes, you will. Pink and orange – like blossom!'

'Admitted, but I also admit we could see something just like it in Stamford Hill.'

'Oh, Lizzy, you really have the sharpest tongue—'

'That you've heard anywhere? I promise you there's sharper.'

'Never on a woman.'

'You can't have been to Edinburgh.'

They talked nonsense. Every word was illuminated. The children were back at the house with Cook Eleanor. They carried nothing but themselves down the street. Such lightness! Even as they approached the gardens, and joined the noisy, pleasure-seeking crowds, even then, the halo encircling them somehow persisted. They were unusual in the scene. Two women sitting at a table alone, unencumbered by children, parents, or noisy husbands pontificating about the American situation or running down the Whigs. Normally she did not care for organized leisure nor the kind of people who sought it out, but this evening she did not begrudge them the eating of shrimp with their mouths open, or their smoking of cigars, or the loud slurping of 'health tea' brewed with dubious water. Although perhaps her face said otherwise.

'Oh dear . . . Cook was right. She said: "Eliza won't like it – she won't like all the people and noise and she won't approve." Eleanor's funny – she worries you're too clever for us . . . And I suppose it *is* a bit of a silly fad . . . We can go home if you prefer? Only, I said to Cook: "Once upon a time there was an Abbey on this very spot and so it will be as good as holy water to Lizzy." '

'All water is holy water.'

It was as if even the little misunderstandings were placed in their path deliberately, to better illustrate the workings of grace.

14.

Grace

Eliza Touchet believed that there was no justification or reason that could possibly be offered for the colour red, trees, beauty, an eyeball, a carrot, a dog or anything else on this earth. Like all human beings she found herself seeking reasons regardless. But what justification can be offered for love? *It is because she is good.* Still, the undeniable fact remained that Frances, whatever else she might be, was also a Baptist. (Soul Competency meant nothing to Mrs Touchet. She knew all too well how incompetent souls tend to be, starting with her own.) On the other hand, it was this same Baptist church, with all its flaws, that had led Frances to the abolitionist cause. And it was Frances who, in turn, had succeeded in transforming a hazy, unformed distrust of human bondage in Mrs Touchet into a burning loathing – a feeling equally undeniable in its force, if a little hard to extricate from other feelings presently burning within her.

Am I not a Brother and a Man?

Previously, whenever Mrs Touchet had considered this sentence, she had found it vaguely distasteful. She had never – when giving alms to beggars, prostitutes and worse – found it necessary to invent a sentimental family relation between herself and those to whom she gave charity. The very first 'meeting' she attended with Frances she had found somewhat comic – overly earnest. But in a few short months Anne Frances effected a revolution in Mrs Touchet's heart and mind. Together they listened to the harrowing eyewitness reports of Jamaican ministers, and were shown shackles and whips – Mrs Touchet had held an iron collar in her hands. She signed old petitions, began new ones, sewed, baked and wrote letters to raise money for visiting American speakers. In Exeter House, in June, she listened to a stolen son of Dahomey, black as the ace of spades, speaking from a lectern as eloquently as Peel himself. And now, when Eliza read the Psalms, and considered the bond-servant Joseph, he was no longer an abstraction. He was a suffering son of Dahomey, with infected, suppurating welts across his back.

What was all of this, if not grace? A grace that kept happening, extending itself through time, as if The Elms and everyone in it had fallen through an un-darned hole in the pocket of this world. Their little life of domestic contentment. A home of women and girls, at ease with one another. Moral improvement, charitable works, quiet prayer. Grace. And William's letters were full of blessed delay: *I have decided to go on to Switzerland.* Two months later: *I am returning to Italy.* Grace. One thing permitted and made possible the other, even if the logic was shrouded, too mysterious to penetrate. Like a finger. Like two penetrating fingers. Like two fingers penetrating a flower. In complete, candle-less darkness. As if the fingers and the flower were not separate but one, and so incapable of sinning the one against the other. Two fingers entering a bloom not unlike the wild ones in the hedgerow – layered like those, with the same overlapping folds – yet miraculously warm and wet, pulsing, made of flesh. Like a tongue. Like the bud of a mouth. Like another bud, apparently made for a tongue, lower down.

15.

Nine Months

It was only when William returned, just after Christmas, that she knew the past nine months had been a dream. She awoke to a different reality. The protective halo became a dark nimbus. Eleanor returned to her spot on the kitchen floor. Mrs Touchet to the silence of herself. During the day, she and Frances performed a strange avoidant dance, known only to them. If one came into a room, the other left it. The children, noisy and everywhere, hid this dance from view. Frances called her 'Mrs Touchet' and she called Frances 'Annie' — just like everybody else. If they ever accidentally brushed past each other — if their fingers met in the passing of a teacup or a plate — Ainsworthian tempests of desire exploded between her ears. As for William, he was in even higher spirits than usual. Full of his travels, of Italy, of Gothic castles and ghostly cardinals and reliquaries containing the thumb joint of John the Baptist and many other follies he mistook for her faith and presumed would interest her. Something stronger than envy — bile — rose in Eliza as he cheerily recounted these adventures. The several borders he had crossed and recrossed, unaccompanied, unencumbered, on a whim, whenever he wanted! She was not interested in the blood of San Gennaro. What interested her was his freedom of movement. His freedom.

16.

A Queer Reversal

That William's interest was in Eliza herself was a fact she did not grasp until the night he came into her room and kissed her. That kiss was a long and queer one: much of the next few years could be said to be contained within it. He had her up against the wall before she knew it, his mouth pressed hard on hers – and yet, when she felt his tongue, she sensed a strange but unmistakeable acquiescence in it, impossible to explain in words. And into her mind, unbidden, sprung the image of that ludicrous boy of fifteen, 'running' slowly across the small space of the basement stage, to better allow Gilbert to 'thrust him through' with a wooden sword. He was not what he seemed. Who is? She grabbed his jaw. At once his knees softened. Now she was taller than him. She heard a moan of pleasurable disbelief. She squeezed a little tighter – another moan. And in this way led him all the way to the floor, his head still held precisely in place by her hand. Her mouth covered his now; all was reversed. His arms fell limp at his sides, she accidentally split his lip with her teeth. Anyone passing would have thought her a vampire, feeding.

She had been invited to stay for Easter. As a young widow, with little family of her own, she was by now practised at securing invitations to join other people's bustling households, especially at those moments of the year that seem invented to torment the lonely. Aside from the Ainsworths, she had a dull niece in Manchester and a disagreeable aunt in Aberdeen. Now she packed up her bags a little frantically and made an announcement of a change of plans over the breakfast table.

'But Eliza – tomorrow is Easter Sunday! You can't mean to travel to Aberdeen tonight? William, tell her it can't be thought of! And the children will miss you!'

William was silent. Eliza put her knife and fork together, and picked up the empty envelope she was pretending contained a letter from her Aunt Maude.

'I will be back before you know it. But I think I must go to see poor Maude, tiresome as it surely will be. I thank you both, as always, for your hospitality.'

Eliza would not go to Aberdeen to see Aunt Maude – that would be ridiculous – but she could not stay here. She needed to be alone, to reflect. In the coach back to Chesterfield she took William's *December Tales* from her satchel and read the first story once more:

Eliza was a woman, certainly of very superior talents; probably of violent and irregular passions. Of these, however, I know little. During the short period of our union, her conduct was without reproach. Her faults (perhaps I am making use of too lenient an expression) were those of a strong mind, unrestrained by prudence, or the force of early restriction. The stream which, if confined within proper limits, would have moved on in gentle calmness, spreading fertility in its course; if abandoned to its unchecked violence, rushes on a sweeping torrent of destruction: so had it been with her, and such will ever be the effect when a too vigorous imagination and talented confidence urge their possessor to pass the bounds which society has imposed upon its members.

How could it be that everything he had ever written was nonsense – with the exception of what he wrote about her?

17.

Visiting Chesterfield

For the next few years, whenever he returned to Manchester, William made a secret detour, to see Mrs Touchet, in Chesterfield. His Manchester alibi – always partially true – was that of his visits to an old school friend, James Crossley, he of 'the finest library in England'. This Crossley person was, in Eliza's view, as responsible for William's graphomania as distilleries are for the drunkards, and sweet tooths for the continued existence of the slaves. Crossley it was who supplied William with his research materials: Defoe's accounts of the old city, the original transcripts of the Lancaster Witches trial, the architectural layout of the Tower of London, *The Newgate Calendar*. He found all the old letters and old books of costumery and armour, and suggested topics, prompting and pushing until William took them up. Much later in life, Mrs Touchet seriously considered the possibility that her cousin was a fraud and James Crossley the true author of all those thousands upon thousands of words. The reality was less exciting. Crossley was a big man with gout, a terrific collection of books, and only one friend: William. He was the kind of fellow who always promised to come to London but never actually did. Nor did he trust the mail coach with his rare editions. So William was obliged to go to Crossley. And on the way – although it was not really on the way – he stopped at Chesterfield.

He transcribed his notes naked, in bed, in the morning, and in the afternoon sat across from her and wrote. She saw for herself how much pleasure writing brought him. He dipped his nib with a smile on his face, liked to speak the especially gory parts aloud, and sang his cockney ballads as he invented them. Not infrequently, he wrote twenty pages in an afternoon. He always appeared entirely satisfied with every line.

18.

Talking 'Cant' in Chesterfield

In the evenings he was supposed to belong to Mrs Touchet, but over dinner continued outlining his first 'proper novel' in a great stream of talk. The plan was to take all he'd learned of the Gothic from Mrs Radcliffe and Sir Walter and apply it to a grand old English house. (For a model, Crossley had suggested Cuckfield Park, a gloomy Elizabethan mansion in Sussex.) For William, this new location meant a new aesthetic. No more exotic counts and princes. No more evil monks or scheming Italian Doges. Instead: lords and ladies, highwaymen, grave-diggers, Newgate types, and all manner of simple, English, country folk. The highwayman Dick Turpin would make an appearance! And gypsies! It would be called *Rookwood* – after the fictionalized house at its centre – and was to be a tale of fate and murder, involving a worryingly large cast of characters, drawn from the high world and the low. Once he stayed up all night, writing a scene in which 'Dick Turpin rode from London to York', although what this had to do with the family saga he had previously described she could not make out. There was no point in asking rational questions. He was besotted with his project, especially the 'flash songs', sung by the criminal and cockney under-world characters and written in the 'cant' slang he had picked up somewhere. Where?

'What do you mean, where?'

'Well, cant is not the same wherever you go, is it? Cockney flash must be different from Scots flash, for example. And surely Manchester cant is different again.'

'Eliza Touchet, what a curious pedant you are. Does it matter?'

'Don't characters have to speak believably? So we believe in them?'

'And so they do. But I can assure you I do not frequent *any* place so low that I am likely to overhear flash talk or cant of any description!'

She wondered about that. Sometimes, at night, she wondered. Sometimes she looked down at him, suckling her breasts, murmuring like a satisfied child, and thought his predilections in these matters were somewhat eccentric, and also that they could not have sprung from nowhere. What had he done and who had he met in all those Italian cities, after dark? Nine months is a long time.

'Well, then, how *do* you compose it?'

'Ah. Thereby hangs a tale.' He tapped a book on his desk: '*Memoirs of James Hardy Vaux*. There's cant on every page. Terrible character. Shocking. Inveterate swindler, pickpocket – the man was transported three times! But later returned to England, repented and converted to the Church of Rome – which no doubt our Mrs Touchet will be very happy to hear.'

'Sincerely converted, I hope?'

'Oh, hang your sincerity! I've no clue. Though *nomen est omen* and all that . . .'

'James?'

'Vaux! You of all people should recognize that name. Old, recusant family in the time of Elizabeth . . . like your blessed, disembowelled Tichborne. In fact, there was a Vaux at Cuckfield at one point, if I'm not mistaken. Married one of the Boyer daughters.'

'Give me an example.'

'What?'

'Give me an example of a line of cant.'

'Happily! *Nix my doll, pals – fake away!*'

Mrs Touchet laughed out loud.

'Marvellous, isn't it? Nonsense to good, upstanding people like ourselves, of course, but to the criminal element it's a form of code. Which may be translated exactly. That one means: *Don't worry, lads, you carry on stealing!*'

'Charming. And you learned all this from a book.'

'Just so. Vaux rather helpfully provides a flash dictionary at the back — it's a treasure trove. You find a phrase or word, look to the translation, and then sort of put it all together in a sentence. I tell you, with this in hand, anyone might speak the cant of the filthiest hole in Whitechapel in a moment.'

Eliza was quite sure this was not how it worked. She held her tongue. He was excitable as the boy she had met in the basement all those years ago, and there was a charm in that, although sometimes, in bed, she put the rolled-up rag in his mouth because she sensed that he liked it and sometimes simply in the practical sense to stop him from recounting the plot of his novel.

VOLUME TWO

It is but seldom in actual life that the tragic and dramatic notes of action and feeling are struck with the force and frequency with which they were sounded in the Tichborne Case. This strange episode indeed may be regarded as having been a species of moral tornado which, sweeping suddenly into the social midst, swept men from their feet. In its rushing and conflicting currents were excited every sort of human passion: prejudice, justice, anger, bitterness, heroic disinterestedness, sordid cupidity, ambition, devotion, cowardice, courage — in a word, every man's strength or weakness — the whole gamut of human motive and emotion raging and swirling about one large, melancholy, monstrous, mysterious Figure.

ARABELLA KENEALY

I.

Moving Again

It had long been William's habit to read the newspaper aloud to servants. It was this pastime that first prompted the unlikely intimacy between William and the new Mrs Ainsworth, and it remained – as far as Mrs Touchet could discern – their only shared activity. Novels Sarah couldn't be doing with. Poetry made her giggle. But she was a great one for the news.

Previously, while William read, Sarah Wells had busied herself with the dusting or polishing. Now that she was the new Mrs Ainsworth she sat in an armchair by the fire, opposite William, while Mrs Touchet, Fanny and Emily wrapped, folded and packed up the contents of the house. She was not fussy about papers: *The Times*, the *Sun* or the *Morning Post* were all the same to her. But she had preferences as to subject. Parliamentary news was boring. American news as unreal as Brobdingnagian news. Reports of revolts in the Caribbean prompted unhinged bouts of hysteria. ('And what if they get it into their savage heads to come over here? And start ravishing English girls and chopping *us* up in our beds, eh? What then?') The Irish Question she did not understand, although she had a large reserve of 'anti-Popish' prejudice to which she periodically gave an airing, and so William avoided the topic to spare Mrs Touchet. In any case, the news she cared for most was not political but social. Anything in the line of rapists, murderers, baby-killers, fraudsters, bigamists, prostitutes, philanderers, sodomites and child-seducers. If such people could be uncovered amongst the gentry, in the corridors of power, the judiciary, or the Church itself, all the better. But no story captured her quite like the saga of the Tich-borne Claimant. It had everything: toffs, Catholics, money, sex, mistaken identity, an inheritance, High Court Judges, snobbery, exotic locations, 'the struggle of the honest working man' – as opposed to the 'undeserving poor' – and 'the power of a mother's love'. And it was a subject that drove all Ainsworths to distraction, which was also in its favour.

2.

Debating Tichborne

'I tell you it's only a few lines. It says here: "*Sir Roger Doughty Tichborne, the claimant to the Tichborne baronetcy and estates, was among the passengers by last week's West India mail from Southampton, his destination being Rio de Janeiro.*"'

'And what else?'

'Nothing else! That is all it says. And I must say I tire of the subject. I feel I've read more column inches concerning this godforsaken fraudulent Tichborne than I—'

'No, no, that can't be it – look again. Why's he gone all the way over there, then? Him being so close to his victory? There must be more. Turn the page, Willie!'

'That is all, Sarah. There is no more.'

'A mercy,' said Fanny, under her breath. But Emily, who was not immune to Tichborne mania, stopped swaddling the ornaments in tissue paper and came to peer over her father's shoulder: 'He's surely seeking witnesses who might remember him. Roger was in South America two years, remember – I mean, before his ship went down.'

The new Mrs Ainsworth stamped her little feet.

'And I tell you what and all: them what say the *Bella* went down with all hands on deck – them people will be smiling on the other sides of their stupid faces! Because no it didn't! Our Roger survived! And took himself to Australia just as he said he did, and took up butchering incognito in Wagga Wagga, just like he said. I tell you I believe Sir Roger. I am a thorough believer in him. Oh, he'll get witnesses all right. And then he'll bring them all here and show them uppity Tichbornes and all their prejudiced lawyers a bloody thing or two.'

'Yes, and all he has to do,' remarked Fanny, drily, 'is explain to the Lord Chief Justice why he's now two hundred pounds the heavier – and a cockney.'

'A fellow may forget all the boys in his class at Stonyhurst,' reflected William, closing the newspaper and his own eyes, 'and all the soldiers from his regiment. He may even forget his own uncle's name. But I cannot for the life of me see how a fellow can forget he once spoke fluent French . . .'

'But no one asked you, Willie, did they? I've said it before, and I will say it again: a mother knows her own child. *A mother knows her own child.* No offence' – a wave in the direction of her stepdaughters and Mrs Touchet – 'but there's them what knows the power of a mother's love and them that simply don't. And that's an end to the matter right there. You tell me, William, you tell me how it is that a mother – *a mother*, mind – can look a body in the face and say: *There stands my only living son, Sir Roger* and not be believed? Prejudice is what it is! Purest prejudice. And now she's dead and gone and there's no one to protect poor Roger from these – these – *vultures.*'

Fanny snorted. 'And no one to pay him a thousand pounds a year!'

'Oh, don't you worry about that. We'll see him right. Don't you worry. His supporters will not forsake him. He's been speaking all about the country, you know, and everywhere he speaks there's *huge* crowds, full of those what are *despised* like him, and *forgotten* like him – and they all put a penny or whatever can be managed into the Tichborne Fund. We feel for poor Sir Roger and vice-a versa. He's for us and we're for him. I'm going to see him talk myself first chance I get – and throw half a crown to his fund if I have one! No, no, no we won't be letting one of our own go to the wolves.'

William thwacked the chair arm: 'One of your own!'

'Now, William, my love, now the thing is, you've lived a very soft life, my dear, so you can't imagine what it is for an honest working man to come up against the gentry, and the Lord Chief Justice himself, and all the bigwigs, with their secret societies – caring not a jot for the little people! Seeing as how they're all too busy answering to the Hebrews or to the Po— or whoever it may be. You can't know what it is for an honest working man to try and get what he's owed in this country. I tell you one thing: I don't fancy Sir Roger's chances in court! I may have come up in the world' – a quick, satisfied look around the half-empty parlour – 'but I ain't forgot where I come from, no, no, no. There's one rule for the rich in this country and another rule altogether for the likes of us!'

Fanny went over to the fire to poke it, as she often did when in a malicious mood. This way her back could be turned to whomever she was insulting.

'But Sarah, surely you see your argument is flawed? For if this man is the real Sir Roger, well, then he *is* gentry, and therefore, by your logic, the courts will treat him fairly . . .' Fanny paused for effect. 'Unless of course he's really Arthur Orton, a common butcher—'

William scaled his eyes tight, in preparation for the inevitable wifely explosion.

'BUT HE AIN'T ARTHUR ORTON IS HE? HE ALREADY EXPLAINED ALL THAT. THEM WHO SAY HE'S ORTON ARE LYING. WHAT HAPPENED WAS HE *MET* A FELLA CALLED ARTHUR ORTON – WHEN HE WAS IN WAGGA WAGGA!'

'Oh, yes, I forgot. In Wagga Wagga, when he was going by the name of Thomas Castro. Rather than "Sir Roger". For reasons yet unexplained.'

'HE WAS LIVING INCOGNITO!'

Fanny wheeled round to seal her victory, poker in hand.

'But why in the first instance pretend to be Castro? Why not, after you're shipwrecked, return at once to the bosom of your *extremely wealthy family*?'

'He had a terrible shock in the water! His mind got all knocked about!'

'Or: he's a fraud. He's really a butcher from Wapping called Arthur Orton. Who went by the name of Castro, and sailed as far from England as could be managed, because – well, who knows why. To avoid bad debts, most likely. Occam's razor, Sarah. In the case of a mystery, the simplest solution will tend to be the right one.'

3.

Still Debating Tichborne

The new Mrs Ainsworth screwed her mouth up very tight, lifted her embroidery hoop and commenced furiously stabbing her needle at the cloth.

'Fanny Ainsworth, you do not know what in the world you are about.'

'We will agree to disagree,' said William, pacifically, and reopened his newspaper.

'I must say I do think he looks rather like Sir Roger . . .' began cautious Emily. 'At least around the eyes. Although of course so very much fatter. Only . . . well, it *is* very strange about Wapping . . .'

William was unequal to Wapping. He stood up and threw his paper in the fire.

'Passing strange,' pursued Fanny. 'For why would a nobleman, recently off the boat from Wagga Wagga, *en route* to Paris – precisely to meet his mother, a lady whom he has not seen in a dozen years – why would such a man decide to secretly stop off in Wapping *of all places* to visit a collection of abject wretches *by the name of Orton*?'

William eased the poker out of his daughter's grip.

'Fanny, must you be difficult? We've been through all this. It's perfectly clear: a fellow called Thomas Castro merely desired to pay a call on the family of his old friend Arthur Orton, the cockney butcher from Wapping, whom he had happened to come across in Wagga Wagga . . .'

'*Thank* you, Willie, I— No, I mean – there *is* no Thomas Cas— SIR

ROGER wanted to visit the Ortons. Oh, you're all trying to confuse me with your blasted cleverness but you cannot get out of the plain fact that A MOTHER KNOWS HER OWN SON.'

'And what of the "plain fact" that no other Tichborne has claimed him?'

'Fanny, I said that's enough. Let's agree to dis—'

'—And then, when poor Lady Tichborne died, your Claimant insisted – *insisted* – on being the chief mourner at her funeral! That is a step too far, Sarah. There is rapacious folly – and then there is mortal sin. To insist on his ridiculous lie at that most sacred of rituals! God help his soul.'

'God help us all,' offered Mrs Touchet, but was not heeded.

'And is it not odd,' murmured Emily, 'I mean to say – is it not odd that people say – that is, those who've heard him speak at his rallies – well, they say that he speaks terribly low, flash talk really . . . and drops every aitch . . . and doesn't seem at all well educated, no more than the black fellow, Mr Bogle, he goes around with, and—'

Sarah laughed: 'Why, that's exactly why we *know* it's him. Let me ask you this: if you were a lowborn butcher *pretending* to be a Lord, wouldn't you talk just so, and dress as you should, and mind all your ps and qs, and keep high company? Course you would. But our Sir Roger don't bother with none of that. He is himself. *He* knows what he's about. And we know him.'

William sighed greatly and sat back in his chair.

'Oh, wife-of-mine . . . If you imagine a man of Sir Roger's breeding, from a family as noble as the Tichbornes, tracing its line back to the time of the Normans . . . If you imagine such a man could in any manner be confused with a common butcher . . . Family tells, my dear. Breeding tells. I would know a gentleman in a moment, as would any gentleman. The difference is profound.'

Mrs Touchet, who generally stayed out of Tichborne discussions, felt moved by this last comment to press mischievously upon the scale:

'But did I not read that the Tichborne family doctor recognized him? And, I believe, a second cousin?'

'So they did! And tell me this, Miss Fanny, if you're so clever – how does Sir Roger know all them things that only Sir Roger would possibly know? About Tichborne Park, and his old fishing tackle, and that cousin Katherine what he loved with a forbidden passion, and all of that? Eh?'

'I imagine the Tichbornes' old negro is feeding him the information in exchange for payment.'

This matter of the manservant Bogle was, in Sarah's view, unfortunate, and she never pressed strongly on him as evidence one way or another. She folded her arms tight across her chest.

'All I know is: a mother knows her own son. And what a mother! Never gave up. For years she paid for them advertisements! Placed all around the world. You think that's cheap? And she was offering a reward – a large one. Why? Cos she loved him so. No price was too high. For she knew her boy weren't dead in that shipwreck! She felt it in her bones! And finally her prayers is answered. Here comes Sir Roger, not dead, very much alive, reading her advertisement in a paper, just as we all did – but he's all the way over in Wagga Wagga, Australia, if you don't mind. Other side of the world. But he says to himself: that's a mother's love, that is. I've done wrong by going incognito and I must forthwith return. So off he goes to Paris. But water journeys don't agree with him so he's sick when he gets there and keeps to his room. Mother sends message after message. Come to me, come to me! But how can he when he feels so bad? So she comes to him, naturally, as any mother would. There he lies, in the dark, a kerchief over his face. She walks in and whips it away – and recognizes him right off. *His ears look just like his uncle's.* Her own words! Months they spent together, before she died! Months! And that's all I need to know, William. No one can change my mind – it's set. And the rest is only conspiracy and lies and prejudice, is what it is. If poor Lady Tichborne said this man is her son, who are we to disagree?'

'Poor Lady Tichborne was quite out of her wits,' said William quietly. From Gilbert he had learned how far a mind may go out of its own bounds, and he would not be moved from this position.

4.

Hurstpierpoint, West Sussex

Eventually all was boxed or wrapped in cloths and carpets and transported to Little Rockley, a red-brick house in Hurstpierpoint, at the
foot of the South Downs. Mrs Touchet was forced to revise her view
of the countryside. It was those fussy little Middlesex enclosures
she hadn't liked. Neat hedgerows dividing higgledy-piggledy
smallholdings – the sense of God's great bounty cut up into so many
single acres. She was far from North London now. And liberated from
dreary Tunbridge. Now the rolling Downs rolled without interruption, and were always in view. Even the most banal activity – buying
sausages! – radiated with glory, for there were the South Downs, over
the butcher's shoulder. Finally, it had happened: she no longer missed
the old Kensal Lodge life. The dinners, the parties. She liked Hurstpierpoint. The quiet tea room, the bakery, the fishmonger's. She liked
that her room was in the attic, distant from all Ainsworths, old and new.
She liked the compact scale of the place, and the fact that she needed no
carriage, hosted no dinners and attended none. The only trouble was
worship. In London, she had been very glad to walk across the canal to
St Mary's and the Angels, where almost everyone in the congregation
was an Irish labourer, and most of them with dirt under their nails – for
Paddington Station would not build itself. But here in Hurstpierpoint
the Anglicans had full dominion. William was well pleased with the
Gothic church at the end of the high street, designed by Charles Barry
himself. But what was Eliza to do? Discreet local enquiries uncovered
a small settlement of Belgian nuns, Augustinians, halfway down the

road to Cuckfield. They had no church, only a crumbling town house. St George's Retreat. On Mondays the Sisters of St George fed the poor. On Wednesdays they were silent. On Fridays they made clothes and worked in the garden. Sometimes, listening to these twelve peculiar women sing in their thick Belgian accents, Mrs Touchet marvelled at so many bad teeth and big knuckles and unfortunate noses and thick leg hairs pushing through worsted tights. Their most ardently held precept – that love cannot be earned, merited or deserved, only generously given – seemed, to Mrs Touchet, to be most severely put to the test on the physical plane.

5.

Another Package

The unpacking felt endless until, finally, it did end. William settled into a new study, and Eliza found herself likewise quite settled in mind and spirit. But then, a few days before Christmas, another package arrived. Same paper, same ink on the brown paper, same handwriting. Posted, this time – a London postmark. This time, she managed to intercept it before it reached William's desk.

Inside was Thackeray's *An Essay on the Genius of George Cruikshank.* Mrs Touchet remembered this as a laborious magazine article, overly flattering to its subject. Now it was apparently a book, fulsomely illustrated with Cruikshank's gross and stupid cartoons, some of them taken from the pages of William's novels. For a moment she was indignant. Thackeray! That pig-nosed moralist! Disturbing her peace! For what possible purpose? Then, remembering, she crossed herself and looked to the heavens: Thackeray was six years dead, and his pig-nose neither here nor there in the Lord's eyes. But then who? Who would send such a thing? Why? She took it to the kitchen and threw it in the fire. She remembered the friendship-ending sentence contained within, as was her habit, although she did not doubt William – whose friendship it was – had long ago forgotten. It was years since the two Williams fell out, and it had never been resolved. In the end the worm Thackeray had simply avoided Kensal Lodge altogether. Strange man. Curious mix of bitter humour, envy and cowardice. Whereas her own William, despite being mortally wounded by the insult, would have made it up with his old friend at any moment, given the opportunity.

Her cousin was never a man much given to grudges, finding them hard to maintain. The truth was he dreaded conflict: he only really knew how to be wounded. It was Eliza's self-appointed task to remember the slights. In this case: *It seems to us that Mr Cruikshank's illustrations really created the tale, and that Mr Ainsworth, as it were, only put words to it.*

6.

Cuckfield Park

All Christmas she was troubled by the mystery of the sender. William meanwhile was trying to finish his 'Jamaican novel'. He was no longer editor of anything and no one ever came to dinner: theoretically the days stretched wide and open. Yet his mood was fragile and required constant boosting. On a sunset walk to the nuns, it occurred to Eliza how close Hurstpierpoint was to his beloved old Cuckfield Park, the original inspiration for *Rookwood*. When she got home that evening – freezing, pink-nosed, radiant with the holy spirit – she suggested a day trip. A boy was hired, a buggy rented, and they went all together. Best fur muffs for Fanny and Emily, curls and a new bonnet for Clara, Sarah in canary yellow, and William squeezed into his favourite suit, whiskers trimmed. The windows were rimy with January frost, William warm with nostalgia:

'I visited often during composition . . . I came to know the family quite well – the Sergisons – and they very much encouraged me in my research, and of course good old Crossley knew the house like the back of his hand, going back to the Elizabethan Boyers who built it . . . Oh, it was a treasure trove. You'll find all of my *Rookwood* in Cuckfield – even the infamous lime tree!'

The older Ainsworth daughters nodded, a little too vigorously, at mention of this lime tree. Clara and Sarah – having the convenient excuse of illiteracy – carried on sticking their heads out of the window to catch snowflakes on their tongues.

William frowned: 'It's hardly to be forgotten. Quite a prominent incident in the novel, if not the central motif . . . The curse of the lime tree?'

'Dreadful curse!' intervened Eliza. 'If ever a branch falls, a member of the family at Rookwood must die . . . Ah! Truly a chilling idea! And the real family – at Cuckfield – they believed it, didn't they?'

'Had reason to!'

'What romance! And so wonderfully put to verse by your father.'

More nodding – too much.

'I have to tell you, girls, they were singing my lime tree ditty in the streets. You could buy the broadsides for a penny from any chaunter in London. Once I walked from Kensal Rise to Charing Cross and heard it sung all the way! And the chapter concerning Dick Turpin – the "Ride to York" – truly *that* had a life of its own. I don't think I overstate the case' – uncertain look at Eliza; promptly dismissed – 'when I say there were at least half a dozen London theatricals with that same title at one point. In the finest houses in Mayfair you could hear flash talk repeated at table. *Nix my doll, pals, fake away*,' sang William, disconcerting everybody. 'Bulwer-Lytton wrote to me, and I was introduced to Lady Blessington and the Count d'Orsay and their circle . . . As Byron had it: "I went to bed unknown, arose, and found myself famous!" "The English Victor Hugo" was even written, I believe, more than once?'

'Just so,' confirmed Eliza, and smiled. The Ainsworth girls, too, relaxed, smiled and left off their frantic nodding. This tale of their father's first great success was, at least, one they knew by the letter.

7.

'I do not advise you to enter upon a literary career'

The park had been re-landscaped and the approach had changed. Or perhaps William misremembered. They went twice round before they found the Porter's Lodge, which was not the Elizabethan, ivy-covered gate of memory but a small turreted building, recently achieved. Nor was there any lime tree. Sarah got out to announce their party. She returned a few minutes later, red-faced.

'This country bint, what can't hardly speak English, has the brass balls to say to me: "Leave a card." No *Madam*. No *If you please*. Just: "Leave a card." Couldn't have looked more put out if I was a little nig just turned up on her doorstep! Silly quim. Says they don't know no one by that name at Cuckfield! Now, who don't know the name of Ainsworth?'

Thirty-six years. Three generations could pass through a house in thirty-six years. And two dozen books could fall out of print. As William pulled the brougham's door shut, Eliza opened her mouth to make this rational case and then realized the folly of it.

The horses set back off down the wide gravel path. William looked mournfully out of the window: 'I do not advise you to enter upon a literary career.' The great house receded into the distance. All the ladies in the carriage wondered who precisely was being addressed. 'It is a very hazardous profession . . .' A sad chuckle. 'Although, of course, ladies don't often think to do anything so foolish.'

While considering this interesting truth, the ladies forgot to direct the driver. They took a wrong turn at the commons, looping through Hayward's Heath. And it was in that hamlet – to the collective disbelief of the Ainsworth dependants – that they found themselves rumbling towards a pub called the Pickwick, with a clear illustration of Mr Dickens' jolly character upon its swinging sign. Every woman in the carriage spotted it before William, and, as if with one mind – though without any opportunity to confer – they now attempted to direct his attention to the opposite window, with overlapping talk of the beauty of the Downs, two magpies on a post, a church that might be of some architectural merit, and – in Sarah's case – a Shetland pony doing a gigantic steaming shit. But to no avail, and the rest of the ride was silent as the grave.

8.

Jamaica, in Fiction

'*Zounds!*' *he mentally ejaculated. 'I suspect the little hussy means to refuse him.*'

Eliza had long understood her cousin to be beyond the reach of editorial intervention.

'*Your notions are strictly orthodox, Colonel, and meet my entire approval,' rejoined Her Ladyship. 'I wonder you do not give effect to them.*'

By now she read him only notionally, skipping over pages – whole chapters.

'*Amen!' ejaculated Oswald, fervently.*

The point was to grasp the fundamentals of the story so as not to be caught out in an interrogation.

The lightning gave a livid hue like that of death to her pallid features. The lifeblood was flowing fast from a deep wound in her side, and he strove in vain to staunch the crimson stream.

9.

Hilary St. Ives, *1869*

No matter how briskly she tried to move through it, this new novel, *Hilary St. Ives*, proved disheartening. Old age had only condensed and intensified his flaws. People ejaculated, rejoined, cried out on every page. The many strands of the perplexing plot were resolved either by 'Fate', the fulfilment of a gypsy's curse or a thunderstorm. It took over three hundred pages for young Hilary to work out that the servant who seemed unusually concerned with his future was his mother, and that the fellow who looked so very much like him that he could be his father was, indeed, his father. And for great swathes of the novel it was hard to distinguish it from the descriptions of a house agent:

> *No material change had been made in the mansion since its erection, and even the old furniture, chairs, beds, antique mirrors, and hangings were carefully preserved, so that it was not merely a capital specimen of Tudor architecture, but gave an accurate idea of the internal decorations of a large house of the period. The hall to which we have just adverted, and which was entirely undefaced by modern alteration, with its gallery for minstrels, its long massive oak table, its great fireplace and andirons, recalled the days of baronial hospitality. A magnificent banquet hall, with great carved oak screen, gallery moulded ceiling filled with old family portraits — dames and knights. What with portraits, carved chimney-pieces, tapestried chambers, and antiquated furniture, you'll find a great deal to your taste at Boxgrove, I can promise you.*

Passages repeated. She read of Boxgrove's 'richly-carved wainscoting' at least half a dozen times. Aristocrats were drowned in obsequious flattery — by the author — while groundsmen and maids were treated as barely sentient. It all ended with a double wedding, 'amid the joyous pealing of bells'. As if marriage — despite all William's painful experience to the contrary — was still the greatest happiness of which he could conceive.

The strangest thing about it all was that he should call it his 'Jamaican novel'. If she had looked forward to it at all it was for this reason, Jamaica being a particular interest of Mrs Touchet. But only in the final pages did that island appear, buried under the weight of an entangling plot like a bobbin at the bottom of a sewing box. For Jamaica turned out to be the secret birthplace of Hilary's secret mother:

Once more she heard the ceaseless screams and cry of the parrots mingled with the screams and chatter of the negroes. Once more her eye ranged over plains studded with dazzlingly white habitations, long savannahs fringed with groves of cocoa-trees and thickets of cactus, plantations of sugar-cane and coffee. Once more she gazed on those bays of unequalled beauty where she had often sailed, and those blue mountains which she had often longed to climb. The whole scene was before her, with its fervid atmosphere, its fierce sunshine, its tropical beauties, and its delights. She seemed to have grown young again — to have become once more an innocent child. Her sad heart beat with pleasurable emotions, and she echoed the light laugh of her nurse Bonita. Yes, her dear devoted Bonita was alive again, smiling upon her as of yore, and bringing her cates and fruits.

This postcard portrait she recognized at once. A *Picturesque Tour of the Island of Jamaica* by James Hakewill. Crossley had sent them a handsome first edition, years ago, and she had sat with Frances in the old drawing room at The Elms, turning over the pages of plantation watercolours, marvelling at how a charnel house may be depicted as a very paradise. This same book had sometimes been held up, at their abolitionist meetings, as an example of successful propaganda, and much scorn poured upon its depictions of little dark women, dressed all in white with white scarves on their heads, moving contentedly through idyllic, pastoral scenes. Only blessed Frances – with her optimistic and forgiving soul – had thought to argue that they might also be viewed as a vision, of what might come to pass, if they were successful in their campaign. Thinking on this, Eliza felt a throb of the old agony. Then reconsidered: thanks be to God such a soul did not live long enough to see paradise lost – paradise never achieved! For despite all the efforts of the Ladies Society for the Relief of Negro Slaves – despite abolition itself – the passage of thirty years did not appear to have made Hakewill's charming watercolours a reality. The recent news from that benighted island was discouraging, to say the least. Civil unrest, a bloody uprising, a state of emergency, and Governor Eyre disgraced: accused of mass brutality, summary executions. None of which as much as grazed the pages of William's novel. There the fantasies of 1820 persisted, like creaky stage sets. But it was all creaky. Everything had been used before or was lifted from life. The paintings on the walls of Boxgrove were by Maclise. The food on the tables Mrs Touchet had cooked herself. And in 'Mrs Radcliffe' – with her 'rich black tresses', decided opinions, Amazonian height and skill with a horsewhip – she recognized a lusty tribute to her younger self. Even Bonita, the mulatto nurse, was a poor copy, with a name half-remembered, half-borrowed from that beautiful day in Brighton, seven years ago, when the Ainsworth clan had stood arm in arm on their own doorstep to watch the wedding procession of the Queen's ward, 'Bonetta', the Dahomey princess . . .

From such worn cloth and stolen truth are novels made. More and more the whole practice wearied her, even to the point of disgust. Now she sighed, straightened the pile of loose paper, tied the ribbon back round it, and walked downstairs, pausing every three steps to save her knees. She could hear him groaning at his desk. As she reached the hallway he emerged. He had that new anxious look upon his face, that so disturbed her. But he had reasons to be anxious. No longer could he count on publication in the respectable magazines, and it was a very long time indeed since the likes of Chapman & Hall had asked to look over a manuscript. She missed the happy and successful William. For years the only sound she had ever heard issuing from his study were the sighs of a satisfied man. Had she really once pitied him for that? Why put such a steep value on self-knowledge? *Victoria veritatis est caritas.* But *was* the victory of truth really love? Sometimes Mrs Touchet suspected Augustine of Hippo of over-egging the pudding. There are easy, self-serving truths, after all. And difficult, generous lies.

'Well? For God's sake – don't keep me in suspense, Eliza . . .'

'A triumph!' ejaculated Mrs Touchet.

10.

St Lawrence's Fair

On the first Saturday in July St Lawrence's fair arrived in Hurst-pierpoint, as it had every July since the Dark Ages. Down the cobbled high street came many curiosities. Garlanded ponies. A Scots pipe band. Three men on unicycles. The Trinity choristers waving silken banners and singing 'Greensleeves'. A group of schoolboys got up as knights in heraldry.

Mrs Touchet – leaning out of her attic window to the waist – was pleased to see the Sisters of St George bringing up the rear, in their unassuming, flat-footed way, trudging in quiet formation. She went downstairs to collect her hat and corral dithering Ainsworths. Dithering, in her view, was a fundamental trait of the clan. Handkerchiefs, change-purses, shawls, umbrellas in case of rain, fans in case of heat, watch-fobs and hats were located and pressed upon their owners. The residents of Little Rockley joined the crowds heading to the village green. There, all was transformation. The villagers were in their Sunday best. Even the grass itself had pushed up many springy clumps of clover, and a joyous yellow archipelago of dandelion. In the centre, two teams of young men battled in a tug of war, for the prize of a barrel of beer. You could guess the weight of the church warden, or the height of the steeple. For the first time in her life, Mrs Touchet saw a carousel powered by steam, without a gypsy or a beast of burden to drag it.

'These are our riches'

The queue of eager riders for the carousel was long, but at last Clara took her turn on this miracle of engineering. Poor Gilbert – who had been brought up from Reigate the night before – was permitted to stand by his niece's painted pony and grip the striped pole boring into its back. His damaged brain, no home for letters, music or conversation, still happily accepted machinery, and he stared with open delight at this piston as it began to move smoothly up and down. Round and round they went. The new Mrs Ainsworth, soon bored, departed for the coconut shy. The remaining Ainsworths stood on the sidelines with their sugar plums. It was hard to say who was the more enraptured, Clara or William. Each time the child circled back into view, giggling and waving, the father outdid himself with hoo-hoo-ing and waving back – and looked the fool doing it. Eliza glanced over at his adult daughters. She saw how they struggled to maintain their fixed smiles. William's especial delight in his youngest child was painfully undisguised. Unprecedentedly, he had chosen a study across the hall from her nursery, and kept both doors ajar all day long, welcoming any interruption on the slightest of pretexts. Whenever he scooped Clara up onto his lap – or pushed his papers aside so she might sit on his desk – he was chided by Fanny and Emily for 'indulgence'. During their own childhood work had come first. They'd counted themselves lucky if their father left his study at six to spend a golden half-hour in their company. After which the evening's steady stream of literary gentlemen began, and the girls were sent upstairs to bed. Aged seven, each girl in turn was sent further, up to Manchester, to Mrs Harding's establishment for young ladies. Only when they grew older, and prettier – and of no little interest to William's friends – had their father truly attended to them.

All fathers should be old, reflected Eliza, young men being barely more than children themselves. Still, she could never have done as Sarah had done. Old men repulsed her. It was one reason – among many – that she had never remarried. Old men brought death to mind. They smelled of death, stored death in their scraggly necks and papery hands, and Mrs Touchet's terror of that inevitable state was her most ardently kept, her most shameful, secret. No. Only young people, gripping the rope, sweaty, hair slick across their foreheads, determined to win a barrel of beer or die in the attempt, could hold her attention.

'I insist on the stocks! I say it must be done!'

Fanny and Emily – having not so long ago been sophisticated literary hostesses in London – did not think the stocks were something that had to be done, or at least not by them. But there was no stopping William. He got down upon his knees amongst the dandelions, put his head and hands through the holes, and gamely paid a farthing for Clara and a number of rowdy unknown children to stand behind a white chalk line and throw tomatoes at him. Mortified, the sisters joined Sarah at the coconut shy. Mrs Touchet stayed where she was, observing her portly, bearded cousin, all youthful beauty fled from him, bent over into a position not at all unfamiliar to her, though now rendered utterly bathetic. A riding crop passed through her mind. An uplifted arm. Tender strips of raised red skin. She wondered if he suffered from these same recollections, and if so, what he did with them. Where he put them. She had the bottomless mercy of Christ for *her* relief. What did he have?

*

72

'The original charter was given, I believe, by Edward the Second . . . and it has been "St Lawrence's Fair" for as long as anyone can remember . . .' William was lecturing, his preferred mode. Unlike so many other men Eliza had known, however, this habit in William sprang not out of a need to dominate but from a sincere overflow of enthusiasm. As he spoke he wiped tomato juice from his face with one hand, taking Clara's little hand with the other. To Eliza's surprise, the child then looked for Eliza's hand and grasped it, as if she were really *their* child, spontaneously birthed from memory. It was in this pleasant grouping that they headed to join the others, at the shy.

'Now who can tell me the tragic story of St Lawrence?'

Clara's face fell: it was tragical indeed to go from squished tomatoes directly to Sunday school.

'He was – um . . . was he – *cooked*?'

'Ah, very good! Very good – very literal. But now *was* he? Mrs Touchet, you are surely familiar with the saints – might you elaborate on "cooked"?'

'You seem to want to tell the story yourself, so you should tell it, William.'

'No, no, no – I cede to the older church.'

Eliza smiled blandly down at the child.

'Well, let's see . . . *cooked* makes it sound rather as though he was eaten with two potatoes and some peas . . . Let us say rather he was martyred – burned alive. It was a time of martyrs. There were many attempts to smash the rock of the church. And St Lawrence was responsible for the treasures of the church—'

'Like a beadle!'

'Well not quite like a beadle. We might say he was the custodian of the wealth of the church. In this period the Roman authorities were executing bishops – indeed, they martyred the Pope himself! And gave Lawrence three days to gather all of the wealth of the church and deliver it to the authorities. But he didn't do that. Do you recall what he did?'

'He was *burned*!'

'Yes, but before that . . . Oh, William, honestly I'm a very poor governess . . .'

'On the contrary: you're doing wonderfully.'

'Well, instead of giving it to the Romans, he gave it to the poor.'

Clara blew a raspberry: 'The poor! The poor are lazy!'

The mother spoke through the child. She even threw her little arms up in her mother's exasperated fashion. Mrs Touchet pressed on:

'And when the three days had passed, he brought the poor, the lame and the sick, the reviled, and the outcast . . . and he – well, he brought them to the Romans and said: "These are our riches. These people, here." ' Mrs Touchet felt tears springing, absurdly, into her own eyes. 'And for this impertinence he was punished. They placed him on a grid-iron – like the one we have in the kitchen – and burned him alive.'

Clara grimaced: 'I shouldn't like to be burned.'

'No. Nor should I. Nor should anyone. And yet, rather than cry out, as you or I would have done, St Lawrence refused to give those dreadful Romans the satisfaction. He said – do you know what he said?'

William could restrain himself no longer: ' "*I'm well done on this side – turn me over!*" But did he? I see an obvious objection. If all the bishops and Pope Sixtus himself were beheaded – as the record tells us they were – why then would Lawrence be singled out for torture? *Passus est* – "he suffered" – is surely the correct text. We can only conclude that a dim-witted scribe copied it down incorrectly, omitting or forgetting the *p*, which any boy who knows his Latin will understand gives us *assus est* – "he was roasted".'

Eliza, who did not know her Latin – no one had ever thought to teach her any – retrieved her hand from Clara's and returned it to her own pocket.

'It is a beautiful story, all the same,' she said.

'On such human errors are churches built! We mustn't tell Hurstpierpoint!'

Clara looked devotedly up at her father with her mother's doll-like blue eyes.

'I will not ever, Papa.' And then, to further solemnize the vow: 'Amen.'

They had reached the coconut shy and the end of Eliza's tether. The sight of poor Gilbert and that idiotic woman slinging wooden balls at coconuts and missing every single one of them suddenly seemed a bitter allegory for the senselessness of all existence. Of her existence. The narrow world in which she lived. The banal company she kept. The other life she might have lived, had only every single thing been different. The cloth backdrop to the coconut shy was a crudely painted tropical scene: beaches, mountains, savannahs, a blazing sun. Five comic negro heads, with broad red lips and protruding eyes, popped out from behind the palm trees, laughing at her and all her hopes.

12.

Jamaica, in Reality

In the gregarious days of Kensal Lodge – amid all that conversation and drink – it had often seemed to Mrs Touchet that there was barely time to finish dinner before midnight arrived, and her duties began anew. Drunken poets had to be reunited with their topcoats and nudged into waiting buggies. Reckless novelists, determined to ride across the fields, helped back onto their horses, and cartoonists, too drunk to stand, led to a spare room. Here, in Hurstpierpoint, she was always in bed by ten. Yet evenings stretched interminably. Sometimes she found a reason to escape upstairs – a letter to write, a headache. More usually, as she cleared pudding, William put a hand to her wrist and looked at her in his old, imploring way. Her own sense of pity would then get the better of her. How could she – how could any of them – leave him alone with that woman?

'Reading, reading, always reading! You'll be doing your eyes in. What you reading now, Eliza?'

'Oh, well, nothing, really . . . only a novel by—'

'Willie's new one?'

'No, but I have already—'

'Naturally we do hope for some money out of this new one. We have hopes of a grand return, if possible, despite so many recent disappointments, as I've never been to the Continent and I'd like to see it. My old man used to say there's a special word you can say what will make a French whore quick as you like—'

'More fruit loaf?' tried Fanny, who believed the effects of sherry could be dented with heavy cake.

'Don't mind if I do. If I didn't know better I'd suspect you of trying to fatten me up! Though I've been doing a fair job of that myself of late, it has to be said, HA HA HA HA.'

'You have an enviable figure,' said Emily, sincerely.

'And I've suffered much envy over it, believe you me. But we can't help what we're born with, for good or for ill. Though I had a cousin flat as a board just like you and she made a point of eating sheep's trotters every day and the change was something to see. And if it can be managed on a penn'orth of trotters, imagine what a side of beef would do! It'd help the both of you, if it come to that, and I'm always encouraging Mrs Touchet not to stint so on the housekeeping for that very reason. In my experience, a gentleman likes a bit of meat on the bones, and it is to be noticed, I always say, that them what never marry will tend towards the lean and bony.'

The clock struck eight. William shook out the newspaper.

'Well. At least that nasty business of Governor Eyre is finally over!'

When in doubt, the news. But he had chosen at random from the front page, without first considering Mrs Touchet, and it was the wrong topic if he hoped for a peaceful evening.

'In what sense over?' Eliza spoke with ominous sharpness, closing her book without marking the page with the ribbon.

'Well . . . I mean to say, he has been acquitted finally of any wrongdoing in the case of Reverend Gordon, and . . . ah, here they mention Disraeli hopes Parliament shall pay his legal fees.'

'How many murderers can hope for such first-class treatment!'

'Oh, come now, Mrs Touchet,' chided Fanny. 'Martial law is hardly to be called murder.'

Eliza's dark brows beetled together. She took on that spiky, Scottish, shield-like aspect to which the Ainsworths, behind her back, had long ago given a nickname: 'the Targe'.

'But that is rather to the point, Fanny,' said the Targe now, rising from the window seat to her full and formidable height. 'That is precisely what all these enquiries have attempted to establish. And one thing that has been made abundantly clear over the past three years is that the Reverend Gordon was some *thirty miles outside* of the area contained by martial law. And Governor Eyre, knowing this full well, ordered that poor man arrested, put him on a boat and deliberately *transported him* to Morant Bay – where martial law could be applied.'

'Surely it is easy for us in our armchairs—' began Fanny, but the Targe would not be deflected.

'—Even by the low standards of martial law, the Gordon case is a stain upon the name of British justice! Tried in mere hours, denied counsel – and hanged from the rafters of a Jamaican courthouse? If that is not murder I do not know what is.'

13.

Debating Jamaica

A meaningful look – *don't poke the Targe* – passed swiftly round the room without managing to catch William's attention. He was preparing his pipe, and seemed to address the tobacco itself as he tamped it down.

'Cousin . . . really, you exaggerate. I've read quite a bit about it and it seems clear that this Reverend Gordon was a rabble-rouser – a mulatto. He whipped up the people, which we know by now these Baptists have a habit of doing . . . And Gordon conspired with the . . . well, with this other negro lay-preacher fellow, and all the other conspirators. Eighteen white men died in the original disturbance. Was that not to be answered? I thought it was put rather well by what's-his-name in *Punch*: "*We really cannot murder a man for saving a colony.*" Droll, but it makes a serious point.'

William sighed – as if at a great burden, dutifully taken up – and attempted to signify the peaceful end of this discussion by putting his pipe to his lips and lighting it.

'William, there is no law, martial or otherwise, that can excuse or justify bloody carnage. If this was saving a colony I dread to think what the Governor's idea of ruin would be. Three hundred and fifty Jamaicans hanged in the public square! Villages burned to the ground, families murdered, women dishonoured, discovered in their beds with their throats—'

'No one is questioning the somewhat disproportionate—'

'—response to an unjust—'

'—a violent uprising—'

'—an uprising which *turned* violent. As I should think it was likely to turn, faced with the local militias, as it was. But the fact remains: the people gathered to complain of an unjust eviction. In Scotland, I hope we remember what it is to have land taken from us, and to not be permitted to work it! To be left to starve in the midst of abundance. Or we might ask the Irish. Or the poor in Lancaster or Liverpool or London for that matter. Did we answer a Chartist gathering with a massacre? Do these people really not have a right to farm land that has been enclosed and abandoned? Upon which they were so recently slaves? *This* was the cause for which Mr Gordon and Mr Bogle were—'

'Bogle!' cried Sarah, through a mouthful of cake. 'Don't tell me that rascal Bogle had a hand in it! He'll lead Sir Roger astray, I said he would, and now look, he's running riot. Sir Roger's too soft-hearted is the trouble . . . I've said it before: you can't trust these people, the Africans no more than the Indians. They'll all cut your throat soon as look at you.'

'Wife-of-mine, we are speaking of a different Bogle, entirely. Yours I believe is a Mr *Andrew* Bogle. We speak of Paul. An insurrectionist Bogle. Who has been executed, along with his co-conspirators. In Jamaica.'

'You must understand, William,' persisted the Targe, 'great parcels of land stand empty!' All Ainsworths now looked to the carpet, just as if this were Exeter House, and they the audience, and the Targe glowering at them over an abolitionist's lectern. 'Meanwhile these absentee landlords half a world away sit with their boots up on the tables of the Bond Street taverns!'

William set down his pipe in despair at ever being given an opportunity to smoke it.

'But who owns the land? And what do Bond Street taverns have to do with – no, no, I'm sorry, Eliza – I'm not sure what you're getting at—'

'Oh, it'll be property he's after! That Bogle wants all the Tichborne land for himself. He's no friend to Sir Roger, mark my words.'

A stricken cry was heard upstairs. Everyone present announced themselves more than willing to go to the child, but – an excess of sherry notwithstanding – Mrs Ainsworth's maternal pride held firm. She rose, unsteadily, to her feet, and brushed aside the great quantity of cake crumb that had gathered in her cleavage.

'I will go, naturally. There is no substitute for a mother's love.'

14.

Agreeing to Disagree

With Mrs Ainsworth safely on the stair, William shifted squarely in his chair to face the Targe. But the moment her penetrating eyes were upon him, his own began to dart between the floor, the wall, the clock, his daughters.

'Now look . . . I mean to say . . . the trouble is, Eliza, freedom has been given. As indeed it *had* to be given – I was ever a supporter of the idea in principle. Even *despite* the great cost to the Lancashire poor – as we both witnessed on our last trip, if you'll recall – not to mention the Liverpool poor and the London poor and indeed all the poor souls who weave cotton and pack sugar and coffee, with whose welfare you do seem rather less concerned I must say . . . But to reach my point: freedom has been given. Yet chaos has followed. Which does rather make one wonder . . .'

Mrs Touchet sat back down, exhausted. Over the years she had concluded that there was no point in becoming furious at sheer ignorance, no more than she found she could blame an unbaptized baby for not knowing Christ. *If he knew what I knew he would feel as I do* was a formula she repeated to herself often, in order to maintain her sanity.

'And I really couldn't bear all those nasty petitions. Never knowing who would or would not agree to come to dinner with whom . . . Carlyle's crowd defending the Governor, and on the other side, your so-called "Jamaica Committee". Couldn't make head nor tails of it. Six of one and half a dozen of the other. Sign one petition and lose half your friends; sign the other – lose the rest. I say: whatever the truth of the matter, it is neither nice nor civilized to split convivial London in twain over a disturbance thousands of miles hence.'

'Here, here!' piped simple-minded Emily, who shared with her father an unassailable preference for nice things over nasty. 'And besides, our old friend Charles is on the Governor's side, *with* Carlyle – and whatever you may think of Carlyle, Eliza' – she spoke quickly, for everybody in the room had already heard at great length over many years precisely what Eliza thought of Thomas Carlyle – 'you must admit that our old friend Charles – as we knew him back in the Kensal Lodge days at least – was ever a friend of the weak and the poor. Famously so.'

'One might even say he grew rich demonstrating the bond.'

This was not at all nice, and shocked Emily profoundly.

'Oh, but Eliza, that *is* unfair! No one could have been kinder. Fanny, you remember that lovely time he came to visit us all in school! And brought cakes and books and was ever so kind and nice. What a surprise that was! For such a great man as Mr Dickens to take the time to do such a generous thing for three little motherless girls, far from home.'

Eliza narrowed her eyes at the South Downs: 'You are too easily surprised, Emily. I accompanied him on that trip, if you recall, and the fact is he came to Manchester in the first place in search of characters – that's where he got his absurd Cheeryble twins.'

'Ah, now that is true, girls,' said William, thoughtfully. 'He wished to meet Whiggish business types in the North, and I told him: "If it's characters you want, Charles, look up the Brothers Grant." I knew he'd make use of them.'

Eliza laughed loudly but without humour.

'That he most certainly did. A nice occupation to take two human beings and turn them into cartoons barely worthy of Cruikshank's inkpot!'

The force of this sent tobacco smoke the wrong way down William's throat, prompting a brief coughing fit.

'Our Mrs Touchet has extended herself from abolitionism to literary criticism . . .'

But as he spoke he allowed himself a coy smile, just as he did on those rare but satisfying occasions when their 'old friend' came up for a kicking in the book pages.

'Well, I still say you are unfair,' complained Emily. 'No one could be said to care more for people than Charles.'

'Fictional people. Those he can control. I was not surprised in the least to see his name on that petition. Even as a young man, he feared chaos. And real life will ever incline towards chaos.'

William scoffed, but uneasily, never knowing quite what to do with Mrs Touchet's occasional flights of philosophy.

'Does any sane man like chaos?'

' "*It is better for a man to go wrong in freedom than to go right in chains.*" Mr Huxley.'

'Well! I must say this Governor Eyre business makes for strange bedfellows! Mrs Touchet finds common cause with a notorious agnostic, and our old friend Charles supposedly on the side of a murderer . . .'

'Oh, what does it matter what that man thinks of anything? He's a novelist!'

Without meaning to, she had spoken in the same tone with which one might say *He's a child*.

'Do you know . . .' said William, after a painful interval. 'I feel quite tired suddenly. I think I shall go up.'

Mrs Touchet was flooded with remorse.

'Oh, please don't leave, not on my account. You were reading the paper, and I rudely interrupted you. Please go on.'

'No, no. I am a novelist. The news is beyond my comprehension.'

'Oh, William, I didn't mean – please do read the rest.'

'There is nothing left to read.' But there was, a little, and reading aloud to a captive audience was a pleasure William found difficult to

84

forgo. After very little encouragement, he lifted his paper once more.

'It appears to have been a fraught decision. The Chief Justice condemned the Governor in "no uncertain terms", and yet the jury still "threw the case out". So: there you are. They agreed to disagree, like Englishmen. As you and I will do this evening, Eliza.'

15.

A Tichborne Addendum

Clara's cries subsided. The clock struck nine. Sarah reappeared in the hall.

'Was you all just talking of the Chief Justice? Bovill?'

William frowned perplexedly at his wife: 'Cockburn's the Justice.'

'Who's Bovill then?'

'William Bovill? Chief Justice of the Common Pleas. Different job.'

'Well, it's him who'll hear the Tichborne case!'

'That so! Poor man. Who'd be a Chief Justice?'

'And I'll tell you something else for nothing: your Guv'nor's gotten a fairer go of it in the courts than poor Sir Roger ever will. It's rigged before it's even begun! You mark my words.'

They had no choice but to mark them, loud as they were, continuous, and long. Leaning like a sailor in the doorway, Sarah now extemporized on the 'shadowy Freemasons' who 'run the Old Bailey' and the 'bitter Catholics' who pay the bribes to the Freemasons who run the Old Bailey, and the 'Hebrew moneylenders' who earn a guinea for every soul thrown in Newgate. She was decrying the many vital Tichborne witnesses presently being 'silenced' in Brazil and New South Wales when Fanny found a gap and interjected.

'But you will have heard Mr Orton got an early boat home from the New World? Leaving his legal team rather in the lurch?'

'*Sir Roger* was taken ill – yes I heard.'

'I wonder if it wasn't the idea of being caught in his lies that turned his stomach . . .'

'Contrarily, Fanny Ainsworth, it happens the Brazilian sun weren't agreeing with him. He's doing much better now.'

'*Much* better – it's all over the Hampshire papers. Father, you'll like this: Mr Orton and his negro – Mr Bogle! – have taken rooms in Alresford, just by Tichborne Park, where they await the trial. Meantimes, the Claimant spends each day drinking in the Swan Hotel. Apparently, the Jamaican fellow behaves with perfect decency – sits there quiet as a vicar, charming everyone with his genteel manners – while our Mr Orton gets drunk, stuffs his gut, spends what's left of the Tichborne Fund and gets into fisticuffs with the locals –'til his Mr Bogle takes him home! Isn't that funny?'

William was very tickled by this and laughed heartily.

'I like this Sir Roger very much! He is better than the original: truly to the manner born. Who could doubt him?'

'Yes, yes, you laugh it up, Mr Ainsworth. I'm sure you're very funny. But I seen many a Lord myself as a child, in the company my mum kept, if you know what I mean—'

'—Yes, thank you, Mrs Ainsworth, that will do—'

'—The kind of company you meet in certain corners of certain streets in Soho, if you know what I mean—'

'WE KNOW WHAT YOU MEAN, MRS AINSWORTH, NOW PLEASE—'

'—And what sort of thing does a Lord like? I'll tell you: fighting, fucking, drinking, and kicking a pigskin about. Now, what does my old man and all my uncles and brothers and cousins like? None different. It's only them on the bottom and top know how to live! The ones in the middle are odd ones out, if you ask me. All that *reading*. They're curious and no mistake!'

William had left the room at 'fucking' but Eliza was privately more impressed by this analysis than anything the new Mrs Ainsworth had said or done since she'd met her, including the floors and the bed linens.

16.

Chapman Sees a Ghost

On a brisk walk with William and the dogs – across the Downs, towards the Reigate coach – Eliza saw a gentleman approaching on the path. There was no one else for miles, and the weather was blustery: scarves, tails, skirt hems and branches waving wildly. Mol and Pol chased the spiralling leaves, with William in lumbering pursuit, out of breath and bellowing. He did not notice the man staring at him as he ran past, nor seem to recognize him. Eliza walked more slowly; her clothes did not permit the same freedom of movement. She knew the man at once.

'Mr Chapman! Mrs Touchet. It's been many years. It *is* Edward Chapman, isn't it? Of Chapman and Hall?'

But he had turned to gawp at William as he disappeared, with the dogs, over the brow of the next hill.

'We met at Kensal Lodge, many times . . .'

Chapman turned back, evidently astonished.

'Mrs Touchet! Of Kensal Lodge – of course. Those were happy days. So very lively! Horne and Cruikshank and Maclise and Kenealy and the rest, all around the same table . . . But what a place to meet! Are you . . . holidaying?'

Mrs Touchet tactfully explained her changed circumstance. She saw that he was hoping to hear certain words and phrases from her: *with my husband* or *and my children* or *thankfully, my granddaughter*. She could only disappoint him.

'Well, it's beautiful country. Wish I lived here myself! But London proves a hard place to leave. Although I am retired, as of last year. My cousin Frederick has taken my place at the firm. Yet I find he still has need of me, or so I tell myself.'

'No doubt he does. Is business good, Mr Chapman?'

'Oh, busy as ever, thanks mostly to our old friend Dickens. Another Kensal Lodge regular! And we shouldn't forget Thackeray – though truth be told it was always rather easy to forget him . . . But I – I – must ask: was that Harrison Ainsworth who just passed? With the whiskers?'

'My cousin, yes! He is the cousin I live with. That I still live with. I'm sorry he didn't stop. He notices little, I'm afraid. He lives in his mind. As writers so often do, although of course you'd know that better than anybody, Mr Chapman, I mean to say, having dealt with so many of them!'

Mrs Touchet was conscious of prattling. She only prattled when anxious, and nothing made her more anxious than the suspicion that she was being considered, by a man, to be a worthy object of pity. She wound her scarf another time around her neck and closed her mouth, resolving to say no more.

'My word. Harrison Ainsworth.'

But it was perfectly clear to Mrs Touchet that what Mr Chapman truly meant was: *I thought he was dead.*

17.

Visiting Gilbert

It was a long, dull ride to Reigate. Several times Mrs Touchet considered opening her mouth to relay this encounter on the Downs. The prospect filled her with a great weariness. Saying the name of Chapman would only prompt, in William, a series of melancholy reflections. She was relieved to reach Gilbert's cosy cottage – a home that words had built, back when William's words still built things – and take her seat by the hearth, with nothing more to think about now than Gilbert's hand in hers, and the slow, circular stroking of his palm, as William read aloud from Defoe. There were pies and cakes on the sideboard, left by a Mrs McWilliam, wife of a nearby farmer, and the red flagstones shone, washed down with milk by McWilliam's daughter, who came daily to clean and set the fire in the grate.

Although Gilbert could neither speak sense nor read, he appeared to enjoy hearing stories. A special favourite was *Robinson Crusoe*. It made him whoop and pull on his whiskers, especially when the cannibals arrived. Such strong reactions left little space for Eliza's feelings. But today the section being read lacked adventure, and Gilbert was quiet. In the silence, Eliza was pricked, on the sudden, by an overwhelming and acute sense of loneliness. A severe, revisionist feeling, it worked upon her cruelly, making her feel that loneliness was all she had ever known. A consequence, perhaps, of what old women called 'The Change'. A special, feminine form of delusion, not to be trusted, and yet apparently impossible to avoid. 'The Change' marked, in the mind of Mrs Touchet, the final hurdle in the ladies' steeplechase:

The humiliations of girlhood.

The separating of the beautiful from the plain and the ugly.

The terror of maidenhood.

The trials of marriage or childbirth – or their absence.

The loss of that same beauty around which the whole system appears to revolve.

The change of life.

What strange lives women lead!

She forced herself to think back, to her prime. No, it wasn't true: she had been the opposite of lonely. Between William's gift for joy and Frances' moral clarity, her younger days were stretched intolerably – almost to the point of breaking. In fact, a long time ago she had sat in this very room, with Gilbert, and thought Gilbert lucky to love animals and machinery instead of people, for people were so fearfully complicated. People were draining. But this, too, now struck her as delusion. Why had she ever imagined she knew what was best for a man like Gilbert – for anyone? Loneliness! Like an affliction it leapt from the page directly into the room with her, seeming to belong not to Gilbert or William or even Crusoe but solely to her:

Here I meditated nothing but my escape, and what method I might take to effect it, but found no way that had the least probability in it. Nothing presented to make the supposition of it rational; for I had no body to communicate it to, that would embark with me; no fellow-Slave, no Englishman, Irishman, or Scotsman there but myself.

18.

A Gift for Joy, 1832

They had run from The Elms, making their escape down the back stairs, and were saddled and halfway to Willesden before anybody knew they were gone. These were the very last days of August: summer was to be seized now or lost for ever. Galloping through Brondesbury, recklessly jumping stiles, the trees shuddered yellow at the merest touch of their branches. At last Eliza overtook William on the Mapesbury Road. She looked back to gloat. Instead, the irresistible vision of a young prince, dashing down a golden carpet, as if in flight from royal commitments.

What was he escaping? Three children under the age of five. No less did Eliza seek to escape them, and this surprised her. Not that she had forgotten Toby – she would never forget him – but whatever illuminated window had allowed her, during his life, to see the world as a place full of children, and intended primarily *for* children – this portal had closed. Other people's children now belonged to the realm of the female: a wearying kingdom. When a child cried, her heart no longer leapt or broke. She only wondered why it cried and who was going to stop it. It was especially wearying to be trapped with children in a sullen and joyless house, in which all residents were driven to distraction by money worries, courtesy of Frances' father, Mr Ebers, who had become a bankrupt.

'But what does this all mean for *you*? Did he even pay her dowry, in the end?'

William groaned.

'Cousin, not only did I never receive the three hundred per annum we were promised upon marriage, now the old fool owes seventy thousand to his creditors – of which I am of course one. Our little publishing concern is *kaput*. I'm afraid my fortunes are tied to those of Mr Ebers and now we shall both crash to earth. Who could have predicted it? But Mrs Touchet: we are escaping for the afternoon! Not another word about feckless fathers-in-law!'

Mrs Touchet could have predicted it. If anyone had less business acumen than Frances' father it was Frances' husband. Their 'little publishing concern' had alarmed her from the start. In two years of operation they had managed one misguided pamphlet on poverty – by William – a squib of Walter Scott's, and a badly written memoir concerning Mr Ebers' decade running the King's Theatre in Haymarket. The theatre itself had been a debt-ridden folly, one which the new publishing venture was supposed to offset. Now debt piled on debt.

'Your face is even longer than usual. Why? It's my trouble, Eliza, not yours.'

'But William, we are all, myself included, dependants in your household, and therefore, unfortunately, your debt *is*—'

'Cousin: look around you. We are in Arcadia, by way of Willesden Green! Give yourself up to joy! For once!'

William jumped down from his horse and pulled at her skirts. She slid off her own horse and fell inelegantly into the long grass. Behind them was an oak tree of perfect proportions. In front, over the next hill, the pretty spire of St Mary's, Willesden. Above their heads, springing out of the nearest hedgerow, an explosion of verbena. Each purple cluster of blossom had its own hovering butterfly. Her cousin put both hands up her skirts, seeking her stays.

'William, whose field is this?'

'What does it matter? You don't believe in private property.'

'I believe in the power of the law that protects it. I don't want to be shot in the rear – or mistaken for a deer.'

'You rhymester, you!'

He kissed her passionately on her neck. This always had an extraordinary effect on her knees. She lay down at once.

'We are in debt. Agreed. Arcadia lost. But I have a plan, cousin. I will finish *Rookwood*. The debt will be paid. Arcadia restored!'

She reversed their arrangement and straddled him. Mr Ebers owed his son-in-law twelve thousand pounds. Mired in paperwork related to the bankruptcy, William had not written a word of his novel since February. Besides, the writing of novels – even good ones – did not seem, to Mrs Touchet, a rational response to a financial crisis.

'It takes more than paid debts to restore Arcadia, William.'

'What about when a brilliant young man hopes to sell a thousand subscriptions in a month?'

She held both his wrists tightly to the ground: 'Even less likely. I will remind you of the camel and the needle.'

'I see. So you would have me be a St Zita and give away my writings *gratis*?'

'The poor don't need literature, William. They need bread. Turn over.'

With his face down in the dirt – a Lord being taught a lesson in reversals by his housemaid – William began a long, profane anecdote about his latest Italian trip. He went to Europe as often as he could, for 'inspiration', and whenever he did, he relied on Mrs Touchet to come down to London and help Frances with the uninspiring task of watching his children. This time he had gone to the walled city of Lucca. There, in the Basilica di San Frediano, he had seen St Zita herself, 'that light-fingered servant girl', dressed in blue and gold and laid out in a glass box, where she had lain these past five hundred and sixty years. There were fresh flowers in her hair – in reference to the miracle of the bread and flowers – and she was, in William's judgement, somewhat small for a saint, being really no taller than Frances. Mrs Touchet imagined what it would be to go to such a place and see such a thing. What she

94

herself would make of it. Mrs Touchet picked up a long stick from the ground and tried it on her cousin twice. It did not stop him talking:

'The *padre* of course insisted she was uncorrupted, but I'd say there was more of pickle than purity about her. Her skin was leathery – almost black as a negro's. Sure sign of the embalmer's art. Of course the old necromancer wouldn't hear a word of it. You should have heard him, Eliza: "*Ha preso ai ricchi per dare ai poveri! Come Robin Hood!!*" With tears in his eyes. Sentimental beyond belief. Honestly, sometimes I think the only thing that keeps you in that superstitious cult is the fact that you've never been to its capital. If you did, I promise you: your mind would revolt!'

A third whack silenced him – bar a burbling murmur of pleasure. Did she really believe in miracles? There was a bracketed place in her brain where things were both true and not true simultaneously. In this same space one could love two people. Live two lives. Escape and be at home.

Afterwards, they passed a long time looking up at the sky. The view was a pleasure. The birds were a pleasure. The butterflies, the verbena, the gold outlines on the clouds, direct from Titian. The light itself. She did not know what face to assume in the face of it all, but turning her head, found William beaming shamelessly. What a gift for joy he had! Resentment, anger, bitterness, shame – all as foreign to his character as they were native to her own.

'You will admit this is Arcadia, and that we have trespassed upon it. Yes you will.'

'I admit nothing.'

A friend to make love with. What could be better? A conversation that began in that basement theatrical was not yet ended, and was almost always full of light and laughter. What would her life be without it? They made themselves decent, got back on their horses and headed home. Coming back round the bend to Kilburn, the sun disappeared suddenly, obscured by a grey squall. A rain sent only for the guilty soaked them quickly and thoroughly. Any hope of a quiet return was dashed by the grim sight of Frances in the front garden trying to make a game of apple collection. Her soggy children were not fooled and knew it was a task that would only be followed by another task: peeling. As the sodden pair approached, Frances greeted them with an apron full of apples and a wounded look. William slid off his horse and vaulted over the front wall. 'Has it come to this? Are we so poor it is apples for breakfast, supper and pudding?'

He hugged his wife until she, too, was wet and laughing. Another emotion to which he was a stranger: guilt. Mrs Touchet struggled to know which attitude to take up. Who was she betraying? It was not safe to look at either party. She joined the children lifting apples.

19.

A Ladies' Outing, 1830

It was Mrs Touchet's first time visiting Leicester. Leicester was not Italy – Mr Ainsworth was back in Italy – but it was somewhere new, and she had Mrs Ainsworth by her side. They sat knee to knee, needing no excuse for proximity. Still, the roads were bad and the coach full. Only Frances' enthusiasm could have persuaded her.

They were off to visit a Mrs Heyrick, whom Mrs Touchet had never met. In preparation, she opened that lady's pamphlet and began reading. It was her first time attending one of Frances' 'meetings': best to be prepared. By the time they'd changed horses, at Newport Pagnell, she had finished the pamphlet, and confessed herself grudgingly impressed, both by *Immediate, Not Gradual, Abolition*, and Frances' description of the author's character:

'Quite your sort of woman. She thinks only of justice! For animals, for prisoners, for the destitute, and for the poor slaves, of course. Her husband died long ago, she has no children: all her energies go to her causes. She has even begun a girls' boarding school in her own home – it must be a large house, she is certainly respectable – and oh! She has set herself the task, along with her friend Susannah Watts, you'll meet her, too – they are knocking on every door in Leicester to persuade the ladies to take sugar off their household lists, and after she has finished in Leicester she means to go to Birmingham! A boycott, you see.'

'That is clever.'

'Isn't it!'

'Gratifying to find someone who practises what they preach.' Mrs

Touchet was aware that their conversation was annoying the old gentleman sat opposite. To further annoy him she now looked down at the pamphlet, turned to a page she had marked with a corner-fold, and read aloud: '*The cause of emancipation calls for something more decisive, more efficient, than words.*'

'Oh, but she is ever so decisive! That is really what I admire about her most . . . Justice has concerned Mrs Heyrick since childhood. They say that she went to rescue a kitten once, with her parents, when she was a very young girl, and well, she chose the ugliest kitten, Eliza, you see, because she loves the despised – and once she even stopped a circle of rough men, bull-baiters, you know, by running off with their bull and hiding it in a barn! She is *very* brave. She visits prisons regularly and speaks to the prisoners. She reminds me of you.'

'Really?'

Eliza was delighted by this comparison – her face grew warm and red – but a moment's self-reflection exposed a harder truth. She did not like ugly animals, dreaded prisons, and would never dare interfere in the pastimes of working men. She could think of nothing worse than running a school.

'I think you only mean that we are both somewhat energetic widows.'

'Well, neither of you are ones for half measures, that's for certain.'

'*So then because thou art lukewarm, and neither cold nor hot, I will spue thee out of my mouth.*'

'Oh, yes, but Eliza, you see, well – I must confess: Mrs Heyrick is a *Quaker* . . .'

It was a lukewarm day in Leicester, drizzling, with a fitful sun that kept promising much and delivering nothing. They had reached their destination earlier than expected; there was time for a little tourism. Standing on Bow Bridge, looking down at the water, their clasped hands were well hidden by a strategically placed shawl. There was no need for words. To Mrs Touchet they seemed to breathe at the same pace, chests rising and falling together, blood pulsing at the same rate, as if one organism. Thus overwhelmed with happiness, she hazarded the possibility that in the silence they were thinking the same thought?

'Oh, I don't think so! Unless you were thinking about Richard the Third.'

Mrs Touchet said nothing. She had not been thinking about Richard III.

'Even in school I never did understand *why* he went on to Bosworth after he struck his spur! The old crone clearly warned him that the next time he crossed Bow Bridge it would be his head – and so it was! But if he had heeded the warning in the first place he never would have gone to Bosworth and been killed, nor had his head cracked open like that on this bridge. Why ever didn't he listen to her?'

Don't you love me? thought Mrs Touchet.

'Men don't listen to old crones,' she said.

20.

Bow Bridge House

Bow Bridge House, home of Mrs Heyrick, turned out to be an eccentric white folly with crenellations and battlements and Gothic windows. Strange dwelling for a lover of justice.

'They do say an Englishwoman's home is her castle . . .'

'Oh, Eliza, please don't make jokes. I think it is quite pretty, really — and *very* original.'

On the doorstep, two old women stood, Elizabeth and Susannah, not yet crones but swiftly approaching that condition. Mrs Touchet readied herself for small talk and dithering. Instead, she was met with quick courtesies and a firm sense of purpose. Decisively the new arrivals were corralled into a double-fronted drawing room to join perhaps fifty neatly dressed women with their hands in their laps, sat in rows of chairs, as if for a recital. Now Mrs Heyrick walked down the middle of the room to light applause, while Mrs Touchet and Frances were directed to their seats by Miss Watts.

'Are you *all* women?' Mrs Touchet enquired.

'Mrs Heyrick believes women are especially qualified to plead for the oppressed. That is one of the things we recommend our campaigning ladies to repeat, when going door to door, speaking against the evils of sugar.'

Frances made a little note in the journal she had just taken out: 'How clever! I shall remember that!'

Mrs Touchet was amused: 'We shall add this task to the lists of harassed lady housekeepers across the nation: *One. Buy no sugar. Two. Remember to get oranges. Three. Plead for the oppressed . . .*'

Silence.

'Do you mean to be funny, Mrs Touchet? I'm afraid I fail to see the humour.'

'No, I only—'

'You'll excuse me, ladies, I must go to my seat: we are about to begin.'

Mrs Touchet waited until the overly serious Miss Watts was out of earshot, then turned to Frances, as she would have done to William, in expectation of comic commiseration, ready to laugh and roll her eyes. But the lovely countenance was stonily unamused: 'You mustn't always *tease*, Eliza. Not everything is funny. And people will misunderstand you.'

Frances turned back to attend to the presentation. Mrs Touchet, chastised, did the same.

'The perpetuation of slavery in our West Indian colonies is not an abstract question,' intoned Mrs Heyrick, very loudly, from across the room. She had a low, booming voice. Interesting, too, that her friend Miss Susannah apparently taught in the boarding school that occupied the east wing of this house – and so presumably lived here, too. Now, what kind of arrangement was that? Were these two, perhaps, like those celebrated Ladies of Llangollen?

'It is not a question to be settled between the government and the planters; it is one in which we are all implicated. We are all guilty of supporting and perpetuating slavery. The West Indian planter and the people of this country stand in the same moral relation to each other as the thief and receiver of stolen goods . . .'

All the women in the room nodded simultaneously, a peculiar sight. Mrs Touchet squeezed the lovely hand of her companion and tried once more to draw her into comic complicity. But Mrs Ainsworth stared resolutely ahead, and with her other hand began taking notes, although as far as Mrs Touchet could make out, Mrs Heyrick was intoning *verbatim* the contents of her famous pamphlet. Lovely as Mrs Ainsworth was, Mrs Touchet realized suddenly that she rather missed the other Ainsworth. She was reminded of a vital difference between that fatally mismatched pair: Mrs Ainsworth had absolutely no sense of humour.

21.

A Ladies' Outing, 1870

Spring came, again. And with it a terrible sense of confinement. Change calls out for change, and it couldn't be that the frost receded, and the daffodils arrived, and the fox cubs, recently born, commenced screaming in the hedgerows – none of this could be borne if Mrs Touchet was to do nothing but sit at the window seat as she had all winter. *To every thing there is a season.* A lowly sentence. It was throned above the commandments in her soul, above even the gospels themselves. (She would never admit this to a priest. Only Frances had known.) In spring, Mrs Touchet always found herself extremely vulnerable to unlikely propositions.

'Wife-of-mine, I don't care if your "Sir Roger" is speaking in Parliament, on the plains of Kathmandu or atop the white cliffs of Dover. You will *not* be attending any such event without a chaperone, and as no one in this house has the least intention of—'

'I'll go.'

Everyone paused what they were doing to stare at Mrs Touchet. Only Clara – a careful student of the antipathy between her mother and the Targe – was too astonished to contain herself: 'You and Mama? Out . . . *together?*'

Thus exposed, Mrs Touchet borrowed a tone from the Edinburgh matrons of her childhood, canny Calvinists ever able to transform the dubious and unlikely into the predestined and inevitable: 'I have anyway been meaning to go to Horsham. We are in need of many things, for the kitchen and the house, and Horsham is surely cheaper than Brighton. I'll put orders in, and have Emily's Sunday shoes re-heeled.'

'There you are! Two birds with one bloody stone.'

'You might take your stone and clock Mr Orton between the eyes with it, while you're about it,' remarked Fanny, but the new Mrs Ainsworth had other things on her mind and did not rise to this.

'A ladies' outing it is, then,' said William, frowning. The mysteries of Mrs Touchet were, finally, unfathomable.

'A ladies' outing,' repeated his wife, a little doubtfully. She crossed the room to stand in sisterly pose next to the Targe, although upon reaching her thought better of attempting to take her hand. 'Won't we be something to see! I'll make a Tichborne convert of you yet, Lizzy!'

22.

Horsham

It pained Mrs Touchet to take a gig instead of the Horsham Omnibus, but she so dreaded the idea of inflicting the new Mrs Ainsworth upon innocent bystanders that she had decided to pay the extra. Now observing the great quantity of lavender fabric wrapped around the woman, the unnecessary ruches, flounces and bustles, the useless ribbons, the decorative combs in the tower of hair, and the comical little hat tilted forward on her forehead, she considered the additional outlay a positive bargain. Eliza herself was unchanged since the '40s. Her waist long, her sleeves tapered, she still wore a horsehair petticoat, a bonnet and a shawl, and parted her hair severely down the middle. She still looked – as one of the Kensal Lodge wits once had it – 'like a narrow bell in a Gothic church'. Alighting in central Horsham, in the Carfax, and consulting her list, she had no doubt she and Sarah were something to see. She refused to be derailed by gawkers. There was a butter dish and table linens to buy, a pair of candlesticks to have soldered, and shoes to mend, and all before half-past five.

But in mercantile matters – as in all others – the two women proved ill-matched. Eliza had a sharp eye for shoddy craftsmanship, political sympathy for the working man (but no cloudy sentiments regarding him) and never, ever parted with a shilling more than she intended to spend. Sarah had no sense of housekeeping in particular nor of money in general. She processed into each low-beamed workshop like a queen, keen to demonstrate the distance between herself and all these lowly joiners, farriers and seamstresses. (Eliza, who did the Ainsworth bookkeeping, knew the distance was not as great as Sarah supposed.) Yet the new Mrs Ainsworth was a capricious Lady Bountiful. Beggars appalled her. She had a very clear idea of how many pennies bought a half-pint of gin. It infuriated her that children in rags with bloody feet should be sent out 'to pluck at the heartstrings'. She had herself been 'on her uppers' many times, had stolen and starved if it came to that, but 'always drew the line at begging' – a point of pride. The only exception she made was for the legless. One missing leg would do, two was ideal, and Horsham – having sent a regiment to the Crimea – provided several moving examples. For these men she wept, bending over their cups in a pose of melancholy dignity, before leaving tuppence.

23.

'Sir Roger'

Errands completed, sun setting, Mrs Touchet fell into a reverie. This was the old Mrs Ainsworth with whom she now linked arms, they were on their way to Exeter House, no time whatsoever had passed . . .

As they neared the King's Head Hotel, reality reclaimed her. She found herself wrong-footed by the gathering crowd. It did not at all resemble those neat, sexless, pious, slightly tiresome women in whose company she and Frances attended abolitionist meetings around the country, thirty years ago. It did not look like any lecture crowd she had ever encountered. There were as many men as women. As many with dirty hands as clean. She saw farmers and hod-carriers and men with faces black with soot, holding their caps to their chests. She saw women for whom she knew no respectable name. Yet here, too, filing under the red-brick arch, were clerks and schoolteachers, dissenters of all stripes, shopkeepers and foremen, ladies' maids, cooks, governesses.

'Justice for Sir Roger!' cried a perfectly sane-looking girl, and thrust a pamphlet into Eliza's hand. Inside the hotel's assembly room, hanging from the rafters, a giant cloth sign hung, carefully stitched:

NO OPPRESSION! FAIR PLAY FOR EVERY MAN!

'See anything yet? Is Biddulph up there?'
The crowd was very large, stuffed in tightly, and what seats there were no one seemed willing to take lest they miss something. Only the

very tall had a clear view of the raised platform at the end of the room, upon which four chairs presently stood, two filled, two empty.

'Who is Biddulph?'

'The cousin! Distant, but not so distant as he don't know his own blood. Country squire, he is.'

As far as Eliza could make out, both men on the dais met this description. Tweedy and high-booted, scarlet-cheeked, and with their knees open wide, as if missing the long guns that more usually rested across them. One was slight, with lamb-chop sideburns. The other moustachioed, and more prosperous-looking.

'There'll be Mr Anthony Biddulph, the cousin, and then there's the moneybags, Onslow. He'd be Sir Roger's greatest supporter. Goes with him everywhere. *Guildford* Onslow on account of that his family owns half of Guildford so naturally they give him the name and as if that weren't enough he's also the MP of the place if you don't mind. Now, could a common butcher make such high acquaintance, I ask you?'

As ever, she spoke loudly, prompting many excruciating conversations with nearby strangers. Eavesdropping, Eliza was amazed. All present had the strongest possible feelings about the Claimant, and many elaborate theories of conspiracy regarding him. No one found the subject, by definition, absurd. It was almost touching to see the new Mrs Ainsworth so undespised, so welcomed in her conversation and opinions, and so much a fount of knowledge, for no one could match her for Tichborniana. In this hall, she was an expert. She knew the Claimant generally came late to these things, 'liking to make an entrance equal to his situation', and that last week, in Budleigh Salterton, he had been mobbed at the train station 'before he got anywhere near a stage'. She knew he generally did two events a day: one like this, for which you bought a ticket, and a 'free gathering' from the window of wherever he was staying, for those 'without a pot to piss in'. The property complications she understood as well as any land agent. Tichborne

Park was leased, at present, to a Colonel Lushington, as Sir Henry Tichborne, the next baronet in line – 'after our Sir Roger!' – was still an infant. Tonight, in Horsham, they would be raising money for a civil trial, so that Sir Roger – who, in this upside-down world, was the plaintiff – might sue the Tichbornes for the removal of said tenant, and the restoration of his ancestral lands. For without the help of the people, Sir Roger could have little chance in that den of papists, the courts.

'But are not the Tichbornes themselves . . . papists?' asked a hesitant young man, a schoolteacher by the looks of him: he carried a pair of dictionaries tied with string.

Sarah swivelled round like a politician on the stump: 'You've hit the nail on the head! And who don't know the power of such clans? Who's not heard of how an ill-timed confession can be turned against you! Girls locked up in convents and all sorts! Never to be seen again! Shadowy, they are. Never got over their royal disappointment, if you understand me. But they're patient, these Catholics. They lay in wait. Sit on their money, and keep it where we can't see it. And here's Sir Roger trying his best to pull back the veil over all that shadowy business! Now, naturally they don't like that! Naturally, they're going to destroy him best they can! Every newspaper's against him – well, what does that tell you? Whose side are *they* on? The people's? Decent, common people like yourself? Not bloody likely!'

This answer – which perplexed Eliza more than anything she'd heard so far – was loudly cheered. Feeling almost faint at the cluster of bodies, the clammy heat, the excessive stupidity, she inched left a little and took the seat she found there. She looked down at the pamphlet in her hand.

A Great Opportunity!
Purchase Mortgage Debentures
in the
Tichborne Estate

For the amount of £100
Offered by Sir Roger Tichborne
All bonds WILL BE Repaid with interest
Once his rightful inheritance is settled upon him!

Beneath this text, two daguerreotypes were reproduced. One was of a sloe-eyed, slender young man in a cravat, radiating the boredom of the very rich. Poignantly unaware of the watery grave that awaited him. The other showed a man of middle age and at least twenty stone, with the face of a simpleton and a chin-strap beard. He as much resembled a butcher from Wapping as any man could hope to without cleaver in hand. Both photographs were audaciously subtitled: SIR ROGER.

24.

Andrew Bogle

Bogle! There's Bogle! That's him!

Strange to hear three hundred people whispering the same thing at the same time, like an emanation of the earth. Eliza stood up. A black man – a very black man – was crossing the stage. His woolly hair was white, neat, and far back on his skull, and his beard was sparse but also neat, pointed like a parson's. He was not unlike a parson, in fact, everything about him being neat, calculated, black – coat, waistcoat, bow tie, the top hat he held in one hand – and all set off by a high white collar, heavily starched. He moved somewhat stiffly, as if troubled by pain. Upon reaching his chair, he was still and could be more closely inspected, and in fact his topcoat proved a size too big, and wrinkled and worn at the arms, and his fingers were likewise worn, long, and ashen. The top hat was frayed at its rim. Dignified, was the word. But a dignity hard won: a dignity in need of constant vigilance and protection. And this appeared to be the role of the adolescent who now appeared at the old man's elbow and gently helped him into his seat. He, too, was a negro, but of lighter complexion. His extraordinary hair – abundant as Bogle's was sparse – had been shaped into a pair of triangular wedges, one pointing up, the other down. Surely a son: they had the same narrow, almost Oriental eyes. But where Bogle's were a shrewd exception in a soft and inconclusive face, the boy's flashed round the room like lightning. A formulation straight out of William's pages! But she could think of no other word.

Speak, Bogle! You know him! We believe you, Bogle!

Later, Eliza could never decide whether it was the influence of the crowd or some mysterious and mesmerizing aspect of Bogle himself that had worked upon her. She was up on her toes, straining for an unobstructed view. It seemed that never in her life had she been more curious to hear a man speak. Before anybody could do so, however, the son left the stage and swiftly returned with the main event: the Claimant himself. A giant! The chin-strap beard had receded many inches – to make room for the several extra stone gained since last photographed – and every button strained at the sheer girth of the man. A gasp went round the room. It took a moment for Eliza to understand that this was a noise of purest approval, even of awe. For all professed themselves glad indeed to see that Sir Roger had been 'enjoying himself', drinking it up and eating it up, by the looks of it, and generally living life to the full, as any man would, given the chance. And why not? He who was so hard done by, the victim of so many lies from so many unscrupulous scribblers and moralists, all of them desperately plotting to bring down this fun-loving, beer-swilling, aristocratic man of the people, Sir Roger. Fellow only wanted what was owed him, after all! And what was justice, if not that? Wild cheering ricocheted round the room. Cries of *Bogle!* And *Tichborne!* Thrown up alternately, like tolling bells. No change came over Bogle: he stayed in his seat. His face retained that impenetrable glaze – impenetrable because so much itself – with apparently nothing hidden or masked about it. It was a confoundment, like honesty itself. Eliza was reminded of someone. Frances! But how ridiculous. And yet: Frances. She who had worn no masks and was therefore almost impossible to understand.

25.

The Claimant

The Claimant was another matter. Nudged onto the stage by the intense young mulatto, his face registered every emotion of the evening, along with that strange 'pouch-mouth' twitch – shared by the real Sir Roger – of which the papers had made much. One saw at once that here was a man who moved as the wind moved. A man with no centre, who might be nudged in any direction, depending. The watery eyes plainly revealed he was out of his depth; but then, too, that he enjoyed this crowd and was willing to believe in their belief if they after all felt so strongly . . . In fact, if it came to that, he *did* believe! In fact, it was an outrage that anyone could doubt him! And yet: what if they found him out? But how could they, as he was precisely who they said he was? How unfair and unjust that I must speak and be cruelly judged – and yet, if the judgement is to be like *this*, so full of jolly cheering and cries of *We're for* you, *Sir Roger,* no matter what I say – even before I speak! – well, then why not speak if they'll hear it and like it and want it so much? Eliza watched all of this and more pass over the Claimant's face, second by second, like weather. Everybody saw it. All that he thought and felt, every angle under consideration, every doubt and every self-defence – it was all impossible to miss, for it was right there, scandalously legible. And what else is honesty – as the new Mrs Ainsworth liked to say – but a face what reads like an open book?

VOLUME THREE

A knowledge of life is the least enviable of all species of knowledge, because it can only be acquired by painful experience.

LADY BLESSINGTON

I.

Kensal Lodge, July 1834

'More port!'

'Yes, one more bottle!'

'Gentlemen, I warn you: what I am about to read is such a piece of puffery, so *horrendously* flattering to its subject, that a mere bottle will hardly suffice. A gallon of port will be required to offset it.'

'A gallon, then!'

'Yes, a gallon! We are eight, are we? Yes, eight – a gallon will do. Mrs Touchet, a gallon of port for eight if you have it!'

They were nine. Mrs Touchet herself was the ghost.

'But let us not annoy Mrs Touchet!'

'Hear! Hear! No annoying of Mrs Touchet!'

'Let the record show: for Mrs Touchet every man present would willingly lay down not just his fork but his life! For is it not the case that where other young women leave as the port arrives, our Mrs Touchet not only brings it, she drinks it? A rare woman! A precious woman! Ah, let Mrs Touchet be anything but annoyed!'

'Observe the young lady's face. The moment for that consideration passed at least an hour ago. Chapman, are you going to read the damn thing out loud or not?'

'Yes! Now: I have in hand a copy of our beloved *Fraser's*, issue number fifty, in which we find our friend Maclise—'

'Hurrah! Arise, Maclise!'

'Stand, Maclise! Raphael of Kensal Rise!'

'Michelangelo of Willesden Green!'

'I prefer to sit.'

'—As you wish – here we find our dear Maclise's entry into *The Gallery of Illustrious Literary Characters*, namely our equally dear: Ainsworth!'

'Boy-author of *Rookwood*! Toast of London!'

'He who hath dug up old Dick Turpin's bones and made the black-guard ride to York very, very fast – really at a somewhat improbable speed!'

'Gentlemen, gentlemen . . . please. You flatter me.'

'*I'll* give you improbable: last week I was on the Great North Road myself, stopped in the Goose and Gander, and right there behind the bar is one of *your* damned illustrations, Cruikshank – torn out and tacked up on the wall – and guess what the landlord says to me?'

'I daren't imagine.'

' "*See that? Right 'ere's where the highwayman Turpin and his trusty Black Bess jumped the fence on their Ride to York*." As if the bloody thing had really happened!'

'What can I say? I take my magic inkpot; I draw; it becomes reality. It is a singular gift I have.'

'Ha! Ha! Ha! Here's to Cruikshank's magic inkpot!'

'All credit to Cruikshank, I'm sure – but have any of you walked into town lately? I counted three dramatic versions of this "Ride to York" on Shaftesbury Avenue alone! Proof that words may travel, too, and without the aid of pictures.'

'*Nix my doll, pals, fake away . . .*'

'Oh, please not that bloody song again!'

'Proof that any Tom, Dick or Harry may slice up a novel as he likes, strip out the speaking parts, and call it a play!'

'Or a song!'

'All of which earns me not a brass farthing, by the way . . .'

'Pity the young sensation!'

'Ah, now, I'm with Ainsworth on that one: I call it theft. Gentlemen, I know I am young and only just now entering your noble profession—'

'Thanks due to Chapman!'

'On the contrary, thanks due to Ainsworth, for introducing young *Boz* to his publisher – and illustrator.'

'—Well, however it was achieved, it seems I am to be published. And what a rum business I find it! One thing I can say in favour of court reporting: I was always certain to be paid for work done. Turn to literature? New rules apply. Good Chapman here binds my book and sells it: very good. Now what's to stop any Soho sneak from copying any section of it and selling it on his own account? Or slicing out Cruikshank's pictures, framing 'em, and making a pretty penny?'

'Alas, nothing at all!'

'I tell you, this is the only business in this world where any man may take the fruits of another man's labour – his sweat and his tears – and pay him not a damn penny for it – all the while getting rich himself!'

'Hear! Hear! Purest slavery! Let's form a charter! Now what about that port?'

2.

The First Insatiable

'Look: it's getting late – is Chapman going to read this whatever it is or not?'

'I'd like to – I am serially interrupted. Where *is* that lovely wife of yours, William – she must hear this, too. It refers to her!'

'Mrs Ainsworth is . . . indisposed,' said Mrs Touchet, with a delicate grimace, intended to imply feminine troubles, and therefore halt any further masculine enquiry.

'Ah. Well, we will respectfully raise a glass in her absence.'

'Your glass is empty, Forster.'

'Tragedy! Um . . . Mrs Touchet, I wonder if I might . . .'

'And now I shall read: "*I have not the pleasure of being acquainted with Mrs Ainsworth, but we are sincerely sorry for her – we deeply commiserate her case. You see what a pretty fellow THE young Novelist of the Season is; how exactly, in fact, he resembles one of the most classically handsome and brilliant of the established lady killers—*" '

'—surely they mean d'Orsay . . .'

'They mean d'Orsay, of course. Though we pray the resemblance is only physical! For the sake of public morality!'

'Gentlemen, I assure you public morality is in no danger from me. The Count d'Orsay's romantic life, as you will have heard, is said to be somewhat triangular—'

'Gossip! Wildest gossip!'

'Whereas mine is a simple, decent and Christian straight line drawn between husband and wife . . .'

'But does not the Lady Blessington herself intend a fresh triangulation? Has she not named Ainsworth and d'Orsay "*the two handsomest young men in England*"?'

'Yes, but where do *I* stand in these rankings?'

'Hear! Hear! I am personally insulted by my absence from this list!'

'MAY I CONTINUE?'

'Must you?' asked Mrs Touchet, but was not heeded.

'It goes on: "*If he escapes scot-free during these first months of his blazing literary success, he is a lucky as well as a well-grown lad. May he — as far as is consistent with the frailty of humanity — penetrate puffery, and avoid the three insatiables of Solomon!*" Now how about that! Who wrote it, do you think?'

'Maginn. I'm a Cork man myself. I'd know that fancified Irish prose anywhere.'

'And if Kenealy says it's Maginn, it's Maginn. Imagine, Ainsworth. You, a subject for Maginn!'

'I am gratified.'

'He's bloody delighted!'

'Let me remind the table — the three insatiables of King Solomon were as follows: women, horses, money. *Do* you pledge to avoid them, young Ainsworth?'

'Well, let's see. I am a poor horseman; you are all presently drinking my money — I believe I can resist everything except puffery. I confess I like to be puffed, and to puff others.'

Mrs Touchet wondered what had happened to the first insatiable.

'And Maclise! What a portrait! Fit for the Uffizi. Have you ever seen such a dandy?'

'That is the mere copy. We have before us the original.'

'The original wears more rings.'

'And now for port! There must be port!'

'I really must insist Mrs Ainsworth be informed of the irresistibility of her own husband, if only for—'

'—The children are on the stairs,' said Mrs Touchet, and left the table.

3.

The View from the Stairs

The summer heat had driven them from their rooms. They sat in descending order of age, peering through the banisters. Anne-Blanche's little toes barely reached the step below. Mrs Touchet climbed high as Fanny, then surprised them all by sitting down.

'Who *are* those men?' Emily's cheeks were dampest and reddest. She spoke in a plaintive way, as if still dreaming.

'I know Maclise. He is the painter,' explained Fanny. She was almost eight. Her rightful place was downstairs, with Mrs Touchet and the clever gentlemen. Instead, she was stuck upstairs with babies and nincompoops and invalids.

'And there's Charles!' Emily considered herself on first-name terms with any fellow who would think to bring round sugar drops and say *one for Emily and one for my horse* and then eat the one for the horse in plain sight, and pretend he hadn't.

'Who is that and who is that and who is that?' Anne-Blanche used a doll's hand to point. Thus were Mrs Touchet's strict rules on pointing evaded.

'Well, next to Maclise is Mr Chapman. He makes books. He is what you call a "publisher". And Mr Horne beside him, he writes about them.'

'Publishers?'

Mrs Touchet laughed. She had never really learned how to speak to children.

'Books. He is writing a book presently: *A New Spirit of the Age*. Your father will be in it, and some of his friends. Mr Horne is a critic.'

Fanny frowned and said it wasn't polite to criticize others, and Mrs Touchet, regretting her previous show of levity, frowned too: 'If wheat is not to be separated from chaff then there will be only chaff.' Which descent into moralizing made the sisters sigh greatly. Mrs Touchet continued: 'Next to him is Kenealy. He is an Irishman.'

'Is he a writer, too?'

'I believe so — of some description.'

'Is he nice?' asked Emily. She always liked to know who was nice and who was nasty.

'He is very Irish. He is of uneven temper.'

Anne-Blanche's doll thrust its hand out again: 'Who's that? Is he nice?'

'That is Mr Cruikshank. He illustrated your father's novel, among other things.'

'You don't like him.' Fanny's powers of penetration Mrs Touchet considered unseemly in one so young. 'Why not?'

There were men who found Eliza spiky, certainly, and probably a tad severe, but also witty and lively in conversation. They chose the seat next to her, even occasionally competed for it. Then there were the men who regarded her with alarm, for here was one of Samuel Johnson's dogs, up on her hind legs. Cruikshank was in this latter camp. The antipathy was mutual. She disliked his early, political work. William had tried to convince her that he had always been 'on the right side', that it was his job to 'ridicule it all, abolitionists included', but she had felt personally ridiculed by his cartoons, and could not forgive him.

'For one thing,' Mrs Touchet improvised, 'he drinks too much, and for another, he has a jaundiced view of the world. You should pray for him.'

All three little girls nodded very solemnly. Prayer was the only power they had to modify the world, and they took the responsibility of it as seriously as any monk.

'Finally, there is a Mr Forster. He is new to me. His chief distinction appears to be that he is the bosom friend of your Charles, Emily. But what time is it? How is your mother?' Silence. 'Crying, still?' Mute nods. 'Did she eat the plate I left?'

'No. She gave it to the dog,' Emily whispered.

'How long will you stay with us?' Fanny wanted to know.

'As long as I am needed. Until your mother feels well again.'

'How long will that be?' asked Emily.

'And now to bed,' said Mrs Touchet, and scooped Anne-Blanche up in her arms.

4.

The Wages of Sin

With all three tucked in, she progressed to the spare room. It was dark, under-furnished, cool even in this heat. Frances lay fully dressed above the counterpane with her back to the opening door. Mrs Touchet sat at the deal table in the corner. There was no purpose in moving closer. In Frances' mind the intimacy of three years ago was forgotten: it had never been.

'I've come to check on the patient.'

'Oh, Lizzy, you are good . . .'

'The children report you ate nothing.'

'You will laugh, you're so sensible . . . But the truth is . . . I have no appetite – not for anything. It's ridiculous but I feel myself . . . fading.'

'Ridiculous thing for a woman of your age to say. Melodramatic.'

'Yes. You have always been older, and more sensible.'

'One of those conditions is permanent, the other a matter of opinion.'

A great roar of laughter came up through the floor. Frances shuddered. It was very hard not to go to her side, but Eliza managed it.

'It goes well, then?'

'Downstairs? It'd be far better if you joined us.'

'No, it wouldn't.'

Frances had this way of accepting the self-evident. And it had become self-evident that William had lost all interest in his wife. She had vanished from his mind – like a character from an early, forgotten

novel – and yet here she still was, in his house! Prematurely aged, physically weak. Whenever he deigned to look over at her Mrs Touchet
thought she spied a deep perplexity in his eyes. How could it be that the
handsome young novelist of the season was also a husband to this
decrepit woman – and a father to three? He did not see as Eliza did.
Frances' eyes had not changed: the gentle gaze was the same. The
oceanic feeling for others. She was still beautiful. And still a stranger to
vanity, still lacking any capacity for rage. Eliza – to whom rage came
as naturally as breathing – felt she had little choice but to take on the
wound herself, although she knew from hard experience that being
angry with William was pointless. It was like being furious with a child.
He was never consciously cruel, only bewildered.

'Do you know, Lizzy, in my twenty-nine years I sometimes think
you are the only other person with whom I've ever really been able to
talk. It's strange. Sometimes I wonder why.'

Eliza gripped the arms of her chair. *Because I am your love!* But it was
not a thing that could be said, and on top of this practical difficulty, it
was also not true. The past few years had made that much painfully
clear. It was William that Frances loved, despite everything. William
she wanted. And now it was William she had lost: to the flush of first
success, to books and ambition, to new friends, to the world. It was
William she mourned, and seemed to mourn sincerely – physically.
Can you die of a broken heart? In novels you did. You could also be
'too good for this world'. These clichés Mrs Touchet abhorred, and yet
here, in this dismal room, they rushed in to greet her, robed as truths.
This young woman's heart was broken. Doctors came and went and
gave different names to it, but whatever they called it, they were unable
to cure it. She was too good for this world. It was impossible to hope
she might understand or even see the indirect and perverse machin-
ations of Eliza Touchet on her behalf. All of it had proved invisible to
her, although so much had happened under her nose – sometimes in
her own house. She was too good to see it. To punish and corrupt a man

for being loved by a woman you loved, whom he himself failed to love, or to love sufficiently. The labyrinthine wages of sin did not occur to Mrs Ainsworth.

'You are unwell. You exaggerate. Potential affinities are everywhere, if we remain open to them,' said Mrs Touchet, and at the same time rose from her chair. Eight literary young men, high in their cups, were calling her name.

5.

Compensations

Downstairs, she found the conversation had taken a political turn.

'It is hard indeed on the planters,' Horne was saying. 'After all, whatever we may think of them, this is their livelihood and they now learn that at the stroke of midnight – four years from now – it is all to be eradicated in one fell swoop. In the circumstances, some compensation for the planters does not seem unreasonable.'

'Twenty million pounds is rather more than reasonable!' objected Maclise, to which Forster replied: 'But, alas, necessary,' and his bosom friend, Charles – as seemed to be their rule – immediately took Forster's part:

'Look, it's a horrid business. Unholy and inhumane, as Wilberforce demonstrated twenty years ago. And so the trade was ended, thank God. And now this scandalous twenty million will, I pray, at least be the last we hear of it. I for one am very tired of hearing of it. We have, after all, no shortage of problems closer to home to which we might now turn our attention . . .'

'Ah, Mrs Touchet! About that port . . .'

'Mr Kenealy, we have no more port. We are entirely drained of port.'

'I confess, I am confused by the question,' remarked Chapman. 'As you say, the trade is finished. Our battalions are in the waters – at great expense to the taxpayer – intercepting the Spanish and the French traders and whoever else, liberating these poor Africans left and right. If that was not already a substantial end to the matter, whatever's left of it will surely die on the vine, in time.'

'No, Mr Chapman, it is not at all an end to the matter. The plantations remain in operation. You might as well say the fire is out while a man still roasts atop the coals.'

'Mrs Touchet, respectfully, we are eating.'

'Respectfully, Mr Horne, I wish I spoke only in metaphor. Fire applied to flesh is a frequent punishment on our islands. I recommend to you *The Horrors of Slavery* by a Mr Wedderburn, in which you will find such a vision of hell—'

'—Mrs Touchet, *I really must insist* visions of hell be reserved for a more suitable venue and occasion.'

It was rare, very rare, for William to insist on anything with regards to Mrs Touchet and the humiliating public sting of it froze her where she stood. The silence extended. Finally, Cruikshank swayed out of his chair to reach the half-empty bottle of claret someone had left on the mantelpiece. And so spoke with his back to her:

'Mrs Touchet . . . Your husband was a Touchet.'

'He was.'

'Manchester name.'

'Of long standing.'

'Cotton family, at one time.'

Mrs Touchet was silent.

'Samuel Touchet was my great-uncle,' said William, genially. 'Cotton was a lively business back then. I must admit as a boy I was quite taken with the romance of those journeys: Liverpool to the coasts of Guinea, then on to the New World, and back to Liverpool, laden with exotic delights! He made a fortune on government contracts and so forth – but lost it all. Over-speculated, I believe, on his fourth trip out. Was even accused of attempting a monopoly, rather shamefully . . . Hanged himself from his own bedposts in the end – great scandal to be a bankrupt in those days, of course – and my poor cousins certainly suffered for it, creditors at the door and so forth . . . Although, in the end, the banks didn't quite get everything. No doubt

Samuel Touchet was an old devil, Eliza, but I must say you have reason to be grateful to him.'

Cruikshank turned and raised his glass: 'To Samuel Touchet. And the money he left behind.'

Mrs Touchet blushed severely.

'It is hard indeed to judge a respectable woman on her source of income, Mr Cruikshank, when so very few means of procuring an income are open to her.'

'Touché, Mrs Touchet.'

That was the first time she heard Mr Charles Dickens tell that terrible joke. It would not be the last. Over the years she came truly to dread it, and one advantage of the sudden end of his and William's friendship was that she no longer had to hear it. Nobody but Dickens had ever laughed at it. Not once.

6.

Dickens is Dead!

Despite being seven years younger, seven times the richer, and in possession of a reputation that had often appeared, to William, to stretch seven continents – despite it all, Dickens was dead, at fifty-eight. It was hard to comprehend. Did Death know nothing of birth certificates and pocket books and annual subscriptions? William was stunned. He sat very still in his chair and stared at the date on the obituary: 9th June 1870. And while Dickens was dropping dead, where had William himself been? At the zoo! Looking at a hippopotamus! Fanny and Emily were 'heartbroken' and wept absurdly. Mrs Touchet concluded this was due to *The Times* informing them that they were heartbroken, just as their skirt lengths had transformed after reading a column in the *Queen*. None of them had set eyes on the man in almost twenty years. And why was Clara crying? 'Because of poor Copperfield! Estella was so cruel!' Children are children, easily influenced by the adult mood. But then, when the coal-boy came, it was *ain't it awful about Mr Dickens* – accompanied by a manly sniff – and an hour later a tearful disquisition on *A Christmas Carol* was offered by the postman. Around eleven, Mrs Touchet was held up twenty minutes waiting for her sausages while the butcher and the vicar's wife took it in turns to quote the various idiocies of the Micawbers. In the afternoon, the Sisters of St George said a prayer for the man. Every one of them wept.

On the high street, at sunset, he was everywhere, like a miasma. Everybody she passed seemed to have Bill or Nancy on their lips, or Gradgrind, or Peggotty, or a dozen others, and confronted with so much prompting, Mrs Touchet herself grew suggestible. She began thinking of that second-hand clothes shop on Monmouth Street, which the young *Boz*, by merely observing, had rendered so startlingly animate, filling all the vacant dresses and coats and shoes in the window with a cast of humans, each one convincing, conjured in a sentence, over-brimming with − life. What looked like life. Mrs Touchet did not believe that souls were fully contained or described by coats and shoes. But she knew she lived in an age of things, no matter how out of step she felt in it, and whatever else he was, Charles had been the poet of things. He had made animate and human the cold traffic and bitter worship of things. The only way she could make sense of the general mourning was to note that with his death an age of things now mourned itself.

Aside from the Targe, only the new Mrs Ainsworth was immune, limiting herself to curiosity about the practical consequences for William. For just as, when one grocer shuts up shop, the one across the street gets more business, she hoped this sudden collapse of Dickens 'might send a little more trade our way!'

7.

Taking the Train

Two days later it happened that Mrs Touchet had to take the train to London, to meet a lawyer. She would have far preferred to go unescorted – she sometimes thought she craved independence more than anything on this earth – but William insisted on accompanying her. He had recovered from his shock. Now he wanted to stand at the edge of a very large hole and observe that he was not the one buried in it. A forgivable satisfaction, slightly marred by the fact that the hole in question had been dug in Westminster Abbey, within spitting distance of the Bard's memorial.

'I really can't imagine what Forster and the family can be thinking,' William complained, but quietly, in case of partisans. There were six commuters in their compartment; five of them were reading novels. 'He never would have wanted it. Would have been furious, in fact – hated fuss. Pure vanity on their part. *The Times* should not have suggested it, and the bishop should never have allowed it. Charles was always against pomp and false honour of all kinds.'

'Yes, a man who names a son Alfred d'Orsay Tennyson Dickens clearly gave no thought to worldly fame.'

It amused Mrs Touchet and it interested her: how hard it proves to take occupancy of our own feelings. There is a tendency to loan them out to others, especially the dead. By the time they reached Waterloo Station, William's indignance on behalf of his late friend had reached a high pitch: his face was red and his top button had to be loosened. Nor was he much cheered by the chaos of the station. No square foot of ground seemed to hold fewer than three people and four carpet bags. Curse the octopus builder, spreading his tentacles across the land, destroying the greenwood! Curse the dismal little suburban terraces where all these dismal people presumably now lived . . . Where had they all come from? Where would they all go? Just then, as if in ultimate answer to her cousin's questions, the arch of the London Necropolis Company materialized on their right. If London was busy above ground, it was full underneath. Graves were being dug atop each other, bodies upon bodies, and too many of them were infectious, and therefore dangerous to move. All those fever-taken Tobys. An epidemic of James Touchets. All Souls and Highgate cemeteries were teeming. Even the mass graves were full. And so a huge suburban cemetery had been built in Surrey to accommodate the overspill, and here was the dedicated platform that took you to it, and the special train that transported the dead and those who mourned them. She had read about these death trains but this was her first time seeing one. As William walked ahead, Mrs Touchet turned back like Lot's wife. Families in black bombazine, boarding, weeping. Stacked coffins in the last carriage, making their final journey.

8.

The Ethiopians

Hackneys, gigs, cabriolets, and omnibuses, all heaving with passengers, were jammed together and pointing in all directions, while people who dared get about on their own two legs streamed between. All around was shouting, singing, speechifying, organ-grinding, and a bright array of signs and symbols, printed and displayed on any spare space: *Colman's Mustard, Hudson's Soap, Cadbury's Cocoa* . . . It was hard for Eliza to disguise her delight at all this human commotion. But William was right: the chances of hailing a cab were slim.

'A walk, then.'

They took London Bridge, which occasioned in William fond memories of his chapter on it in *Jack Sheppard,* and the even more pleasant recollection that this same novel of his had once outsold *Oliver Twist,* thirty years ago. Mrs Touchet did try to attend to what he was saying, but was overcome with stimulation. A chaos of beggars and costermongers, of flower girls and fruit boys; two Chinese in incomprehensible conversation; all manner of fascinating women. And the clothes! Undreamt-of in the sartorial philosophies of West Sussex . . .

And every ten yards you heard a new song. As you caught the melody of one, the next began, like a dozen newspapers come to musical life. Who wrote these heavy rhymes and scandalous narratives? They were sung – not very tunefully – by well-fed fellows with red faces, dressed like swells. A few were songs for poor Dickens, set to familiar, melancholy tunes. But the majority were lively jigs of murder and mayhem. The most popular concerned a baker who'd slit his own mother's throat in Lambeth, a week past. Some sang the murder; some the subsequent hanging. Then, just as they stepped off the bridge on the Middlesex side, Eliza caught wind of a sweeter music up ahead, and upon turning a corner, spied a band of Ethiopian minstrels, of the kind she had always favoured. They had joined forces with a chaunter, singing the broadside he was selling for a penny a sheet. She was struck by their obvious poverty and odd composition. Three of the men – Irish or Scotsmen by the look of them – had the usual burned cork smeared over their faces, and their red hair poorly hidden, tucked up inside broken top hats. But there was also surely a Lascar Indian in their number – his hair was silky and black – and the two other singers were full-blooded Africans. All were barefoot, despite their tailcoats. So transfixed was she by this unusual arrangement she hardly noticed the song.

'Can you believe it? Incredible. There's fame for you! They should bring *these* fellows to the Court of Common Pleas. You know you're a Lord when they're singing you on the streets of London!'

Mrs Touchet listened:

In olden times the poor could on a common turn a cow,
The commons all are taken in, the rich have claimed them now,
And even poor Sir Roger is denied his rightful claim,
The Lawyers call him Orton – Bogle swears that's not his name!

'Not too near, Eliza . . . you never know with these fellows . . .'

Eliza roused herself to make a joke: 'I've a penny here. Hadn't we better buy a copy for your wife?'

It pleased her that she could still make her cousin laugh. It reminded her of the young William: so full of energy, so infused with good humour, so accepting and generous of other men's talents, so willing to be guided, directed, amused, and swept away by almost anyone – even a woman. So free of the desire to dominate. She had never found another man like that. And so, in some ways, that ghostly, long-vanished William had done her more harm than good. He had created an impractical expectation within her: the hope of regularly encountering further examples of the type.

'If you do,' said William, laughing as he spoke, 'I'll make sure you hang for it.'

9.

The Lawyer Atkinson Makes His Recommendation

'As I have said: I am not legally bound to inform the dependants, and I shall *not* inform the dependants – that is, unless the dependants insist upon knowing. But it is my firm recommendation,' continued the lawyer Atkinson, 'that you consider this surprising development *only in so far* as it affects your own material circumstances, accepting the happy change *solely* as the evident boon that it is, and with the *firm understanding and proviso* that any ancillary information concerning it is precisely that, *ancillary*, and of no use or purpose to the new beneficiary, Eliza Stuart Touchet – that being yourself – and therefore need not be divulged, for it has, as I say, no bearing on the material change referred to above, the financial implications of which are clearly and gratifyingly stipulated in the last will and testament of the late Mr James Touchet, to which document I presently refer. If this ridiculous Tichborne business has taught us anything, Mrs Touchet, it is surely that wills, imprecisely proved, will go on to cause all manner of mischief . . .'

Later – much later – Eliza would come to understand that within this dense paragraph of legalese there lay a fundamental choice. A crossroad. Had she known it at the time? There were no signs along the route. No rainbows, no burning bushes. Nothing remarkable about either the setting or the cast. The lawyer Atkinson she had met once a year for twenty years, and he was unchanged in himself, although, as he put it, 'in sadly and vastly reduced circumstances'. For the old Doctors' Commons was demolished, and all its proctors and advocates displaced to new offices, and Atkinson – a proctor himself – now did his civil business in a narrow set of rooms next door to Cordwainers' Hall, on Distaff Lane in the shadow of St Paul's. This proximity to the Worshipful Company of Cordwainers did not please him; it merely made the whole street smell of leather. Nor did he find anything inherently charming in the idea of an ancient guild of shoemakers. For Atkinson it was a coming down in the world: 'But I call you here today, Mrs Touchet, to discuss the opposite: a coming up! A most decided coming up!'

Coming up, to a man like Atkinson, could mean only one thing: money. But before she could congratulate herself on the finer points of her own morality, she reflected upon what independence truly meant to her. What else was money but a material form of freedom? She wanted to recoil from this venal and pedantic man. Instead, she leaned forward in her chair and listened very closely. He had a bird's blank, beady eyes and a beak for a nose. He droned on. His head went forward and back, like a woodpecker. Back and forth went that beak, tapping away at Eliza's practical ignorance regarding her own finances, until it broke open the most astonishing nest egg. Her annuity was to change – to double. As much as it pained the lawyer Atkinson to reveal it, there had been another beneficiary to the will of the late James Touchet, and the truth of this had been kept from his widow all these years, Atkinson explained, for 'reasons of delicacy'. But now this beneficiary had died, and although 'the beneficiary had dependants' it was the professional opinion of Mr Atkinson that these dependants had no solid legal claim, and were anyway extremely unlikely to press any such claim. In which circumstance, the deceased's annuity reverted to the widow, that is, to the aforementioned, that is, to Mrs Touchet.

'To me?'

'Your annuity is to be doubled. All you have to do is go to your banker. He has the document awaiting your signature.'

'But you still have not said to whom the will pertains. Who was the deceased beneficiary? Who are the other dependants who might make a claim?'

At which point the lawyer Atkinson sighed and began upon his recommendation. There it was: the crossroad. The choice of knowing, or of choosing not to know. It is at such moments, Mrs Touchet believed, that our souls lie in the balance. If only William had been there! But William had walked on, to the Abbey, to pay his respects to Dickens. She stood alone, at the crossroad.

Other people are our obstacles. They are the force that we are up against. She felt this most strongly when in her lowest moods, that is, when furthest from Christ. Other people are our stumbling blocks and hurdles, our impediments and obstructions – they are sent to try us. And yet, left untried, left to our longed-for solitude – with no one to witness our many hypocrisies – how easily we deceive ourselves!

'I will accept the money and follow your recommendation, Mr Atkinson, thank you. I think, all being equal, it is probably best if I know nothing more of these . . . these claimants. I feel certain no good would come from it.'

'A wise decision, Mrs Touchet, if I may say so. A prudent decision.'

10.

Distaff

Outside, Mrs Touchet looked to the heavens for guidance. Instead, she found herself considering the facade of Cordwainers' Hall. High up, upon the pediment, was engraved the coat of arms of all those who work in leather. It showed a peasant, a girl, spinning cord on a distaff. As if this ancient livery hall worried itself over the apprenticeships of lady shoemakers, the pensions of lady shoemakers, the wages of lady shoemakers! Mrs Touchet was reminded of the girl who spun gold for the king in the fairy tale. *Rumpelstiltskin!* And just like that, the little demon man was quite exploded. Simply by calling the Devil by his right name you vanquished him. Only in fairy tales.

What Can We Know of Other People?

All her thoughts were disturbing. They arose in the gap where a name should be. And in that same gap, lurching up to meet her: freedom. The thought that she might live somewhere of her own choosing! In her own rooms, paid for with her own money. It was dizzying. She stopped and looked at her shoes. They were old, and needed new soles. Why was it easier to think of shoes than freedom? How could she feel so wrong-footed by the very thing she had prayed for?

Seeking relief, she turned her mind to the streets in front of her. To the people who walked them, so very many people, and so varied. She had always noticed a great many Chinese and Indian seamen in this area, and they were all still here, but there were also several newer shops with their signs written in the ancient script of the Jews, and a small delegation of Turks – or at least men in *fez* hats – peering into the windows of a jeweller. One of the surprises of this new and busier London – compared to the city she and William had known – was how many more foreigners there now seemed to be in it, perhaps because she walked so near to the river. She spotted black maids-of-all-work and black cooks and housekeepers, a black man with deep angular scars on both cheeks, watering a horse outside a pub, and two others sat on the ground, utterly destitute by Waterloo Bridge, and then a brown shop boy in the doorway of a furrier. She was old enough to remember when it had been fashionable to have Carib boys in livery at the threshold of fine houses, got up like Princes of Arabia. But the servants she spotted now were dressed plainly, in the clothes pertaining to their labour. And not only servants. Working men of various kinds, and a superior-looking African – he carried a doctor's bag – climbing into a cab. Mrs Touchet liked to examine her thoughts as she had them, and now, as she deliberately took an inconvenient road to keep sight of two curious women – one white, the other black, both dressed theatrically and walking at a clip, arm in arm – she asked herself what precisely was the nature of her interest in the foreign and unfamiliar. She knew she was often bored. Profoundly bored by the life around her: its familiar contours, its repetition, and the several people she knew very well, really too well. All Ainsworths, for example, were by now an open book to her. Nothing they said or did could at this point possibly surprise her. She compared this deep boredom to the enlivened sense she had when in the presence of strange strangers, like these two mysterious women. Why did they walk so fast and laugh so often? Why were their clothes bright and yet at the same time cheap and somehow disreputable? How had they come to know each other, and so intimately that they walked in arm in arm? What world did they live in, and what unknown and perhaps unknowable mental landscape formed it? Could it be deciphered? Guessed at? What can we know of other people? How much of the mystery of another person could one's own perspicacity divine?

12.

Consider Bogle!

Since that strange afternoon in Horsham she had considered him often. His very person seemed to present her with that same question. For here was a man who had truly surprised her. It was a fleeting surprise – a flicker between one state and the next, like a flame changing shape – but she had been unable to forget it. It happened in the moments after he finished his sober, articulate and apparently heartfelt testimony on behalf of 'Sir Roger'. His son came to his elbow once more, to help him, and as they progressed slowly across the stage together – there it was! A change. In gesture, in movement, in the expression of his face. She had no very precise words for it and yet she had seen it. An unreadable intimacy between Bogle and son. The last time she had seen something like it was between a couple of servants of Lady Blessington, years ago. Something deeply private, encoded, not intended for the crowd, and yet spotted by Mrs Touchet, at least, who tended to flatter herself that she 'saw all'. It was disconcerting. For she thought of herself as having several faces to show at different times to different people – as all women have, and must have, to varying degrees – but she had never seriously considered the idea that there might exist also a class of men (aside from the obvious case of the sodomites) who, like women, wrote the stories of their lives, as it were, in cipher. To be translated only by a few, and only when necessary. Attempting to translate such ciphers wherever she encountered them was Mrs Touchet's private delight. Unlike most decipherers, though, she was particularly intrigued when proved wrong. As she had been about this

Bogle – not realizing that such a man could even possess an ulterior or private world – and as she was now proving to be about the two fast-walking ladies, who appeared not to be women of her own peculiar persuasion after all, but rather simple thieves! The black one distracted the 'mark' with her chatter and feathers and laughter, while the white one slipped a hand behind his back to pick his pocket.

13.

Visiting the Lady Marguerite Gardiner Blessington, Spring 1836

'You are welcome, you are welcome – we delight in your presence! Ye young literary lions! Lucky be the fine steeds pressed between your thighs – oh, don't look so shocked, William – so they are lucky! And I am indebted to you for this introduction! But I have read all your sketches, young *Boz* – I consider us old friends! I will call you Charles at once, if you don't mind, or even Charlie – and have no polite English protest about it. I am a bloody Irishwoman in my heart and mean to stay one! Welcome to Gore House! Oh, and a third gallops through the gates – ah! Well, now I am embarrassed: boys, you should have warned me. Excuse me, madam, I did not realize – oh, and look at me in my damned Indian slippers!'

Eliza looked down from her high horse. The slippers were ridiculous, as was the woman. Meanwhile, behind the Lady, in the doorway, a little black boy in a red silk turban held up a platter of something, while his female counterpart beat the air with a huge plumed fan, although it was March, and cold.

'William, really you are a damned pain! Silly boy: why not say a lady was coming . . .'

She had come out of curiosity. As much as Eliza hated awful people, she also could never resist them. Now she looked pleadingly over at William to make the necessary introduction, but found her cousin oblivious, as ever. The astonished Lady Blessington, meanwhile, stared straight back up at Eliza:

'But to whom do I owe——?'

'I am Eliza Touchet. Mr Ainsworth's cousin. By marriage.'

'Ah, the cousin! And a fellow Celt, if my ear does not deceive me . . . A fine horsewoman, too, by the looks of it. Well, you are welcome. Pardon my surprise and my tongue. I thought for a moment you were a wife, and wives, in my view, will cramp the style of any *salon*.'

'My husband is dead,' announced the Targe, prompting William to laugh lightly and jump from his horse:

'Our Mrs Touchet is a woman after your own heart, Lady B. She is likewise famed for her blunt clarity of expression.'

'Indeed?'

'But let me put your mind at rest: Mrs Touchet has no husband – as she mentioned she is, like you, a widow, though of somewhat longer standing – and I . . . well, I have presently mislaid my wife——'

'In*deed*?'

'——Alas, she has moved back in with her father, Mr Ebers.'

'And I am merely engaged,' said Charles. 'May we come in now?'

14.

Weightier Matters

At the door, the children moved aside. William, as he passed, took a bonbon from the platter of the boy. The girl, walking behind them, sent a steady stream of cold air down Eliza's back.

'And the Count?' William asked.

'He will be with us presently. He is about his *toilette*.'

'A matter of no brief duration, I'm sure . . .' said Charles, under his breath, amusing himself thoroughly. And mustn't it be wonderful, thought Mrs Touchet, to be one's own best entertainment!

From the hall they were ushered into a grand salon. It was difficult for Mrs Touchet to decide what repulsed her most: the red walls, the giant gold harp or the luridly coloured bust of Bonaparte. There seemed to be a chaise in every corner. Into one of these the Lady Blessington now reclined. It was covered in a peach silk damask and made her look even peachier, if such a thing were possible. Her young guests meanwhile were encouraged to sit together on the great green ottoman opposite, like an audience, or three clerks on an omnibus. The children took their places either side of the hearth and stood still and expressionless as statues.

'What a beautiful home you have, Lady Blessington.' Aside from permanent amusement, this appeared to be Mr Dickens' other mode: obsequiousness. 'And so full of character. I know I am in Kensington and yet I feel I could be in Arabia, or perhaps' – an amused nod at the children – 'some spot even further south.'

'Ah – Charles! – I thank you! It is gratifying indeed to have a fellow scribbler – if I may refer to you in this way – it is very gratifying to have a scribbler admire the furnishings. As a *dilettante* scribbler myself I know well how we writer characters furnish the houses of our imaginations and with what fine attention . . . And Gore House has been a particular challenge. To "do" a house is no small matter – not that literary young men like yourselves need know a thing of these tedious matters of midlife – but still, there are so very many decisions to be made, of a banal and practical nature. Not to mention the aesthetical questions. Although of course, I had the Count's help there.'

'D'Orsay is *taste itself*!' exclaimed William, as if this were an original or interesting thing to say. Mrs Touchet saw his new friend Charles wince, a little.

'Just so,' agreed the Lady, 'and yet still there was a great deal to do. Wilberforce was the previous owner – not a man given to fancy in any area. I would like to tell you it looked like a Methodist church when we took it over, but as the Count put it, it was hardly as *chic*. Ha! Now I've shocked you.' Eliza smiled thinly. One of her least favourite things was to be told what shocked her. 'Yes, our Mr Wilberforce was a dour one, to be sure, and with a very poor sense of curtains . . .'

'With respect, Lady Blessington, Mr Wilberforce surely had weightier matters on his mind than curtains.'

The Lady Blessington – who had not looked at Eliza since she came down from her high horse – now turned and frowned at this brazen attempt to get back up on a new one.

'Indeed. We are all indebted to Mr Wilberforce, to be sure. I am of the opinion that no man or woman can sleep peacefully while their country sins, and who can doubt the sin of bondage?' – a sentimental glance across at the child-statues – 'but did not Wilberforce live his whole life on the proceeds of the sin he so reproved? His grandfather was in sugar, I believe, and certainly Wilberforce never made an independent penny . . . I can't help but remember our beloved, departed Byron on the subject of hypocrisy . . .'

Back in Kensal Rise, saddling the horses, Dickens had opened a sweepstake on the first mention of Byron, having it on good authority that their glamorous hostess 'rarely got through five sentences without dropping the name of Byron on the carpet'. But William had trouble believing in the vulgarity of titled people: reluctantly had he placed his bet for 'a reference to Byron within the hour'. His new friend bet half of that. Only Mrs Touchet, a natural cynic, had put her money on the five-minute mark, and so was now owed three shillings.

15.

Conversations of Lord Byron

'I have the page right here,' said the Lady, opening her own book. It had somehow materialized in her hands: ' *"When you know me better you will find that I am the most selfish person in the world; I have, however, the merit, if it be one, of not only being perfectly conscious of my faults, but of never denying them; and this surely is something, in this age of cant and hypocrisy."* I can hear him saying it like it was yesterday. Never was a man more clear-sighted on his virtues and his flaws.'

'A remarkable man,' said William. 'Our greatest poet.'

'My greatest friend! How I loved those Italian days, our long afternoons of conversation . . . and yet we were often sadly at odds, and argued as much as we agreed. The poetical temperament is a complex matter indeed . . . Ah, d'Orsay! We were just speaking of Byron and the poetical temperament! Oh, boys, I am cold; my Irish soul yearns for fire; do sit with me.'

The many curves of the Lady Blessington now came to the hearth where she sat on her not insubstantial bottom, dismissed the servants, and beckoned her 'boys'. They came at once, William on one side, the Count d'Orsay on the other. Mrs Touchet remained where she was, on the couch. Charles – whose restless legs had been bouncing ever since he sat down – now took the opportunity to walk about the cavernous room. On his travels he picked up *Lady Blessington's Conversations of Lord Byron*, traced a finger down the back of a wooden St Lucy, plucked a string on the harp, and claimed to admire them all. But Mrs Touchet, watching him keenly, saw only the voracious court reporter, making notes for the prosecution.

16.

Triangular Arrangements

A discussion began upon the poetical temperament. The 'boys' admitted to having one, Charles denied the same – 'My temperament is prosaic' – while Mrs Touchet said nothing whatsoever, for no one asked her. Instead, she studied d'Orsay. If anything, she had been even more curious about him than about his benefactor. She was not disappointed. He was the ludicrous dandy of fame, with the much-imitated Parisian drawl. It was said he resembled William, but now that she saw them together it was clear the resemblance was manufactured and aspirational on William's part. His new yellow cravat was a clear *homage* to d'Orsay, and his curls had grown longer to match, his trousers tighter, his buttons larger. But d'Orsay, strikingly feminine in face and manner, was far and away the more beautiful. That the Lord and Lady Blessington should have betrothed their only daughter to this young Ganymede did not now seem so strange to Eliza: viewed from a certain angle it must have seemed the simplest way to keep the boy within their orbit. But this did not answer the question that thrilled the gossips of Kensal Lodge. Who was this dazzling Ganymede *for*, exactly? Zeus or Hera?

Eliza let her back sink into the couch and reviewed the evidence. By all accounts, the Lord, when he lived, had been besotted with his pretty young friend. Then, in death, he left d'Orsay his fortune, precisely on the peculiar condition he marry the daughter. Yet, when the daughter fled the marriage and the household, the Count d'Orsay had remained with his mother in-law, sharing the Blessington fortune and – so the scandal-mongers claimed – her bed. But exactly what age was this childish woman? Forty-four? Forty-eight? It was mysterious, like so many other things about her. Even her name was dubious. Back in Tipperary – or so Mrs Touchet had heard – Marguerite Gardiner had begun life as plain old Maggie Power, married off at fourteen to a drunken gentleman farmer, who conveniently died not long after, in a debtors' prison. After which, it was said, the young Maggie had become something one down from a courtesan but one up from a common whore. A mistress. The mistress of powerful men. For this reason, she was shunned by the society women of London, and her many tedious essays on feminine etiquette and morality – published in the *New Monthly*, and widely ridiculed – had not yet managed to turn the tide. Perhaps sensing the intractability of her position, she had written her scandalously successful Byron book, and thus given up entirely on the approval of respectable women, settling instead for the company of brilliant young men. She certainly had the looks for salon life – and the luck. To reel in Lord Blessington had been tremendous luck; it had funded the whole enterprise. But looks *are* luck. Eliza's own looks, by contrast, she had long understood to be too specific, an acquired taste. They had never garnered sufficient general interest to be useful, or never at the right moment. If she was quite honest with herself, their most ardent tribute had come in the form of a sheaf of very bad handwritten poetry, sent from the law offices of her husband's young cousin. The verses themselves she had long ago forgotten. But she remembered the flattering accompanying note:

All these poems were written in my nineteenth summer – let this plead my excuse for their volatility, childishness and crudity with my fair friend – <u>she</u> knows what they originated in, or the mirror will inform her . . .

But it is the perverse business of mirrors never to inform women of their beauty in the present moment, preferring instead to operate on a system of cruel delay. So it was that she had looked in the mirror, aged twenty-five, and seen only an angular crone, without attractions. Yet more recently, looking at a pretty watercolour of herself – painted around that time – she saw at once what William had seen: a black-haired Diana, pale as the moon, as mysterious, as beautiful. Still, it could not be denied that the Lady Blessington's was a beauty of a different order. Full-blown, round and pink, with a décolletage as open as Eliza's was buttoned up. Which comparison, when brought to mind, somehow made Eliza feel the more exposed.

17.

On Cruelty

She watched the Lady put a proprietorial hand on William's thigh. It was several weeks since the cousins had laid a hand on each other. For God and sanity's sake Eliza prayed that door was closed for ever. Nor had either of them seen Frances these last three months. Not since the children went back up to school and Frances moved to her father's to 'convalesce'. Eliza was the only female left at the Lodge, surrounded nightly by brilliant young men, a situation which, if she were quite honest with herself, she had come to enjoy. Most nights the thought of Frances felt very far away. Drowned in port. Now Lady Blessington's hand moved up an inch. To her own surprise, Mrs Touchet felt hatred go through her chest like a hot poker. But even worse was the thought that some form of envy was at work, and so the resourceful Mrs Touchet quickly assumed the wound on behalf of another – as was her habit – and in defence of whom her heart now leapt. *Poor Frances! So forgotten! So humiliated! So publicly unloved!*

'Mr Dickens, am I not flanked by the two handsomest men in London?'

'Lady Blessington, I fear I am not the best judge.'

'Ha! I believe you're jealous.'

Sometimes envy is so much like a recognition of fundamental similarity that the two emotions prove hard to separate. Were not she and Blessington both dogs up on their hind legs? Making the best of trying circumstances? Surrounded by men? Not especially liked by women? Considering these parallels, the hate drained from Eliza and was replaced by a surfeit of self-loathing, against which her defences were thin. But wasn't she, at least, respectable? Whereas this 'Countess of Cursington' was notorious from London to Lake Garda!

'*Madame*, I have no need of external judges. I can judge very well for myself, *merci*, and I say you are entirely correct. We are very handsome.'

'Oh, d'Orsay, what terrible vanity!' cried William, but his cheeks were rosy with the compliment.

'Vanity indeed!' Lady Blessington nudged her Count in his ribs. 'But to be serious for a moment: Byron once claimed to me that he could sooner pardon crimes – because they proceed from the passions – than any of the minor vices, like vanity. And he meant it! He was adamant. And yet surely one *cannot* compare the minor vices – selfishness, conceit and so on, which carry their own punishments – to the mortal sins that destroy the lives of the innocent!'

'I disagree.'

'Indeed, Mr Dickens? With what part?'

'I find I don't differentiate between vices. All the smaller vices can in my opinion be made crimes very easily – it is only a question of degree. Selfishness, vanity, self-deceit – all are often enough the basis of our very *worst* crimes. Other people suffer our selfishness, for example, as surely as we do. Wouldn't you say so, Mrs Touchet?'

Mrs Touchet was very struck by this. Firstly, because she agreed; secondly, because he spoke directly to her and seemed desirous of an answer; lastly, because she had so far refused to read this too-celebrated young man and had not, in her personal dealings with him, thought him up to much.

'Yes. I would agree.' She spoke slowly and carefully. 'Except I would add that cruelty stands apart. In any degree, cruelty is a crime. It is the very worst we can do.'

From far across the room, Dickens looked up with sudden and sharp interest, as if Mrs Touchet were a strange ship just appeared on the horizon. The Lady Blessington, noting this, determinedly steered the conversation back to shore:

'Well, I can assure you, Mrs Touchet, the Lord Byron was never cruel. Like most people of a poetical and aristocratic temperament, he was a stranger to the very idea. And still people persecuted him as if he were the worst bloody sinner alive – an experience with which I must say I am sadly familiar . . . Were you an admirer of Lord Byron, madam? Or were you one of the many ladies who disapproved?'

'I cannot say I ever gave the matter much thought,' replied Mrs Touchet, airily. She had committed almost all of *Don Juan* to memory. Nor had she ever forgotten the poet's visit to the Ladies of Llangollen. That visit was inscribed upon her heart.

'Oh, reputation!' The Count suddenly flung a gloved hand at his own forehead. 'It is my opinion that given how quickly we are forgotten we would do just as well not to attempt anything at all!'

Lady Blessington hit the boy playfully on the arm: 'd'Orsay, you are impossible . . . And yet, in essence, did not Byron agree with you? You will recall that moment in my book when he so poignantly quotes Cowley: "*O Life! Thou weak-built isthmus, which doth proudly rise up betwixt two eternities . . .*"'

'Well, there we are! All is for nothing!'

Charles laughed: 'But d'Orsay, now you speak in favour of chaos and sin – as if the two eternities were at all alike! Yet where we end up for the second surely depends very much on the Christian humility and piety we are able to muster precisely *while we are still upon* that "weak-built isthmus" . . .'

'On theology I am lost,' said William, glumly. 'It is Mrs Touchet's department.'

For the first time, all heads turned to Mrs Touchet. It was what she had wanted and yet now she felt that too many eyes were upon her. She spoke past them all, to a silver monkey on the mantelpiece:

'As long as we speak of an island upon which people can suffer – and can cause pain the one to the other – I do not see that an eternity at either end is necessary to render that island of the utmost importance. Our duties on the island will be many. They will be never-ending, in fact. And *that*, I should think, is enough of eternity for any man, woman or child.'

This brought silence to the company.

18.

On Mobility

The Count, having accidentally begun this detour into moral philosophy, felt a responsibility to lighten the mood. He began cajoling the Lady to give the party 'one of zose epigrams she writes in ze nighttimes in her leetle notebook'. She took him up on the offer:

'Well, this is from yesterday: "*The genius and talents of a man may be judged by the quantity of his enemies, and his mediocrity by the number of his friends.*"'

William burst into laughter: 'What a mediocrity I must be! For I have a great number of friends!'

The Lady Blessington laughed and the Count laughed, but before Mrs Touchet and Mr Dickens could laugh, they made the mistake of meeting each other's eyes.

'And you, young Dickens – you have only enemies, I'm sure,' purred the Lady Blessington, prompting more laughter, from all except Mrs Touchet. She kept her eye instead on this chameleon, Maggie Power. How she moved in a moment from Irish bawd to city sophisticate, from coquette to Lady, from mother to lover and back again! Some lines from *Don Juan* came to mind:

Some doubt how much of Adeline was real:
So well she acted, all and every part
By turns – with that vivacious versatility
Which many people take for want of heart.
They err – 'tis merely what is called mobility,

The Fraud

A thing of temperament and not of art,
Though seeming so, from its supposed facility;
And false — though true; for surely they're sincerest
Who are strongly acted on by what is nearest.

19.

Le Monde Bouleversé

Mrs Touchet was in urgent need of fresh air. Could you sicken from too much wit? She claimed a headache, rose quickly before she could be accompanied, turning left at the front door. Round the back of Gore House, through a double trellis of briar rose, she found herself standing in a walled kitchen garden, aimless between lines of lettuce. A strong east wind blew strands of hair into her mouth. Glancing down at her riding habit, black and heavy, she wondered at herself for wearing it. How like the Ladies of Llangollen! Except lonelier, for there was only one of her. Taking shelter behind some tall tomato plants, tied to their stakes, she heard somebody whistling somewhere.

'Yer milk, yer Majesty!'

She spotted the whistler: a milk-boy in his Welsh whites, over by the kitchen door. Opposite him, standing on the doorstep, were the two servant children. But everything about them had undergone a sea change: their gestures, their movements, the expressions on their faces. The stiffness, the stillness – evaporated. The boy had removed his turban to reveal a head of dense black hair that no wind moved. The girl, bonnet loose at her neck, was just now placing the fan up the back of her skirts, in imitation of the buxom rear end of her mistress.

'Who needs your bloody milk!' – she did a passable Irish brogue – 'I do squeeze it out my bloody tit I do and then my darling boy drinks it up, so he does! Lap, lap, lap!'

She accompanied this with an obscene mime. Both boys looked on, rapt.

'*Pardonnez-moi, madame.* Am I your son or your husband?'

This from the black boy, in the accent of the Count. But later, replaying the episode in her mind, it occurred to Mrs Touchet that the child's native tongue was just as likely French as English.

'*Madame, répondez, s'il vous plaît.* Who am I to you?'

The milk-boy stuck his chin in the air and held on to a pair of imaginary lapels like a toff: 'He's a bit of both, I'd say. Wouldn't you say so, my lady?' His little audience erupted in filthy laughter. And how deluded we are, thought Mrs Touchet, to assume anything gets by our servants!

'And who are *you*, exactly?' asked the girl. Her tone was imperious. The milk-boy, abashed, pulled off his cap and looked at the floor:

'Oi, Annie – let me be the Count now, Annie . . . be fair. Nero, you can be the dead husband. A girl like you, well . . . they say every fella's got two girls or more in the savage lands, and vice-a versa, least that's what I've heard . . .'

It was as if, in this upside-down world, the girl really was a lady, and the milk-boy a nervous suitor far beneath her. But the girl was unmoved. She looked him up and down and made a strange, contemptuous sucking noise with her teeth:

'*Lawd! Protek wi fram di wikkid!*' Mrs Touchet could not tell any more if the girl was being the Lady Blessington, herself, or someone else entirely. '*Wha' mi fi wan' wid two fool like you?*'

Mrs Touchet accidentally stepped on a twig. All three children froze where they stood. Mrs Touchet blushed to the tips of her ears.

'Good afternoon, children.'

The Arabian Prince managed a reply; the girl was dumbstruck. Her fan dropped to the floor. The milk-boy took another look over his shoulder and seemed to intuit Mrs Touchet's fatal lack of authority. Real ladies did not eavesdrop in kitchen gardens, or stand blushing and tongue-tied. They did not say 'Good afternoon' to the likes of these two. Emboldened, he pulled his cap low over his eyes and restored normal relations:

'This here's the two quarts for the Lady, fresh from our finest Suffolks — and don't you be getting your inky little fingers in it. And you can tell Cook from Nichols there's money owing on them cheeses, and Nichols says that it can't be scratched no more, or the Lady B will get to be hearing about it herself. You hear? Well, what you two doing staring at me like a couple of Congo halfwits? Ain't got no work to do?'

He kicked some gravel into the house. Someone will have to clean that up, thought Mrs Touchet, reflexively, although she knew who the someone would be, and by the look on the girl's face so did the girl. Playtime was over. The child replaced her bonnet, nodded, lifted the first pail from the doorstep and was gone. Her companion stayed where he was. He looked past the milk and the milk-boy, past Mrs Touchet, past the horses and the gates of Gore House. Also past caring, past toleration, past patience. Finally, he turned towards the lettuces to smile directly at Mrs Touchet. Not a nice smile. A sharp smile, with a threat in it. Then bent down, took the second pail, and walked off towards the pantry, past all the kitchen drawers so full of sharp and threatening things. The milk-boy started up again with his whistling and ran off. The lettuce heads blew about. Mrs Touchet thought, inexplicably, of Saint-Domingue. Walking quickly back towards the house she was unsure as to what had so disconcerted her. Yet here was her heartbeat, loud, in her ears.

VOLUME FOUR

'From One Who Loves the Despised.'

PSEUDONYMOUS SUBSCRIBER TO THE TICHBORNE

CLAIMANT'S DEFENCE FUND

I.

The Artist & the Author

Their third February in Hurstpierpoint was polar: the garden filled
with snow. Beautiful, but of little use to anyone but Clara, who dug
'sea-channels' and built icebergs, never seeming to 'catch her death' no
matter how many of her elder, rheumatic sisters warned her she would.
Somehow this child had grown into an affectionate and happy girl of
whom even the Targe could feel fond. Happy, and usefully incurious.
The type of child not to wonder when she found an old riding crop in
the back of a wardrobe, nor ask any questions if some handwritten love
poems fell out of a copy of Audubon's *Birds of America*. Upon discovering Mrs Touchet destroying a different sort of evidence one morning,
she was very easily sent off course:

'What are you doing? Was that the package for Father?'

'It was.'

'But why did you just throw it in the fire?'

'It was not a nice package.'

'Oh! Well, better poke it and move the coals about – it'll burn
quicker.'

It had arrived in the same brown paper as the previous packages.
Inside, a first edition of one of William's midlife novels, *Old St
Paul's*, with every one of its illustrations razored out. The significance of this only dawned on Eliza weeks later. The snow was gone,
the sun was out, the cousins were taking tea in the garden, and a
furious William was reading aloud a letter from the paper:

'*To the Editor of* The Times: "*Sir – under the heading of 'Easter*

Amusements' it is stated that Mr W. Harrison Ainsworth's novel The
Miser's Daughter *has been dramatized by Mr Andrew Halliday, and produced at the Adelphi Theatre, and as my name is not mentioned in any way
in connection with the novel—" '*

'—But who on earth—?'

'—Eliza, please don't interrupt: you have not heard the half of it.
*"And as my name is not mentioned in any connection with the novel – not
even as the illustrator – I shall feel greatly obliged if you will allow me
to inform the public through the medium of your columns of the fact
(which all my private friends are aware of) that this tale of* The Miser's
Daughter *originated from ME"* – Blackguard! Liar! – *"and not from
Mr Ainsworth."* Can you believe it? How can it be believed? It beggars belief!'

Mrs Touchet sighed profoundly: 'Poor George.'

'*Poor George* she says! Are you mad, cousin?'

Not mad, but distracted. All the mystery packages of the past two
years were now lining up in her mind and pointing in one direction.

'He continues: *"My idea, suggested to that gentleman, was to write a
story in which the principal character should be a miser, who had a daughter, and that the struggles of feelings between the love for his child and his
love of money, should produce certain effects and results; and as all my
ancestors were mixed up in the Rebellion of '45, I suggested that the story
should be of that date in order that I might introduce some scenes and circumstances connected with that great party struggle, and also—" '*

'William – I've heard enough. You will choke on that scone.'

'On he goes, with his lies and insinuation – and then we have this: *"I
do not mean to say that Mr Ainsworth, when writing this novel, did not
introduce some of his own ideas"* – Ha! That's big of him! – *"but as the
first idea and all the principal points and characters emanated from me, I
think it will be allowed that the title of originator of* The Miser's Daughter
*should be conferred upon, Sir, Your obedient servant, George Cruikshank,
263 Hampstead Road."* Is *that* where you live, you scoundrel!'

Mrs Touchet wrung a napkin in her hands: 'Well. It is very unfortunate.'

'Unfortunate? First, he sends a letter to the American papers, claiming to be the true author of *Twist*, no less – and now it's my turn? At least he had the good grace to wait until Dickens was dead! What on earth can have possessed the man?'

Mrs Touchet looked over at the novelist's youngest daughter, sitting cross-legged on the lawn, humming to herself, constructing a daisy chain. What possesses people? Unhappiness, always. Happiness is otherwise occupied. It has an object on which to focus. It has daisies, it has snowdrifts. Unhappiness opens up the void, which then requires filling. With things like angry letters to *The Times*.

'It is clear enough,' said Eliza, thinking back, 'that he holds a grudge. Against Charles for his enormous success, I suppose, and with you . . . well, if you remember, William, he did think he was to work on *Old St Paul's* . . .'

'*Old St Paul's: A Tale of the Plague and the Fire*,' William amended, bitterly. 'And if I may say so I have not been without my own "enormous success". You will recall *Jack Sheppard* outsold *Oliver Twist*, at the time.'

'Of course, yes—'

'—By a factor of four, as it happens.'

'Yes, William – I really didn't mean to . . . I only meant: without warning, you hired another man to do it instead. I mean, to illustrate *St Paul's*. George had illustrated all the others. He felt dropped, I suppose. You *do* sometimes drop people, William. And Charles dropped *everyone*.'

'And this is revenge? Thirty years after the fact?'

'Cruikshank was always a terrible drunk.'

'Don't excuse him. Besides, he is teetotal these days – he writes endless pamphlets upon the topic. Honestly, you are too provoking! Why do you choose now to excuse a man you've always hated? I can remember when you were half ready to murder him — and over a few cartoons about the negroes! It really is a very annoying habit of yours, Eliza. You become fond of people at the very moment that they should be most severely condemned.'

This, being close to home, stung. Eliza fell silent. She picked up her book and tried to read but the words swam. A goldfinch came to the bird-bath and washed itself. The novelist's youngest daughter ran up the lawn to show off her daisies. His new wife could be heard singing tunelessly somewhere. There are always so many things to attend to, but when the void opens up there is only the void. *Two hundred pounds a year, two hundred pounds a year, two hundred pounds a year.* She heard this sentence running through her brain, every day, hourly almost. The money remained untouched. She had not gone to see her banker. Here she still was, in Hurstpierpoint. Her mind froze around the matter: the only safe course was to do nothing. She had tried praying on it, but had been disappointed, not receiving the answer she wanted. Instead, in its place, had come a startling question: *In whose debt am I?*

2.

Contemporary Fiction

'My God, does it never end? Ridiculous!'

He was now glowering at the front page, upon which, convenient to his mood, a drawing of the Claimant could be found, fatter than ever, and due in court on May 11th, a month from today.

Eliza squinted at the headline: 'They expect full galleries. It will be the fashionable thing to attend, apparently. Even the Prince of Wales plans a visit. I did wonder whether *we* should go . . .' She laughed lightly, as if the idea had only just occurred to her. 'You *have* been looking for a contemporary subject . . .'

William let Clara onto his lap and looked over at Mrs Touchet as if she had lost her mind.

'*You* wear it, Papa!'

William accepted the offering, placing the flowers round his neck and kissing the child on her forehead. But then turned back to his cousin with a querulous look upon his face:

'I am perfectly capable of finding a subject for a novel without your assistance, thank you very much. But don't let me stop *you* from going – and why not take Mrs Ainsworth? Yes, there's an idea; in fact, I shall suggest it. I know how much you two enjoy your ladies' outings . . .'

Cruelty did not come naturally to William. But every now and then he lunged like this and landed a clumsy blow. She felt the injustice of it, especially as she no longer had any arena in which to counter-parry. A long time ago there had been the riding crop, the silk ties, the tight grip.

Nowadays, she only bit her tongue, like every other woman she had ever known.

'What is that you're reading, anyway?'

Mrs Touchet glanced down at the book that sat idle in her lap.

'Oh, only the second volume of that novel. I'm rather enjoying it.'

'The Eliot fellow?'

'Her real name is Mrs Lewes. But yes. I like it.'

William made a face like a dog eating a lemon.

'Couldn't get through volume one – and aren't there seven more to come? Once upon a time decent men satisfied themselves with three . . . What on earth does the woman need with so many? No adventure, no drama, no murder, nothing to excite the blood or chill it! I must say I can't understand the glowing notices. As if she were a new Mary Shelley! But there isn't an ounce of Shelley's imagination. Just a lot of people going about their lives in a village – dull lives at that. Even more boring a topic than a trial. Are we meant to be amazed it's a woman? An obvious publicity trick by *Blackwood's*, and look at how the public falls for it! Is this all that these modern ladies' novels are to be about? People?'

'I like it,' repeated Mrs Touchet, and lifted a scone to her mouth, the better to obscure a smile.

3.

The Court of Common Pleas, 11th May 1871

As much as Eliza hated awful people, she also could never resist them —

And now that she sat in the gallery with the new Mrs Ainsworth, she had to admit to being glad of the company. Neither woman had ever been to a trial before; it turned out there were many *longeurs*. Clerks had to be sent across town to strong-arm reluctant jurors, or out into the Palace of Westminster to retrieve witnesses lost in the corridors, and in these slow moments — were it not for her companion's constant chatter — Eliza would have reverted to reading. But the new Mrs Ainsworth had a way of making all reading, indeed all private contemplation or mental escape, entirely impossible. She kept a person usefully tethered to the present, like the stays on a hot air balloon.

4.

Dramatis Personae

'Now that one there's Mr Ballantine. Willie claims he used to come to dinner, back in the old days, but who knows with Willie! Anyway he's the one who's for Sir Roger. Funny-looking if you ask me – jowls like a bloodhound. But of course, I'm a great believer in people looking like what they are. Your insides come to your outsides eventually, and a bloodhound lawyer like that is just the thing to sniff out these Tichbornes and their lies . . . Though I see Judge Bovill's quite another cup of tea. He looks a right toad. Now, men of the toad persuasion are not to be trifled with, Mrs Touchet – I've surely told you that before – and a toad judge will be a bother to Sir Roger, naturally . . . What a lot of horsehair and powder! If they knew what them moth-eaten wigs look like from this height they'd naturally fork out for some new ones.'

Sarah leaned forward and peered through the opera glasses Mrs Touchet had tried very hard to dissuade her from bringing. But the glasses did not now seem out of place. The line between courtroom and theatre was far thinner than she would have supposed. Sir William Bovill, flanked by his three Justices, sat on a raised stage, underneath a high wooden canopy shaped like a proscenium, and behind him hung a lion and unicorn painted on muslin, just like a backdrop. Eliza could very easily imagine an Icarus suspended from this rigging – wooden wings tarred with goose feathers – or a weird sister with a kitchen broom pressed between her legs. Meanwhile, immediately in front of this 'stage', facing it, sat a collection of interchangeable bewigged clerks and barristers, arranged in a half-circle precisely as if sitting in the orchestra, and onlookers were packed into two ground-floor 'boxes'. And what else could you call Sarah and Eliza's view but the one from the 'Gods'?

'What do you make of Coleridge, Sarah?'

'Which one's him again?'

Mrs Touchet pointed discreetly: 'Sir John Duke Coleridge. A descendant of the poet. He's representing the Tichbornes.'

To her surprise, Sarah found this very funny:

'What a specimen! A milksop if ever there was one. And did you ever see such a lamb's face! Whoever brings a poet to a battle can't know much about war! Ha ha ha! Oh, I'd say Ballantine can deal with him all right. But the one what's with him, Coleridge's second, that Hawkins fella – he's hawk by name, hawk by nature. Look at that nose like a beak. We'll watch out for him!' She swung round – somewhat theatrically – to train her glasses on the dozen or so harried-looking men sitting in the reporters' gallery.

'But not as closely as we'll watch them snakes. For a snake is a snake is a snake is a snake . . .'

Thanks to the thorough work of such snakes in the daily papers, there was not much that was new to either woman in Ballantine's opening remarks. But Sarah was glad to have it confirmed in a court of law – and in front of such an audience – that a shipwreck could indeed affect one's mind and memories of childhood, and that aristocrats often enough 'got no more book reading' than common folk, and could hardly be expected to write grammatical letters to long-lost mothers or for ever remember all the silly French words they had supposedly been raised speaking. Mrs Touchet, meanwhile, was interested to hear that Roger's father had been cruel, and his childhood unhappy, and spent mostly in France. In the misery of aristocrats she found proof of the ancient wisdom regarding camels, rich men and the eyes of needles. After an unedifying spell at military school, Roger had gone into the military itself, serving in Ireland. During holidays at Tichborne Park, home of his uncle, he had fallen in love with his first cousin, Katherine 'Kattie' Doughty. But both the Doughtys and the Tichbornes had vetoed the match. Unable to marry, Roger had bought himself out of his commission, and gone to seek adventure in the New World. There he had not drowned, but rather survived. And was certainly *not* Arthur Orton, who was a separate man altogether – 'A butcher, of the butcher type, of Wapping,' according to Ballantine. Although, unfortunately, this Mr Orton could not, at present, be located. Still, there was no shortage of people who had met the Claimant and did not think him a fraud. The court was promised – threatened – hundreds of witnesses. The jury, noticeably reluctant to take their seats in the first place, were now to be heard groaning. Mrs Touchet, looking eagerly below for Mr Bogle, or the Claimant himself, and seeing neither, surmised this was likely to be a long affair. The new Mrs Ainsworth, entranced, expressed her desire to come again at the first opportunity.

5.

The Uses of Improvisation

But another trip was an inconvenience to William: he had writing to do and disliked his daughters' cooking. Having only suggested the original outing out of spite, he had naturally not expected it to be repeated. Now he grew suspicious of his cousin's motives, and Mrs Touchet, sensing danger, improvised. She spoke movingly of the moral necessity of 'finally teaching Sarah to read and write'. Was not this trial the perfect opportunity? It being always 'easier to instruct where interest already lies'? They might even use the transcripts from the *Daily London News* as reading material, and the new Mrs Ainsworth could surely be taught to form her letters by way of a little court reporting. When trying to get what she wanted, the Targe was ruthless: she could make almost anything sound not only necessary but inevitable. William was swiftly defeated.

Eliza, almost as quickly, realized she had inadvertently provided a useful cover for her own activities, for she might now take a great deal of paper and ink into court without arousing suspicion. And when, on their second visit, she was informed by a nearby journalist that the large-nosed woman in the public gallery was the famous lady novelist herself! Well, then she permitted herself the indulgence of believing in coincidence – those dropped stitches that permit a glimpse of the infinite tapestry – taking it as a sign from Providence that she was on the right path.

6.

Comedy in the Court

On their third visit, they found that the audience for *Tichborne vs Lushington* had grown so large the whole company had been forced to move, from the Court of Common Pleas to the larger Queen's Bench. Mrs Touchet looked about hopefully for any further sign of the admirable Mrs Lewes but if she and her big nose were present, they could not be spotted in the crowd. This time the people had come prepared: they had winkle-pots and paper cones of chestnuts to accompany the entertainment, and laughed and applauded the cross-examinations exactly as if at the music hall. (Truly eminent visitors – who could not decently be seated with this mob – were provided with chairs and invited to sit beside the Judge himself.) The morning was taken up with several former Carabineers from the 6th Dragoon Regiment, swearing on the Bible that the twitch of the Claimant's eyebrows was the very same they recalled on Sir Roger, or that his ears were oddly familiar, or that they'd know those elbows anywhere. Absurd. The new Mrs Ainsworth received it all in a spirit of utmost seriousness. And yet, at other moments, could surprise Eliza with her shrewdness:

'Now, please notice, Mrs Touchet, how that maid girl from Tichborne Park mentioned the mouth twitch just as the Captain did? But seeing as how the Captain's wearing all that bleeding gold braid *he* gets his fair hearing, while the likes of Ethel gets spoken to like she's something on the bottom of Coleridge's shoe! And would someone please tell me why this Coleridge person keeps saying *Would you be surprised to hear* every time he opens his bleeding mouth? I don't find a thing that man says a surprise. Thinks he can talk to a decent working girl like she's nothing! What's so surprising about that? But he won't be doing that with Mr Lushington, you'll see.'

Eliza consulted her notes. She credited herself with a quick mind, but it was Sarah who seemed to have much more rapidly gained a thorough grasp of proceedings.

'But Lushington's merely the *tenant*, isn't he? He hasn't really anything to do with the case, as far as I can see, Sarah, except in name.'

'Exactly. Got no bloody horse in the race. But in the morning papers it says he's already promised to vacate Tichborne Park early, to make space for the "real owner". That's how convinced our Mr Lushington is. So what does *that* tell you?'

'Well, as he never knew Sir Roger in the first place, I'm afraid I don't at all see how—'

'No more did I know the bugger, nor any of them snakes, nor any of this lot' – Sarah gestured at the avid chestnut-eaters all about them – 'Don't stop us lot from having a right to our opinions, does it?'

After lunch, Sir Roger's military tailor, a Mr James Greenwood, took the stand to confirm, to the delight of the court, that Sir Roger was now 'Considerably stouter. The only thing left of him is about the eyes.' As was becoming very clear to Mrs Touchet, no amount of solemn questioning on the part of the lawyers could repress or deny the people's sense of a comic carnival. Mr Coleridge, in particular, had an unfortunate habit of asking the sorts of questions that too easily lent themselves to comic treatment:

COLERIDGE: *We have heard you are a tailor. Who is your clerk?*
GREENWOOD: *My sleeping partner.*
COLERIDGE: *But who is that, Mr Greenwood?*
GREENWOOD: *Why, Mrs Greenwood of course!*

The new Mrs Ainsworth, applying handkerchiefs to both eyes, pronounced it funnier than anything you'd get at the London Pavilion.

7.

Negative Capability

On the twenty-ninth of May it was reported that the Claimant would take the stand the next day. Sarah traced her forefinger slowly underneath this sentence, sounding it out. Eliza felt something flutter inside her – anticipation. For wherever the Claimant went, there went his friend Mr Bogle, and she had her papers and her pen and her inkpot and the timing was impeccable. On the train, she could barely control herself, fingers thrumming on the window. She had known the giddiness of love, and the febrile sensations of hate and fear, but this feeling was different. It was an excitement of the blood that was yet under the total control of her mind. Was this what the admirable Mrs Lewes felt as she worked? What William and Charles had known, all those years?

8.

Are *You Arthur Orton?*

Arriving early, they entered the court at the forefront of a mob, and took their seats on the ground floor, not twenty feet from where Mr Bogle sat with his son, both their faces visible to Mrs Touchet in profile. She could draw no better than a five-year-old, but she now tried to get them down in sentences. Mr Andrew Bogle's wispy beard, his sparse white tufts of hair, and owl-like watchfulness. His son Henry's striking good looks and narrow, penetrating eyes. She noticed, too, that Henry was quite as busy as she was herself, scribbling furiously on a legal pad, filling twice as many pages. Meanwhile, on the stand stood – wilted – the Claimant. It was a warm day. Having proudly refused a seat at ten a.m., now, at eleven, he appeared to be suffering from his choice. To Eliza he looked exhausted, sickly. His mouth twitched with regularity and his voice was weak, seeming to struggle to get out of the bulk of himself. Eliza felt sorry for him. He appeared so defeated, avoiding even the eyes of his own counsel, Ballantine, who was presently trying to lead him gently through his testimony. The court grew quiet. What they needed was a reasonable explanation for that incriminating, clandestine visit to a certain Orton family, in Wapping. Could it be done? Why, if he was truly an aristocrat, did he know those lowly Ortons at all – and why on earth had he gone to visit them? Together, lawyer and client agreed that while it was true that the Claimant – *en route* to meet his mother in Paris – had gone to pay a call on these Wapping Ortons, this visit had been merely a 'courtesy'. Acting as 'Mr Orton's representative and friend from Australia', the Claimant had wanted only to let these Ortons know that their son had 'done well for himself' in the New World, and that he sent his love. And no, he was not Arthur Orton himself, and he did not know why so many people in Wapping seemed to think that he was. Eliza wanted to laugh. But as this part of his testimony was being greeted with respectful silence by the crowd – and as she was used to finding many things funny that others didn't – she bit her tongue.

Now Ballantine waded into the murky visual evidence. It was true that Sir Roger had earlobes in his photograph, and that the Claimant did not, but daguerreotypes had no firm place in a courtroom, being too new-fangled and often of uncertain origin, as well as so very easily doctored and changed. With this Mrs Touchet found she broadly agreed. Then Coleridge approached. Mrs Touchet looked across to check the effect on the Bogles. She saw no change whatsoever in Mr Bogle's calm stolidity, and only a little stiffening in the writing hand of his son. The Claimant, for his part, finally conceded the need for a chair. His great body sank down; a glass of water was brought to his elbow; he folded his arms across the lip of the witness box, cast his eyes down like a tired bull, sighed heavily. Coleridge began. Would it surprise the Claimant to know that a private detective had discovered that at least two members of the Orton family were receiving secret payments? Presumably from the Claimant? Presumably in return for their silence? Would it surprise him to hear that Roger Tichborne never was in Wagga Wagga in his life? Would it surprise the Claimant to hear that he had been spotted by a local Wapping man and identified as none other than Arthur Orton? That they had ship records of a Mr Orton leaving Wapping as a boy and sailing to the other side of the earth? The Claimant hedged, groaned, muttered. Coleridge tried to assert himself:

'I ask: would you be surprised to hear it?'

'I am not surprised to hear *you* say so.'

Hilarity in the court. It was a long moment before poor Bovill could corral them all back into silence.

Then Hawkins stood up, thrust his gown out behind him like a toreador, and asked the Claimant directly: '*Are* you Arthur Orton?'

9.

Not Her Pen

A silly gasping went up all about Mrs Touchet, as if this question above all others was particularly astute and unanswerable. Sarah squeezed her hand. As well as comic timing, the Claimant had a flair for drama. He waited a long moment, stood up briefly, and brought his hand to his breast, like a man pledging his faith: 'I am not.' Wild applause. Mr Bogle was seen to nod his head several times, while son Henry cheered with the rest. But this glory was short-lived: the next round of questions concerned Sir Roger's time at Stonyhurst College, about which the Claimant appeared to remember less than nothing. He did not know who Virgil was, or whether he was a writer or a king. He thought Latin was Greek and couldn't tell either of them from French, his supposed native tongue. He did not know Shakespeare from Galileo or Physic from Biology. He could not describe the contents of a sealed packet Sir Roger had apparently left with the main steward of Tichborne Park – a Mr Gosford – before he sailed for Brazil. Or if he knew, was refusing to say. The court was by now oppressively hot: guilty sweat ran down the Claimant's face. It was really very hard not to feel sorry for this man. So obviously out of his depth, caught in an ever-widening lie that had outgrown even his own substantial girth. Not to mention all these gullible, mal-educated, no doubt well-meaning people who had so foolishly championed his cause . . .

When the court at last broke for luncheon, Eliza reminded herself to be a good Christian. She would not crow or appear too pleased with herself. She would be gentle and mindful of Sarah's hurt feelings, always remembering that false beliefs are precisely the ones we tend to cling to most strongly. Before she could speak, however, Sarah erupted in enthusiasm:

'Ain't it a marvel how he ties all them stuffed shirts up in knots! The more them lawyers talk, the more he proves himself! If he was false, naturally he'd have ginned up on every subject like false people always do, but he's a Lord so he don't bother. He knows what he's about and that's all that matters. Virgil! Who's Virgil when he's at home?'

Back in the courtroom, to convince herself she wasn't going mad, Mrs Touchet resolved to simply write down whatever passed between Coleridge and the Claimant, without further commentary:

    C: *What is chemistry?*
    TC: *It is about chemistry, of course.*
    C: *I know. History is about history, and so on. I ask you what is it about?*
    TC: *About different herbs and poisons, and the substance of medicines.*
    C: *Do you mean what is in a chemist's shop?*
    TC: *I think a dose of it would do you good.*

But there was just too much of it, and too much laughter from the crowd, and whatever the shortcomings of photographs, they could at least take in a whole scene at once, as a pen never could. At least, not her pen.

10.

What is Real?

Just in front of Eliza, in the orchestra seats, a big-boned young woman had been sketching all day. Looking over the girl's shoulder, Mrs Touchet felt envy at this display of superior skill. In a few light strokes the girl had caught Bovill's toad-like pomposity, Coleridge's badger face, the Claimant's heavy-jowled exhaustion, even young Henry Bogle's lightning eyes. Oh, for a muse of coloured pencils! The big-boned girl, sensing someone at her back, turned. She had a broad, plain, intelligent face. Beady blue eyes. Cheeks that went fiercely red, like a Scot's. A flutter went through Mrs Touchet of quite another kind again. Then: clamour in the courtroom! Gasps! For a perplexing moment Eliza had the belief – as we sometimes do in nightmares – that the whole world and everything in it was just a dream of her own making.

'Do you mean to swear before judge and jury that you *seduced* this lady?'

But Coleridge was not talking about Mrs Touchet or her Lady Illustrator. He was speaking to the Claimant and pointing at Katherine Doughty, the love of Roger's youth, presently a timid-looking late-middle-aged woman, seated in the second row and married to someone else. The Claimant nodded. Gasps!

'And on *oath* you are claiming that in the infamous sealed packet – now sadly destroyed – you had in fact left Mr Gosford instructions of what to do in the event of your own cousin's . . . *confinement*?'

'I most solemnly to my God swear I did,' replied the Claimant, causing an uproar, although as far as Eliza could discern, he had spoken as much out of boredom – and perhaps a desire for an early dinner – than any more calculated motive. If he was Roger he would know what was in the sealed packet, and it might as well be something thrilling, if only to break up the tedium of cross-examination. Meanwhile his 'cousin' fled the room in tears.

'Bloody hell – we're in for a show now!' whooped Sarah, standing and grasping the seat in front, but instead the court dissolved into chaos and had to be adjourned.

II.

All is Change

After which Eliza was in need of a long walk.

'Well, you do as you like, Mrs Touchet, naturally, but I wouldn't be the type to walk to no purpose . . . If you'd ever had to walk from Brighton to London barefoot, as I once did, that'd naturally cure you of ever again desiring to walk nowhere for no reason. No, I'm going to sit my pretty arse down somewhere and eat a pie, excuse my French. Imagine he went and got her up the duff! What a cad is our Sir Roger! And I will see you at the station at four.'

Eliza Touchet prided herself on her walking. It was her way of understanding her age, or rather, of defying it altogether. If, as you neared sixty, you could walk as far and as fast as you did at forty — at twenty! — did that mean no time had passed? From the courthouse she reached the Edgware Road without any signs of breathlessness, spurred on by the vision of poor, maligned Katherine Doughty, a dough-faced woman with nothing of her youth left in her. But in Kilburn she caught herself breathing heavily, and sighing, for so much had changed. Mapesbury House was sold, and a little further on, so was The Grange. All the old estates were either shut up, dilapidated or demolished. Railways cut across fields, and sometimes the fields themselves vanished entirely under rows of little houses, built comically close together, with railings replacing hedgerows, and lamp posts where elms had been. She oriented herself by pubs and churches — everything else was transformation. The Kilbourne river ran no more — a railway ran instead — and the Wells were closed and the Bell knocked down and replaced with a new establishment of the same name. Only by the wet flapping of a barnacle goose did she know she now approached the River Brent, obscured as it was by a brickworks and yet more houses. Eliza chided herself for vanity. Time was so much harder on land than people. She was still Eliza Touchet. But what was this place?

12.

A Memory

At the bridge she paused and looked down at the stagnant water, in the spirit of reflection. And all at once her Frances was with her once again, still young, not sick, not dead at thirty-three, bending over the bridge beside her, looking down . . .

They were both a little breathless, in the memory, having run the distance from Elm Lodge with a small crowd of farmers and excited children. His Majesty's huntsmen, rarely seen this far north, were charging through the neighbourhood. Scarlet-coated, on horseback, surrounded by hounds! The local crowd pursued the riders through the lanes, but Eliza and Frances, knowing better, had hitched their skirts and jumped stiles for four fields, only to lose the whole hunting party near Kilburn Woods. They were resting on the Grand Union bridge – having given up the chase – when the stag appeared suddenly below them. Magnificent animal! In its panic, it must have changed course and made for Paddington. Now it hesitated a moment; then leapt into the river and swam for its life. Its maladapted legs churned the water, it seemed about to drown – but was soon struggling up the opposite bank, like a newborn foal. A gang of schoolboys, gathered on the verge, cheered this rare example of the weak escaping the strong. The dogs howled. The horses snorted hotly and turned round. Frances wept tears of joy. They had walked home happy, hand in hand. Later, Eliza heard from a church warden that the stag fled straight from the water into St Mary's churchyard, was cornered there, and torn to pieces. A tale she kept to herself.

13.

All Souls

On the other side of the bridge, Mrs Touchet now accepted that her legs ached and turned left at the cemetery, to begin the long walk back to town to rejoin the second Mrs Ainsworth, and catch their train home. Beloved Kensal Lodge would be in front of her in a minute, and then Kensal Manor House, if they had not both been knocked down by the builders like all the rest. In another test of her faculties, she tried to remember the year they had moved from the Lodge to that second, grander, property. '41? '42? At the height of William's fame, anyway.

On a melancholy whim, she turned back and retraced her steps, passing through the gates of All Souls. The dead stay where they are, at least. More join them, but that is the only change. She took a seat on the first bench that presented itself, and, looking up, grimaced at the twenty-foot monument before her, unchanged, except for a growth of ivy around its preposterous foot-long dedication: TO HER. When she had lived beside this graveyard, and taken her morning constitutionals here, she had liked to pretend the HER in question was Frances. That this ornate display of grief – the flying cherubs, the cameo engraved into the stone, the giant statue of 'Faith' embodied as a beautiful young woman – that all of this was for Frances. A comforting thought. Nor was it an entirely illogical or sentimental connection: they had known the lady, not well, but they had met her. Emma Soyer, the painting prodigy. Frances had liked her very much. Oh, but Frances liked everybody. She had been amazed at the girl's precocious skill, and Eliza supposed it was amazing, to paint so well so young, though she could not consider talent a merit in itself, talent being as much a case of luck as beauty. But it was true that the girl, at only eighteen, had contributed a fine painting to the movement, which they had then auctioned off, raising significant money for the cause. It depicted two little black sisters, the elder looking to heaven with a book in her lap, while the younger stared straight at whoever looked at her, so as to prick the conscience. Pretty dresses they wore and pretty expressions, patient yet determined for liberty, with a palm tree waving behind them. They looked like what they were, human beings, which was the point.

The artist herself had been a pale, strange-looking girl with a long, pointed nose like a Frenchman. Later she married the head chef at the Reform Club — he was the Soyer; before that she was plain Emma Jones — and so, like Mrs Touchet, had found herself in possession of a dubious French name, although it had clearly been of more practical use to her. She was famous in France: *Madame Soyer*. At home, she was more of a curiosity, another one of Samuel Johnson's dogs, paintbrush in paw. Yet despite all her success in the world of men, Madame Soyer's baby had died, too, and she with it, aged only twenty-eight. Poor woman. On the other hand, here was this giant monument TO HER, and her paintings were presumably still somewhere, on some wall — in fact, weren't they said to be on King Leopold's? Witty and acute feminine conversation, by contrast, could not be hung on any wall. No one builds a monument to it. Even Lady Blessington, for all her silliness, had understood this, wisely smuggling herself into print between lines of Byron.

14.

A Single Soul

A crippling dose of self-pity, more suitable to a child, surged through Mrs Touchet. She stood up and looked about for a sadder story than her own to cheer her. She did not have to go very far. Only a few hundred yards to the left lay the tragic Hogarth girl. Dead without issue. Dead without making art or books or any kind of name for herself. Dead before womanhood had even come to claim her:

> *Mary Scott Hogarth*
> *Young, beautiful and good*
> *God in His mercy numbered her among*
> *His angels at the early age of seventeen*

Only Dickens, thought Mrs Touchet, sourly. Only he could imagine those first two adjectives as having any possible relation to the third. Sentimentalist. And never more so than on this subject of his dead sister-in-law. The heaving tears he'd shed at this young woman's graveside! The animal moan as they lowered the coffin! An inconvenient, revealing grief, unnatural and unmanly. He'd cried more than his wife! Just as, only a year later, Eliza would cry more for the loss of her Frances than she had ever cried for her own husband. More than William ever cried for Frances . . .

She remembered the Hogarth girl's funeral as a warm May day like this one, heavy with the scent of rotting blossom. After it was over, on the short, silent walk home, William had seemed troubled. Did he wonder, as she did, if Dickens' domestic arrangements were as singular as his own? Perhaps it didn't occur to him. So many things didn't.

If she did not leave now she would miss her train. She walked quickly back towards the main gates, past husbands and wives buried in the same hole for all eternity; once more past TO HER. Designed, commissioned and unveiled by the uxorious Mr Soyer, who had yet turned up to the unveiling with a ballet dancer half his age. Mrs Touchet allowed herself a private smile. As long as we profess to believe that two people may happily – or feasibly – invest all love and interest in this world solely in one another, till death do them part – well, then life, short as it is, will continue to be a human comedy, punctuated by tragedy. So she generally thought. Then there were these moments of grace when she startled herself with the idea that if anybody truly understood what is signified by the word 'person', they would consider twelve lifetimes too brief a spell in which to love a single soul.

15.

Adjourned Until November!

Overnight, the newspaper writers turned puritan, like so many Methodists fainting in the aisles. This despite the fact that Mr Gosford, the steward of the estate, had long ago destroyed the secret packet and had never looked inside it. But into this narrative void the Tichborne Claimant's tale of forbidden love and potential pregnancy fit perfectly – it was the kind of scandal with something for everybody. Not for the first time Mrs Touchet was struck by how much more passion may be aroused by phantom damages done to female 'honour' than by anything actually done to a woman herself. *We are only ideas to them*, she wrote, at the top of a page. But it was not in keeping with anything else she had written so far – she could not explain even to herself what she really meant by it. Frowning, she scratched it out.

Downstairs, Sarah's analysis was, by contrast, plain-spoken and frustratingly accurate:

'He only went and mentioned the unmentionable! Don't he know that these gentlefolk find their babies in the cabbage patch? Oh, he's in for it now. Now he's lost the toffs and gained the mob! For I should say *we* know what's between our own legs, or I should hope we do. What's more, we remember using it! I'll tell you when court will be recalled, Mrs Touchet: when all them dozy gentlewomen stop their blushing!'

Eliza, much dispirited, put her pen and papers back in their locked drawer and did her best to re-enter the life of the household. But what had previously been only irritating now felt unendurable. Why this house and this garden? Why Hurstpierpoint? Why these weekly visits to Gilbert? Why the Sisyphean task of breakfast, lunch and dinner, made and cleared and made again? What was the point of it all? William was hard at work on his twenty-ninth novel. Why must it feature Catherine Howard and Anne of Cleves? Why did she have to hear about it? *Two hundred pounds a year.* But it was Touchet money: it had blood on it. And to give it away, meanwhile, was to have to know to whom, and why.

She was annoyed with William for teasing her. ('Pity my two court reporters! They suffer without their trial! You'll find a very amusing piece in *Punch* about "Tichborne Withdrawal", Eliza. I'll leave it out.') Almost equally irritating were Sarah's attempts to establish a sisterly commonality between them. ('I should say we *are* suffering. It's very boring out here for girls like us.') She did not want to talk to any Ainsworths nor listen to any. There was someone else. One night she even dreamt of him. They were at a table somewhere in the centre of London, and she was reaching her hand out for his, saying: *Tell me everything.* But when she woke, she was still in Hurstpierpoint.

16.

An Amusing Piece in Punch

A SURPRISING SUGGESTION

The British Public is suffering. A long indulgence in the stimulant known as TICHBORNE, BOVILL, BALLANTINE, COLERIDGE and Co, has produced an unhealthy state of excitement which is followed, now that the stimulant is not on tap, by a corresponding state of depression. The papers, which contain the ordinary amount of murder and violence, pall on the public appetite. The constitution of the people is deranged. Respectable householders wake up in the night, shrieking, 'Would it surprise you to hear?' and declaring they see Claimants climbing up the walls. Elderly ladies cannot return to browse in the cool pastures of good books, and sigh for cross-examination. Young ladies have left off reading novels to an extent that must alarm MRS MUDIE.

Under these circumstances we ask, 'Is it too late to adopt a suggestion thrown out by the correspondent of a contemporary, and to assemble the Claimant and counsel and bench on the beach at Brighton?'

By combining business with pleasure, and rendering the proceedings attractive, the trial might not only be rendered more endurable to both parties, the counsel, the judge, and the jury, but it might even be made to pay a portion of its own very heavy expenses.

The Court, by modelling itself upon the Christy Minstrels' form, with the Claimant and Solicitor General as 'End-Men', would draw a tremendous crowd.

The proceedings might be opened with a solo and chorus, the latter of the usual nigger type –

> Here's old JOE (or Bo, as the case may be)
> VILL!
> And he's so
> ILL!
> Ching-a-ring, jiddy jiddy, Juba, Bang!

The examination would carry on in a jocular vein, until Bones's turn came for a song, after this fashion: --

> Supposin' he ain't you,
> And supposin' I was me,
> And supposin' we both were butchers of Wapping.
> How very surprised we'd be!

This would naturally conclude with a break-down. After which Tambourine would take the floor –

'I thay, MR BONES, why am dis child like St Paul's Cafeedrill? Gib it up? Yah! 'Cos, wid all yer drivin', ya can't git round him!'

This is the merest outline, of which the talent and ability of those concerned could supply a finished picture. We are only expressing the opinion of thousands when we cry: 'The silly season is here! Give us – Oh, give us our TICHBORNE case once more!'

VOLUME FIVE

Bogle: I am never surprised at anything myself.
Hawkins: You are never surprised at anything?
Bogle: Never in my life. I never recall that I was.

COURT TRANSCRIPT

London Daily News,
Friday 10th November 1871

With court back in session, the first witness called was Andrew Bogle, the man of colour, whose name has been so frequently mentioned in the course of the trial, and we need not say that his appearance in the box excited considerable interest. He is an elderly, respectable looking man, with hair slightly tinged with grey, having an intelligent face, and a very soft voice and manner. He asked to be accommodated with a seat, and one was immediately placed in the box. His dress was made more conspicuous by a bright blue necktie, which on the preceding day had been the subject of some facetious remarks by counsel. Mr. Sergeant Ballantine examined him as follows:

SB: I believe you have been very ill lately.

B: Yes, for some little time.

SB: I believe you are now staying at Harley Lodge, the residence of Sir Roger Tichborne.

B: Yes.

SB: How old are you, Bogle?

B: I am 64.

SB: Are you a native of Jamaica?

B: Yes.

sb: Do you recollect, when you were about 11 years of age, the late Mr Edward Tichborne?

b: I do.

sb: He was the gentleman who afterwards became Sir Edward Doughty?

b: Yes.

sb: Do you recollect his being in the island of Jamaica?

b: Yes.

sb: He managed I believe some estates belonging to the then Duke of Buckingham?

b: Yes.

sb: How came you to know him?

b: I used to go to his house in the morning.

sb: And did he employ you as page?

b: He sent me with messages.

sb: And it ended in your being taken as page. And did you continue as page as long as he remained in Jamaica?

b: Yes.

sb: And when he returned to England did you return with him as page?

b: Yes.

sb: And did you remain six months in England? Did you stay at Tichborne Park and Upton Park?

b: Yes.

sb: Tichborne Park was your home, and you often went to Alresford?

b: Yes, very often.

sb: At the end of the six months did you and your master return to Jamaica?

b: Yes.

sb: Did you reside with him for eighteen months on the Hope Estate, which belonged to the Duke of Buckingham? And at the end of that time did Mr Tichborne give up the management of the estate?

B: Yes, and he brought me with him to England.

SB: Shortly before his arrival in England a Miss Doughty had died.

B: Yes, and that put him in possession of the estates.

SB: Did you continue in his service until March, 1853?

B: Yes, and for the last 20 years of his life I was his valet and always in attendance upon him.

SB: Upon his marriage you accompanied him upon his foreign tour? You were more or less acquainted with all the members of the Doughty and Tichborne family?

B: I was.

In further examination witness said:

B: I myself married twice, the first time to the nurse of Lady Doughty; and second to the schoolmistress. They are both dead.

SB: When did you first see young Tichborne?

B: A great many years ago. He was a mere child just beginning to walk about. That was when he used to visit Sir Doughty at Upton. I knew his parents very well. His nurse was Sarah Passmore. I recollect his going to Stonyhurst, and he spent his holidays generally at Tichborne. There was one room between his bedroom and mine. I used to go out shooting and fishing with him and hunting, of which amusements he was very fond. He used to smoke night and day.

SB: Was there much company kept at Tichborne?

B: Sometimes.

SB: Was he much fond of gentlemen's society?

B: No, he used to be fond of being downstairs with the servants more than of being with the gentlemen.

(Laughter)

SB: Was there more than one gamekeeper?

B: Only one and a boy, and he used to associate a good deal with them.

SB: Was he at all musical?

B: Yes; he used to make a good deal of noise with the French horn.

(Laughter)

SB: How did he talk English?

B: Very badly at first – broken; but he improved a good deal before he left England.

SB: After Sir Edward Tichborne died, did you continue in the service of Tichborne's father?

B: Yes; about four months.

SB: No fault was found with you?

B: Not that I know of.

SB: Having left the service, did you and your wife determine on going to Australia?

B: I married afterward and we went in the spring of 1854 to Sydney.

SB: Used you to communicate with Lady Doughty?

B: Yes. I received money from her to pay our passage, and up to the time of returning to England with the plaintiff I received an annuity of 50 pounds from Lady Doughty. Since I have been in England the annuity has been stopped.

2.

Walking to Willesden

If witness examination was a form of stimulation, it affected the two women differently. Provoking in one a great hunger — easily satisfied by a braised pork chop — and in the other, a compulsion to walk, despite the cold. But Eliza's was a hunger, too. Some afternoons, she felt there was really no telling how far she might go. She might walk for ever. Instead, cresting the hill at Kensal Rise, she was surprised by exactly what she'd been looking for. A powerful sense of *déjà vu*. Made no less powerful by the knowledge that what she was recalling was not an episode from her own life but rather a fictional echo, lifted from the pages of *Jack Sheppard*, which was the only one of her cousin's many books she'd ever really liked:

> *Immediately beneath her lay Willesden — the most charming and secluded village in the neighbourhood of the metropolis — with its scattered farm-houses, its noble granges, and its old grey church-tower just peeping above a grove of rook-haunted trees . . . Every old country church is beautiful, but Willesden is the most beautiful country church we know . . .*

Towards this spot Mrs Touchet now directed her steps. The farm-houses were less scattered, and the granges enclosed, but the medieval church remained. Silent and remote, lost in time. Approaching the gate, she thought the churchyard different, but only because memory had preserved it in an eternal May. At the height of their friendship, she, William and Charles had galloped to St Mary's every Sunday, leaping recklessly over stiles, racing each other . . . Getting down from her horse she would find blossom in her hair. Now it was drear November. Mrs Touchet's riding days were behind her. She bowed her long body to pass through the low arch, and spied the Roundhead bullets, still lodged in the stone. She heard the shuffling of a church warden somewhere. In this empty church, before an empty alcove – where a Black Madonna had once stood, before Cromwell's despoliation – she now crossed herself, as she always had, although she no longer worried herself over the soul of Cromwell. She moved to the easterly corner to light a candle for Frances. Then, on a queer impulse, lit two more: one for each of Mr Bogle's dead wives.

March the sixth, 1838. Next March, thought Mrs Touchet, my Frances will have been dead for longer than she was ever alive.

3.

Jack Sheppard, *1838*

In the end it had all happened very suddenly, while everything was tumult and anxiety. Frances was still in her father's house, and her family, the Ebers, had accused William of 'marital neglect', and secretly withdrawn the children from their school. Mrs Touchet meanwhile was back at Kensal Lodge, turning her hand to housekeeping, in the absence of anyone else to do it. The *Rookwood* money was gone. Frittered away on port, gold buttons, constant entertaining. The follow-up – set in the French court of Henri III – proved confusing and unpopular: the publisher had failed to recoup his costs. And in the middle of this perfect Ainsworthian storm, suddenly, Frances died. They had not seen her in three months – yet she died. Mrs Touchet was to have been sent to the Ebers' as emissary, to encourage her to come home – but she died. In the fantasies of a bolder Eliza, she had even imagined taking the runaway young wife to Italy, where the sun cures all ills, and there they would have found a little house, nestled in an olive grove, and sent a letter back to Kensal Lodge, a few months later, confessing their intention to stay. *We have decided to live like the Llangollen women, only in white cottons rather than black worsted . . .*

Instead, she died. The Ebers buried her in a family plot in Oxfordshire, a funeral to which William was not invited, much less his peculiar cousin. Mrs Touchet gave up Chesterfield and moved to Kensal Rise permanently. *My Frances is dead.* No matter how many times she said it to herself it had remained an impossible fact. Yet not to believe was to go mad. Weeks of tearful agony. Now, more than thirty years later, she found she barely remembered that time, and it was only what came after that had remained. The void. The way it opened up inside her. Sitting in this same Willesden pew day after day, staring at the same empty alcove, with a mind just as empty.

It was during that tumultuous year of 1838 that she felt she had finally understood what writing was *for*, or at least what it was for in William's case: escape from the void. Distraction. Within a week, true to type, he was back at work, writing to his old friend Crossley. Did Crossley have any materials concerning the year 1724, or the reign of George I? If William came up to Manchester, would he be able to borrow a copy of *The Newgate Calendar* . . .

By that April, his *Jack Sheppard* was well under way. She read it as he wrote it. She read it before anyone. It was Jack's mother, Mrs Sheppard, who had stood on the crest of a hill looking down at St Mary's. And it was here, in this same church, that young Jack began his life of petty crime, picking a congregant's pocket. Eliza considered herself a sophisticated reader, but *Jack Sheppard* brought out the child in her. She gasped as the boy-thief scaled the walls of Newgate. Cried tears of moral frustration when Jonathan Wild, the government's chief 'Thief-taker', proved just as much a thief as any of the poor sinners he'd sent to the gallows. By the time young Jack had made his third escape from gaol, she knew there was more life in this infamous Newgate house-breaker than a dozen French dukes. Finishing it, she thought: *vulgar, violent, sensational, ridiculous.* But she also understood that she would not have to worry about the price of port for some time. She gave no edits, only strongly protesting a scene of seduction, in which Jack submits to two prostitutes simultaneously: the 'Amazonian', black-haired Bess Edgworth, and the blonde, pert-nosed Polly Maggot. It 'shocked' her. Or so she had said at the time. So she had strained to believe. Now she wondered whether she hadn't confused frustration and regret for piety and disgust. Why had William left it so late to imagine, in fiction, what reality itself had just foreclosed?

4.

The 'Newgate Controversy'

What she couldn't for the life of her remember now was whether the real Jack Sheppard had been a Willesden lad or not. At the height of *Sheppard* mania — when it was outselling *Twist*, and on various stages in dreadful musical versions — she often heard the claim that the boy's final resting place was that little cemetery, just off Willesden Lane. Perhaps William had made it so. Over the years, despite everything, he had made a lot of things so that weren't. Flitches of bacon and lime trees and Dick Turpin riding through Cricklewood. Eliza attributed this not to any special skill on her cousin's part but to the fact that the great majority of people turn out to be extraordinarily suggestible, with brains like sieves through which the truth falls. Fact and fiction meld in their minds. Songs William had written years earlier returned to the stage and were mistaken for history. How many Londoners still believed that Sheppard, waiting to be hung on the Tyburn gallows, sang to the waiting crowd: *Nix my doll, pals, fake away . . . ?*

Keep stealing, my friends! From life for fiction, and from fiction for life. What a terrible business. At least William did it clumsily, with benign incompetence. Whereas his friend Charles had done it like a master — like an actor. That was precisely what was so dangerous about him. Charles Dickens played a part, always. For this reason it had not in any way surprised Mrs Touchet that the role of 'William's best friend' should turn out to be such a temporary one. In fact, as soon as *Sheppard* began its serialization in *Bentley's* — while *Twist* prepared to leave that same organ — she had sensed trouble on the horizon. She saw the way

Charles winced when the two books were spoken of together, as 'Newgate novels', usually in articles worrying about the pernicious moral effect of Newgate novels. A collision was due. Their sensibilities were in opposition. Charles – careful, ever conscious of his reputation – hated unlicensed theatrical versions of *Twist*, but William loved any *Sheppard* play, no matter how poorly done, horribly abridged, or punctuated by terrible songs. He made friends with the same unscrupulous impresarios Charles already counted as enemies. And when Charles relinquished his editorship of *Bentley's*, passing it on to William – who delightedly received it – only Mrs Touchet seemed to understand that this was the younger man's way of offloading not only the magazine but the friendship. Not long after, Dickens sent in his dog, John Forster, to finish the job, with a vicious hatchet job in the *Examiner*. The whole purpose of which – as far as Mrs Touchet could see – was to establish a wide berth between poorly written, morally corrupting books like *Jack Sheppard*, and whatever it was his good friend Charles wrote.

How much all of this hurt William she was never sure. Back then, his skin was thick – it had to be – and his spirit was ever sunny, irrepressible by instinct. Sales were booming. The children were returned to Kensal Lodge. The Ebers were easily bought off, and suddenly there was the money to buy them. Her cousin did not see trouble heading his way until it struck, like his beloved Ainsworthian lightning, on the front page of the *London Daily News*:

LORD WILLIAM RUSSELL MURDERED!
BUTLER CONFESSES
INSPIRED BY AINSWORTH'S 'JACK SHEPPARD'

It wasn't true. Russell's butler had – perhaps – read *The Newgate Calendar*, and been inspired by the heroic criminality to be found within. But the connection was enough. Sales slumped. Hysterical, self-serving condemnations of the Newgate novelists were fired from all quarters, from the very people who had sung the songs, watched the plays, devoured the serials. But by that point, Charles had moved out of range. Two-faced as Jonathan Wild.

The world is full of hypocrites: that could neither surprise nor sadden Mrs Touchet. She had lived too long – and visited the Queen's Bench too many times – to be in any way astonished by that fact. Far worse, in her view, was the cruel redirection or perversion of any natural course, as when we force a river underground, or bend a child to our will. Thinking back on it now, she sincerely regretted the course William had been set on, as a consequence. Off into the distant, storied past – where he felt safest – or up and away into the ether, the super-natural, where nothing is real and nothing matters. All those court intrigues, kings and queens, muskets, lace, wainscoting! All those magical gypsies, witches, ghosts! Never again would he properly attend to the kinds of stories that were right in front of him. Stories like her own – or for that matter like Mr Bogle's. Stories of human beings, struggling, suffering, deluding others and themselves, being cruel to each other or kind. Usually both.

5.

Like Two Peas in a Bushel

Sergeant Ballantine: Did you ever go beyond Sydney in the colony?

Bogle: Never further than five miles.

SB: You were never at Wagga Wagga?

B: No.

The witness under further examination explained that sometime in August 1866, his son, a hairdresser, shaved a man who said he had seen Sir Roger Tichborne in a nearby hotel.

SB: In consequence of that did you go to the neighbourhood of the Metropolitan Hotel, Sydney?

B: I did.

SB: And when you were near the hotel, did any persons pass you?

B: No one that I knew.

SB: Did you see any persons whom you thought you knew?

B: No more than the Claimant. He was the only person I saw, and he and another were in the yard of the hotel – behind it. I sat to wait for him in the gateway of the hotel.

SB: Had you received any description of his appearance at that time?

B: No more than what my son told me.

SB: What was your opinion?

B: Why, directly I saw him I knew it was Roger Tichborne; at the very first sight.

SB: How near did he pass to you?

B: About three or four yards.

SB: Did he see you?

B: He saw me, and stopped and looked. I looked hard at him and smiled, and he came up to me and said, 'Well, old Bogle, is that you?' and I said, 'Yes, sir.' He said something to me about his going upstairs, and I think he said, 'I'll see you again directly.' That was what I understood him to say, and in a very few minutes the waiter came and asked me step that way. I went upstairs then, and saw Roger in his room alone. I said, 'I beg your pardon, I called to see Sir Roger Tichborne, but you are not him, are you?' He said, 'Oh, yes, Bogle, I am.' I said, 'How much stouter you are got!' He said, 'Yes, I'm not that slender lad I was when I left Tichborne.'

SB: Did he ask you anything further?

B: He asked me how long I had been in Sydney, and I told him about twelve years. He then asked me if I lived at Tichborne with his father, after he left. I said I lived with him about four months. He asked me why I left, and I told him it was because Mr Gosford, the steward of the estate, said there was to be an alteration made. I told him that after a conversation with Sir James, I left him. He asked me if the brothers Godwin were alive.

SB: Who were they?

B: They were farmers near Tichborne, and one of them rented a farm there. He then said the older Godwin was a very stingy old fellow, and would never allow those two sons a half-a-crown a-piece to spend.

SB: Did he mention any other persons?

B: Yes. I was not aware there were two sons of Godwin till then. I thought there was only one. He asked me after Mrs Martin and whether she was alive.

B: Who was she?

SB: She was nurse to my master's mother. I told him she was alive when I came away; that Mrs Martin was a very old woman, quite 80 years old, and never by chance seen out of the house by anyone. He also enquired for two brothers named Guy, well known people in the village.

SB: Who were they?

B: Well, they were rather low characters.

(Laughter)

SB: Did he mention anyone else?

B: Yes, he enquired after Etheridge, the blacksmith in the village.

SB: Do you recollect whether he mentioned anything else?

B: He asked me if I remembered going out rabbit shooting with him and Brand, the gamekeeper. That had happened often.

SB: How long did the interview last?

B: About an hour, and he asked me whether I remembered that his uncle Edward used to blow up sometimes.

SB And did his uncle Edward really 'blow up'?

B: Sometimes.

(Laughter)

SB: Anything else?

B: Yes, I told him what I had heard of the shipwreck and his loss, and he said it was dreadful, and that he nearly lost his life. That was the only time I ever mentioned the matter of the shipwreck to him.

SB: Did you name these people to him or he to you?

B: He to me. I had never thought about any of them except Mr Gosford. He then told me he was going to England by the next mail, and I told him that they would be very glad to see him back.

SB: Had you any intention of going to England?

B: Not at that time, but I had intended to go before. After that interview I called upon him every day, but he was always out, and I only had four interviews with him.

SB: Now then, having seen him so much, have you any doubt he is the Roger Tichborne of former days?

B: Not the slightest.

SB: Have you ever given him information of his early days for the sake of getting up his claim?

B: None whatever. I could give him a great deal of information if he had asked me, but he never did ask me a single question.

SB: Were you, after this conversation at the hotel, convinced that he was Roger Tichborne?

B: Yes, I was. In fact, he was so like one of his uncles that I could not mistake. I never knew anyone in my life so like the late Sir Henry Tichborne.

SB: They were alike, were they?

B: Yes, as like as two peas in a bushel.

(Laughter)

6.

Forgiveness in Stereoscope, 1845

Mrs Touchet's nerves were such that she left the setting of the table to the girls and went to pace the front garden. Back at Kensal Lodge this would have been a reasonable course of action; in Kensal Manor the garden was so much wider and more beautiful, there was a perfect oak, and a rustic seat beneath it – she sat down. Took the distressing note from her skirt pocket and re-read it:

Dear Mrs Touchet,

I am writing with haste to catch the four o'clock. Perhaps you remember William's announcement of his editorship in The New Monthly? He hoped for contributors 'eminent not only for talent, but for high rank'. To be brief: I took exception to this, perhaps more than was warranted, and wrote a somewhat intemperate piece answering it in Punch, for I do not believe we need talk about 'high rank' in our republic of letters. Be that as it may, I wrote it, sent it off, and then did not think of it again. In the meantime, I received an invite to Kensal three days ago for this evening and happily said yes, and am coming as planned – but now realize that Punch was published yesterday. I have written to William, to explain and apologize. Do you think I shall be forgiven?

Yours,

William Thackeray

It was almost seven o'clock. The other guests were:

Maclise

Chapman

Chapman's brother

A young lawyer called Sergeant Ballantine with a long face like a horse

A terrible lady poet whom William had met 'at the theatre'

The girls

She bit her thumbnail and looked over her shoulder to the windows of the dining room. She watched William and his three graces laughing and goosing each other instead of neatly laying the pink and yellow bonbons at the head of each sitting, as they had been instructed to do. He looked more like an elder brother than a father. Had he seen the four o'clock post?

Five minutes later it was in a sort of a daze that she stood at the threshold, opposite William, welcoming people, interested only in whether the face in front of her had a nose squished flat as a boxer's and a joyless cast. Then suddenly there it was: very red, and looking at her imploringly, as if she had any power to freeze time or turn it back or otherwise halt the necessity of Thackeray turning at some point to face his host on the other side of the door.

'Ho! Thackeray!'

'Good evening, William.'

'Oh, what delights we have for you this evening! In order of delightfulness they are: my daughters—'

'Well, they are always—'

'—I haven't finished: the daughters, a stupendous goose, seasoned by our own Mrs Touchet, some literary bonbons straight from Paris, fresh peas from this very garden, many things in aspic courtesy of I don't know who and from where I couldn't say – Mrs Touchet will know – a brilliant young lawyer who talks sense – unlike your host – a limpid lady poet I am taking under my wing, several old friends AND a wonder of the age: a stereoscope.' The red had drained from Thackeray's face, and now he took the hand his host offered. 'And not a Lord or a Lady anywhere in sight, I can promise you that.' The red returned. William laughed: 'Come in, come in. I say your hot head does you credit. No injustice will ever pass you by, that's for sure.'

Mrs Touchet, in wonderment, closed the door behind them.

Perhaps it was William's gift for joy, perhaps Mrs Touchet's seasoning, Cook's grapes in aspic, the girls' radiant beauty, or the quality of the port. Dinner was perfect. The only hitch came towards the end, with the bonbons, which Mrs Touchet had chosen precisely because their mottoes came from novels. But after the table had correctly guessed lines from Austen, Richardson, Bunyan, and other dead masters, Mrs Touchet opened her own bonbon only to be confronted by the lines of one who continued to irrepressibly live, although he was too busy these days to come to dinner.

'Repeat it could you?' asked Chapman. 'You whisper.'

'Oh, it is not much of a line: "*We never see ourselves – never do and never did – and I suppose we never shall.*" Mr Chapman, I'm afraid you of all people really *should* know it.'

'Well, well, the immortality of bonbons already . . .' William stared down at his own motto, which was from Sterne. In the silence everybody else, too, seemed to find their own motto newly fascinating. Finally, William raised his head to look over at his cousin with a haunted face of enquiry:

'From *Pickwick*, is it?'

Mrs Touchet stood up and scrunched the motto in her palm:

'*Nickleby*. Now to this stereoscope. Anne-Blanche got it only yesterday in Covent Garden and we have saved it up especially for this evening . . .'

*

The girls went first, and were so besotted with a set of images from the Congo that William had to remind them of the line of eager oglers behind. The lady poet's favourite was a very banal view of the new London Bridge. William and Maclise were astounded by a square in Florence, which they both attested was 'like standing in the very spot'. This they knew because they had both stood there, many times.

The young horse-faced lawyer bent down and put his eyes to the holes:

'Ah, now this one's very good. Kandy Lake. My own brother is in Ceylon as we speak. Incredible. You can see the trees, the water, the land – all in three dimensions, just as if you were standing there.'

'Perhaps I am being very dense,' remarked Mrs Touchet, 'but can I not see the very same thing right in front of me every day of my life? Am I not always, in effect, "standing right there"? The real world presents itself in three dimensions, after all. Four, if you believe in a dimension of the spirit.'

This made everybody laugh, but when it was her turn to put her eyes to the strange machine Mrs Touchet lost her sense of humour. A view of Ceylon. A distant mountain, a lake, three mysterious people in a curious boat. All framed by unknown trees she would never see, not for herself, not in this lifetime.

7.

At the Dolly Shop

December brought a cold snap. The Thames froze, the cobblestones were slick with ice, all horses were to be pitied. The lawyers wore gloves indoors. Judge Bovill was besieged by ladies anxious for his health, bearing hot tea and soup. After a long morning of cross-examination, Sarah and Eliza walked the Embankment, blowing on their fingers, talking. Sarah had changed her mind about Bogle:

'I'll say this for him: he knows which side his bread is buttered. Went looking for gold in them streets down there – turns out there weren't none. Finds he prefers London to New South Wales, after all. Well, that was right and decent of him to say. I'm sure we've given him more English liberty – and treated him better – than anyone on that godforsaken prison island!'

'Hmmm . . .'

Abruptly, Sarah stopped walking and looked out over the ice, upon which a brave man was sitting, fishing through a hole.

'I do know what you think of me, Mrs Touchet.'

Mrs Touchet, Scots-red, tried to cut her off at the pass.

'Never mind all that. All I want to say is that I know we ain't always seen eye to eye, and that it was your home, naturally, before it was mine, and all that. Now, I may not have the airs and graces of—'

Mrs Touchet tried once again to deny she had ever—

'No, you'll let me speak,' said Sarah, with a new authority. 'I say: I know what you think of me. But where I've come from you can't imagine. And that's all I want to say.'

She pushed her bosom up and rested her chin upon it. This was meant to signify an end to the matter. But all her life Eliza had refused to be the servant of pathos, and could never accept any argument on the basis of emotion alone:

'With respect, Sarah, I am aware of your . . . previous circumstances. And I can assure you I have never passed judgement upon you in the light of them.'

Sarah snorted and pushed her bosom up an inch.

'On my life I have not. I have known privation myself. When my husband died, he left me in poverty, and were it not for William—'

But she could not finish over the laughter of the second Mrs Ainsworth.

'Poverty, was it? Poverty, she says!'

'I don't see what's so amusing about—'

'You're coming with me.'

'The next session is at three. Where am I to come, exactly?'

'Wapping. Orton Country. My country, too, as it happens. I'd like to show you something. Poverty! Ha! What's that face for? You like to walk, don't you? It's only an hour if you walk fast.'

They walked briskly, following the frozen river. By Tower Bridge the ice appeared total and unpassable, but the further east they progressed, a quantity of docked ships broke it up into floes and islands, until there seemed no ice at all or even water, only ships. Mrs Touchet expressed surprise that she had walked so far to be shown industry and wealth, river-facing town houses and a seven-storey sugar refiner, taller than Babel.

'Well, that's all Camden, Calvert and King – they own all of that, the refiner, all them ships, far as the eye can see. There's plenty of money in Wapping, always has been. You can go down the pier and see *palaces* down there. See how the big boat men lived . . . *still* live. When I was a kid, we called them Con Men, Cunts and Kidnappers.'

Mrs Touchet almost objected, but then remembered they were

alone. And in the absence of an audience, she realized, nothing really offended her, except cruelty.

'My poor grandad? Nicked a bag of coffee off the back of one of them ships. They sent him to New South Wales. Eighteen. No one never saw him again. Poor boys went off on them ships all the time, sometimes in irons, sometimes not – but none came back. Look at Orton! And that's just how it was. All the money was in them waters and these Camden types made the most out of it, and we made the most out of them. Don't all them sailors need feeding and watering and a good seeing-to? Before they sail to darkest Dahomey or wherever it is they're headed? Still do. And we all did our bit. My gran used to say ships need stealing from, too, for the insurance. We're doing them a favour, she'd say. Funny one, my gran. Worked on her back, all right, yes, she did, but people round here respected her, naturally. She had her pride. Two things she swore she'd never do: go to a workhouse or go with a black fella, like some did round here. Standards. And I've never forgotten that.'

As they approached the Hermitage Wall, the smells changed, the noises changed, and Sarah took a sharp turn towards the water, grabbing Eliza's hand and not allowing her a second glance down a narrow street of tumbledown dwellings, their roofs set at angles, and all the barefoot glaring boys in the doorways.

'*I'd* walk down there happily, Mrs Touchet, but it's no place for you. I know you suppose you know things from reading your storybooks and what have you, but it's a different matter down here, I can promise you that. Follow that road and in five minutes you're in Stepney!'

'But what's *in* Stepney?' asked a bewildered Mrs Touchet. She had never been this far east before.

'What's in Stepney, she says!' Once more Eliza endured the second Mrs Ainsworth laughing at her. 'A crowd you don't never want to meet, Mrs Touchet. I'm Stepney myself, originally. Know who else was purest Stepney? Jack bleeding Sheppard. Born and bred. My grandmother's mother's mother I think it was – she saw him hanged. Didn't read about it in no storybook, she was there! Willesden *my eye*. God love our Willie but there's times I think he really don't know his arse from his elbow . . . Jack Sheppard was from *Stepney*. And my people are Stepney, going back and back to Domesday. Moved up to Wapping to avoid the Relief. I come from proud, free people, Mrs Touchet. We don't take the Relief for no one if the price is to be our liberty. I come from the kind of people 'd rather die than go indoors. No Wells ever saw inside a workhouse and never will. We'll take the streets, thank you very much. Now, it's just down this lane.'

They took a series of twists and turns until they reached a covered alley. The only light came from the very far end, where a low arch opened onto a set of steep seamen's steps and beyond that, the lapping Thames.

'Now what would you call that?'

Halfway down the alley, another tumbledown building with a lop-sided roof. Eliza peered at it.

'I would say it's a pawnbroker.'

'Well, it ain't.'

'—*Isn't*,' interrupted Eliza, from force of habit.

'—Ain't a pawnbroker and ain't a marine store, neither. It's a dolly shop. There's a difference. Look in the window.'

It was piled high with miscellaneous items. Parts of things rather than things in themselves. Pipes and screws and planks. A small mountain of chair legs. Shoes without soles, bustles without fabric, the heads of hammers. Torn handkerchiefs. Lamps without wicks. The backs of mirrors, glass gone. Nothing whole. Nothing clean. And above the door, instead of the usual brass bell, there depended a little black doll, in a long white dress, with a white headscarf on her head.

'And what would you *call* all that?'

'Well, I—'

'It's rubbish, Mrs Touchet. The dregs. You go to the likes of a pawnbroker to pawn your emerald ring or your solid gold watch. Knowing you can get it back, when your ship comes in. You've probably seen the inside of one of those, I'll grant you that. Before your ship came in. When you was in "poverty". But your marine stores are something else again – they're a step below. In a marine store you pawn a chair, a nice suit, your bed, and you ain—you *aren't* expecting to be seeing none of that again. But it'll pay your rent another quarter, so you do it. I may be wrong, but I don't think you've ever been quite in need of a marine store, have you, Mrs Touchet?'

Without meaning to, Mrs Touchet looked down at the garnet on her finger, long ago reclaimed. Sarah smiled. Not a nice smile. A sharp smile, with a threat in it.

'Now, your *dolly shop* is a whole other kettle of fish. Dollys are for them who've got half of nothing and are fucked to boot. If you ever find yourself in a dolly, Mrs Touchet, you'll know you've reached the very bottom of the bucket. *That's who you are and that's where you live.* At the bottom.'

Mrs Touchet looked away, down the alley, to the dark water. She felt afraid.

'You've never been anywhere near a dolly shop, Mrs Touchet, I can promise you that.'

Sarah pushed open the door, sending the doll spinning. A loud male voice hailed her from behind the counter: 'Sarah Wells! As I live and breathe! That you?' Eliza stayed where she was, on the outside, looking in. Above her head the doll kept turning, turning, turning. Hanging from its rope.

8.

No One to Send

Sergeant Ballantine: Did you make any communication to anyone?

Bogle: Yes, when he agreed to take me to England. I said, had I not better write and say I was coming? He said, 'Yes, perhaps you had better write to my aunt Lady Doughty.' And then I got my son to write, and I signed the letter.

sb: How came you to go to England?

b: Well, it was partly my own doing. When he said he was going to England, I said, 'There will be plenty of people glad to see you, and I wish I was going too.' He said, 'I'll take you if you like.' I thanked him, and said I would go. I then got rid of my little furniture, and gave up my little room, and then he said he could not take me, as he wanted money. I was very much annoyed; and when he saw that I was annoyed he said he would see me the next morning. I did see him the next morning, and then he said he had made arrangements, and I was to go with him.

sb: Did you keep a copy of your letter to Lady Doughty?

b: No, no copy at all.

sb: And when you returned you informed Lady Doughty of your return?

b: Yes, I called, but she refused to see me, and the 50 pound annuity has never since been paid.

Cross-examination by the Attorney General:

AG: What are you doing now?

B: Nothing at all. I am living in Sir Roger Tichborne's house, doing nothing.

AG: And is that what you have been about since you left Sydney?

B: Yes.

AG: Did your wife come home with you?

B: She is dead.

AG: Your children?

B: One came home with me.

AG: Where is he?

B: At school.

AG: And does Sir Roger Tichborne, as you call him, pay his schooling?

B: Yes; he pays 6 pounds a quarter for him, and when he comes home for his holidays he comes to the house.

AG: Did you live with the Claimant at Sydney?

B: No, not an hour. I never had a sixpence from him at Sydney.

AG: You are very precise.

B: No, not so much as you suppose.

AG: And you swear you never lived with him?

B: Yes, I swear I never lived with him ten minutes.

AG: Then if he has stated to anyone that his uncle's valet – meaning you – was living with him in Pitt Street, it is not true?

B: No, it is false.

(Laughter)

AG: You say he never asked you for any information about his early life and family?

B: No, never.

AG: And all the time you were coming home with him, and living in his house here in England, he never asked you a question for the purpose of obtaining information?

B: Not a word that I can recollect.

AG: Did you ever give him anything connected with the family?

B: No, nothing.

AG: Did you ever give him, not information, but any articles or things?

B: Well, I think I gave him a likeness of Sir Edward Doughty and a leaf out of a book that I had.

AG: When was this?

B: In Sydney.

AG: How came you to give him the likeness?

B: Well, I did not give it to him. I took it to show him, and he sent and got a copy taken of it and I have mine now.

AG: What for?

B: I don't know. He never told me what he wanted it for.

AG: Did you ever give him a plan of part of the property?

B: A plan? Yes, I showed him a plan of Upton House – a picture, rather – and that is all I have got.

AG: Had you any picture, plan or map of the Hermitage area of Wapping?

B: No, and I had never heard of it till I saw it in the papers.

AG: Then, if he ever said that if you happened to have his uncle's likeness and, likewise, a plan of a portion of the Hermitage Estate, he would get it copied, that would not be true?

B: No, certainly not, as regards the map. I did give him his uncle's likeness.

AG: And the leaf of a book?

B: Yes, I did.

A paper was here handed to the witness, who said it was the leaf in question.

AG: Out of what did it come?

B: I have a book with these papers.

AG: What book?

B: Lady Doughty gave it to me.

AG: Where is it?

B: At Roger Tichborne's house.

AG: Will you send for it?

B: I have nobody to send.

(Laughter)

9.

Believing Bogle

After Christmas, William put his foot down. The trial had run six months, it showed no sign of concluding, and a man could not reasonably be expected to pay weekly train fares in perpetuity. If the ladies of Little Rockley wished to see Mr Bogle & Co. more regularly than once a quarter, well, they were most welcome, but would have to find the money themselves, or else walk there. *Two hundred pounds a year*, whispered the Devil, in Eliza's ear.

Consequently, in January they visited only twice, on both occasions catching portions of Coleridge's speech for the defence, which lasted a month in itself. They found him boring and long-winded. Eliza passed the time eavesdropping, and, in this way, discovered a common paradox of feeling: it was possible to 'know' Sir Roger was a fraud and yet still 'believe' Bogle. In fact, whatever side of the thing a person was on, admiration for Bogle appeared universal. He was of 'noble' and 'loyal' spirit, 'spoke plainly' – unlike the lawyers – had 'never wavered'. In a storm of absurdity, Mr Bogle was the calm eye. Perhaps he gained something in comparison with his fellow deponents, who had a tendency to cast spells upon themselves in the witness box, making up stories from whole cloth, which then became indistinguishable from the truth, even in their own minds. The past came to be patterned like the present. The present manipulated with an eye to the future – and to the main chance. By contrast, Bogle's story never changed. It was this very persistence, this loyalty, that had cost the poor man his annuity, and whatever else anybody claimed, this fact could not be denied. All he had to do was agree with the Tichbornes that 'Sir Roger' was a fraud and his annuity would be restored. Instead, he stood firm. To take a guaranteed capital sum and freely exchange it for the uncertain rewards of the truth! In the opinion of the winkle-pot eaters in the nosebleed seats there was no greater sacrifice, nor any nobler gesture, no, not on God's green earth.

IO.

All is Lost!

Given their irregular attendance, it was sheer luck that the women should find themselves in court for the very last day of the trial, for nobody in the Queen's Bench that March morning had any inkling it would be the last day, least of all the Claimant. He had decamped at the beginning of the week to the Waterloo Hotel in Jermyn Street, to be wined and dined by an optimistic circle of Tichborne Bond investors. He was therefore not present to witness a middle-aged soldier take the stand and swear on the King James Bible that he had personally tattooed a heart and anchor on Sir Roger's left arm, years earlier, when both men were boys. Astonishment in the court! Every man and woman in the place had seen the Claimant's heavy arms resting on the witness box, sleeves rolled up, bare as the day he was born. Would this be the fatal blow? And yet the Claimant's claim had overcome so many more outrageous obstacles. Missing earlobes, a forgotten language, an absent education, a body and accent transformed, the sudden death of his 'mother'. Still, if the jury knew anything it was that tattoos do not simply vanish from left arms. Now the foreman stood up to say they had heard enough and were ready with their verdict. The foreman spoke; Bovill nodded; the world turned upside down. Now the plaintiff was not Sir Roger but a criminal by the name of Orton, herewith charged with perjury. The wardens of the court received new instructions. The criminal Arthur Orton was to be apprehended, arrested, taken to Newgate. All was lost!

*

The court exploded. Only Bogle and son stayed in their seats, heads slightly bowed. There were so many people rushing for the exits that Eliza feared a tragedy – a stampede. When she turned to Sarah, to suggest waiting up here in the balcony – at least until the clamour had passed – she found the new Mrs Ainsworth already on her feet, purse in hand:

'I'm heading Regent's Street with the rest of them! Sir Roger needs his people by his side. He ain't abandoned! We won't let him rot!'

Why dissuade her? Here was a moment of peace in which to gather one's courage.

II.

A Proposal

The jury was released. The courtroom rapidly emptied. The man to whom Mrs Touchet had so hungered to speak was just now stepping out into Parliament Square, and from there — if she did not boldly step into his path — he would escape her grasp, float off to some corner of the city she could not know or imagine and would never be able to reach —

'Mr Bogle, I'm so sorry to accost you in this manner, but my name is Mrs Touchet, and I would very much like to take you to tea . . .'

12.

Andrew & Henry & Eliza

She had imagined this encounter. Pictured herself accosting father and son, just like this, outside the court, and then the walk down Great George Street to a chophouse, the corner table by the window, even what she would say as the arthritic Mr Bogle slowly took his seat. But nowhere in these mental projections had she imagined being asked to explain herself. No more than she expected the figures in her dreams to stop what they were doing and ask their sleeping author why they flew in a hot air balloon, or visited China, or dined with the Queen . . .

'It is surely not a difficult question, Mrs—'

'Touchet.'

'Mrs Touchet. My father has had a very long and trying day. I con-sider it my duty to protect him from any further exertions. I'll ask again: what is it that you want with my father?'

He did not say *my farder*. Had no hint of that Caribbean lilt she had expected and heard at various lecterns over the years – and for a moment this threw her. Nor was this young Master Bogle, like those musical voices of memory, pleading his case. On the contrary, it was Eliza who now found herself pleading:

'Well, I – I only wish to speak with him. But perhaps he might answer for himself? Mr Bogle?'

The elder Bogle put out a steady hand to still his excitable son:

'Madam. I have spoken. I have spoken and I have not been believed. I think I have now finished speaking. Sir Roger is ruined. And if he is ruined, how much more ruined am I? No. Now I will go home. Come, Henry.'

'But Mr Bogle – *I* believe you.'

And saying it aloud, she realized it was true.

He looked at her narrowly. He had been holding his top hat in his hands; now he sighed and put it back on his head.

'Well. It's of no consequence now.'

'On the contrary, Mr Bogle – there is to be a criminal case, in which no doubt your testimony will prove consequential. Particularly given that the public interest in your situation is at present so lively.'

Henry frowned: 'You are a journalist, then?'

'I – well, no. I am a writer,' improvised Mrs Touchet, colour flooding her cheeks. She had hoped not to stumble into a direct lie. But something about the shrewd, dissecting gaze of the son pushed her onwards: 'That is to say, I write occasional pieces. For a periodical. *Bentley's.* And I feel certain our readers would be very curious to hear more of your father's story.'

'I see. And what would it pay?'

'Pay? I'm sorry – I don't understand.'

'Mrs Touchet, with all due respect, if my father has something that is of value to you then it is only fair that he should be paid for his trouble. We have been told that these London papers sell twice as fast on the days when my father's testimony appears. And yet so far we have seen no advantage from it whatsoever.'

Mrs Touchet struggled to hide her disappointment at this open display of venality. She clutched her reticule a little tighter in her hands.

'Mr Bogle, I'm afraid I cannot pay for interviews. As far as I am aware it is not common practice.' A private look now passed between the Bogles that she did her best to read. Offence? Hunger? Pride? 'But if there is some other way in which I might be of assistance? Perhaps, well . . . I wonder whether you and your father might not join me for a good hot meal? You must be in need of sustenance after such a long and trying day.'

Had she gone too far? She could see with what defensive care the son was dressed. Kept his gloved fingers tucked into his palm to hide the holes. Wore a stopped brass pocket watch in his threadbare waistcoat. His shoes were of the kind found in the marine stores, serially resoled, and in three different shades of brown leather. Perhaps he was sixteen. The two of them stepped back from her for a moment and consulted, and it seemed Henry's counsel would win out. But then the father put a hand to his son's wrist once more and stepped forward:

'I will come. My son will walk with us as far as Regent Street. He must go to Sir Roger; he will be needed there. But I will come with you and eat.'

13.

A Public Spectacle

The walk was not long, but never in her life had she experienced anything like it. The Lady Godiva could not have attracted more attention.
At the coffee stalls queues of people turned to stare, and a dozen heads
whipped round on the omnibus. Taxi drivers revolved on their boxes
to examine from behind what had already been scrutinized from the
front. Some recognized Bogle and cried out his name – *Ho! Bogle!*
We believe you, Bogle! Send our regards to Sir Roger! – but most mistook
the three of them for a family of some kind. A not unknown sight in the
slums – so Eliza imagined – but surely rarely to be seen promenading
through town.

Being English, most commentary was quiet, poisonous, patient.
She strained to hear it but could never catch it distinctly: she had
always passed half a yard in front before the speaker began. But children, having fewer scruples, laughed openly, and could be heard
asking each other what happened if you gave an Ethiope a bath, how
such woolly hair might feel in your hand, advising each other on
defence against cannibals. It would have been Mrs Touchet's inclin-
ation to fill the air with chatter, but neither Bogle nor his son said a
word. They walked in silence until they reached a likely chophouse,
through the window of which Mrs Touchet could see at least one
respectable-looking woman dining. Here Henry took his leave of
them, and a startled doorman led the party of two to a booth behind a
pillar, far from any natural light.

'Mrs Touchet, I have repeated, over and over, all that I have to say, and all that I know of the matter. I have spoken to the gentlemen of the press and in the courtroom. What else can I say that I have not said?'

Mrs Touchet looked at the table. It was for some reason very difficult to look into his eyes.

'With respect, Mr Bogle, I think it would interest people very much to learn how you came to be in such an unusual situation. Your whole history would be of interest, far beyond the narrow scope of what we have heard in the courtroom. What was your life in New South Wales, for example – or in Jamaica? We learn very little of our Caribbean possessions since the terrible trade ended—'

'Alas, Mrs Touchet, that trade is also a part of my history . . .' He spoke distantly, looking past her towards the kitchens. A set of pewter candlesticks sat between them. He picked one up, weighing it in his hands. 'Do you suppose they serve pork chops here?'

'They are famous for their chops, Mr Bogle,' murmured Mrs Touchet, and was quiet for a moment. Had she ever gone without a meal, even once, in her whole life?

'I am fond of chops.'

'Then we will have them. Mr Bogle, do you think you might like to tell me something of your story? I mean, tell me something of your life?'

Mr Bogle sighed, put down the candlestick, and seemed to come back to the table, back to the present moment, from a place far away.

'A life is a long business, Mrs Touchet. What should I tell you of my life?'

She almost reached a hand across the table.

'Tell me everything.'

14.

A History of Bogle

'My life has had many parts,' said Bogle. 'It is difficult to say how many lives I have lived, or where my story truly begins. One thing I know for certain: my story is not what it should be. I should have been a great man. I come from great men, on my father's side. But I hardly remember my father and can only speak of what Myra told me. Myra was my mother, and much of what I know of my father's life she gave to me. Poor woman, that she should have nothing else to give me but that! What more I know of his story I was told by Peachey, who worked first in the mill house and then the boiling house, and came from my father's village. Peachey out-lived my mother and my father. For all I know she lives still. Peachey was not her true name, any more than Nonesuch was my father's name, but so they were called, on Hope, where I was born. (My mother was born on Hope and Myra was her only name.) Hope is in the parish of Saint Andrew, Jamaica. I have no other name to call it but my home, though it angers my son Henry if I say so. My son is a very fine and fierce young man. He has been educated here in England. I received what education I have on Hope, and my father died there, even though it was so far beneath him. But I will do as my son would prefer and tell you first of the life I should have known, that is, the life my father intended . . .

'My father was an African. He was called Anaso. His name has a meaning. It means: "The child must avoid what the earth forbids." His people had a name for everything, and were called the Nree, I believe. I cannot say how these things are written down, but that is the sound. They came from forests in the north of their world. When I asked

Peachey what his name meant she said: our people forbade all murder, and all blood upon the ground, and had no army because of that. What you call God we called the earth and our name for this was CHI. Great men ruled. They were called oh-zo. So Peachey said. These were all strange names to me, but they were not strange to Peachey or my father. This was his own world, and he was one of the high-born men within it.

'But in my father's village there were also the low ones. They had been taken from our enemies, who were called the Arrow, I believe. We kidnapped these Arrow and made them low. We owned them, and they laboured for us, and the name for them was oh-hoo. But even the oh-hoo were higher than Peachey. (Peachey must have had another name but I never knew it. She never told me it.) Her family were of the very lowest: they were born low. They were called oh-soo, which means a person who is an abomination. To live near Peachey's mother or even touch her mother's hand was unlucky, and all of Peachey's mother's babies died, excepting Peachey. Peachey's family belonged to my grandfather, who was I am told a great oh-zo and a free man. He received slaughtered animals from his village as a tribute to his greatness and had a seat on the council, as a judge, like Mr Bovill. Together with the other great men he protected the village and the oh-hoo and the oh-soo and did nothing that the earth forbid. No man or woman among them had ever heard the name of Our Lord, but their rule was as wise and good as any to be found in the gospels. Nor was it just one house or one court that my grandfather ruled, but far and wide, over many people. The people said *Igwe!* when he passed by. This was a mark of respect. He wore a red cap with eagle feathers in it and carried a tall staff, which surely had a name. I wish I knew it. There were statues of our ancestors in his home. He poured water upon burned ground, at their wooden feet, and this was also a mark of respect. I never myself witnessed such things and don't know if I say the names correctly. But Peachey swore that as a small child she had seen these things, and my mother never doubted her, so then why should I?

'I will speak now of how my father was kidnapped. He was nine years old. That is the time that childhood ends and the road to greatness begins. His face had just been scarred in the way of his father. The blood ran down the ridges in his cheeks but he did not weep or cry out. To cry would have been a great shame, and he was very proud, and ready to become a man. But first he had to have the secret of the mask revealed to him. In his village, there was a tradition: masked men danced through the village on certain days at certain times of the year. They came as judge and jury, but masked. They passed a sentence of judgement upon those who had done wrong. It was believed that the dead people of the village spoke through them, and it was a great secret who these masked men were. No woman must ever be told: it was a secret only to be revealed to young men with ridges in their cheeks. And my father was such a one. But a terrible thing happened! One day a masked man came to my father when he was walking alone and said he would take my father to a special place, where the secret would be revealed. This was the tradition and my father went with the man. But this masked man was a fraud. He was not one from my father's village. He was one of the Arrow. He did not take him to the special place. He took him through the forest to the water and sold him to a Scotsman who put him on a boat. My father kicked and fought and struggled, but he was a child and the Scotsman was grown. Peachey was on that boat and many others in chains. My father was added to their number. All around him the people wept bitterly to find themselves so low. My father did not cry (I have been told). He did not cry when the elders marked his face with a knife, and he did not cry in the ship, although the journey was very long and hard, and his suffering was great and many died. My father never saw his home again, nor his mother or father or sisters or brothers or anyone that was kin to him. The ship was called the *King David*. It sailed to Bristol and then on to the harbour in Kingston, Jamaica, leaving behind the life I should have known.'

VOLUME SIX

Andrew Bogle
Black 25
Creole
Taken off the Country
by Edw: Tichborne: Esq

FROM THE SLAVE LIST OF THE HOPE ESTATE,
SAINT ANDREW, JAMAICA, 1826

I.

On Hope

Some great men carry their pride with them – despite all cause for pride having vanished – and it was this way with Anaso, although he was not yet ten. Noting this, Mr Ballard renamed him Nonesuch. Mr Ballard had a Glaswegian sense of humour and prided himself on witty naming. The ugliest woman on Hope was called Aphrodite, the lame watchman, Hercules. The surname 'Bogle', meaning scarecrow, he gave to anyone who attempted to pride themselves on their appearance or behaviour. And during the period of seasoning, Ballard had observed this boy grooming the horses pridefully, polishing the guns pridefully, and picking up pig shit with a certain look on his face, as if he considered even such light labour beneath him. This from a saltwater African, black as any Hope had ever seen! Still, the boy proved quick-minded, and Ballard began bringing him on his morning rounds. An error. Here was a shrewd child, who knew how to make himself indispensable in many unlikely places and situations. Providing small services to the coopers and wheelwrights, for example, or to the Creole nurses in the hothouse, and even to the bookkeepers, whose pencils he sharpened. His rightful place was the small gang: banking cane, shovelling horse manure. It was Ballard's mistake – but nothing was quite right that winter. There was trouble in the negro village – of Ballard's own making, but still trouble – and also in the Main House, where the housemaids no longer waited for him to leave the room before sniggering. He was in a bitter back and forth with the first gang about the need for a plough, two of the cane pieces had been ratooned to death – despite his warnings about the soil – and a hurricane had taken the roof off the trash house. All was commotion and change and humiliation, in other words, and, as a consequence, stitches were dropped, and trouble seeded that would bear fruit much later. A case in point being the fact that this Bogle was right there with him in the parlour when Ballard first learned that his employer had dropped dead:

Nov 28th, 1775
  Alas sir, having lost our only child – and sole heir – last month, I must now write with worse news. I have lost my dear husband and in him my only certain friend. Words are inadequate to express my grief for this unexpected and immeasurable loss! This event has plunged my mind into such a state of stupification that I am scarcely able to support myself or do anything that is necessary for me to do in my present state of affairs, though the responsibility of Hope now lies solely in my own person,
  Anna Eliza Elletson

The death of Roger Hope Elletson could hardly stupefy Mr Ballard – he had never met the man. But he had been warned by his predecessor – another hard-working and much-abused Scot – that the only thing worse than an absentee English owner was the interfering, sentimental wife of such a man. So it proved:

I am extremely concerned at your account of the sickness that has prevailed among the negroes, particularly that you seem to despair the recovery of Long Phoebe and Hope Beneba as I am afraid they are of the number of old negroes that Mr Elletson had most affection for . . . I know he regarded them all, and it was always his wish and desire that they should be well taken care of in sickness or in health and their respective situations rendered as comfortable as possible. I therefore beg the favour of you to continue the humane plan, and

never to use any correction on them, unless you see it as absolutely necessary to preserve that authority with which you are invested. I beg you will assure them of my affection towards them and I firmly rely on your goodness and humanity to comply with my wishes for their welfare. I am very glad that you have a prospect of succeeding in the plan of watering the estate,
   AEE

Ballard read this letter twice, and considered his options. He knew that the last estate manager, Ruthland, had been chased off Hope for deviating too severely from this 'humane plan', having punished four boys for abandoning a cane piece in the middle of the rainy season. They had left their holes half-dug, and the holes subsequently flooded, ruining the crop. The boys themselves were later discovered up in the provision grounds, tending to their own crops. Ruthland burned off their ears. Some unknown informant wrote to the sentimental Elletsons about all this: Ruthland lost his position. Now it was Ballard's turn to work in impossible conditions for a sentimental Englishwoman who wouldn't know a ribbon cane from a lollipop.

2.

Correction

If he wanted to correct Big Johanna, he would have to proceed with caution. Either she was at the Sunday market, selling provisions, or in the negro village, a maze of a place designed to frustrate any reasonable man. He had worked on other estates where the negro quarters were laid out rationally and orderly, like a barracks. On Hope, the negroes lived in a higgledy-piggledy collection of individual dwellings, and the Main House, built by the Spaniards, was for some reason level with the rest of the estate, rendering it useless for the purposes of surveillance. Thus, when he looked through the tarnished glass of his bedroom window each morning, towards the cottages – trying to locate Johanna's – all he could see was a grove, and now that he was inside the damned grove, all he could see, as ever, were too many paths, too many trees. Stopping suddenly, he snapped at Nonesuch, as if the silent boy had just accused him of being lost:

'Well? D'ye know the way to Johanna's or don't you?'

Anaso could have walked to Derenneya's blindfold. He knew all these labyrinthine pathways and where they led, each little whitewashed place, and who lived in them. He knew the Creole cottages from those of the saltwaters, whose sweetwood rafters were rotten, whose pristine, who grew breadfruit and ackee, who ginger and avocado pears, and what price they got for it all on Sundays. He knew Derenneya's compound was by far the largest and most respected, and that this was not because she was having another of Mr Ballard's babies – as Ballard himself seemed to believe – but because she fed three branches of her family on the products of her kitchen garden alone. Her portion of the provision grounds, meanwhile, was pure, enviable, profit.

'Something amusing, Bogle?'

Pity the man who must search for the mother of his own child! Pity the man who never hears her true name!

'Oh, no, no, Mr Ballard, this way.'

They stood in Johanna's yard. It was empty: most people were at market. But a small crowd of old women in white had gathered at the periphery. They stood with their elbows resting on the fence, peering at Ballard, in their Sunday headcloths.

'Go in. Tell her to come out.'

'Yes, Mr Ballard.'

Anaso set off, making sure to walk as naturally as possible over the bumpy ground, as if nothing hindered him. This calmed the women. Privately Anaso believed such caution unnecessary. He spent all day with Mr Ballard, week in, week out, had made a study of his character, and knew that you could dig up every single coin jar hidden in this yard and rebury them in the floorboards by Ballard's own bed: the man would not notice. The man noticed nothing.

'Well?'

Nonesuch re-emerged, shaking his head. Some of the women began to laugh. The door of Johanna's cottage lay open. From here, Ballard could see three statues, carved from cottonwood, with white cowrie shell eyes, and one smaller, balsa wood figure wearing a ram's horns, backwards.

'On you go, the lot of you!'

He flapped his arms and bellowed, like a man running at birds. Nobody moved. It was Ballard himself who had to move, striding into the house. Anaso followed.

Inside, Derenneya was kneeling in a corner, her broad back to them both. They watched her pour water upon burned ground. Anaso stepped forward, transfixed. Remembering! Ballard clipped him round the ear:

'What d'ye think you're looking at?'

Sag-sack belly. Duppy complexion. Two yellow tusks, all that remained of Ballard's teeth.

'Not a thing, Mr Ballard.'

Never room saltwaters with saltwaters: experience teaches a wise estate manager at least that much. Upon arrival, Ballard had placed the Bogle boy in the hovel of a mild, feeble-minded Creole freewoman, Old Phoebe, who called Hope home and swore she would never leave. But now Old Phoebe was in the hothouse, face half-eaten by the Yaws. Who knew where Bogle spent his nights? Who knew how much of this Obeah hogwash the boy had already witnessed?

'And the baby?'

Anaso pointed to the bundle on the bed. Ballard went over to look. Ballard nose, Ballard eyes. Indisputably a Ballard. Yet with Johanna's lips and hair, and for some reason even darker than Johanna. Darker even than Nonesuch! Which explained the sniggering, and the general fascination. The unfortunate impression given was of some form of magical domination on the woman's part. A triumph of her blood over Ballard's own.

'Bogle – pick it up. Take it outside.'

Feeling watched, Ballard turned. More white headcloths, two dozen of them now, still peering. He must act now or else lose the moment.

'Bogle, *take the baby outside.*'

Little Derenneya stared up at Anaso. He knew that her name meant *stay with mother, give her company*, and that she was the first child of Mr Ballard's that her mother had permitted to live. A special child, then. Powerful. Anaso stared right back, not wanting to be thought of as one without power himself. He had the sense that he was holding one from his own village. She was very dark and very beautiful, just like her mother. Like his own mother. He closed his eyes. *Stay with mother*. He wished he could promise that, but Mr Ballard did not want whatever was coming next to be witnessed. As Bogle walked out of the cottage, he felt the child's tiny hand reach up and cling to his ear. He heard Ballard close the shutters.

3.

Nonesuch Bogle & Mulatto Roger

The sentimental young widow Anna Eliza Elletson did not stay a widow long, marrying someone called the Marquis of Chandos the very next year. Ballard got the blacksmith to fashion a new brand, reflecting this change. From then on, all children and new arrivals to Hope had MC burned into their shoulders, instead of RE, as it had been in the time of Elletson.

Two years later, a child was born to the Duchess of Chandos, a girl – also named Anna Eliza. All of Hope was instructed to stay home and pray for this little Anna's soul one Sunday, thus wasting a perfectly good market day, causing much resentment. Soon after, a young man arrived at Hope, on the packet from Liverpool. He was a mulatto, of the same age as Nonesuch, and came with instructions:

> *If Roger can be made a useful tradesman he may have his choice,*
> *but I would not have him employed in any laborious work, as I mean*
> *to give him his freedom, if he behaves well and you approve it.*

What Ballard was meant to do with one of Roger Elletson's bastards he was sure he didn't know. The boy's mother was one Polly, taken off the estate before Ballard's time, and ever since a maid in the Elletson town house, on Curzon Street. He was notably pale, more like a quadroon. This seemed to have had the predictable sentimental effect on his owner. Yet if the new Duchess of Chandos ever deigned to set foot on Hope, she would soon enough discover that she owned a great many people no darker than this Roger, and more than a few pale as Ballard himself. A fact that sometimes had the power to surprise visiting Baptist women, but could no longer surprise Mr Ballard. He was a man of fact not sentiment, charged with producing at least two hundred high-quality hogshead of sugar and a hundred and twenty puncheons of rum per year, and it was a plain fact that if he manumitted the bastards of every attorney, owner and manager on Hope, well, then the ribbon canes would rot in the fields. Even as it was, margins were tight: one had to be continually prepared for losses. Someone was forever falling into a copper of burning molasses, coming down with the Yaws, losing an arm or leg to the rollers, or simply keeling over and dropping dead in the middle of a half-planted piece. Even the saltwaters succumbed at an alarming rate. The climate was impossible, the labour hard. It was hard on everyone. Nor was Ballard of the outdated opinion that lower administrators and overseers should be necessarily picked from the coloured class. In his time, he had hired many Scots overseers, some blacks, a few Irishmen, and could draw no general rule from them. But he had never, ever known a mulatto overseer to be anything but an unmitigated disaster. *If mi for have massa or misses, give mi Buckra one – nah give mi mulatto, dem no use wi people well.* So went the familiar saying among the blacks. Two decades in the sugar trade had taught Ballard the truth of it.

He read the letter through once more and looked the new arrival up and down. Compared to Bogle – who took a step away from his new companion, as if to avoid the connection – the child was a poor specimen. Knock-kneed, skinny, weepy. Another fact: Hope needed no more 'useful tradesmen'. A generation of boys had been trained thus ten years prior, with the consequence that, of the fifty-odd masons, coopers and carpenters, only a handful were presently over thirty. And a boy like this, raised in England, who knew nothing of the medicinal plants, would never be welcome in the hothouse. In there, Jenny and

Moira prevailed, flattering themselves with the title 'nurse', although as far as Ballard could tell, all the real medicine was done by one 'Doctor Paul', a tall negro, said to have received some kind of medical training in Kingston. Whatever the truth of that, these superstitious labouring negroes would be seen by no other medic. Ballard himself had been forced to put an ulcerated foot in the hands of the 'doctor' only last month, when a felled tree blocked the Kingston Road.

'But what exactly did you *do* in London?'

The boy seemed baffled by the question. He looked over at Bogle, who answered for him:

'Errands, Mr Ballard. Ran about the place, here and there. A page.'

Ballard made an exasperated sound and stamped his foot. It no longer gave him pain.

'Can't speak for himself? Cat got your tongue?'

The boy started weeping again.

'I've been told I can't work him – and it seems he won't speak. What earthly use is he to me?'

'Mr Ballard, he can ride with me. Tend the animals with me.'

Lower administrators and overseers were best started out in the pens, with the animals, or trained as drivers, to get them used to breaking in a horse, and patrolling the cane pieces. With boys this young, such training could be done with foresight and correctly, on donkeys. Bogle was already well on his way, and perhaps would prove a good influence. Ballard told Bogle to write *Mulatto Roger* in the General List of Negroes, under the column headed: 'Chickens and Pigs'.

4.

'im who speak sense here nah speak true'

Over time, only Big Johanna recalled the true name of Nonesuch Bogle, but they did not see each other much in any given day. The very sound *Anaso* grew strange to Anaso. Until he was Nonesuch. Until he was Bogle. Johanna's own true name was one he would no longer have dared say aloud, even if he could remember it. Her hate stalked her everywhere. She cursed those she hated; often they died of it. Johanna lived in a different world. She spent her mornings ferrying huge harvested bundles in her arms from piece to trash house, heaving her axe, quartering cane. Afternoons were passed in the boiling house, wielding the longest ladle, withstanding that furnace heat. Nonesuch meanwhile fed the animals, assisted the carpenters, accompanied Roger in his schooling. Sharpened pencils. He watched the bookkeeper write *notorious runaway* next to Johanna's name, three years in a row, and marvelled at her persistence — at what it cost her. Two toes. A breast. The cleaving of her face, a scar that ran from eye to chin.

Peachey worked the mill house. She fed cane into the new horizontal rollers, which were part of the humane plan, being less lethal than the vertical. They still ate limbs, but not nearly as often. One day the roller caught Peachey's left hand. Nonesuch and Roger happened to be passing. Roger sat mute on his donkey, horrified by such a quantity of blood, but Nonesuch leapt from his mule, ran in and pulled her free of the machinery. He carried her to the hothouse. Her hand was gone and her arm mangled to the shoulder. Roger explained it was her own fault for getting too close. Just before she fainted, Peachey looked up at Nonesuch and cried: *Igwe!*

That same night, in their cottage, Nonesuch slept badly. He looked over at Roger, deep in dreams. There was such a strange mix of cowardice and cruelty in the boy, which his companion found hard to excuse or explain, but which Big Johanna, with her second sight, had swiftly diagnosed. A divided soul. Most people have only one animal spirit within them, but Roger had two: the mouse and the snake. Nonesuch could not deny it. He had watched the shadow of mouse, snake, mouse, snake, pass over this boy's face many times; it was happening even now, as he slept in the moonlight. Pity the man who lives in his own dream! Roger knew nothing of what the earth forbid. He had never known any world but this one. Why should he have any idea that this world of his was upside down? Instead, he tried to find sense in it. It was pitiful to be a woman, pitiful to be mad like Big Johanna, or black as Nonesuch, or poor and now one-armed like Peachey, and it followed from all this in Roger's mind that pitiful people should suffer most, for was that not the natural order of things? Better Peachey than him! The low were surely low for a reason. Big Johanna spoke in tongues. She thought her little black daughter had the power of prophecy. When you told her to hush up and speak sense, she never listened – and look where that got her. She put the evil eye on people. She claimed that *im who speak sense here nah speak true*. She could not be corrected.

Roger, by contrast, felt he spoke sense. He had two arms. He was almost as pale as Mr Ballard. The only thing that did not make sense to Mulatto Roger was the fact that he had, for some reason, been placed on an equal footing with Bogle the saltwater, although he himself was the son of a great man. Didn't he deserve his high horse? Didn't he sit on it proudly?

5.

A Dinner

Ballard had heard it said that a man's insides come to his outsides eventually, and sitting opposite Thistlewood, listening to his tale of making one negro shit in the mouth of another, he was struck afresh by the truth of this. There was something very wrong with this man. His skin was diseased, as if some internal corruption had burst forth. The tongue was tombstone grey and the mouth hellish red with ulcers. No doubt his tears of amusement were forty per cent proof.

'Then I gagged him and let him stew in the sun for the afternoon. And that was the last time the bastard stole a breadfruit from *me*!'

Ballard smiled blandly. He placed a hand over his own tumbler, refusing Nonesuch's pouring, in the hope that this might encourage Thistlewood to do the same. Thistlewood held his cup high, nodding only when the rum troubled the rim. Yet even in his utter degeneracy, the man still drove a hard bargain:

'Now to my point. You'll take Caesar and another ten like him, and four women, until next May – though I will insist on the same rent. Your water situation is neither here nor there to me, Ballard, and the price was long agreed. No one from Breadnut Pen will give you any trouble, that I can promise you. They know by now it's their head on a pike if they do.'

Ballard had sat opposite Thomas Thistlewood like this for dinner, at crop season, once a year for over a decade. Never had it been a pleasant experience. Privately, he considered the man a lunatic, and a poor businessman besides, for it was bad business to put heads on pikes: headless men can do no labour. He pitied the man altogether. A farmer's son of dubious family, with poor manners, no sugar and only one hundred and sixty acres, all of it provision grounds. His main source of income appeared to be the thirty-two negroes he rented out, although he had beaten most of them already half to death – another example of bad business. Given the choice, he would far rather never see this man again, never listen to his stories, or watch him pickle himself in rum. But Hope's own great size was its liability. There was more cane to be got out of the ground than there were able hands to pull it. This year, as it was last year, Thistlewood had him over a sugar barrel.

'—So I says to him: what do you do out here with *your* prick? Bathe it in asses' milk?'

He stank. His shirt collar was black with dirt. Everything that came out of his mouth was lewd or bloody or dripping in devilry, and he seemed entirely lost to the present, unaware of Mary and Deirdre coming in and out with the food, Nonesuch leaning over to place a pork chop on his plate, or Big Johanna listening in, furiously slamming pots in the kitchen. In his mind, he was back in his glory days. Still overseer on Egypt, where the first women's gang had been his personal harem. By the time he struggled to his feet, deal done, dinner mostly down his shirt front, he could barely stand. Johanna had to be brought out to help him back to his carriage. Bogle opened the door. Ballard stood on the front steps, waving. He certainly noticed Johanna muttering into Thistlewood's ear in a foreign tongue. But she often did that.

6.

The Great Storm

The great storm came that night, barely touching Hope, staying in the west, and it was ten days before Hope came to hear of the destruction over at Breadnut Pen. Thistlewood's provision grounds were entirely razed, along with his own house, and even his friend Wedderburn's estate next door was damaged, for Johanna's wrath was enormous and knew no bounds. Rumours flew. It was said that the same words Johanna had whispered in Thistlewood's ear she had spoken over each of Ballard's bastards, just before they died. Someone claimed to have seen her dip her thumb in chicken blood and draw a cross on the back of Thistlewood's neck. All nonsense of course, but nonsense has to be reined in, or else chaos rules. Ballard, as a man of facts, felt he had no rational choice but to correct Johanna again, and publicly this time, although of course he had never meant to kill her. A miscalculation. On Hope, names drifted from people over time, and Big Johanna, as it turned out, was no longer the strong, hearty girl of times past.

7.

Inheritance

Little Johanna inherited her mother's good looks, her mother's strength, and those labours that had once fallen to her mother. She had her mother's gift, too, or her madness, depending on who you asked. She had prophetic dreams and spoke in tongues. Nonesuch envied her. She had inherited something – she came from somewhere. When she babbled, he thought: *Your mother's tongue.* He knew this was an unworthy thought, but he couldn't help it. At thirteen, she was already in the boiling house, scooping the scum off the largest copper with the longest ladle, like her mother before her, and through the shimmering heat was easily mistaken for her mother. Would she soon run? Could she, too, kill those she cursed and despised? The people of Hope took a constant interest in Little Johanna and her progress, for she was a child of Hope and her family history known to all. They remembered her mother's murder, and the vivid, anonymous letter that had so moved the sentimental Lady Chandos that she fired Mr Ballard, only to replace him with a Mr Macintosh, who turned out to be no better. Nobody knew who had written that letter. What difference would it have made if they did? Nonesuch had no lineage that anyone knew, or cared to know. As far as Hope was concerned, he came from nowhere. He had even come to feel this way himself. Sometimes, very late at night, he looked past Roger to the little window and tried to conjure his own mother's face there, amid the sweetwood. Nothing.

When Nonesuch tried to picture Lady Anna Eliza Chandos of the humane plan, only a milky circle came to mind. It was hard to square this indistinct image with the recent news from England. This same Lady Chandos – while at a party and in 'high spirits' – had pulled a chair out from under her beloved Marquis as he went to sit down, and the fall had killed him. Part of the humane plan? Or another form of inheritance? While blotting the account books, he noted the dead Duke's money flowing in to Hope, rebuilding the trash house and extending the boiling house, among other improvements. There were no more letters from Lady Chandos. Many on Hope entertained themselves with visions of the Lady in chains, or with her head on a pike, or transported to Botany Bay with the other husband murderers. But Nonesuch, privy to all Hope's correspondence, knew better. The Lady had gone 'mad with grief'. The Lady was in an asylum. Hope and every soul upon it now belonged to a twelve-year-old girl, on whose behalf the estate was entrusted to two London attorneys, until this new Anna Eliza came of age.

Roger confessed himself amazed: he had known of no mad women in England and had thought it a condition peculiar to Jamaica. But Bogle did not think of madness as belonging to any particular person. Every letter that came in and out of Hope was mad. Every column of numbers, hogshead of sugar, and puncheon of rum. The world was sunk in madness. It covered everything, like weather.

8.

Myra

Was it mad to value sanity in such a place? Myra was not beautiful, perhaps, but her mind was clear and bright like a stream, and for Nonesuch this was everything. They had first met as children, when he was in the hothouse, sick with dysentery, and it was her job to collect medicinal plants for the nurses. Now they were past grown. He was in charge of the small gang on Indigo. She was in the first women's gang, on Derry – Roger's cane field. Sundays were all they had. When he was inside her he couldn't imagine why men wanted power or money or land or anything but this, it was everything. Amazing that you didn't see people coupling on the open road, in the aisles of churches, anywhere they could find! He loved her, and lived from Sunday to Sunday. It was not like that for Myra. Derry was notorious. In Roger, the snake had ultimately triumphed over the mouse, and anyone who laboured under him was truly to be pitied. There were Sundays when seven days seemed to have aged her seven years. Sometimes it was as much as she could manage to stroke the ridges in his cheeks before falling asleep.

Nonesuch wanted children, for the same reasons men have always wanted children, but he also understood that for Myra it might mean a respite. There would be at least some nursing time away from Derry, and then, perhaps, a period of looking after the motherless and the unweaned. But each month she bled and no baby came. Other people in their position went to Little Johanna. A chicken was killed, the blood dotted around the perimeter of a cottage, and a baby soon arrived.

Myra was against it. Her mind was bright and clear but she could also be rigid and stubborn. She spoke of Jesus and the Devil yet did not seem to understand that poor Mercury was being ridden by the spirit of his dead aunt, or that the soul of Abba's daughter was caught in the roots of the silk cotton tree, or even that Little Johanna, when in her trance and under the Convince, could speak to the long-dead Indians, or prophesize about the world to come. All things that were perfectly obvious to Nonesuch, for he had seen and heard them. He badgered Myra about it, but she wouldn't change her mind. They went on hoping, and being disappointed.

One Sunday, she showed him an abscess behind her left ear, and asked if he would still love her if she was ugly? She had tears in her eyes. He said yes but did not know if what he had said was really true. In the hothouse they gave her wild cerasee to drink, and a paste of the same to rub on her skin. One of the nurses took him aside and warned him: '*Woman nah get child if she feed pon cerasee.*' But what could he do? In a far corner, curtained off from the others, lay the worst cases. Some were noseless or eyeless or both, or had lipless mouths that were now mere holes into the void, with a few stray teeth poking through. The Yaws had terrified Nonesuch as a child, and the sight of these people still filled him with horror. He should have visited Myra more than he did. But she had come to the nurses in time and was spared the worst. She lost an ear, and the skin around her neck remained for ever scaly, but she lived.

9.

Barren

Over the years Nonesuch had many children although none yet with Myra, and he found the spirit of this angry and unborn child to be an endless trouble. It pursued him, blighting his vegetable patch, bringing him frequent illness, and deceitful friends. Despite this, he still loved Myra and relied on her bright, clear mind. She was the one who explained to him that if they took up an offer to be married in the Moravian church, well, then they would be hounded by the Moravians for ever. As for all the giddy talk of 'amelioration' – which had been presented to him as good news – Myra knew that if they were to no longer work on Saturdays, this would only mean they'd work twice as hard on Fridays. No, she did not put much store in any news from England, preferring to be precise and careful with her provision money, in the hope that her freedom could one day be bought. Perhaps she was wise. But Nonesuch worried that without a child, bitterness would swallow Myra entirely.

10.

'Myra's Andrew'

The century was about to turn. Soon Myra would no longer bleed and it would be too late. Just before jonkonnu, Nonesuch went in secret to Little Johanna. She told him to go to the aqueduct and look around the marshy base of each pillar for a plant with small violet flowers and the smell of mint. It was called pennyroyal. A trickster of a herb, it could 'bring child but throw away young belly, too'. Nonesuch thanked Little Johanna for this advice and went to jonkonnu in good spirits. There was no battle between Christmas and jonkonnu on Hope: the sentimental Lady Chandos had long ago assumed it was something like the mild revelries of her own English peasants, and had approved it, on the principle that it came 'but once a year'. More recently, the attorneys wrote letters condemning the 'frenzied dancing' and 'heathenish drinking and noise' but the Lady was shut up in her asylum and did not answer. Jonkonnu continued. The man dressed in red with the white mask and the little house on his head processed through the estate, blowing his conch, and the masqueraders danced, the singing exploded, much rum was taken, and it didn't end till the sun came up:

Jaw-Bone, Jaw-Bone, John House Canoe!
You know us and we know you!

Nonesuch slipped pulverized pennyroyal into Myra's cup.
When their son Andrew finally arrived, the next September, jonkonnu took on a special meaning. Each year, Myra put the boy on

his father's shoulders and they danced after the one they called John House Canoe, who wore his home on his head, and so knew of no exile. *Myra's Andrew.* It was Nonesuch himself who wrote the name into the General List of Negroes, blotting it carefully, and with great pride. He could do very little for any of his children. But with time, and a certain amount of cunning, he could do his best to prevent *Myra's Andrew* from appearing in those long columns that contained the first and second gangs, instead placing their son within those safer margins Nonesuch had known himself:

House Boys
Drivers
Carpenters
Coopers
Masons
Overseers

II.

The Final Return

When Andrew was six, the news came from England of Mr Wilberforce's triumph in the parliament of Mr Grenville. At jonkonnu that
December the people celebrated. Later in life Andrew had few memories of his mother, but he always recalled that she had remained
cautious and unconvinced. She spoke bitterly of England, preferring
the example of Saint-Domingue, where the people 'took matters into
their own hands'. She did not credit the promises of Prime Minister
Grenville. If no fresh African hands came, didn't that mean they were
the only hands they had? Perhaps it was 'the end' for somebody, somewhere, but not for them.

Nonesuch, disloyally, glanced down at Myra's hands and thought
they resembled those of a witch or a hag. So worn out! He missed
young hands, young love – especially when the bougainvillea flowered
in the spring. On Palm Sunday, he was in the Main House showing
Andrew how to press a wax seal on a letter, when his son noticed the
strange open wound on the back of his father's neck. He had left it so
long it could not be hidden by a neckerchief any longer. Later, in the
hothouse, a very old saltwater spotted him and cried *Igwe!* Nonesuch
wept. His cheeks with their proud markings had collapsed, he looked
like a skull. But he came from somewhere. He lay down in the corner
with the worst cases. He lost his eyes first, then his nose, then con-
sciousness itself. On the twenty-fifth of October 1808, Anaso, son of
Cuffay, left this world and returned to the realm of his ancestors.

For Love & Profit

Andrew Bogle thought himself very likely seventeen, or thereabouts. He was small-boned, not tall. Some people spoke to him as a child, some as a man, he found it hard to settle the question in his own mind. It was never tested by hard labour. He had inherited the name Bogle, and so was understood to be, like his father, good with inkpots, wax seals, letters, errands, overseeing, gun-polishing and animal husbandry. He stayed within the columns of his father, in other words, as his father had hoped. His mother stayed on Derry. She had a child with Mercury, whom she called Leda, and then a son called Jasper, whose father was a mystery. The effort wore her out. She was moved to the second gang, and in this way – or so Andrew dared to hope – received some little respite. In the end, though, it all came to nothing: Leda died at eight, Jasper at nine. His mother's spirit broke. She 'went under'. Andrew took up the responsibility of tending her provision grounds as well as his own, and visited her on the frequent occasions she ended up in the hothouse. He marked her as 'sickly' in the General List. She had the look of death about her. He mourned her as she lived, knowing it could not be long.

Just as Nonesuch had valued a bright, clear mind, his son Andrew valued strength. He was in love with Little Johanna, although she was old enough to be his mother. Nobody understood this love, he was a laughing stock. Even Little Johanna laughed. She called him 'boy'. He called her 'wife'. When he tried to speak of love, she liked to tell him to go back to the Main House and play with his inkpots. Still, he loved her, and they were married in his heart. Ellis, the other boy in the Main House, thought his friend mad and worried for him. He tried turning Andrew's attention to pretty Dorinda, the housemaid. Only last month, Dorinda had walked the fifteen miles to her father's estate in St Elizabeth, presented herself to him and declared: 'Sir, I am your daughter, and yet I am imprisoned like the Israelites in Egypt!' This bold speech had impressed the Englishman very much. He was considering buying her freedom, if she herself contributed fifty pounds towards the sum. She had raised thirty: it was a good prospect. Ellis was interested in good prospects and liked to lecture on the topic. He had seen much on Hope, and felt himself to be a kind of philosopher, or at least one who knew something of human nature, and it was his conviction that wise people never considered the question of love without also considering the question of money. This new Lady Anna Eliza, for example, had been engaged to the future Duke of Buckingham since the age of six. This was what Ellis called an 'add-up marriage'. It meant that what was hers would be added up to his and vice versa. After they were married – and upon the death of her mad mother – Anna Eliza had inherited Hope, many mansions in the city of London, all the Chandos estates in England and Ireland, and yet more property in a strange place that Ellis called the 'Isle of White'. All of which was then added up to the tens of thousands of acres belonging to her husband, the Duke. Amongst the Duke's haul was a property called 'Stowe'. Both Bogle and Ellis had been given a chance to examine this estate when it slipped out of an envelope onto the writing desk. A small engraving of a very big house. When the Duke's father died, the new Lady Anna Eliza would become Duchess of Chandos and Buckingham and Countess Temple of Stowe, while her husband would be Duke of Buckingham Richard Brydges Chandos Temple Nugent Grenville, Earl Temple of Stowe, for when you married in this adding-up-way, your name got much longer and took for ever to copy out. Now, you tell me, said Ellis, what any of that has to do with what you call love?

Added-up acreage: 57,465

Added-up annual income from rent: £70,420

Ellis blotted these figures himself. He was therefore in a position to advise those labouring under false romantic ideas. *Add-up, bwoy, add-up!* Andrew liked Ellis and enjoyed listening to him. But he could not think of love as profit. When he was inside Little Johanna, he thought not of money or land or 'adding-up' or anything really other than the feeling of being inside her, safe and rooted. If anything was added-up it was their souls, fused together in the moment of ecstasy.

13.

Mr Edward Tichborne

In January, the Duke's agent, Mr Edward Tichborne, returned. He was, as ever, concerned about the drought, writing many urgent letters to England regarding the need for irrigation. But the Duchess of Buckingham and Chandos had read her own dead mother's correspondence on that subject and took her mother's view. The poor soil of Hope would not survive the process: 'the remedy would be worse than the cure'. It was Bogle's job to copy out the monthly cultivation figures for each piece, in the hope that these dire numbers might convince the Duchess of the wisdom of the plan. Letters went back and forth: she remained unconvinced. In the meantime, he performed the services of a page, as he did whenever Mr Tichborne visited. Mr Tichborne liked to talk. His page learned a lot by listening. For example, that it was possible to have five hundred pounds a year and yet feel hard done by. That a gentleman always wore a topcoat – even if it was hot as the Devil – but never the same cravat twice in a week. To be the third-born son of seven was a terrible tragedy. It meant you had to scrabble for your living on godforsaken islands like this one. Too much port was bad for the feet. In September, Bogle learned he would be leaving Hope for a period, to accompany the talkative Mr Tichborne to London, England.

14.

Wild Talk

A house was rented in Dean Street until Christmas. Bogle slept in a warm room next to the kitchen. Three other people lived downstairs: a maid-of-all-work, the cook, and a boy with no title who did the dirtiest jobs. Bogle was amazed by their existence, and by everything else. He had seen the Irish poor in Kingston, and destitute Germans in Mandeville, but the English poor were of a bewildering variety and extent. Running daily messages from Tichborne to the Duchess on Pall Mall, he often wished he had Ellis by his side, for when the time came to return to Hope, he doubted he would be able to do justice to all he had seen. Legless men lying in gutters, half-naked whores in the doorways, children begging for pennies on the steps of churches! Nothing was 'added-up' here. The English turned out not to be a single tribe of well-fed top hats and silk skirts, as Ellis imagines, but rather a wild struggle of factions, all intent upon their own survival, and therefore, in a certain sense, not strange or unfamiliar at all. Sometimes the talk below stairs reminded him of late-night gatherings in the cottages. The maid-of-all-work was, for example, very like Bella from back home. Bella had previously laboured on a different estate, in Saint Catherine, upon which everything, to her mind, was richer and more impressive and run on a grander scale. So it was with this maid, who mourned her previous position in a 'great house in the country' and refused to add his own clothes to the wash on account that she hoped she 'hadn't fallen so low in life as to scrub a nig-nog's things'. Cook meanwhile put him in mind of Little Johanna. She liked to mutter darkly to herself, and could be heard wishing death upon a startling variety of enemies, from the costermonger up to the Prime Minister. But she was not beautiful like Johanna and lacked Johanna's gifts. Nobody she cursed died.

The boldest and most astonishing talk came from the boy Jack, who had no last name and 'no parents to speak of'. This, too, reminded him of Hope, where the mouths that ran wildest tended to be the hungriest. Jack cleared bedpans and chimneys, shovelled horse muck, shovelled coal. He said the French war had been a 'dirty trick', and a 'game of soldiers for rich men' and that the Duke of Wellington could 'shove his victory right up his arse'. He was especially vexed by the recent 'outrage up in Peter's Field', where the cavalry had 'murdered the poor people of Lancashire in cold blood, on government orders'. And all the while the Prince Regent 'jes floated about on his yacht, eating beef and getting fatter!' Several nights a week Jack sneaked out of the window of their shared basement room to attend a 'politicking meeting', in a chapel on Hopkins Street. There he listened to 'men who love freedom and ain't afraid to speak on it' – although the whole town was 'riddled with government spies'. You could be sent to Botany Bay for saying one man one vote. For complaining about the price of bread. Bogle was told of one John Baguely, a hero of Lancashire, presently 'banged up in Newgate', simply for repeating the phrase: *Liberty or death!* Yet despite all these dangers, Jack urged Bogle to accompany him to Hopkins Street, if only to hear a preacher called Wedderburn, the natural-born son of a slave and her master – 'coloured like yerself' – who did well to say: 'The slaves should murder their masters soon as they please!'

15.

Pragmatism

On a trip out of town — they were visiting Sir Henry Tichborne, in Tichborne Park — Bogle found himself trapped for two hours outside Newgate Prison. A huge crowd had flooded the street to watch a hanging, and all passing traffic was held fast in this human mass, as if in treacle. Three boys faced the gallows for the theft of a sheep. Bogle liked Jack well enough, but not enough to be hanged for him. Whenever he heard the basement window being opened, he closed his eyes and feigned sleep.

16.

Lineage

Where would the Chandos-Buckinghams decamp for the autumn?
There were many possibilities, it was their annual argument. The
Duchess preferred her own Avington. The villagers loved her
there, protected her from radicals, and the Tudor panelling kept out
the draughts. The villagers of Stowe, by contrast, she found 'morose'. The Duke prevailed: they went to Stowe. If Tichborne now
wished to conduct any real business with the Duke before Christmas,
he would need a better carriage than he had, a change of horses and
somewhere bearable to stay overnight. All of which cost money, and
he would far rather conduct his business by post. But the Duke's
spending was out of control, and the man was notorious for ignoring
letters from attorneys and creditors. He had to be confronted in
person.

On a wet day in mid-October, knee to knee in a rented gig, they
headed north, with Tichborne talking and Bogle listening. Eight hours,
during which Bogle learned many things. He had always known a man
could be high born and yet go unhonoured – his own father had suffered this fate – but had never imagined this might be the case for such
a one as Mr Edward. Tichborne himself seemed amazed. How had a
man from a family 'as noble and ancient as my own' come to be 'working like a slave' – and for such a notorious spendthrift and fraud? The
answer had something to do with being a Catholic – Bogle could not
follow the logic of this very precisely – but something more to do with
the old, frequently mentioned, problem of being the third-born son of

seven. The Duke, by contrast, was the lucky firstborn of his clan. 'And as for their dukedoms! Look up their lineage why don't you!' Bogle could not, lacking the means. 'Sheep farmers! Sheep farmers and merchants. Oh, and a few crooked soldiers with government sinecures. But didn't these Temples and Grenvilles know how to marry. These boys can find an heiress in a haystack! They know which side a lady is buttered!'

Bogle admired a gold and russet forest as it went by, swaying in the gathering wind. One lifetime was not enough to understand a people and the words they used and the way they thought and lived.

17.

Staying Overnight at the Brown Hen

Bogle tied up the horses, brushed their coats, cleared their hay-flecked shit from outside the entrance, filled their nosebags, led them to the trough, took Tichborne's bags upstairs, unpacked them, laid out Tichborne's nightclothes and a suit for the morning, shined his shoes, lugged half a dozen buckets of water up two flights of stairs, drew him a bath, set the fire in the grate, replaced the counterpane on the bed with one from a carpetbag containing linens of Tichborne's preference, lit and covered six lamps, went back downstairs. Tichborne was slumped in a wingchair by the fire, having just opened a bottle of port. Bogle tried going to bed.

'Oh, sit yourself down, boy. Keep me company!'

Bogle sat. The bottle was large, and empty within the hour.

'This much I'll say for her: she treats the poor like her own children. Sometimes she can be over-indulgent in that direction – as you would know yourself, Bogle – but at least she's careful with her money and uses it well. Which makes her worth twenty of him, in my eyes – and the bank's. How shamefully he treats her!'

The Duke, it turned out, was like Mr Ballard: he thought of women as property and had sired children in many houses, far and wide. Money ran through his fingers like sand.

'As for the pretty boy – the second Duke, as he'll soon be . . . Four months that wastrel spent on the Continent and damned if there was a piece of coloured glass or a Medici statue left in all of Venice. He'll put his mother in the poorhouse yet. Like father like son. Incontinent – in all things. Why d'you think we had to fetch the boy back from Rome? Wouldn't be surprised to find a Buckingham bastard born in every whorehouse in Italy . . .'

Bogle learned that the Duchess, who had married at sixteen, was now forty and no longer spoke to her unfaithful, spendthrift husband, preferring the company of her little dog. It sounded an awkward arrangement. Tichborne laughed:

'Oh, don't you worry, Bogle. They manage. A fellow might be married like a sultan at Stowe – have twelve wives and still never set eyes on a one of them! You'll see.'

18.

A Very Big House

The next morning the skies darkened, then opened. On the long, stormy approach through the grounds, Bogle had his first glimpse of a house like no other, into which Tichborne Park could be fitted perhaps twenty times. A pair of soaking footmen ran down the front steps and directed the carriage to the bad weather entrance. Tichborne and his page stepped bone-dry straight into an underground cavern, fashioned from white stone. Here the walls sloped inward and the ceiling was low. Two ghoulish creatures – half cat, half woman – lay in wait for them at the bottom of some stairs that led who knew where. Everything was stony white, cold to the touch. Engravings of bird-headed men lined the wall. Startled, Bogle turned quickly, stumbling against a stone casket large enough for a dead child. Tichborne laughed; Bogle was afraid. Whose ancestors were these?

Out of nowhere, a manservant in livery appeared – 'The Duke is glad you are here, and that you have arrived through the Egyptian Hall. It is a recent addition. He is very proud of it' – and led them out of the ghastly chamber and into a vast underground tunnel, like a long, covered street, lined on both sides with racks of guns. It seemed to Bogle that they walked a long time. Turning right, then left, then right again. Sometimes servants hurried past. The tunnel branched off into other tunnels. Here the smell of something baking. There the sound of struck metal. A house like a city, with an armoury to defend it.

*

Then they were upstairs. Light streamed through giant windowpanes. Bogle had not thought it possible to walk so far and still be inside. A great round room with a circle of glass in the roof. A long thin room like a train station, filled with books. A room of musical instruments. A room of statues. A room decorated with little decapitated heads on pikes, painted straight onto the walls. On the way out of this room, Bogle looked again: the pikes were in fact green vines set off with yellow bows, and all the heads were pink and smiling. A room full of couches. A room like a trash house: it would have taken the cane from ten pieces piled horizontally to fill it. Another barn of a room, with River Mumma's golden table stretching from one end to the other. Then another, with a ceiling of gold. More stairs. A glimpse of a bed, big as a boat, robed in velvet. This house wore silk and gold and velvet like a woman. No room was naked, no wall bare.

They came to a hallway, domed like a church, with a curved staircase winding up. Here the walls seemed, to Bogle, to be painted with scenes from home. At least, he felt he recognized the palms and cedars, the forested hills, the sparkling blue-green water. Here and there, in the groves, someone had whimsically added little groups of naked, unmurdered Indians, as if anything was left of them besides their moaning laments in the conch shells. Climbing the stairs, he turned back, seeking Kingston, and almost collided with two young lads in aprons with brushes in hand. They slopped white paint over a bay at sunset. 'We have more paintings to be hung than wall space to hang them.' The servant explained this with peculiar pride, as if the house were his own property: 'Space must therefore be made.' Bogle watched a cascading waterfall disappear under a fresh coat of white. 'The Rembrandt Room,' announced the servant, and opened a door.

19.

A Young Negro Archer

Tichborne was caught off guard. He hadn't expected to find the couple together: he was used to playing them off against each other. The Duke sat at a card table by the fire, the Duchess in a far corner by a window, with a snoring pug dog in her arms. Tichborne took a deep breath and began upon his unhappy speech. Bogle walked over to the Duke, placed the sheaf of relevant papers before him, undid the purple ribbon, stepped back, and stood silently by the door. Bad harvests were in that sheaf, and hurricanes, and too many dead babies, severed arms, cases of the Yaws, interfering Baptists and sickly old saltwaters who would never now be replaced by new ones. As Tichborne spoke, the Duke groaned, and paced up and down. The Duchess stayed where she was at the window. Bogle found a golden spiral in the wallpaper and followed its repeated path across the room.

'Enough, enough – it's no *use*, Tichborne. You can talk of soil and hurricanes till the cows come home: it's only a matter of time. Not even on Saint-Domingue were the poor French outnumbered as we are. Parliament is the only possible route, but we need cool heads, and at this moment the West Indian Interest are in a state of extreme anxiety. Who can blame them? Abolitionists and Whigs in one ear, a lot of damned Baptists and Methodists in the other. The situation is extremely combustible. I have reason to hope that I have their trust, and that they believe I will serve their interests – not least because they are also my own. But you must understand: the name of "Grenville" can hardly be pleasant to them. No fellow in Jamaica dreams of making his fortune any more – only of preserving what little profit he makes – and we know who we have to thank for *that* . . . Between Hope and the other place – Middleton! – it truly is a wonder we survive. But my wife finds all of this terribly ironical.'

Tichborne feigned innocence: 'Oh? In what sense?'

No one answered this. The Duchess walked to the next window. What was the point of having had a Prime Minister for an uncle if this same uncle then worked against the family interest? Tichborne watched the Duke leaf through the papers on his desk, as if the answer to this conundrum might be found there. Silence. There was only Mimi the pug, snoring. Since coming to England, Bogle had grown used to silence, and to standing like a statue, eyes straight ahead. He found ways to occupy himself. The patterns in wallpaper. The sconces round lamps. The carvings on a fireplace. The paintings on walls. If there was a negro face in a corner of any painting, anywhere in a room, he prided himself on finding it in a moment – he supposed he was homesick. Yet only now did he notice the boy archer, on the opposite wall. It was not a small portrait, and maybe that in itself was the cause of the delay, for he was accustomed to finding such faces in the corner of canvases, or buried in a crowd. This boy took up the whole frame. Bogle liked him very much. He had a bow in hand and a quiver on his back, and looked just like Ellis by the side of Mr Macintosh, off to hunt wild pig. Only, this young archer was not carrying anything for anybody. These were his own bow and arrow, and he hunted on his own behalf. Bogle felt a throb of sadness welling in his throat, and swallowed hard. How he looks like Ellis! Oh, how homesick I am!

20.

The Order of Things

In the afternoon, the wind and rain relented, and the sun emerged. Tichborne walked out through the southern doors to wait for their driver. Bogle watched him flop defeated onto a stone bench under some dying orange blossom. Bogle, given no direction, stayed where he was, between the doors that opened onto a 'North Loggia' and another set that led to the South. A private country in front, another behind, both stretching to the horizon.

He looked about him. To his left, four naked men on a pedestal wrestled a snake. The stone was black. The men did not seem to be. Bogle did not know why they were naked or wrestling a snake. They did not interest him; he turned away. To his right, above his head, more stone people surged from the walls. This group were suspended in mid-air, like duppies, but there was no reason to be frightened, no, they did not move, and there was no magic involved, only craft, as when you carve a figure in a cottonwood tree. He took a step closer. The tableau was fashioned from white stone, and it seemed to tell the story of a great man – a king of some sort. Below him, a woman knelt, preparing to pass over a crown. Soldiers and onlookers and children were gathered all about this pair, reminding Bogle of the nosy old women of Hope, leaning on their fences. Watchful. Curious about power. Finally, on the ground, naked, at the king's feet – craven as a dog at the heel of his master – was a black man, just like himself.

Bogle did not know how a house came to be as big as a city, with two private countries either side. He did not know why men might wrestle snakes. He did not know in what world a boy like Ellis would be free to hunt on his own behalf. But this tableau in white he understood from top to bottom – it was as familiar to him as his own name. The order of things. On Hope it was his job to put the order of things into neat columns, in a clear hand, into the General List, as it had been his father's job before him. But mere ink and paper were beneath such a place as this. Here you wrote it in stone.

21.

In the Event of Universal War

On their first night back in London, Bogle surprised himself. He said: 'Wait.' It was not easy to collect his things in the darkness, he was not practised at it, as Jack was, and he tried his new friend's patience during the search for some shoes. But then he was ready and following Jack through the window and out into the night. The lights and the glass made unpredictable shapes and shadows in the darkness, revealing people and places in odd flashes. He walked quickly past all the Soho women, trying not to look too green, too surprised. Then, on Hopkins Street, at the door of the chapel, a red-haired girl said it would be a shilling. For this you got a ticket with a printed head upon it – Jack already had one – and admission into 'any debate, and the Sunday Lectures besides'. Half-relieved, Bogle turned to go, but Jack kicked up a fuss: 'Now, are we *for* the poor and ill-used or ain't we?' The red-haired girl scowled: 'You've a big mouth, Jack, we know that much by now.' But then sighed, and stepped aside: 'If it's just the once, a penny will do.'

The chapel was a makeshift thing. You walked up a narrow wooden staircase until you arrived at something like a hayloft, where perhaps a hundred people stood, facing a 'chairman' at a desk. They were late, the first speaker was just finishing, and now the chairman stood and repeated the proposal under debate: 'In the event of universal war, which of the two Parties are likely to be victorious: the Rich or the Poor?' The second speaker rose to a chorus of emphatic whoops, Jack's amongst them. Bogle felt himself clapped on the back: 'Your man's up next – Wedderburn!'

His man? The hair was rather flat, and he was closer to Roger's colouring than his own. He had a pug's nose and a disputatious face. The only truly familiar thing about him was the name – it had an air of home about it – but before Bogle had time to consider this last point more closely, the man was on his feet and had begun. He had a thrilling way of speaking. The familiar lilt of the islands combined with the fervour of the Soho barrow boys. He drove each point home with his hands – grasping the air as if wringing the neck of some invisible government agent – and he was full of questions. There were but two classes of people in England, the very rich and very poor, and how did this happen? The crowd did not know but bellowed enthusiastically. Why was the land held by four hundred families alone who took special care to marry only each other? No more did Bogle know but found himself cheering with the rest, and thought of Ellis, who would have been amazed at the scene. Could this truly be the son of a slave? Every eye was upon him, and every ear. He held the very soul of the crowd in his palm, and Bogle realized that he had always thought of this commanding spirit as a feminine gift, because of the Johannas. But this man's hate likewise stalked him everywhere. It flamed: you felt its warmth just being near him. He was just as enraged by 'Peterloo' as Jack, and listening to him now, Bogle realized how many of his young friend's striking ideas and phrases were, in fact, borrowed. Cut from this brown man's cloth:

My motto is assassinate!
God gave the world to the children of men as their inheritance – and
they have been fleeced out of it!
I am with Thomas Spence: any person calling a piece of land his
own private property is a criminal.
The 16th of August was a glorious day for the blood spilt on that
day has cemented our union.

Could blood be glorious? All around a cheer went up, confirming the glory. And what had happened in France was to happen here, and all the Lords and Ladies were fleeing abroad, because by now they knew that the starving poor were determined not to put up with their base condition a moment longer. Various men Bogle had never heard of would *lose their heads* and the Prince Regent, whom he had heard of, was a fat-faced fool, a drunk and a whoremonger. 'He don't care a damn about the people's sufferings!' Here Wedderburn strangled the air, and the crowd echoed him, like those strange puppet shows Bogle sometimes spied in Covent Garden: *HE DON'T CARE A DAMN!* For a long moment, no more speech was possible. The crowd was just too loud. The chairman banged the table, seeking order. Wedderburn unlocked his strangling hands and pointed ominously out of the only window:

'And they tell us to be quiet like that *bloody spooney Jesus Christ* who like a *bloody fool* tells us when we get a slap on one side of the face turn gently round and ask them to smack the other! But I like jolly old St Peter! Give me a rusty sword, for they have declared war against the people! They burn Carlyle's printing of the rights of man – but they can't burn it out of my head! Not even if they hang me! Glory be to Thomas Paine!' A roar went through the loft like a hurricane through the trash house. Bogle turned to Jack to ask him a question but the boy had his arm raised, clutching St Peter's sword, and now he rattled the invisible thing in the air, and roared with the rest, spit flying from his mouth.

On the way home, Bogle got to ask his question. Jack frowned. It seemed to Bogle that Jack liked to talk but not to be questioned.

'How d'you spell it? P-A-I-N, I expect! And Thomas *Spence* is him who looked up the matter in the Bible of all places and *rat-ifi-cated once and for all* that the land ain't owned by no one, for it was given by God to every man! And Thomas Pain . . . Well, he was him who said all men have rights and *that*, if you must know, young Bogle, is who Pain is.'

But why Pain had been saddled with such an unfortunate name Jack could not say. Then Jack asked Bogle what he had made of it all and Bogle said he had hoped to hear more about the slaves and Jack said what did he mean was he stupid that was the whole point of the thing for without their rights weren't all men slaves? Bogle said nothing. They walked in silence to Shaftesbury Avenue where Jack in far too loud a voice asked if he would come to Hopkins Street again, and Bogle, mindful of spies, said he would not.

22.

Bitter Harvests

To miss jonkonnu, for Bogle, was an ominous feeling, but Tichborne insisted on Christmas at Tichborne Park, and then New Year at his Doughty cousins' house, in Dorset. Finally, on the third of January, his page was sent back to Jamaica, alone. A month later, the first person Bogle saw as he stepped off the boat at Falmouth was Ellis, dressed in black, clutching a hat to his chest.

Peachey swore that Myra *'jes lay down quiet pon de ground and died'*. But Peachey still thought of him as a boy, and had always tried to protect him. By 'the ground' she meant the sticky floor of the boiling house, although who had put his mother to work there, and why, nobody seemed to know or would dare tell. Only Johanna could comfort him, and she was nowhere to be found. She had taken the shape of a wild horse and run for the hills, or else her soul had migrated into a cotton tree, or she was with old Obboney himself, cursing them all from the other side. It was planting season and Bogle was meant to be overseeing the ratooning. Instead he went up to the Main House to get the truth about Johanna's location from Ellis, who looked at him pleadingly. The truth would only add-up pain to pain: why should he be the deliverer of it? Reluctantly, he opened the drawer of the armoire and passed Bogle a copy of the letter that had started the trouble. It was from Macintosh to the attorneys:

She is forever predicting the end of the world. Both our world on Hope and the world itself.

It was true enough that Johanna had been seen walking under the windows of the Main House, speechifying, singing, and threatening Roger – but she had always done these things. The mystery was why Mr Macintosh was of such a nervous disposition:

She is perhaps under the influence of a congregation: we have seen much baptizing of negroes of late. She recites certain troubling verses from Leviticus, which are easily misunderstood by the others and surely intended as a form of incitement to rebellion or riot. She has a millenarian cast of mind.

This last was hard to understand. But on the next page Mr Macintosh had taken the trouble of writing out clarifying examples:

And ye shall hallow the fiftieth year, and proclaim liberty throughout all the land, unto all the inhabitants thereof: It shall be a Jubilee unto you, and ye shall return every man unto his possession, and ye shall return every man unto his family.

The land shall not be sold for ever: for the land is mine, for ye were strangers and sojourners with me.

And if thy brother that dwelleth by thee be waxen poor, and be sold unto thee, thou shalt not compel him to serve as a bond servant.

The attorneys, frightened by so many recent outbreaks of rebellion across the island, referred the matter to the Justice of the Peace. Little Johanna was sentenced to three months' correction on a treadmill in Kingston Prison.

23.

Automaton

For a period after hearing this, Bogle found he couldn't feel anything. Whenever someone tried to hurt or deceive or get the better of him in some way he was only confused. Why did they think that he was even *in* there, and could still be hurt? If Ol' Higue herself had come to suck the life out of him, she would have found him already empty. He discovered you could live in this way: like an empty skin after a visit by a soucouyant. Nobody noticed. In fact, in the view of Mr Macintosh, his efficiency only improved, and he was entrusted with more tasks, some of which came with little freedoms that he could not feel and no longer cared about. On Sundays, he drove Macintosh's wife to church and sat beside her throughout the service. On Mondays, he rode to Kingston for letters from England and whatever copies of *The Times* had come off the boats.

24.

Cato Street

In mid-May, while placing the newspapers on the sideboard, he spotted a black face in a strange cartoon on the front page: *The Spencean Philanthropists*. A group of men in wigs and gowns and topcoats and spectacles danced in a circle, as if round a maypole, but at the top of this pole were five heads on spikes. Four pink heads and one black. Bogle sat down where he was and read their names.

> *Brunt*
> *Ings*
> *Thistlewood*
> *Tidd*
> *Davidson*

Davidson's was the head that had drawn his attention: he turned out to be a Creole from Kingston. Together these headless men were 'radicals'. Like Jack, they hated Lord Sidmouth, and claimed the land belonged to all, and they wanted 'universal suffrage', and the return of something called 'habeas corpus'. In a hayloft on Cato Street these men had conspired to murder the rulers of England, as revenge for Peterloo, and to free the English from their present 'state of slavery' – a phrase Bogle re-read three times before dismissing it as a printer's error. He read on: the plot was foiled. There was a spy in their midst. With trepidation he traced his finger down the remainder of the long column, looking for the name 'Jack', and finding instead another familiar name: Robert Wedderburn. But Wedderburn, who had many prior dealings with the condemned men, happened to be already safely in gaol on the night in question – imprisoned for 'seditious writings' – and so still had a head on his shoulders. Bogle looked at this strange cartoon a long time, feeling something at last. But what? An irritating mental itch which, as he went to scratch it, he found he couldn't reach.

25.

Thistlewood! Wedderburn!

It was almost harvest time. Bogle set off on the long ride to Saint Catherine's to collect the five men Hope had rented for the season. Around midday, he came to the burned-out remnants of Thistlewood's old place, Breadnut Pen, where it bordered Wedderburn's estate. He stopped his donkey in its tracks. Thistlewood. Wedderburn. Could it be? But Thistlewood was thirty years dead! He only lived on in the memory, a species of bogeyman whom old women employed in their stories, to scare misbehaving children. Wedderburn's estate, meanwhile, was neither closed up nor sold. Besides, why would any young Wedderburn or young Thistlewood conspire against their elders? People added up, they did not tear away, or turn the world upside down, it made no sense — and no doubt England was as full of Wedderburns and Thistlewoods as Jamaica was of Cudjoes and Pompeys. Then again, children are sometimes a bitter harvest. He had heard old women say so. Sometimes they did not come to add-up. Instead they undid — they destroyed. They cursed their fathers, and burned their houses to the ground. This was called the revenge of the young. Bogle looked out over the pieces, remembering London and Wedderburn and his strangling hands, so full of feeling. He himself was younger than Wedderburn, but he had always been quiet by temperament, watchful. He knew by now that hate would never come to him as easily as despair, or the feeling of no feeling. And if this headless Thistlewood was in reality one of the Jamaican Thistlewoods, he thought it must have helped in some way to at least have a father to curse, and a home to destroy. That was surely like having a target for an arrow. Bogle meanwhile sat on his donkey and despaired. What did he have?

26.

The Eternal Return of Johanna

When the bougainvillea began to shrivel and the rains stopped, Johanna returned. She was not the same woman he had loved. They tied your hands to a giant treadmill, as if you were a donkey, and whipped you as you walked all day, until the trough beneath your feet filled with blood. He tried to speak to her of love, as he had once done, and to tell her of what he had seen in England. Her eyes rolled in her head. She would not listen to anything but her own voice. She laughed at him. She had always laughed at him but this laugh was different. She said: 'You are a fool, Bogle. I had a dream. I see it all.'

27.

The Prophetic Circular Dream
of Little Johanna

will SEE that we have done what the earth herself FORBID. But I have a DREAM and it is the TRUTH and believe me it will come to pass. I tell you the world is UPSIDE DOWN. These people are BAHAMA GRASS! Wherever they PLANT DEM ROOT they SPREAD and DESTROY! This is hidden from FOOLISH BOYS but not from ME. I have a DREAM. I know that this time will END and a new time will BEGIN, as it is written in their books and in the DIRT IN MY MOUTH and in the shit of that old Devil OBBONEY himself. I have seen the SECRET ENGINE OF THE WORLD! Some fools say the world rests on the back of a turtle, but that is a FAIRY TALE FOR PICKNEY! The world rest upon THE TREADMILL! I have SEEN it. I have a DREAM. The TREAD-MILL TURNS, it never STOPS, and atop it rests every SHINING CITY and SHIP and GOLD COIN and all KINGS AND QUEENS and LORDS AND LADIES and all CHURCH MEN for it is a TREADMILL WET WITH BLOOD and it is the SECRET ENGINE OF THE WORLD! Whoever walks it will WEEP and say look at me brought so LOW! But I say ALL THINGS MUST TURN and who stands now SHALL FALL and all land that is closed SHALL BE OPEN and every BLADE OF BAHAMA will be CUT DOWN and THE DEAD WILL LIVE and the living die and KINGS SHALL WEEP and the people will enter their palaces and SHIT ON THEIR FLOORS and THERE WILL BE A RECKONING! Everything taken from us I WILL RESTORE! We shall have noses and eyes again and mouths and WE WILL SPEAK OF THE TREADMILL until the day of MOSES' JUBILEE! I dreamt that NOTHING DIES and NOTHING IS FORGOTTEN for the TREADMILL IS A CIRCLE and there will be no end to circles until all have seen the TREADMILL and waded through its BLOOD. And even the BLIND WILL SEE IT, but it will be TOO LATE! *CHUKWU SELA AKA, UWA AGWU!* This world will BURN, it will cast us off, EVERY LAST ONE OF US, for she is TIRED OF US, and nothing will live and we

28.

Bahama Grass, 1826

Four years passed before Tichborne returned to Hope. The first thing he did, upon arrival, was send Bogle for the accounts. Within a single year, two hundred and eighty-eight hogshead of sugar had declined to fifty, one hundred and forty-five puncheons of rum to only fourteen, and every corner of Hope that could be rented out had been, as if the Duke were a poor man in need of every penny he could squeeze from the ground. Tichborne wrote to the attorneys and discovered the true extent of the Duke's debts. One hundred and fifty thousand pounds, relating to 'Stowe and other expenses'. A two-night visit of the Russian Tsar, for example, had involved a redecoration costing ten thousand pounds. The King himself was 'a regular visitor' and this, too, had proved expensive. Tichborne dictated a letter to the Duke. It did not speak of his spending – that was unmentionable between them – but he asked the Duke to consider securing a water contract with the military camp downhill. The run-off from Hope's mill could be easily redirected, it was a simple and practical plan, and would bring in some two thousand a year. The Duke disliked talking practically: a reply might take months. In the meantime, Tichborne worked himself into a fury about Bahama grass. It had been planted years ago by Ballard, intended as a pretty border round the estate, but had proved rapacious and near impossible to eradicate. It dug itself in everywhere, spread rapidly, sucked the life out of the soil, killed off native species, and was altogether a blight upon the land. Tichborne did not understand why Little Johanna laughed as he explained all this. He got Macintosh to task the women's gang with the pointless task of pulling it up, root by root.

29.

Taken Off the Country

In June, a small, vicarious pleasure came to Bogle: Ellis was to marry
Dorinda. A dissenter church in Black River had agreed to it, and the
sentimental Duchess had given special permission, writing a long letter
describing marriage as a seal of virtue, a check on the passions, which
no right-thinking Christian should ever try to keep from either the
wretched poor nor the Africans, given their particular need of it. Bogle
put on his white cottons and accompanied his dear friends to Black
River. It was market day: the church was full of people. But when the
banns were read and Ellis and his bride stood up, the people in the pews
burst into laughter and mockery. It was several minutes before the minister could restore order: 'And how do ye live yourselves? In sin, I'll
wager!' The congregation bowed their heads as the minister spoke and
fell silent. Dorinda wept. But his friends were married. Bogle tried to
be happy for them, though it was a bittersweet feeling: his own Johanna
refused to step foot in such a place. Still, he held out the hope of Johanna
recovering her sanity, and the law changing, and of persuading her, one
of these days. But even this idea – that he had such a thing as 'days' and
hopes that might take place within them – turned out to be presumption. The next morning Tichborne still had not received his answer
from the Duke, and in a fit of pique, quit his job and left the island,
taking his page with him.

30.

A European Honeymoon

They stopped in London for only a few days, to collect a woman – 'Bogle, this is Mrs Kathryn Tichborne. We were married in May' – and then left for Europe, on 'honeymoon'. Here was a new word. Everything was new. Nobody ever explained where they were going or how long they would be staying once they got there. He soon learned it was better to sleep on dusty red tiles than the beds he was occasionally offered: cooler, fewer fleas. It was high summer. People assumed he should be used to the heat, when in fact he found it unpleasant, being so much drier than Jamaica and with no relieving rains. In Spain, a schoolboy pricked him with a pin, to see if he would bleed. In France, a chambermaid confessed to cutting a tuft of his hair as he slept, curious to know 'if it truly grew by itself'. In Germany, a philosophical stable boy explained that as 'one of the meek' he would soon inherit the earth. Every church they visited was a golden palace, and yet the priests seemed, to Bogle, to be very sly, with their sandals and frayed gowns, playing at poverty. In Italy, more than a year into their travels, the Duke and Tichborne almost collided. Tichborne was heading to Venice and the Duke, as it turned out, was already there, sailing in the harbour, hiding from his British creditors. His boat was called the *Anna Eliza* and had cost sixteen thousand pounds. They were informed of all this one night in Rome, by a Viscount named Byng who himself owned 'half of London and most of Bedfordshire'. Contemplating this fortunate young man of property seemed to depress Tichborne: he drank too much and retired early to his rooms. The next morning, he announced they would be doubling back on themselves and heading home, by way of Spain.

In Paris, awaiting their final crossing, they received extraordinary news. A distant Doughty cousin had died, leaving Tichborne her entire estate, on the condition that he change his name to Doughty and produce a male heir. Mrs Tichborne was already pregnant: it was a good prospect. The estate included a large portion of Bloomsbury, as well as Upton House in Poole, Dorset. Tichborne was excitable, he kept jiggling around, making it difficult for Bogle to pull up his master's trousers or fasten them.

'Good news, Mr Edward. You are uprising in the world.'

'*Rising up*, Bogle. But yes, I do rather seem to be.'

Tichborne had always tracked the progress of his many brothers closely, and with a heavy heart. Now he began to wonder if his luck was turning. One brother had died in China, another in India, and a third on home soil. This placed him second in line. Meanwhile, the youngest Tichborne was still childless, and the eldest had been recently cursed with a seventh daughter, to add to the six he already had. Was it possible there would be no male heir? Back in England, Kathryn promptly gave birth to a little boy called Henry. Nothing could dent Edward's new-found optimism. Not even the news that his little brother's ridiculous French wife had just been blessed with a son of her own, called Roger.

VOLUME SEVEN

Then why suppose yourselves the chosen few?

ROBERT WEDDERBURN

I.

D is for Doughty

With the arrival of their baby Henry, Edward and Kathryn renounced the name of Tichborne and became Mr and Mrs Doughty, losing their temper with anyone who forgot this. For a while, Bogle inked a D into his own palm, as a reminder. The household moved to Upton. The property came with its own estate steward, a Mr Gosford, as well as a cook, a drunken gardener, three nervous ladies' maids who had never before seen an 'Ethiopian', and two stable boys. It was a big house, but Bogle had walked the halls of Stowe, and felt himself to be a man who could no longer be surprised. When Mrs Doughty became gravely ill, he was not surprised – even less so when she recovered – but the Doughtys were stunned both by this visitation of ill luck and by its reprieve. Mr Doughty built a church across the road, visible from the front windows, so that Mrs Doughty might remember the grace of God from her sickbed. This reminded Bogle of Little Johanna dropping four stones in a line to ward off duppies. It did not surprise him.

One night in August, Mr Doughty ran downstairs without a stitch on and told Bogle to get dressed and have the coach ready. Fifteen minutes later Bogle drove to Poole Harbour, as instructed, eyes half closed with sleep. On the pier, two men were bowing deeply to a third man wearing a lot of gold braid but with bucked teeth like a donkey. Tichborne seemed very agitated. His bandy legs were shaking: 'It is the Count of Ponthieu, Bogle. Hold the door open.' Bogle held the door. Why was everybody dressed so finely at one in the morning? He drove to Lulworth Castle, as instructed, left the men there and drove all the way back to Upton to the sound of Tichborne snoring. The next morning the whole thing had taken on the quality of a dream, although he had not slept. After dinner service he was so exhausted he could hardly balance the bottle of port on its tray. The new Mr Doughty, having slept most of the day, was full of energy, eager for company. He wanted to know what Bogle had made of the Count of Ponthieu, but Bogle didn't really make anything of him, aside from those teeth. Mr Doughty laughed till tears came out of his eyes.

'What if I told you that your "donkey-tooth" passenger was the exiled King of France!'

He was so tired. He just nodded.

2.

Upton Park, Poole

Life at Upton had a regular rhythm. It revolved around heavy meals, different beverages at different hours of the day, newspaper deliveries and daily visits to Upton's chapel. Sometimes Bogle thought that if he had attended any church as frequently as he went to this chapel, well, then, he would have believed something quite different and perhaps even thought of 'God' entirely differently, like a Mohammedan or a Protestant. But he lived at Upton and went to mass, and very soon there was no other God for him than the one to whom everyone at Upton prayed. He went to chapel twice daily, and soon gained a reputation for piety, for which he was praised. From this, he gathered that prayer must be harder for others than it was for him. Nothing felt more natural than directing his thoughts to an unseen realm – or resting his tired knees in the pews. Even more obscure was the connection between this growing reputation and the fifty pounds that Doughty now informed him would be given to him per annum, for his service to the family. With as little fanfare as that, he joined the rank of paid servants.

3.

The Christmas Uprising, 1831

Christmas came, smelling of raisins and sherry. Nobody danced or wore a house on their head. They sat in their chairs and cracked opened bonbons and read the little mottos inside. Christmas passed. It was another month before anyone in Upton got to hearing of the 'Christmas Uprising'. Bogle had to paint over his yearnings for jonkonnu with a fresh portrait of slaves burning their trash houses, Maroons and militia men hunting the culprits, mass executions. His island was on fire.

Every evening, in the newspapers, the tale of this negro uprising expanded, and Mr Doughty expressed some variation on his relief to no longer be in any way involved with the 'cursed sugar trade'. Bogle snuck the newspaper back to his quarters after dark and read the long columns by the light of a single candle, trying to understand if only the north coast was burning and who exactly was being executed in the town squares for refusing to work. But of all the negroes in Jamaica there was only one with a name, as far as *The Times* was concerned – Sam Sharpe – and after a while he understood that he was only upsetting himself. What he wanted to know no English paper would ever tell him.

In the dining room, in February, a woman in a low-cut gown shivered dramatically and put down her knife and fork: 'Yesterday I read that the first fire was lit by a woman, and what do you think she said as she did it? *I know I shall die for it, but my children shall be free.* No doubt it's sentimental of me, Edward, but I was moved.'

Mr Doughty snorted, and accepted a fresh pouring from Bogle at his left shoulder.

'Entire business is unsustainable – I knew that much the moment I stepped off the boat. We'd do well to let the whole island slip into the sea.'

Later that night, in his bunk, Bogle closed his eyes and submitted to a sentimental vision. He put the first torch in Johanna's hand, the words from the newspaper into her mouth, then lay back and watched the whole thing go up like a bonfire.

4.

Reform, 1834

He pored over the explanations and arguments for weeks. No matter how many columns he read on the matter, it all seemed like madness. Could Parliament be mad? He had heard it said that heat affected the English mind – July was especially steamy and oppressive – and on August the first *The Times* informed him that the bill had passed. He folded the paper back up neatly and placed it on a tray beside the port and the cheese.

'Bogle, the trouble is you *will* look for sense where this is none. I'll give you one word: *reform*. It is the mania of the day, and I suppose you could call that a kind of madness . . . Everything must be "reformed". Why? That is the part nobody seems able to explain to me. But nothing must escape our new passion for reform, at home or abroad! We've only just finished deciding every fellow in England who sells boiled sweets or runs a brickworks is to have his own vote, and now that we've tired of meddling in our own affairs, we seem to be turning to the Indies. I'm afraid that's all the sense I can make of it, and it's not much. Apprentices! You only have to think of your what's-her-name – your Johanna. That one wouldn't work when they whipped her! Do they imagine she'll work as an "apprentice"? But that's the Whigs and their "reform" for you. Want to "abolish" the very thing that gave them their high positions in the first place, for God only knows they've no nobility of birth. I say: give me an honest Tory any day. Perfectly obvious landed men should be listened to on political questions, here *and* abroad. Are we not the only ones with something truly at stake? A blind man could see that far. Instead, we busy ourselves making rods for our own backs. Remember our sentimental old friend the Duchess? Would you believe she's begun sending her own peasants out there? To cover the shortfall? Irish, mostly. And there you have it, Bogle. Reform or no reform: someone's got to cut that bloody cane. Thank God I'm out of that accursed business!'

This was stunning news. Jack on a cane piece?

'Well, that's the sad joke of it all. They're mostly dead within a week of arrival. Can't take the climate. Dropping like flies, I heard.'

In bed, he tried to envision this freedom that was not quite freedom. That was and was not. That was 'here', but also 'not now', and would arrive later for Johanna, because she worked outside, but sooner for Ellis, because he didn't. A two-faced freedom, which already belonged to boys like Jack, even if they did the same labour and died like flies. His mind blanked at the paradox. As when that philosophic German stable boy had tried to describe a flying arrow that flew and yet somehow did not, was launched and yet never arrived at its target . . .

5.

Miss Elizabeth

Miss Elizabeth was Mrs Doughty's nurse. She was not beautiful, and it was not the love he had felt for Little Johanna, but he thought it unwise to compare them. Here, in England, love was not a passion but a kind of adding up – a consolation – and Elizabeth's parents were very poor but clean, as was she, and all his life he had been in awe of nurses, beginning with the ladies of the hothouse. By marrying Elizabeth, his own good reputation might be added to hers, Elizabeth's meagre stipend consolidated with his own, and they were both under the patronage of the Doughtys – it was a good prospect. With his two years of partially preserved wages, he might lease a cottage in the village, and he had often noticed this Miss Elizabeth noticing him. From the gardener, Guilfoyle, he learned that if he were to try, he would not cause offence. He began considering marriage.

6.

Black Bogle

When she accepted him, he was quietly pleased, but before he could ask the Doughtys for their blessing, young Henry – Mr Edward's only son and great hope – sickened and died. The boy was just six, and Elizabeth worried that her own failure to save him would count against her. They waited. When, at the end of the year, a fresh confinement of Mrs Doughty's was announced, this seemed as good a time as any. Bogle entered the drawing room fearful, stumbling over his words, but soon realized the Doughtys had expected more inconvenient news, and were glad of the prospect of a pair of married, settled servants who intended to keep working, rather than losing one or both of them to marriage, which was the usual trouble. The only difficulty was that the mania for reform had not yet, as Mr Doughty explained, 'deigned to reach as far as the one, true faith'. They would have to be married in the nearby Anglican Church, at Great Cranford.

At the church door, Bogle held his breath. There were of course the usual whispers and stares from strangers, but almost everyone in the church was known to them and the patronage of the Doughtys proved iron-clad. Nobody laughed. He was, to the people of Poole, 'Black Bogle', the pious, quiet, trusted valet of Mr Doughty, and a unique figure in the village, like the boy at the tollgate with five fingers, or old Miss Ellen who had always lived with Miss James. Marriage only consolidated his position as local curiosity, and he settled into the role, surprising no one and for the most part remaining unsurprised himself, though he could occasionally be startled when he overheard his name in the mouths of Doughty or his guests, invoked as proof, at the dining table, of the 'malicious exaggerations of the Quakers'. For was not our own Black Bogle, husband of our dear Nurse Elizabeth, as content and healthy a fellow as anyone in Poole could ever hope to meet?

7.

Who Am I, Really?

Their first son, John Michael Bogle, was born the next year – a few months after the Doughtys' daughter, Katherine – and then baby Andrew John arrived the year after that. Sometimes Bogle caught a glimpse of his own face, in the small mirror, above the hearth. Who was this well-fed fraud, with a home and a hearth, and a small mirror above that hearth, and two brown boys, and his own evening paper in his lap? At night, in bed, this false figure disappeared, to be replaced once more by the original. Elizabeth grew familiar with the sounds of groans and weeping in the night, gasps, even screams. She sat up and watched her mysterious husband as he thrashed beside her. He seemed to writhe beneath the pressure of some invisible force, as if trying to get out from under a powerful restraining hand.

8.

'slavery'

When John was about two, the word 'freedom' returned to Bogle's evening newspaper. This time it claimed to be unqualified, total, and the date was set: August the first, 1838. He tried to imagine it. All that came to mind was jonkonnu – a foolish vision, he knew. The question was not what the celebrations would look like but what would happen the day after they were done. Still, his eyes were very wide as he read, and when he closed the paper, they filled with tears. So many people, caught in the turning gears. Women, men, children, babies. Generation after generation. His father. His mother. The noble line of Johannas. Ground down. Minds ploughed. Bodies mangled. Souls boiled until they evaporated. Human fuel. Round and round went the treadmill. A hundred years? Two? The philosophical stable boy had claimed three. Cut the people down, plant new ones in the holes. Cut off their hands and their ears and their breasts. The trough of blood. In his dreams, this trough was infinite. In his dreams, he walked alongside it for ever, barefoot through the Bahama grass, screaming. Yet all that the readers of *The Times* would ever know of this treadmill was that it had ceased operations.

He turned his face from Elizabeth and looked to the fire. People in Poole rarely asked or were even curious about anything that had happened to anyone outside of the district of Poole, but every now and then, when the subject unavoidably arose, Elizabeth would swiftly and yet delicately take charge of the enquiry, like the nurse she was after a doctor has left the room:

'Mr Bogle was Mr Doughty's page, as a child, and was of great service to him, on the island . . .'

Of all Little Johanna's extraordinary gifts, perhaps the most treasured had been her skill at 'naming'. She alone knew the secret word which, if said aloud by either party in a marriage, would curse that union and destroy it. Couples on Hope came to her to discover their own secret word – different for each pairing – so that they might not stumble across it accidentally and ruin their happiness, although, as time passed, either the man or the woman would usually invoke it on purpose. Tonight, Bogle's own secret word was all over *The Times*. When Elizabeth got up to attend to the crying baby, he took the paper and thrust it into the fire.

9.

Adding Up & Taking Away

When John was eight and Andrew seven, Elizabeth's lungs filled with a persistent fluid that could not be drained. She gurgled and seemed to be drowning. John ran the half-mile to Upton but by the time Bogle was brought to his wife's bedside she was dead. Everything he had worked for, every hope, every possibility and prospect for the future—

'Bogle! Remarkable news: we will be moving to Tichborne Park in the autumn. My poor brother died on Tuesday – his title has passed to me. A move like this will always have its difficulties, of course, and I don't forget your recent misfortune, but I can promise you Hampshire is beautiful country and a fine spot for a fresh beginning. Mrs Doughty – Lady Doughty-Tichborne! – is keen that you bring your boys. She has even taken the trouble of finding a good Catholic school, it is not far from Reading. I do hope you will consider following her recommendation. She thinks of your welfare always, and an apprenticed boy with a little education is worth his weight in gold – and can usually be counted on to stay clean, besides.'

He was so tired. He nodded.

10.

Tichborne Park

Tichborne Park was a big white house like a wedding cake, and Sir Edward dedicated it to the principle of pleasure. Hunting, eating, drinking and cards were the proper business of the place, and anyone who sat at table and tried to speak of quarterly profits, cotton, sugar, imports, exports, or anything that smelled of merchants and markets, was quickly diverted:

'Bogle, get this man a drink! We'll have no commerce of any kind conducted at dinner!'

It was impossible not to notice the change in Sir Edward. Previously, he had dreaded any contact whatsoever with his surviving brothers and their families. Now that he was the unchallenged head of his clan, much of Bogle's time was spent delivering invitations to Tichbornes near and far, who were suddenly welcome to come for lunch or dinner and even extended stays. His Frenchified young nephew, Roger, visited his pretty cousin 'Kattie' every school holiday – whenever he was down from Stonyhurst – and Bogle often used the example of these two growing young people to imagine the heights and manners of his own boys, over the years. He saw John and Andrew rarely. They sent regular letters home in neat copperplate, a few each term, thanking Lady Doughty for a Christmas pudding, an Easter Basket, a small statue of the Virgin. Tucked behind these formal greetings was usually a page for their father's eyes only, scrawled at great speed, complaining of cold rooms and cold treatment. What could he do? They were motherless boys. If Cook didn't make him a late meal after table was cleared, it was rare that he made an evening meal for himself. What would he do with two motherless boys?

11

Love or Property?

Years later, in court, Bogle was asked if he had been surprised by the 'unnatural closeness' between Katherine 'Kattie' Doughty and her cousin Sir Roger, as if any love between cousins could only be 'unnatural'. It was not so on his island, but he added it to his private list of notable English aversions. At the time, he had held his tongue, and let Sir Edward 'blow up', as was his habit. Bogle listened closely, but he never learned whether the root of the trouble was love or property:

'I want to sell Upton – as is my God-given right – and so off I went to him, and I said: dear nephew, as it happens it appears that now that you are of age, I for some reason cannot proceed without your signature of approval on a legal document. And what do you think he says to me? *'I love Upton and I love your Kattie and I won't let you sell it unless I can marry her.'* I tell you, Bogle, I almost throttled him with my bare hands. His own first cousin! My own damn house to sell! Useless blighter with a frog mother who's mad as a hatter anyway. Over my dead body, Bogle.'

Roger was not to set foot in Tichborne. Sir Edward gathered Bogle and all the servants to tell them this and to explain what each man and woman should do in the event that they spotted the young guardsman on the property. These instructions were martial in tone and comically improbable given Bogle's rheumatism, Cook's substantial girth and Guilfoyle's permanent state of drink. Also, Roger had always been popular below stairs. He drank as heavily as Guilfoyle, out-smoked

Cook, and amused the maids with his attempts to play jigs on the French horn. There was something ludicrous and sad about his banishment. For the first time since they met, Bogle had a feeling about Sir Edward that he had firmly resisted until this moment: pity. Second sight, perhaps. That was the last time Sir Edward's servants would stand together in front of him, listening.

12.

Patronage, 1853

A loud thud came from upstairs. Bogle knew exactly what it was at the moment that he heard it: a body falling to the floor. His first thought was: *How will I live?* After the funeral, he waited two agonizing days, before knocking on the door of Lady Doughty's chamber, hat in hand. She listened to him in a silence he couldn't gauge, dismissing him without an answer. A bleak night in the cottage followed, envisioning the inside of a poorhouse. The next morning, she sent a note asking to see him. She explained that she herself was returning to Upton, but that even out of her employment, Bogle must bring no shame to her dead husband's family, neither through his own conduct nor that of his sons, who were both soon to be out of school and would be in need of gainful employment. She advised him to seek fresh employment with Sir Edward's brother, the new baronet, Sir James, who was moving to Tichborne with his difficult French wife, Henrietta, and their son, Roger. Bogle nodded.

He had been wrong about Hampshire. No one respected or loved him here: his life was patronage, only. Nobody came to the cottage with condolences or sympathy, and he had worked for the new baronet only a few months when Gosford took him aside and explained that Sir James 'wished to make a change'. No reason was given. Bogle tried to catch the wily steward's eye. They had both heard Lady Tichborne refer to Bogle as 'that ape'. She made no disguise of wiping every cup he passed her with a handkerchief before deigning to drink from it.

'I'm sorry about it, Bogle,' said Gosford, speaking to a patch on the wall just above his head. 'The decision has been made.'

Bogle nodded.

13.

Surety

All efforts he made on behalf of his sons came to nothing. He could find no apprenticeship for his eldest and so had to appeal to Lady Doughty, who agreed to make enquiries. But the chemist she found in Nottingham was a failure. The chemist claimed John fought with the customers. John said the customers would not take advice from him, and feared his remedies were poisons. He was let go. Bogle travelled to Upton once more to appeal to Lady Doughty in person. He tried to explain how bleak the prospect was for his boys, 'their colour being against them', and wondered aloud if it would be better if they all left the country. The Lady sighed and informed him that although Sir Edward had 'left no legal provision whatsoever', she would, in the name of charity and Christian conscience, continue the sum of fifty pounds in perpetuity. Bogle nodded. He stood still a beat longer than was polite, in the hope of receiving a piece of paper, something signed, anything whatsoever that he could hold in his hand as surety, after all these years.

'Good luck to you, Mr Bogle – and goodbye.'

14.

Jane Fisher

Lady Doughty's annuity would keep him in his cottage, just about, but the problem of his sons remained. Both young men despaired of England in a manner their father rarely had – he had not often had the time for despair. Even now, despair had to wait, as love intervened, or at least convenient affection. She was a local spinster, the daughter of a soldier. She taught at the village school – another profession for which Bogle had only respect – and went by the pretty name of Jane Fisher. He had spoken to her for a few minutes every market day for a decade. Curious-looking, flame-haired, with eyes that sprang too far from their sockets, she knew something of what it was to be stared at. They had that much in common. It was Jane's idea to sail to Australia – as Guilfoyle the gardener had done the year before – and he felt glad then that he had chosen a woman and not a girl, and one who also felt she did not belong, and therefore did not feel the complacent caution of those who have always been safely rooted. She was a good prospect. This time, he would be married in the church of his choosing.

15.

Saltwater

Although glad to leave England, he was terrified, as ever, of the sea, and it was a fear that never abated, not for a single day in those three long months. His rheumatism was tormented by the movement of the boat. But upon arrival in New South Wales, he found his annuity went a little further. They were able to lease a cottage of five rooms, and soon added a child, Henry, to their happiness. Within the year, his eldest, John, was making a living playing the fiddle wherever people wished to hear it, and young Andrew was apprenticed to a hairdresser. When a letter arrived from Lady Doughty with the news of the death of her nephew, Sir Roger, at sea, Bogle wept. Not for Sir Roger. Out of a delayed and ecstatic relief, that he himself should have successfully crossed an ocean once again, as his father had before him, and yet not died in the attempt.

16.

Johanna's Warning

Im give wid one hand. Im take wid de other. On the island, forty-three was not an impossible age to have a child nor even an unlikely one, but he was not on the island, and at forty-three Jane was delivered of a second child, called Edward, only to die three weeks later of 'uterine haemorrhage'. Bogle stared at these incomprehensible words on the doctor's report and heard Johanna's warning just as clearly as if she were in the room with him. He helped dig the grave himself. The next day he held his fourth motherless son in his arms, so tiny, so in need of sustenance. In despair, he tried sheep's milk. A week later, he dug another grave.

17.

Lady Mabella de Tichborne's Warning

Long before the Conquest, when the greenwood abounded, there were already Tichbornes in England. But their first real dent in the historical record occurs in the reign of Henry II. By that time, they were settled in Hampshire. The sentimental Lady Mabella de Tichborne had long been married to a Sir Roger, who was not sentimental, and this difference in temperament had been the cause of much misery between them. She was generous, he miserly. Where she was soft and forgiving, he was harsh and unrelenting in his judgements, once they were formed. Now, on her deathbed, she wanted a guarantee from Sir Roger that he would do 'something for the poor'. Sir Roger bent over his dying wife and told her that if she could manage to get out of bed, and crawl around their landholdings with a lit torch in her hand, well, then he promised to give the poor exactly as much grain as she could enclose before her torch went out. She managed twenty-three acres. Just before she collapsed and died, she declared that if the grain thus enclosed were not doled out annually, as promised, then a curse would fall upon the Tichbornes. Seven sons would be followed by seven daughters, and the line of Tichborne would end. Ruin would befall them.

Thus began the Tichborne Dole. The family prospered. Two hundred years later, when young Chidiock Tichborne lost his impractical head over the Scottish Queen, it must be admitted that the family's faith in the protection of the Dole wavered. Some years later, James I handed them a baronetcy: faith was restored. For the next two hundred years, the portion of land called the Crawls continued to provide grain for Hampshire's poor, until the seventh baronet, a Sir Henry, grew tired of the indigent mob convening on his land once a year, and put a stop to it.

But witchery is patient. That baronet had seven sons. His eldest son, another Henry, had seven daughters. His third son, Edward, did manage to have a son, but he was short-lived, dying at only six, and Sir Edward's next child was a girl. Another grandson, born in the same year, lived longer, and took the name of Sir Roger, seven hundred years after his predecessor.

18.

What is Real?

'It was my son Andrew who paid for my passage back. That was good of him. But only my youngest boy came with me — my Henry. We sailed on the *Rakaia*. Sir Roger sailed first class, on the money that Lady Tichborne sent him. We were in second class. It was very difficult with my rheumatism. And by the time we returned to England, my pension had been stopped. Lady Doughty stopped it, because I swore Sir Roger was true, when Lady Doughty and all of the Tichbornes believed he was false — excepting Roger's own mother. Then his poor mother died. And now it seems all is lost. But I shall be staunch for Sir Roger. I have always been staunch.'

Bogle reached into his tattered coat pocket and drew out a carefully clipped and yellowing square of newspaper. He placed it on the table between them:

A handsome REWARD will be given to any person who can furnish such information as will discover the fate of ROGER CHARLES TICHBORNE. He sailed from the Port of Rio Janeiro on the 20th of April, 1854, in the ship La Bella, and has never been heard of since; but a report reached England to the effect that a portion of the crew and passengers of a vessel of that name was picked up by a vessel bound to Australia, Melbourne, it is believed. It is not known whether the said Tichborne was amongst the drowned or saved. He would at the present time be about 32 years of age; is of a delicate constitution, rather tall, with very light brown hair and blue eyes. Mr Tichborne is the son of Sir James Tichborne, Bart. (now deceased) and is heir to all his estates. The advertiser is instructed to state that a most liberal REWARD will be given for any information that may definitely point out his fate. All replies to be addressed to Mr Arthur Cubitt, Missing Friends Office, Bridge-street, Sydney, New South Wales.

'No reward has come to me yet. But I am staunch. I will remain staunch.'

19.

The Door Opens Inward

Wonder had reduced Mrs Touchet to nunlike silence. All her life she had been trying to open a locked door. She had pushed as hard as she could upon it – using means both personal and metaphysical – in the belief that the door opened outwards, onto ultimate reality, and that this was a sight few people are ever granted in this lifetime – particularly if they happen to be born female. Now, without any effort on her part, the door had come loose on its hinges. Finally, she could open it! But to her astonishment, it opened inwards. She had been standing inside the very thing she'd been looking for.

'Oh, here is my son, Henry! But – Sir Roger?'

Mrs Touchet roused herself. The young Bogle stood just behind their table, rigid as a soldier in a sentry box.

'Sir Roger is occupied. And I should not have been gone so long. Excuse us, Mrs Touchet – my father tires easily. We must go. At present I am not liquid in funds but Sir Roger assures me he has an account here and it will be added to his bill.'

Mrs Touchet blushed: 'That is completely unnecessary, the very least I——'

'Sir Roger will attend to it. Goodbye, Mrs Touchet.'

The senior Bogle took back his newspaper square, folded it carefully, and placed it in his pocket.

As he stood to leave, Mrs Touchet thrust her hand inside her reticule and drew out a *carte de visite*:

'If I can be of any assistance whatsoever.'

Henry stepped forward to take the card, frowning at the name – it was William's – before closing it in his fist: 'Thank you. And goodbye.'

On the train back to Hurstpierpoint, Mrs Touchet felt that the train itself was still and that it was her mind that raced forward, faster and faster. The door opened inwards! The exotic island of her conception was not some utterly different and unimaginable world. It was neither far away nor long ago. Indeed, it seemed to her now that the two islands were, in reality, two sides of the same problem, profoundly intertwined, and that this was a truth that did not have to be sought out or hunted down, it was not hidden behind a veil or screen or any kind of door. It was and had always been everywhere, like weather.

That evening, as soon as she reached Little Rockley, Mrs Touchet went straight to the small *bureau plat* in her bedroom and wrote it all out, just as she remembered it.

VOLUME EIGHT

Come, all ye jolly covies, vot faking do admire,
And pledge them British authors who to our line aspire;
Who, if they were not gemmen born, like us had kicked at trade,
And every one had turned him out a genuine fancy blade,
And a trump.

'Tis them's the boys as knows the vorld, 'tis them as knows mankind,
And vould have picked his pocket too, if Fortune (vot is blind)
Had not to spite their genius, stuck them in a false position,
Vere they can only write about, not execute their mission,
Like a trump.

If they goes on as they're begun, things soon will come about,
And ve shall be the upper class, and turn the others out;
Their laws ve'll execute ourselves, and raise their helevation,
That's tit for tat, for they'd make that the only recreation
Of u trump.

FROM 'THE FAKER'S NEW TOAST', *TAIT'S EDINBURGH MAGAZINE*, 1841

I.

Appeals to the Public, 1873

Mrs Touchet was under the singular delusion – common at this stage of the process – that everything was connected. On the one hand, she wondered if she might be going mad. On the other, the schoolchildren on the common were hopscotching to a new rhyme:

Now I wonder what he thinks of,
As in Newgate he does stop,
How he'd like to be at Wapping,
In a big old butcher's shop!

Lively Tichborne debate was everywhere. It became the baker's sole topic of conversation. The Hurstpierpoint Working Men's club advertised a free lecture – *Betrayal of Sir Roger! Can Right Prevail against Might?* – to be presented in the club room, above the old Horse Inn, Tuesday week. She noted an especially devoted Tichbornism among the drinking and gambling interests. Every pub counter in Horsham had its Tichborne Fund Box, and Sarah came back from the races with the going odds for the criminal trial.

Only William was immune. He was busy with his Jacobite novel – *The Manchester Rebels of the Fatal '45* – and with the 'Great Pretender' so much on his mind, he found any mention of the small-time fraud 'Sir Roger' completely exasperating. Mrs Touchet became expert at hiding a new kind of contraband: Tichborne Toby jugs and figurines, Tichborne pamphlets and newspapers, a Tichborne biscuit tin with a badly drawn portrait of the Claimant upon the lid . . . All ordered by Sarah, paid for on subscription, and delivered straight to the house. It was like the Garibaldi mania all over again. Except this time she found it impossible to maintain an amused distance. She got into the habit of retrieving something called the *Tichborne Gazette* from the kitchen woodpile and staying up till the wee hours reading it, intrigued by its heady mix of Tichborne advocacy side by side with articles on land reform, jury reform, republicanism, trade unionism, payment for MPs, 'universal suffrage' – if the universe excluded women – Anti-Catholic screeds and whole pages given over to the anti-vaccination movement, for who knew the true intentions of these rich men and their needles? She read that a reinforced bed of wooden planks had been provided for the Claimant, as the regulation prison hammock could not hold him. She read that the Claimant's bail was set at ten thousand pounds. Then, on the twenty-fifth of March, Mrs Touchet read a plea from the man himself, on the front page of the *Evening Standard*:

> *Cruelly persecuted as I am, there is but one course that I could see, and that is, to adopt the suggestion so many have made to me, viz. To 'appeal to the British public' for funds for my defence, and in doing so I appeal to every British soul who is inspired by a love of justice and fair play, and who is willing to defend the weak against the strong.*

> *All donations to The Tichborne Defence Fund, 376 The Strand.*

For a wild moment she considered going to the address given. What would she find there? A round table, perhaps, with Bogle and son seated at it, and Guildford Onslow, and that distant Tichborne cousin, and the family friend with the glass eye, what's-his-name, the gullible antiquarian, oh, what *was* his name – Francis Baigent! – and perhaps a few publicans and racetrack owners, and Guilfoyle, the gardener, back from New South Wales, half-drunk in his chair, with his dirty boots up on the table . . .

'Eliza. *Eliza*. Are you listening to a word I say?'

Eliza looked up from the forgotten sewing in her lap. William was in the doorway, very red-faced, with what looked like a thin book in his hand, held high like a piece of evidence.

'What is it, William?'

He walked over to her and put it into her hands. It was not a book, but a pamphlet, encased in handsome dark-green Morocco with gold trim:

THE ARTIST AND THE AUTHOR

A STATEMENT OF FACTS

By the artist, GEORGE CRUIKSHANK

Proving that the Distinguished Author,

Mr. W. Harrison Ainsworth, is 'labouring under

a singular delusion' with respect to the origin of

'The Miser's Daughter', 'The Tower of London', etc.

'But when did it arrive? I was reading very late last night – I must have oversl—'

'First post. What has *that* to do with anything?'

Mrs Touchet bit her lip.

'*Etcetera*. What does the blackguard *MEAN* by "ETCETERA"?'

'Oh, William. Nobody takes George seriously, and anyone who employs the phrase "statement of fact" is surely expecting disbelief. If he's not back on the drink he is evidently deranged. My advice is to keep your distance.'

'I will reply in kind. I will *not* have my reputation dragged through the mud in this manner.'

'But how many copies of this thing can he possibly have printed – or sold? At sixpence? No, no, William, I've thought about it and I would advise you most strongly to ignore this – this – provocation. To respond would surely only bring more publicity to what is, at the moment, a very obscure—'

'I intend to write to him directly, and to directly confront him.'

'Well, that is not at all like you, William.'

'I can't think what you mean – it is entirely like me. Things can hardly be left as they are. The one thing I cannot abide is bad blood between old friends.'

The one thing you can't abide, amended Eliza, silently, is not to be liked.

2.

Freedom!

They had arrived early, and were rather pleased with their position at the front of this giant crowd. But then the great doors of Newgate heaved opened, the crowd pushed forward, Sarah was swept out of sight, entirely lost to Mrs Touchet – and here came the Claimant! The noise was tremendous. Banners waved, hats flew, the crowd surged once more. She looked for Sarah but it was impossible. The carnage of Peterloo flashed through her mind. Her face must have betrayed her panic: through the cacophony she heard someone very close by calling her name. She looked up and saw Henry Bogle. He was on the same jerry-rigged platform as the Claimant, alongside his father and several others, with one brown hand outstretched to her:

'Mrs Touchet! Quickly! Take my hand!'

She hesitated for a long moment, for reasons she obscured even from herself. The crowd surged once again. She took his hand. Space was made for her among the peculiar collection of people on the dais. They were about a dozen, all told, huddled together in the substantial shadow of the Claimant, for whom the crowd cried out.

Speak, Sir Roger!

We believe you, Sir Roger!

But it was Guildford Onslow and his walrus moustache who stepped forward:

'Friends! Supporters! Make no mistake about the facts. If it were not for the working classes – which I call the noble part of the British public – our Sir Roger would still be in gaol!'

A great cheer met this 'statement of fact'. But was it true? From her freshly elevated position Mrs Touchet could see far across the human sea. Flat-capped men and poorly dressed women were certainly not hard to make out, forming little groups, holding up curious banners:

Cabinet-Makers Unite for Tichborne!
The Whitechapel Debating Club Has No Faith in Tattoo-humbug!
MIGHT AGAINST RIGHT IS ALWAYS WRONG
Working Men of Croydon Are Lovers of Fair Play
THE WILLESDEN TICHBORNE RELEASE
ASSOCIATION

Even to the unsentimental Mrs Touchet there was something inspiring and moving in the idea of all those earnestly collected pennies and donated subscriptions. A snatch of Shelley came to mind: *Ye are many, they are few . . .*

If only Onslow were a poet! But he was a country squire and spoke like one, arguing his case persuasively but without beauty. How could it be right that all the money and power of the state should once again be levied against this poor man without a penny in his pocket? Who would defend Sir Roger in his second trial? Would the injustices of the first be repeated? Why had that court been packed with aristocrats? Why were no decent working men allowed in? How many Jesuits had been on that jury? Another roar went up, accompanied by the sound of small coins hitting the sides of buckets. Mrs Touchet did not recall an excess of aristocrats or Jesuits at the first trial, and was quite certain she'd seen many a poor man. And what choice did government have but to accept the cost of cases imposed upon it? But such dry and inconvenient facts were of no consequence here, in this ocean of feeling. Now Onslow ceded the stage to the Claimant. Considerable space had to be made for him: Mrs Touchet found herself shuffled to the very edge of the dais, with a squint-eyed woman she recognized as the wife, and several of the Claimant's ragged children, all clinging to their mother's ugly skirt. Here was an opportunity to examine 'Sir Roger' from the back. He had not yet reached the proportions of a Daniel Lambert, but seven weeks of Newgate rations had somehow added several stones to his frame. Nor had prison time made him any more eloquent, or rid him of his Wapping taint:

'I am no talker, my friends. Am I here to tell you I'm Sir Roger himself? Not a bit of it. You'll decide that for your own selves, like free Englishmen. I am only here to say: *Every man deserves a fair trial.* Even a poor one. And that's all what I ask for and all what any man deserves. And I'll say this and all: no doubt lawyers are very handy at many things, and they can often make black appear white – but more frequently I am sorry to say they make white appear black!'

If the Queen herself had appeared on this little stage – out of her widow's weeds, whistling a jolly tune – she would not have received a more jubilant response. *Go it, Roger! Right against might!* Mrs Touchet observed this peculiar man as he accepted the public's adulation without a moment's anxiety, as if it were only to be expected. A pulse of doubt ran through her mind. Wouldn't a fraud be nervous? Wouldn't a fraud make more of an effort to convince?

The crowd began to chant for Black Bogle. He stepped forward, slowly removing his battered hat. A spontaneous, urgent, respectful silence spread, for the people knew he spoke quietly. They had listened to his tale in court, read it in the sheets, heard it sung in the street – even watched it upon the stage. They were not tired of it yet. *I first knew Sir Roger, when he was still a boy, at Tichborne Park . . .*

Eliza listened along with them, but felt that she alone truly heard the man, pierced as she was by a new awareness, a subterranean insight. A person is a bottomless thing! She might rush the stage to proclaim it: *A person is a bottomless thing!* The people saw only the battered hat, the rigid fingers, the sparse tufts of hair, the dark skin, so unlike their own.

They heard only the quiet voice, speaking lilting words in a certain arrangement. And mistook all of this for a person. Kindly, simple, old 'Black Bogle'. They could not know what he had seen, nor where he had been. But perhaps, reflected Mrs Touchet, this is always the case. We mistake each other. Our whole social arrangement a series of mistakes and compromises. Shorthand for a mystery too large to be seen. *If they knew what I knew they would feel as I do!* Yet even once one had glimpsed behind the veil which separates people, as she had – how hard it proves to keep the lives of others in mind! Everything conspires against it. Life itself.

With this train of thought Mrs Touchet had brought herself almost to the brink of tears. She did not immediately notice that Mr Bogle had already finished, and now, as he turned back towards her to make his exit – unmoved by the wild applause he had provoked – Mrs Touchet once again felt an urge to rush forward, to let him know that she, alone, understood. Since their transformative day at the chophouse she had, indeed, 'kept him in mind', and now stared beseechingly at him, so as to convey the sentiment, but Mr Bogle only smiled politely at the queer lady journalist, stepped round her, and joined his son at the very edge of the dais.

BOGLE SPEAKS TRUTH screamed a man, very close to the left eardrum of Mrs Touchet, spraying spittle on her shoe. She looked down to examine the screamer, one poor man among many, in a flat cap and a worn pair of trousers, with hands blackened by his labour. How had Mr Bogle managed to so captivate this inarticulate stranger? Why did Mrs Touchet – with all her good intentions, her facility with language, her capacious imagination – still struggle to make herself understood?

3.

Magnetism

Magnetism, Mrs Touchet supposed. The ability to hold the attention of a crowd. She had often wondered about this quality. Women spoke in public so rarely, and those few she had seen attempt it generally depressed her. Too much prevarication and pleading, nervous babbling, pious lecturing. An exception was Elizabeth Heyrick. *She* had spoken well. But that had been in a Leicester drawing room. Public speaking requires the freedom to speak in public, without fear of masculine censure or ridicule, which was never in short supply, even in supposedly enlightened gentlemen. Take Dickens! Remembering his well-aired opinions on the matter of feminine public oration, Mrs Touchet felt freshly murderous: she wished she could raise him from the grave with a stroke of her pen the better to put him back down in the ground again. How could a woman ever improve when fenced in on all sides by contempt? When given so few opportunities? Then again, Mr Bogle had the gift, as did 'Sir Roger', and neither of them could be said to have had much practice. Was magnetism a natural attribute, then? The most magnetic person she'd ever known was Dickens himself, and she counted herself among the few who had understood that the source of that man's attraction was not success or fame or even money but rather something innate, for she had sat next to the obscure, twenty-two-year-old *Boz*, and watched the whole table turn to him whenever he spoke. Of course, most men had no such gift: on the contrary, they bored her to tears. And heads have always turned for women, too, in tribute to their beauty. Being so tall and narrow and punishing of aspect, Mrs Touchet had been largely excluded from that arena of influence in her youth. Now she was old. The exclusion was total. No one wanted to sit beside her at dinner any more, and even at those long-ago literary affairs all her conversations had been private. Still, more and more these days she suspected that women, too, could possess magnetic powers of attraction – above and beyond mere beauty – and that she might herself be such a woman, and that, moreover, there might be a great deal more of such women than was commonly supposed. But how to test this theory?

4.

A Public Literary Dinner, Manchester Town Hall, 12th January 1838

The trouble was a lack of clarity. The original invitation was so worded as to make it very difficult to know who this 'public dinner' was for, exactly. The mayor spoke of 'honouring Manchester's prodigal literary son'. But on the second page ominous mention arrived of 'your friend "*Boz*",' whom it was hoped would 'also consent to be present'. Mrs Touchet steeled herself: she was expert in the management of masculine pride. But William wrote back without betraying a hint of envy or professional anxiety: *I need not enlarge upon the merits of Mr. Dickens, as by common consent he has been installed in the throne of letters vacated by Scott.* It surprised her. Then again, William loved Manchester, dinner, being in public, being honoured. He decided to make a five-day trip of it: 'Pick Crossley's brains – and steal from his library!' Mrs Touchet had never known her cousin to visit Mr James Crossley and return without a new novel in mind. And a new novel, once begun, would soon be finished, necessitating a large, celebratory publication dinner at the Sussex Hotel, in Blackfriars, which many literary young men would inevitably attend, in the fullness of time producing their own novels, which would only necessitate yet more literary dinners. Thus the treadmill of literature turns . . .

To be busy, for William, was to be alive. Not content with writing three chapters a day, he began interfering with Mrs Touchet's administrative arrangements, writing letters willy-nilly to Manchester, arranging accommodation, deciphering timetables, and other matters that she had long ago perfected and with which she required no assistance. Thwarted, she hovered about his desk, tutting and sighing. She tended to think of thirty-three as the age of burgeoning wisdom. It was the age at which she had begun, finally, to know herself. Now William was of Christ's age. Was he wise? She did an accounting: estranged from his wife, with money troubles and litigious in-laws, he was certainly no longer the carefree literary young man she had first met, and first loved. Did *he* know that? Reading over his shoulder, she thought that the only thing more obscure, to William, than the motivations of other people, were his own:

Now, in respect of the public dinner. Is it to be given to me or Dickens — or to both? Acting upon your former letter, I invited my friends to accompany me, imagining the dinner was to be given in my honour: but I have no feeling whatever in the matter, and only desire to have a distinct understanding about it.

He had feelings; they needed careful management. To this end, Mrs Touchet set up a separate channel of communication between herself and Crossley, with the aim of ensuring, behind the scenes, an equal honouring. It was a business of some delicacy and secrecy, but it was managed. The twenty-six-year-old genius and the thirty-three-year-old prodigal son reached Manchester on the last day of Christmas, with snow on the ground and a bitter chill in the air, but only warm feelings towards each other.

5.

Doubly Blessed

Knowing that both men loved to walk and 'work up an appetite' – for a day's writing as much as for their lunch – Mrs Touchet advised William to take Charles on a tour of Manchester. William bored his brilliant friend with the facade of the old Ainsworth town house, the gates of his school, and the inside of the Cross Street Chapel – 'My grandfather preached here! I'm from a long line of dissenters!' – before embarking on a more interesting series of wrong turns, which spat them out unexpectedly at the very edge of St Michael's and the Angels. Charles was enthralled. Here, on the putrid wasteland, amid the whores and the beggars, he watched two men hammer planks over a mass grave. It was the outcasts and the superfluous that fascinated him. Such people interested William, too – up to a point. He was a King Street boy: the poor lived elsewhere. Charles, by contrast, had an instinct for the desperate corners. In one morning, they saw more ragged schools, men's hostels, shelters for fallen women and orphanages than William had seen during his entire youth in the city. Finally, with fingers numb and stomachs growling, they made their way to Mount Street. Crossley met them on the steps of the Friends Meeting House – as prearranged by Mrs Touchet – and carefully set the tone of equal esteem:

'Dickens and Ainsworth! Ainsworth and Dickens! Manchester is doubly blessed!'

'You have grown, James.'

'Only in one direction. Reading is poor exercise!'

'Well, your mind outruns most men's. Dickens – Crossley.'

Back in Hurstpierpoint, Mrs Touchet met the post-chaise each morning and did her best to read between the lines. From William's letters, she gathered that both men were honoured and delighted, but also that Dickens had been forced to endure, at table, an extended retelling of her cousin's romantic, highly unlikely, childhood memories of Peterloo. Picture fifteen-year-old William, leading his small 'brigade' of King Street boys, 'hearts filled with Jacobite dreams', to the edge of Peter's Field, where they throw stones at the Manchester Yeomanry, jeer at the magistrates, cheer Henry Hunt, and narrowly escape with their lives . . . William's letter was very long. Towards the end, she permitted herself to leap over paragraphs.

Charles' letter was short. She had meant to savour it with a cup of tea beside the fire. Instead, she read it stood stock-still in the street, unable to stop once she'd started. Crossley had a disreputable book he wanted to give William – a first edition of *The Newgate Calendar* – and so the young literary men reconvened the following night, at a chophouse. They found Crossley and his sizeable belly in a quiet corner, wedged between wall and table, already encircled by a half-dozen steaming dishes. *I was wondering all night however he should be got out, but still more amazed how he ever got in.* Mrs Touchet laughed out loud. Reading *A Christmas Carol,* many years later, she replaced the Ghost of Christmas Present in her mind with this vision of Crossley, looming over his cornucopia of food, wedged into a corner . . .

William returned to Sussex in a lively, bright-eyed mood. He tickled her from behind when she passed him on the stairs and looked more handsome than ever. How easy he was to love when he was happy! How easy everyone is to love in that state. Looking back, she always considered this smoothly organized, perfectly stage-managed trip to Manchester to be her last, great domestic success. It was anyway the last one she cared about. Six weeks later, Frances died. The children returned to school in Manchester. William dived into his new novel. Mrs Touchet, bereft of occupation, confronted the void.

6.

Summer 1872

It was like the old days. She was standing in the very same town halls and corn exchanges and theatres she had stood in with Frances, only now she was old. Getting old turned out to be a very strange business. She was learning so many new things about time. It could twist and bend until the past met the present, and vice versa. She was both here and there, then and now, it was invigorating, but also sometimes confusing.

Once again, a young son of Africa stood, like a challenge, before her.

But this time he was not at the podium, demonstrating the inner workings of a manacle, he was by her side, in a ticket office, ensuring she purchased a return.

Once again, she had to lie to William. She claimed to be passing her days in the Reading Room of the British Library, researching the history of the Touchets, an idea he found eccentric in the extreme, but did not debate as long as she came home in time for dinner.

In reality, she was on a train, heading to a meeting.

Sometimes it was impossible to travel and return within a day.

On those occasions she told him she was 'staying overnight in Manchester, with my niece'.

And today that part, at least, happened to be true.

7.

Manchester Free Trade Hall

For reasons of convenience, they had travelled on separate trains and now Henry was late. She stood outside the Free Trade Hall on Peter Street, on the opposite side of the road, as he had instructed. He had been surprisingly firm about this. Over the summer, Tichborne meetings had grown ever larger and more unruly, until they were 'no longer suitable for a woman to enter alone'. *Old woman* he meant, but did not say. In return she pretended not to notice the stares and commentary that followed this young son of Africa wherever he went. Waiting for him, it occurred to her that she, too, had become an object of fascination: people did not expect an old woman to be so tall.

Preferring to stare rather than be stared at, she examined the crowds streaming towards the entrance. It was the biggest rally so far, and would also be the most lucrative, at a shilling a head. She had attended them all, since the Claimant's release, in April. By now, they tended to merge together in her mind. First the Claimant and Bogle were mobbed at a train station. Sometimes Bogle stood on a bench and spoke directly to the people, but more often than not they were rescued by a local publican or racetrack owner or jovial lord of the manor, and whisked off in a private carriage to be taken to lunch, or out shooting, or simply paraded through the streets of a town already plastered with their pictures. Then, in the early evenings, the event proper would begin. The speakers took their turn at the podium: a representative of the town, then Onslow, Tichborne, Bogle. Sometimes soldiers from Roger's old regiment spoke, or the army doctor, or the cousin, or the friend of the family: Francis Baigent. Rallying cries, pleas for donations and stump speeches followed – many of them reckless. More than once she heard Onslow claim that the Chief Justice was a secret Jesuit, in league with the Tichbornes, and had been promised a pay-off, in the form of land and property. This was the sort of talk that could jeopardize the next trial, or gaol a man for contempt of court. And all around the stage, in the cheap seats, the hysteria grew. Any mention of King's Counsel, Justice Bovill, the jury or the Tichbornes themselves prompted wild howling from the crowd. Frequently, she heard the cry: *A hanging's too good for them!* She tried to remind herself that what she was witnessing was a sincere mass emotion – dispossession – being twisted and manipulated for ulterior purposes. Still, they frightened her. Were these 'the people'? Were these *her* people? Only Bogle kept his head. Her admiration for him grew daily. His story never exceeded its bounds, never turned to conspiracy or illogic. He never raged, never accused. He was simply immovable for truth, even if Mrs Touchet found she could not accept that what he so steadfastly repeated was, indeed, the truth. But just as she preferred a Mohammedan to an atheist, she felt she would always choose Bogle's breed of conviction and belief over the cynicism and venality of a man like Onslow. Was there something else? Perhaps there was also something in aesthetics. Onslow was such a red-faced walrus of a man! When young she had not found kindness attractive: she had overlooked it. Goodness, yes, magnetism, certainly, but kindness had not registered. Now that she was old, kindness seemed to her to be the only thing that really mattered. The only truly attractive quality. And what a kind face had Mr Bogle . . .

At first, she had been conscientious in getting all the business of a Tichborne meeting down, however mad. Now, under the weight of repetition, she did not often take out her pen, preferring to limit herself to noting the surroundings. For example, this hall. Such a mammoth orange *palazzo*! The last time she was in Manchester, the Corn Law had not yet been repealed, and all this was still a field of grass. Yet it remained possible to fall under the building's charming spell of fraudulent antiquity – even to forget that Peter's Field had ever existed. Lovely how the sun played upon the sandstone! She had never been to Italy – she had never been anywhere – and felt grateful for these local imitations.

8.

The Facade

Where *was* Henry? She felt the vexing pity of passers-by. Did they think her a tragic old woman with nothing to do? She tilted her head defiantly upwards, towards the facade. Nine allegorical stone ladies, spaced at intervals, looked back down at her. She thought that the one in the centre must be *Free Trade* herself – she was covered in barley and looked smug about Repeal – while the lady with the lyre and the pen, face frozen in self-regard, was surely *Art*. But was the woman with the boat *Trade* or *Commerce*? The elegant, classically draped girl with a cotton distaff and a lot of packages and machinery was probably *Industry*, but Mrs Touchet had visited the lady cotton workers of Manchester, many moons ago, and felt that the resemblance was slight. She was on safer ground with the continents. *Europe* looked like Athena, with one hand open, in expectation of payment. *Asia* had a box of tea on one side, a barrel of spice on the other, and treasures in her lap. She, like Europe, was fully dressed. *America* was half-naked, barbarous. She had boxes of cotton and molasses, wore an Indian headdress, and kept a handful of cigars close by. How the cotton and molasses had come to exist in the first place was a mystery that Mrs Touchet thought might be answered by the next lady along. But on this topic *Africa* was silent. Like America, she had misplaced her clothes, and around her bare feet was gathered the bounty she had provided to the world. Ivory, lions, grapes, some exotic fruits which Mrs Touchet could not identify, ostrich feathers, pots and carpets. Nothing else.

'Mrs Touchet – forgive my lateness. Are you well? What are you looking at?'

'Oh! Henry!' She had recently extended the pockets in all her skirts until they comfortably accommodated a pad and a pen. The result of this feminine ingenuity was that she often had large ink-spots on her wrinkled fingers, just like a schoolgirl. 'Nothing. Nothing at all. Shall we?'

9.

Visiting the Ainsworth Girls, 28th October 1838

God preserve me from novel-writing, thought Mrs Touchet. God preserve me from that tragic indulgence, that useless vanity, that blindness! In a cold dormitory, two hundred miles away, three heartbroken, motherless girls had hoped to be visited by their father. But William was busy at his desk, dreaming up Jack Sheppard:

'Eliza, it would help me very much if you would go in my place. Dickens is eager to make the trip – he's determined to try the train. Forster will accompany him. I've written all the necessary letters of introduction, our Miss Harding at the school expects you, and these jolly Grant Brothers await Charles. You know the city well enough. I wish I could go but this is a vital moment for me – I am knocking on the door of the third volume. May I count on you?'

On the journey up she resolved to say absolutely nothing of interest. She would address all necessary conversation to the gruff and unappealing Mr Forster, and ignore his brilliant friend, whom she suspected of being a vampire. She had no wish to appear in any more novels. But it was her first time on a train: she clutched the sides of the seat in terror, amusing Charles greatly, weakening her own defences. Here was an irresistible and irrepressible young man. She felt equally fascinated and repulsed by him. He was somehow too easy to talk to. And far too good at listening.

'Now, Forster, what d'you say? *I* say we take a very good cake to these poor, motherless Ainsworth girls before we do anything else. Cotton mills can wait and so can these prosperous Grants. Cake and comfort must come first!'

Was he really so good or did he only want to be seen to be good? Does it matter?

10.

The World of Sentiment

She remembered a baker's shop in King Street: a lemon cake was selected. All three of them put a hand to the cake-box in the cab, to steady it, and the silliness of this meant that they arrived at Miss Harding's School for Young Ladies in too light a mood for the errand upon which they had come. Charles recognized this before she did. In a moment his face transformed, from levity to sympathy, and found its reflection in three melancholy girls, walking the long corridor as if towards an execution. Mrs Touchet remembered that about school: no information was ever given ahead of time, the better to keep you in a permanent state of submission and fear. But now smiles broke out on their faces, and Fanny – always the boldest – began to run. Charles was exuberantly hugged, and hugged each girl in turn. Mrs Touchet, who had known these girls as long as they'd known anything or anyone, stood to one side with her hands folded neatly in front of her.

'And here is Mrs Touchet,' said Emily, who always remembered her manners. 'And it's Mr Forster, isn't it? What a nice surprise. How kind of you all to come.'

Mr Forster, who seemed just as uncertain as Eliza Touchet in this world of sentiment, busied himself cutting the cake.

II.

Cotton & Confidence

The traffic was incredible, they had the devil of a time moving through the town. As ever, the driver had a lot to say about the matter. Charles bent halfway out of the carriage to catch it all, but the man's Lancaster accent proved too thick, even for Charles. Mrs Touchet was tasked with translation:

'Well, in essence he blames Villiers.'

Charles was fascinated: 'In what way blames him?'

'Blames him for the traffic. If you gather five thousand men in one place for a protest – or so this man feels – traffic will inevitably be the result. I must say, I see his point.'

Charles laughed. Forster frowned greatly: 'Men are perverse. Working men especially. How rarely they seem to know their own interests!'

It was said with weary superiority and decorated with a sigh. Mrs Touchet couldn't let it stand:

'Perhaps not all working men enjoy having their interests explained to them by the sons of earls, Mr Forster.'

'You DISAGREE with repeal, Mrs Touchet?'

'I didn't say that.'

'It is obvious to me that the law should be repealed – FOR THE AGE OF THE LANDLORD IS OVER.'

Not for the first time, Mrs Touchet wondered why this Mr Forster could not modulate his voice as other people do. His whispers were perfectly audible; his normal voice was a foghorn. When even slightly excited, he sounded like a castaway trying to attract attention.

'Agreed. And as far as the Honourable Mr Villiers risks his own family's profits – *if* he does – I will salute him. But when one age passes, shouldn't we ask what is to replace it?'

'It is the age of MEN WITH IDEAS, Mrs Touchet! The age of men of INDUSTRY AND CREATIVE ENERGY. Better a benign manager than AN IMPERIOUS LORD. And from what William tells us of these goodly Grants, no pair of employers could run A MORE CHRISTIAN OR HOSPITABLE place of employment for a working man, OR INDEED WOMAN. That is, in fact, EXPRESSLY WHAT WE ARE HERE TO OBSERVE.'

Charles put on a face of mock-solemnity: 'As you can see, Mrs Touchet, Mr Forster and I have great confidence in the Grants, and in the middling class in general. And we have it on good authority that these Grants are good men of the middle. Ainsworth himself has assured us of it.'

'THAT HE HAS.'

'Better to have laws,' said Mrs Touchet, quietly, in the hope it might encourage a more general modulation of voice. 'Better to have laws, and not rely on the Christian kindness and hospitality of anybody. You have great confidence in the middle class, Mr Dickens. But confidence is a very uncertain political quality, in my experience. As for Christian kindness and hospitality – they may always be revoked.'

'And laws can be repealed.'

'Yes, but it's harder.'

That took the smirk off his face. He was looking at her as he had that time at Lady Blessington's: like a strange ship just come into port.

'DICKENS, WE ARE DRIFTING FROM THE POINT.'

'How so, Forster? Explain.'

'All that I am trying to explain to THE LADY, who perhaps IS NOT

WELL VERSED IN POLITICAL ECONOMY, is *THIS*: if the price of corn goes down, well, that is an unarguable good for THE WORK-ING MAN, and though he may indeed *be* the *HONOURABLE CHARLES VILLIERS*, that gentleman is still ON THE SIDE OF THE WORKING MAN and doing his damnedest to repeal this CURSED LAW, which, as the lady must be aware, has sent many a DECENT FAMILY TO THE POORHOUSE – and made so many LANDED MEN RICHER THAN EVER BESIDES. I don't see what the lady CAN object to in repeal, *IF* she is on the side of progress, AS I UNDERSTOOD HER TO BE.'

'After all, a bigger loaf is a bigger loaf, Mrs Touchet.' How he loved to say her name! It amused him. Everything amused him. Even the misfortune of having a humourless best friend: 'And if food is cheap, Mrs Touchet, our driver friend up there will have a little more money in his pocket, and if he has a bit more money in his pocket, then he'll buy more things, including more of the kinds of things his *fellow* work-ing man makes – and thus, Mrs Touchet, the wheel of free trade turneth!'

It was a good story. Mrs Touchet could think of another one: if food was cheap, so then wages could be lowered, too, by 'benign' managers, and their profits increased in turn – but she could feel herself becoming animated and perhaps comic, or comically monstrous, and she did not want to appear in any more novels. She held her tongue. She held it through the remainder of the drive, and through their tour of 'the most modern calico factory in Europe'. The Grant Brothers were every bit as prosperous-looking as William had promised – a pair of globular, rosy-cheeked, grey-whiskered fellows – and excessively jovial. Everything either of them said concluded in an exclamation mark. They had been desperately poor in Scotland! But were now very rich in Lancashire! And so had good reason to be happy! And more than enough money to be benevolent! Mrs Touchet stood silently between Mr Dickens and Mr Forster, and listened to the tale of how this happy transformation had come to pass. The low price of cotton was at the heart of it. The story went on a long time. She looked about her. She found that if she squinted the place looked less like a factory spinning distant human suffering for profit, and more like a series of hard-faced local girls turning an endless row of printing presses.

12.

What If?

'But that's enough of our adventures in calico! We're very sorry to bore a lady! We will soon have tea at Grant Lodge, in front of the fire! Where we hope you will find company more suitable!'

In her imagination, Mrs Touchet was already there, in the company of a couple of tall, dour, narrow, Northern women, the inevitable companions of such spherical, exclamatory brothers. She was already, in her mind, being dragged to some chilly feminine antechamber – far from the fire and masculine debate – to further discuss recipes for plum pudding, plans for a ragged school, the discouraging sex lives of the poor—

'Are you quite all right, Mrs Touchet? You look pale.'

Part of what people mistook for his goodness was his close attention, which was everywhere on everything, always. It was unbelievably hot in this room. The noise was deafening. Yet the women passed from machine to machine with quiet industry, as if they noticed neither, and Mrs Touchet refused to be the first to wilt. If Mr Charles Dickens could stand it, so could she. She shook her head and held her tongue. The Grant Brothers continued to explain the significance of a large coin now being passed from Dickens' hands, to Forster's, and then finally into her own. It was not a coin of the realm. It was stamped: Grant. And in this Grantian coin, the visitors learned, each girl was partially paid, and with this she was free to buy clean cottons for herself, and provisions for her family, in the adjoining shop – also owned by the Brothers Grant.

Forster praised the economy of this. Charles praised the result: such neat and pleasantly turned-out girls! Mrs Touchet felt cotton in the back of her throat, and coughed. This being the first sound they'd had out of their lady visitor, the Grants paid it special attention, and began a twenty-minute discourse on the importance of open windows, and the benefits therein, and the goodness thereof. *And what if you weren't so good*, thought Mrs Touchet, *and chose to keep the windows shut?* And what if, instead of providing good, clean clothes for 'your girls', you instead let them go about in rags or sackcloth? What if you are less rich next month? Is benevolence to rise and fall like a market?

Such were the thoughts of the young Mrs Touchet. Much later, when she was older, she wished she'd voiced them. At the time, four talkative men — two of them jovial, one vampiric, and the last just incredibly loud — were altogether too much for her. They were four sides of a box through which no noise of her own could escape.

13.

Regina vs Castro, *23rd April 1873*

The world is so much, and so various, and all the time – how can it be contained? Language? *When does the trial begin?* one woman asks another. *Today*, comes the reply. But the word 'today' may hide multitudes. For April the twenty-third was the day the *auld enemy* celebrated itself. The day when Mrs Touchet, in protest, liked to wear tartan underskirts and re-read *Macbeth*. The Bard's birthday. Also, his death-day. The day Eliza Touchet had first set eyes on Mrs Anne Frances Ainsworth. Yes, today, for Mrs Touchet, was a fictional day, an illuminated day, a day of coincidence – of magic! And yet, for Sarah, what was 'today'? Wednesday?

'Will you only look at these lawyers, done up in blue this time! I must say I like them fur collars: *very* fancy. But what a bunch of old rough boys they've dug up for a jury!'

Back in the nosebleed seats of the Queen's Bench. The judge, this time, was indeed Sir Alexander Cockburn, a name Sarah could not be persuaded to pronounce without sounding out all of its consonants. To counter claims of class prejudice, this time the jury had been stacked exclusively with labourers, tradesmen and publicans. Bogle, being plagued by joint pain, was not present, but Henry had been sent in his place. He sat at the Claimant's right hand, making his copious, mysterious notes. Months ago, Mrs Touchet had tried to explain to the new Mrs Ainsworth that although it was true that 'the Crown' was now prosecuting the Claimant, this did not signify that the Queen herself would be in attendance. Sarah, ignoring her, had a dress 'made up special'. It was pink and yellow, puffed, flounced, trimmed to an extent that even Louis XV might have balked at. Her hair was braided in the back like an Easter loaf.

'Oops here's old Hawkins again! Hawk by name . . . But we're ready for you this time, Mr Hawkins!'

Not quite. The prosecution opened with a devastating summary of the facts. Arthur Orton's siblings had received secret payments from the Claimant. The Claimant had given the court a list of sailors lost on the *Bella*, but none of these names were on the *Bella*'s crew list. Instead, they were discovered amongst the crew of the *Middleton*, which was the ship upon which a certain teenage Arthur Orton had sailed from Wapping to Tasmania, many years ago. (How like a novelist! thought Mrs Touchet. How he lies to tell the truth!) Almost everyone who had ever met Sir Roger remembered a tattoo on his left arm. The Claimant had no such mark. All across South America, the Claimant had called himself 'Tom Castro', only becoming 'Sir Roger' in Australia, after Lady Tichborne's adverts reached those shores. In conclusion, his supporters were either nitwits, fraudsters or both. Francis Baigent, the 'family-friend and antiquarian', was a weak-minded fool who kept muddying the waters, inadvertently feeding the Claimant more information than he ever managed to get out of him. As for Andrew Bogle! Well, when all was said and done, he was a negro:

'And though I do not like, as a rule, to abuse whole classes of men, I cannot forget that there are some portions of the negro race who are not proverbial for truth . . .'

Laughter in the court. Mrs Touchet looked down anxiously to see the effect on Henry, but his back was to her, and she would have to wait for a day without Sarah to stop him in the hallway and make reference to it in some form or another, before making her own way back to the station. The next week just such an opportunity arose, but she dithered and did not. To speak of it would be to erase humiliation? Or only to add to it?

14.

A Question of Length

Once Hawkins had summarized the main points, he proceeded to reiterate them in great detail, a process that took seventeen days. After which Cockburn wanted to know how many witnesses counsel intended to call. Hawkins looked down his beak at the brief before him: 'Two hundred and fifteen, My Lord.'

The only person who did not react to this, as far as Mrs Touchet could make out, was the Claimant himself. He sat to the left of Hawkins, alternately sighing, yawning and doodling. Sometimes he sketched the jurors, sometimes the lawyers, sometimes Cockburn himself.

'Bloody hell, I thought we'd be out of here by May, naturally, at the very latest. I've racing season to consider, mind. How long do you think this whole business likely to last, Mrs Touchet?'

Mrs Touchet shrugged her shoulders. Her private and silent approximation was: about eight volumes.

15.

The Twelfth Messenger

It occurred to Mrs Touchet that the law – much as she idealized it in her own mind – did not itself have sufficient rules, and some of the ones it had felt somewhat arbitrary. Why, in a criminal case, was the accused not allowed to speak on his own behalf? And how did a man *become* a lawyer, exactly? Every lawyer in the room practised 'the law' differently, although all were long-winded – they had that much in common. She had been listening to the French evidence for two months already, and there was no rhyme or reason to the modes of questioning. No one ever seemed to know how to begin or where to end, which information was pertinent and which purely extraneous. It was like reading a novel by William. Old Jesuits from Roger's Parisian schooldays were lined up by the prosecution, only to have the opposing lawyer – an eccentric Irishman called Kenealy – attack them on various points of Catholic doctrine. This, though popular with the crowd, had nothing whatsoever, as far as she could see, to do with the case in hand. A digressive fortnight was passed arguing about the true nature of confession. Was it not the case that the Jesuits practised 'equivocation'?

'S'not right, is it, Mrs Touchet? You lot don't lie for your God, do you? Even in court?'

Before Mrs Touchet could defend herself against such calumny, the peculiar defence lawyer began interrogating an old monk called Lefèvre about the significance of his last name:

'And are you not named after the notable saint, sir? I am speaking of course of the fifth-century saint Alexis Lefèvre? And did not that saint, like our much-abused Sir Roger, leave the bosom of his family for years, only to return, years later, as a beggar? And was he not taken in by this old family *as* a beggar, and yet never recognized . . . ?'

'Ooh, he's got him on the ropes now, Mrs Touchet! You'll "confess" to that, at least . . .'

There was something unhinged about this defence lawyer, something supremely bothersome about him, and the workings of his mind. Bearded as Moses in the desert, his eyes – tiny behind bottle-thick glasses – had a fanatical cast. He brought to every debate the quality Mrs Touchet dreaded most, and from which she most hoped the law was secure: sentiment. Most of his sentiment was fury. He thrived on it. Jesuits and Catholics of all stripes infuriated him, but also 'the establishment', 'men of the press', 'bewigged judges', 'corrupt government' and many more eccentric groupings: 'deceitful sailors', 'Wapping cobblers', 'the devious French'. Any rational evidence offered to the court he seemed able to confuse and derange through exposure to his own derangement. Hawkins called forty-eight consecutive Wapping men to the stand, each of whom pointed at the Claimant and called him Arthur Orton. Kenealy managed to find fifty-eight from that same neighbourhood to just as vehemently deny it. He badgered a Captain Angell – who had known Orton's parents, and met Arthur himself, in Hobart – until he mentally collapsed:

'I suppose it is just possible, Mr Kenealy, that he may not *know* he is Arthur Orton. I mean: he might forget his own identity . . . There may have been such things in the history of the world as a man not knowing himself!'

This struck Mrs Touchet as a beautiful and philosophical idea. But Mr Kenealy leapt up like a man giving a toast: 'A man who does not *know himself*, My Lord? Is such a thing to *be imagined in our wildest conceptions*?'

And it was right in that moment that all of a sudden – she knew him! Kenealy!

The Irishman – the poet! Friend of Maginn? Yes! The passionate versifier from Cork! So changed! So bearded, bespectacled, thin-lipped, jowly, mad-eyed – could it be? His young face had vanished entirely. The red hair was grey. The stomach protruded. But it was him. She ransacked her memories. *Kenealy*. Edward Kenealy. From Cork. Eccentric, relentless. Studied the ancient languages. Wrote ponderous, indecipherable poems full of dense mysticism. Had become disillusioned with writing – she remembered that much – scorning all literary company. Stopped coming to dinner. Disappeared from view. Years later, there was some scandal connected with him . . . she could not now remember what. She would ask William, when she got home. What else? When had she last seen him? Perhaps twenty years ago. On the crest of Parliament Hill. He looked strange, seeming to sport four collar points, and she remembered thinking: *He has hocked his coat and must now wear two shirts against the cold.* It was in this vulnerable attitude that she had agreed to be accompanied through the woods and talked at all the way, in the same frantic, monomaniacal manner. A peculiar monologue, about the world falling into darkness every six hundred years, it was a cycle of sorts, and each time the people awaited the arrival of a spiritual messenger who would bring the light – yes, that was it exactly. There were a certain number of messengers prophesied – twelve! Eleven had come already, the Buddha, Muhammad and Jesus among them. The crux of the thing was that apocalypse would follow the last. By the time they'd emerged at Gospel Oak – unless Mrs Touchet's memory was very faulty indeed – it had been heavily hinted that she was in the company of the twelfth . . .

She swivelled in her seat to tell Sarah of this astonishing coincidence. But in those Kensal Lodge days of port and literary young men, the new Mrs Ainsworth had been still a child, in fact, was perhaps not even born. She turned back and folded her hands in her lap. She would tell William, when she got home. He would understand. He always did. Theirs was a fellowship in time, and this, in the view of Mrs Touchet, was among the closest relations possible in this fallen world. Bookended by two infinities of nothing, she and William had shared almost identical expanses of being. They had known each other such a long time. She still saw his young face. He still saw hers, thank God.

16.

Only Half the Story

She practically ran through the house to the garden. William sat in the shadow of the apple tree, a large book in his lap. As she approached, a magpie alighted on the little iron table between them. Sarah caught up and took off her hat to salute it: '*Hello, Mr Magpie, how's your wife!*' The exuberance of this caught both her husband and her housekeeper by surprise. 'What you two looking at me like a couple of Bedlamites for? You have to say it, otherwise it's seven years' bad luck: *Hello, Mr Magpie—*'

William closed his book with a weary expression: 'No, dear. You say: *One for sorrow, two for joy, three for a—*'

'Maybe on King Street! Round *my* way they say: *Hello, Mr Magpie—*'

'William: the most extraordinary thing has happened.'

Eliza removed her own hat, and began rattling off the events of the day: the moment of recognition, the delightful literary coincidence.

'Kenealy! I remember him. Brilliant man. Uneven temper. Very Irish. We used him a lot in the magazine at one point. Then he wrote some rather sharp verses about *Chuzzlewit*, I think, and I had to take him aside, you know, and tell him it just wouldn't do . . . To run a serious literary magazine, Eliza, you must always ensure that only nice things are said and all the writers kept happy – particularly the famous ones.'

Eliza was quite sure this was not how it worked. She held her tongue. Sarah meanwhile was making her escape up the lawn, having bolted at the word 'literary'.

'But William – there was a scandal around him somehow – years later. Do you remember?'

'I do. He had a son – a bastard son, I'm afraid – in Ireland, and he took the boy from the mother and brought him here to raise him alone . . . eccentric idea, but there you are, and one night—'

'He beat the child. I remember!'

'It was something more than a beating. Black and blue with rope marks round his neck. They found the poor boy wandering the streets.'

'Rope marks?'

'Half-strangled. Kenealy did a few months in Newgate for it.'

'But how did he become a lawyer, after that?'

William scoffed: 'If every man who ever hit a child lost his livelihood because of it, what a country of beggars we'd be!' Eliza made a face of revulsion. William was wounded: 'Never have I put a hand to my girls, Eliza – as you well know. Nor would I ever. But poets are not always the gentlemen we imagine them to be. Although perhaps the same might be said of novelists . . .' He tapped the cover of the book in his lap and winced.

'Oh! How is it?'

'Well, I see Forster tells only half the story.'

It was said with great bitterness, and though Mrs Touchet had never really liked the man, she also did not see how Mr Forster could have done otherwise. What was he meant to say? Spirits of the age sometimes leave their wives for actresses half their age? Spirits of the age have been known to bully their children and drop their friends? The people wanted the Dickens they had.

'I suppose literary biographies are always more or less partial . . .'

'Yes, but Eliza, *I* have no Forster. I have Cruikshank.' His face fell into despondency. 'Sometimes I wonder *what* I have.'

It was a domestic policy of Mrs Touchet never to encourage morose thinking: 'Well, you have a hundred pounds a year, to begin with.'

' "*For services to literature*". So much and no more from Mr Palm-erston. It was a bad day for me when Disraeli was got out!'

He tried to laugh it off in his old way, but bitterness had a hold of him, and what came out was closer to a strangulated sigh. Mrs Touchet tried to imagine what it might feel like to have the highest authority in the land pension you off, in recognition of your vocation. She tried to imagine finding such recognition insufficient. Until this moment she had not guessed that her cousin hoped for a knighthood, and she could not, from this distance, discern how likely it was that his old friend Disraeli would ever have given him one. What really interested her in it all was the presumption. Of recognition, of respect – of attention itself. Why did he assume such things as his due? Was this what men assumed?

17.

A Celebratory Party at the Sussex Hotel, Bouverie Street, 12th December 1840

'How about it, old girl? Shall we walk? Can you manage it?'

'Don't call me "old girl", William. I am not yet forty. Let me get my muff.'

There was no snow yet but it was cold enough: a hoar frost rimmed every hedgerow from Kensal Rise to Maida Hill. After which, lamp posts and lamplighting, shops with fogged windows, mitten-less children with their hands in their armpits. The smell of burned coffee. Town!

'What a year it's been, and what a Herculean effort, if I say so myself . . . I truly feel as if I've hardly seen you – or the girls. I'm excited to show you the scenes of my labours!'

Eliza was curious to see them. She had been keeping house, back in Kensal Rise. When she wasn't doing that, she was consoling three mourning girls during their all-too-frequent school holidays. William meanwhile had been ensconced in the Sussex. It was a shabby enough hotel, but he was fond of it, primarily because it was so near to his publishers. The result of this convenience was that two novels, written simultaneously, had been completed within the year: *Guy Fawkes* and *The Tower of London*. Both of them serialized in what was now – since Dickens had relinquished it – William's own *Bentley's Miscellany*. He had produced four chapters a week since January, walking them over to the printers himself, without commentary from Eliza nor any opportunity to modify them. For years she had more or less resented being William's *de facto* editor, but not to be asked at all was provoking in a different way. She was no longer needed. Did she need to be needed?

'And when you think back,' said William, who had not paused for breath since Marble Arch, 'I mean, to our recent misery, it really is remarkable how things have brightened up.'

'Well, yes, I suppose. Although, Anne-Blanche still cries herself to sleep . . .'

William stopped in his brisk stride to look confusedly past Mrs Touchet, towards Kensington Palace.

'I was speaking of that business over *Sheppard* . . .'

'Ah.'

'At the time so excruciating, and yet! All things pass. Blackballed at the Trinity Club! Blocked at the Athenaeum. Practically accused of murder—'

'Let's not exaggerate, William.'

'—and yet now that the *Sheppard* storm appears to have passed, it really *is* very gratifying to feel the sun rather shining upon one, once again. I don't even mind those who perhaps tried to put me in the shade at one point or another – Forster and Thackeray, for example. I don't begrudge them, and I can't understand these literary fellows who *do* hold grudges, as if a bad review were a mortal wound! I say: let bygones be bygones. I shall be glad to see them both this evening. Did I tell you the *Tower* in particular seems to be selling with incredible speed? We can barely print the damn thing fast enough.'

How easy it is to treat people well when things are going well for you! thought Mrs Touchet. Aloud she said: 'Happy news.'

'*Very* happy. I only wish we could have persuaded Crossley to come down. I should have liked to celebrate with him.'

'William, Crossley has never come down to London. He never will come down to London. You are a fool to keep asking him.'

'Ha! What you call foolishness, Mrs Touchet, I call eternal optimism. I always hope for the best and the jolly thing is I am almost always rewarded!'

'Hmmm.'

They turned into the Strand, where it was apparently already Christmas. It was a sin to dread Christmas, but it distressed her to spy paper chains in the shop windows. At Christmastime, her domestic resentments boiled over. Who would cut all those ribbons and pick mashed holly berries out of the floorboards? Who would put all those pigs in their blankets? Who would remember to buy cloves and oranges? Knowing the answer, Mrs Touchet felt a general tetchiness descend into a Targe-like rancour, ill-suited for a party full of literary young men. But here they all were, in the dining room, cheering the late arrival of their host who had a twig caught in his famous curls and really should have taken a hackney like any other self-respecting novelist. Hanging her overcoat very slowly on a hook, Mrs Touchet made a surreptitious, inverted survey of the company in an etched mirror. Maclise, Dickens, Kenealy, Maginn, Thackeray, Forster, as well as several new faces, not all of them young, but all red-cheeked and in a state of advanced inebriation. A pair of well-scrubbed girls were just now bringing in plates of chops and potatoes, a case of too little, too late. The rounds of toasts could not now be halted. William threw his hat into the ring at once:

'Let me speak for Major Elrington! If you do not know him, he is the Governor of the Tower, and without his help Cruikshank and I – where *is* Cruikshank—?'

'Coming! From deepest East London!'

'Pity the man who knows neither North nor West!'

'Pity him indeed! Now: without Major Elrington, the architectural wonders of the Tower would have remained unknown to Cruikshank and I, and therefore, this book – which we are gathered together to celebrate this evening – would never have existed. Well I remember the evening George and I progressed to the little beach at Hungerford Stairs, a boat to await, with the noble Tower barely visible in the moonlight, and yet seeming to beckon to us, from across the roiling Thames . . .'

Mrs Touchet, sensing a lengthy narrative, took her best chance, swiftly crossing the room to seek a seat furthest from the circle of self-congratulation. She found herself next to Kenealy.

'And have you been called upon to toast yet, Mr Kenealy?'

'No. I am afraid I believe in speaking to a purpose.'

Mrs Touchet laughed: 'Ah, you consider yourself in the wrong place, then?'

Mr Kenealy did not laugh: 'I consider that I came to London for substance and find myself forever buffeted by hot air.'

'I see. But are they really so serious in Ireland, Mr Kenealy?'

'They know God,' said this strange man, and crossed the room as if they were not in conversation at all. Mrs Touchet was still gathering herself from the shock of such Irish abruptness when she heard her own name ringing out:

'A toast to Mrs Touchet!'

'Hear! Hear!'

'An ode to Mrs Touchet! A ballad for her! Champion of women! Defender of the slaves!'

'Queen of Exeter Hall!'

'What news of the Convention, Mrs Touchet? Will the American slaves be freed at last?'

Mrs Touchet stood up, returning to the circle, so as to stop this nonsense and attempt to speak on her own behalf:

'The Anti-Slavery Convention was held in June. But women were barred from it, Mr Dickens. I was not able to attend, much to my fury and dismay.'

There was a collective comic sigh, which was interrupted by Cruikshank, just in the door. To Mrs Touchet's experienced eye, he was already in his cups:

'Barred? No, no, I don't think so, Mrs Touchet – no, I'd say you are mistaken. I went to see Haydon's painting of the whole business, you know, only last week, at the Academy – we lowly caricaturists have been known to visit the occasional art gallery – and it was ill-done if you ask me, and with a child's conception of perspective – looked more like a barn than Exeter Hall. But there are definitely ladies in it! I remember their faces.'

'Let it never be said that Cruikshank forgets the face of a lady!'

Mrs Touchet felt her own face burning.

'American ladies, we'll wager!'

'Persistent American ladies!'

'Very persistent American ladies wearing Turkish trousers!'

'If only Mrs Touchet was as persistent as these Turkish-trouser-wearing American ladies!'

Encouraged, perhaps, by the mention of Turkey, Cruikshank launched into a full-throated rendition of 'Lord Bateman', adding more verses than Mrs Touchet had ever previously known existed. She was glad of it: her face still burned. Only when Bateman was released from that fabled Turkish prison – having exchanged his plentiful lands in Northumberland for his freedom – did she feel the colour leave her cheeks.

In her embarrassment, she had not looked about her or noticed that Thackeray was sitting to her left. Now he rose and announced a fresh toast for the disgraced newspaper man and political agitator, Richard Carlile, that 'hero of the poor', whom Mrs Touchet considered to be generally right about the press, police, women and sex, but entirely wrong about God:

'I do not mean to dampen this jolly occasion,' said Thackeray, immediately doing so, 'but I feel it incumbent upon me to raise a toast to our most brave, most shamefully mistreated, Carlile, whose office stands next door to this fine establishment, and who stood in his own person with the people all those years ago, at Peterloo. Carlile it was who published our beloved *Rights of Man*, and the much-missed *Republican*, only to be gaoled for his trouble – and it is Carlile's example, I hope – I *pray* – which will both ennoble and *humble* all of us who scribble for a living, and yet make no such sacrifices for it, as that great man has. To Carlile!'

'All hail Carlile!'

'Hear! Hear!'

Thackeray sat back down between William and Mrs Touchet, his pig nose dilating with pride. William turned to him cheerily:

'Well said, sir! Very well said! Whatever *did* happen to the *Republican*? We all loved it as young men in our hotheaded days and yet it *has* rather fizzled out . . . Seems to happen to many a journal, especially the political ones – who knows why? But my *Bentley's* is in rude health, if I say so myself! Speaking of which, do you know, I must just speak to Charles about a matter . . .'

Mrs Touchet and Thackeray watched William corner Charles, across the room. She could feel exasperation rising off Thackeray like steam.

'Fizzled out! Good God, the government taxed it out of existence. It was a deliberate policy of repression.'

Mrs Touchet decided to be disloyal:

'My cousin is a sweet and generous man, Mr Thackeray, but politics are not his forte.'

'What *is* his forte, precisely?'

Mrs Touchet was silent. It was somebody else's turn to blush.

'Excuse me, Mrs Touchet. I've drunk too much. He is your cousin. And your cousin does very well, by all accounts, far better in fact than I do. No critique of mine can harm him.'

'That may be – but you are supposed to be his friend.'

She watched him take a big breath. He was the kind of man who felt obliged to tell the truth at all times, no matter how uncomfortable this might prove for others. She hated people like that.

'In my view, Mrs Touchet, if I may be very honest with you, I believe that you have put your finger on the whole trouble. What we so foolishly call "the literary scene" – a vulgar, ludicrous phrase to begin with – is really just *"butter me and I'll butter you"*, done in the name of friendship, day and night. I am sorry to say it, but our dear Ainsworth . . . Well, for one thing, he too easily mistakes titles for talent. Every other page of *Bentley's* is presently written by a Lady So-and-so or a Sir Whatever-your-name is. And what is the result? Unreadable dross. Though I don't know why anyone imagined this editorship would be a discerning one when the editor himself so often mistakes—'

Mrs Touchet's glass was gripped very tight in her hand – she had drunk two large glasses already – but the rest of Thackeray's dreaded sentence did not arrive.

'Forgive me. I really have taken too much drink.'

'You have said what you meant to say in a free country. Please finish.'

'Well, it is not such a terrible critique – I was only going to say that . . . well, perhaps your cousin too frequently mistakes information for interest. Especially in this latest volume.'

Mrs Touchet sighed and held her tongue. She had, in the past, stopped reading William's novels near the end, midway through, and, on one occasion, after only the second chapter. But she had never before been defeated by the first page – until now.

'I rode out to Kensal TWICE last week. EACH TIME only to be TOLD you were "NOT AT HOME!"'

Mrs Touchet turned to discover the source of the raised voices, and found not the expected Mr Forster but Cruikshank and William, the author hunched in the window seat with the artist looming over him.

'Nor was I! I was *here*, Cruikshank, writing. George, I am very sorry if you're upset – but we had no contract for *St Paul's*, and when one is approached by the *Sunday Times*, one naturally—'

'We shook on it, sir! And that is usually contract enough for any honourable man! Unless he is some kind of a FRAUD?'

Mrs Touchet, sensing disaster, stood suddenly and proposed a toast to the young Queen.

'Good idea, Mrs Touchet! To the Queen!'

'And to the new princess!'

'Well said! A toast to the young Queen and her new princess and to the health and glory of the realm!'

'Better yet – let's sing it!'

All the literary young men stood up to face the portrait of Victoria. Flushed with wine, gripping each other's elbows, they sang heartily of what Britons never, ever, ever shall be.

18.

The first page of
The Tower of London

ON THE 10TH OF JULY, 1553, ABOUT TWO HOURS AFTER NOON, a loud discharge of ordnance burst from the turrets of Durham House, then the residence of the Duke of Northumberland, grand-master of the realm, and occupying the site of the modern range of buildings, known as the Adelphi; and, at the signal, which was immediately answered from every point along the river where a bombard or culverin could be planted – from the adjoining hospital of the Savoy, – the old palace of Bridwell, recently converted by Edward VI., at the instance of Ridley, bishop of London, into a house of correction, – Baynard's Castle, the habitation of the Earl of Pembroke, – the gates of London-bridge, – and, lastly, from the batteries of the Tower, – a gallant train issued from the southern gateway of the stately mansion above-named, and descended the stairs leading to the water's edge, where, appointed for their reception, was drawn up a squadron of fifty superbly-gilded barges, – some decorated with banners and streamers, – some with cloth of gold and arras, embroidered with the devices of the civic companies, – others with innumerable silken pennons to which were attached small silver bells, 'making a goodly noise and a goodly sigh as they waved in the wind,' – while others, reserved for the more import-ant personages of the ceremony, were covered at the sides with shields gorgeously emblazoned with the armorial bearings of the different noblemen and honourable persons composing the privy council, amid which the cognizance of the Duke of Northumberland, – a lion rampant, or, double quevée, vert, appeared proudly

19.

A Theory of Truth

It was time for Mrs Touchet to decide what she really believed. To separate fact from fiction once and for all. She had worried that 'the law' needed a theory of law. Eighty-five court days later, she was having similar trouble with 'the truth'. Did the truth require a theory of truth?

Falsus in uno, falsus in omnibus – so went Kenealy's. He used it liberally, brandishing it against witnesses, lawyers, the judges, Cockburn himself, the Catholic Church, the press, Westminster, the entire judicial system. Any resident of Wapping who could be shown to have ever lied to their rent-collector, grocer or beadle was not to be trusted on the question of Arthur Orton. Soldiers who had once skulked off a day's training to go into the village for a pint of cider – such men had no scruples, and might say anything whatsoever about the existence or otherwise of tattoos. It turned out that Gosford, the steward, had lied about his personal finances. He could therefore not be trusted on the possible contents of the sealed packet nor anything else:

'*False in one thing, false in all* – it is a fundamental principle of the law. And *this* man' – Kenealy had a habit of accusatory pointing, as at a martyr tied to the stake or a witch strapped into her dunking chair – 'hath broken it!'

To this, Cockburn took exception, reminding the jury that there was in fact no such principle in common law. Under his breath, Kenealy replied that it was the law of heaven and a great shame that the Queen's Bench dwelt in the ninth region of hell. But his *sotto voce*, like

Mr Forster's, was perfectly audible to all. He received the censure of the bench. He received it frequently. For whining, ranting, swearing, sermonizing, lecturing and embarking upon incredible rhetorical tangents, some lasting a fortnight or more. The people adored it. The spectacle of a Cork man taking on the establishment enlivened an oppressively hot summer and proved a pleasant distraction from the financial crisis. If Mrs Touchet did not get the first train into town, she could not be guaranteed her seat, and by the end of a day's proceedings, the crowds outside were sufficient to fill the court five times over.

On the train back home, she and Sarah enjoyed the caricaturists. Tichborne as the Jabberwocky, Kenealy as the Hatter, Hawkins as the Rabbit and Bogle as the Dormouse. Tichborne and Bogle drowning in the Thames, Kenealy pushing them towards the shores of Westminster, and Cockburn kicking them both back into the water – the word JUSTICE painted on the sole of his shoe. Kenealy as St George, plunging the Sword of Tichborne into the dragon of the judiciary. Kenealy as lion-tamer, the Claimant as clown, Bogle as tightrope walker and Cockburn as the ringleader, all of them under a Big Top. Which last suggested, to Mrs Touchet, another potential theory of truth: *Of all the places the truth may appear, perhaps the least likely is a circus.*

20.

The Mysteries of Bogle & Luie

Andrew Bogle entered the court and took the stand once more. Impossible to imagine him being false in one thing or any. Calmly, with great clarity, he repeated everything he had said in the civil trial. One theory of the truth is that those who tell it betray no anxiety: such a one was Mr Bogle. But might a person be sincerely false? That is, false and not know it? She found it almost inconceivable that he could have fed the Claimant information except, perhaps, unwittingly. Yet she knew him to be a shrewd and intelligent man . . .

What a mystery was Mr Bogle! Since the day of the pork chops, she had made many clumsy and unsuccessful attempts to revive the intimacy of that afternoon, but if she contrived to bump into him in the corridors – or to catch his eye from her nosebleed seat – he seemed startled, uncomfortable. When their paths crossed, it was only Henry who spoke to her, while the elder Bogle made his excuses – painful joints – wished her good day, was gone. Did he think her a vampire? She only wanted to know what could be known of other people! In trying to understand other people, Mrs Touchet generally followed the principle of Terence. Not only was nothing human alien to her, but she assumed that if she had ever thought or felt something, well, then it was extremely unlikely that she was the only one to have ever done so. And if a slave like Terence could consider himself an example of the general case, why not Mrs Touchet? In this spirit, she now considered her own tendency to believe what she most needed to be true. Yes, perhaps Bogle needed to believe, could not *afford* disbelief. And if that were true of him, it was surely also the case for Henry, and for Mr Onslow and Mr Baigent, not to mention all those optimistic people clutching their 'Tichborne Bonds' . . . Good money had been thrown after bad, annuities annulled, reputations wagered, all eggs put into the Tichborne basket. Mrs Touchet drew yet another theory of truth from these melancholy reflections: people lie to themselves. People lie to themselves all the time.

The other possibility – that Bogle was the mastermind of the whole affair – she rejected outright. Such a calculated conspiracy was not to be imagined from such an even-tempered, quiet, simple, honest, elderly negro as Black Bogle, and Hawkins, sensing a general disinclination in the courtroom to see this gentle old man too forcefully interrogated, chose not to linger upon him. Instead, the question of the *Osprey* returned. This was the ship that had rescued the Claimant from the waters, bringing him to Melbourne – according to the Claimant. A witness recalled an *Osprey* in Australia around that time; another remembered a ship by the same name in Rio, as well as a steward who had sailed upon it: a Dane by the name of Jean Luie. *Where is this all going?* wondered Mrs Touchet. She wished that life's pages could be flicked forward as in a novel, to see if what followed was worth attending to in the present. She was completely unprepared for what came next. Kenealy approached the bench, his brief held high like a tablet of Moses: 'I call to the stand: JEAN LUIE.'

A luxuriously bearded man in a cheap hat and a peacoat entered the box. His accent Sarah identified as 'foreign'. Yes, he had rescued Sir Roger. Yes, that was Sir Roger sitting right over there. No, Sir Roger had no tattoo. Mr Luie had personally nursed him back to health and should know. Mrs Touchet, astonished, expected triumphalism from her court companion, but Sarah had her arms crossed tightly over her bosom, as if to prevent the entry of this Mr Luie's testimony into her heart:

'I tell you I don't like it. Too convenient by far. Also, his eyes are too close together. And I don't like the look on his face. That's a con man's face, believe me, I've seen 'em. I tell you I've a bad feeling in my particulars. Say what you like about old Black Bogle, but that's an honest face even if it *is* dark as the Devil! Where was Luie when we had the first trial? I tell you, it's a trap! Poor Kenealy will live to regret this Luie speculation. He's a bad bet, Mrs Touchet, you mark my words.'

Many of Mrs Touchet's liberal passions had their original source in the proverb *Give a dog a bad name and hang him*, the truth of which had struck her with great force in childhood. The purpose of life was to keep one's mind open, never to judge on appearances or bad names, and always to make decisions based on evidence only. She had continued to take this idea seriously in her maturity, long after most reasonable people abandon it. She chastised Sarah for her prejudice, and in this way backed herself into a corner. For almost a month she joined the Jean Luie partisans. There were eager sightings of different *Osprey*s, examinations of crew lists, witnesses who had never heard of this Jean Luie, others who thought the name sounded familiar, the entering into evidence of shipwreck logs, and much interrogating of custom clerks – until the morning two wardens entered the court and identified Mr Luie as a recently released convict, actually a Swede called Lundgren, and presently living with an active member of the Tichborne Defence Fund.

21.

Open Land

Although long fascinated by Ethiope singers – authentic or painted, melancholy or comic – Mrs Touchet had never imagined attending a formal concert of such music, much less with someone like Henry Bogle by her side.

Yet a week from Tuesday this was exactly what she intended to do.

She could not help but notice the boundary lines around her person smudging and shifting with age. Whereas, in many other people of her acquaintance – especially the men – these same lines had grown only more defined. New fences went up, sometimes walls, sometimes battlements. She was not above congratulating herself on this difference.

She told William she was going to Wigmore Hall to hear a Frenchman play Bach.

22.

Grace

Mrs Touchet did not often cross the river. As she and Henry approached the southern bank — and the Metropolitan Tabernacle came into view — she grew uneasy. She had of course heard of this monument to Protestantism but the scale of it shocked her. From the water it looked impressive, almost as large as the Vatican. Once inside, though, the design proved reassuringly rational and without beauty, like Protestantism itself. Henry, in his fastidious way, took out a handkerchief to lay on his seat. Together they calculated the number of seats at about six thousand. It was a hot, close night, but as the hour approached every seat was filled.

'Their reputation precedes them. First, they sang for the Queen. Today to six thousand Britons. What a day of progress for your people, Henry!'

'And for yours, Mrs Touchet.'

Before she could reply, applause, huge and echoing, filled the vastness. Just behind her ear, a woman cried out *Well, they ain't black as all that*, in a tone that implied she meant to pursue the matter through the courts. Mrs Touchet, curious, peered through her opera glasses to the little circular stage below. Four men and seven women had emerged. Some of them favoured Andrew, others Henry, but there were several other shades, besides. Most perplexing to her were the three young women who might, from this distance, be mistaken for William's daughters. No Topsys in childish crinolines or End Men in battered top hats. Only sober suits and modest dresses. Mrs Touchet, always sensitive to the public mood, sensed confusion and dissension in the audience, transforming – after a few minutes of urgent whispers – into a new accommodation. If these Fisk Jubilee American negroes did not look quite like the ones you saw down St Giles's way, that was surely to be expected. They were bound to do things differently over there. And if they were dressed for church, well, wasn't this a church, and a grand one at that? But a church, to Mrs Touchet, had a different connotation: a church was only another form of human error, to be counted with all the others. She could be persuaded aesthetically by many, spiritually by some, but would never be wholly convinced. Not by any temple made by hands. As for this 'Tabernacle', it had been built on the site of a notable martyrdom and was therefore calculated not to please her. She did not like to be reminded of the excesses of the Catholic Queen – nor of her own hypocrisy upon that point – and once she had begun upon this accusatory train of thought, she found it very difficult to get off. Human error and venality are everywhere, churches are imperfect, cruelty is common, power corrupt, the weak go to the wall! What in this world can be relied on?

When Israel was in Egypt's land
Let my people go
Oppressed so hard they could not stand
Let my people go.

Rapture. Beauty. Grace translated – made visible! Had she ever truly heard music until this moment?

23.

What Can We Know of Other People?

Afterwards, collecting herself in front of the Elephant and Castle, Mrs Touchet was moved to tears once more. The living jubilee! That those so recently in bondage should lift their voices in joyful song! As she tried to convey some of this agitated emotion to the younger Bogle, he nodded and fanned himself with a playbill, agitated in a different way, distracted; she suddenly realized he wasn't listening. Not for the first time this evening she wished she was standing here with the elder Bogle instead. Despondent, she watched Henry scanning the exiting crowd, as if seeking one particular face amongst the six thousand, although he had not mentioned any plan to—

'Mrs Touchet, may I introduce you to Miss Jackson.'

Mrs Touchet blushed severely. She dithered, not knowing what to do with her hands. She did something strange with her head, a sort of rearing back, in response to which the young negress in front of her nodded minutely. Nothing more.

'But you are – you – are you not – one of the singers? What beautiful singing! What a symbol, if I may put it that way – and what an actuality!'

Another tiny nod: 'You are kind to say so, madam.'

'Last week I left my card,' explained sheepish Henry, 'offering my services, as a guide. We were given permission by her chaperones, and as you can see Miss Jackson has taken me up on the offer, and now does me the honour of allowing me to give her a tour of the city.'

He was just a boy, saying the sorts of things he thought a man should.

She noted the young people's grim similarity of dress: old-fashioned, overly formal clothes, intended to give an impression of unimpeachable decency. The drawing-room conventionality of it all disappointed her profoundly. Was this, then, to be freedom?

'Rather than make a tourist of Miss Jackson, Henry, you might think to ask her for her story. It is sure to be a remarkable one.'

This she delivered in the admonishing voice of her own, long-dead mother. In response, Miss Jackson smiled tightly and said nothing. She seemed oddly resistant to Mrs Touchet's own sense of a momentous event. Why was this young lady so determined to behave as if she had done nothing more remarkable this evening than clean a kitchen or serve a meal?

'Miss Jackson is very curious to see our "Big Ben".'

Mrs Touchet frowned, momentarily wrongfooted by Henry's use of the possessive pronoun.

Aloud she said: 'Ah. Well, that is not too far.'

'We intend to walk along the river. Won't you join us, Mrs Touchet? I know how you like to walk.'

Mrs Touchet quickly said she would not. Undisguised relief passed over Miss Jackson's face. Mrs Touchet was bewildered. How dark this Miss Jackson was, and yet how prideful, how self-contained. Was she beautiful? Mrs Touchet could make no judgement, having no criteria. As an expert in longing, however, she felt herself on surer ground with Henry. He had the unmistakeable look of a besotted boy. He looked just like van Dyck's page, gazing up at his moon-faced Princess Henrietta. But this comparison only threw Mrs Touchet into further confusion, not least because Henry, being taller, gazed down. And the only moon-white face was her own.

The three of them stood in place for one of those strange, attenuated silences, perhaps unique to England, in which a conversation seems like a thing no one has ever been able to achieve, no, not since the dawn of creation. Mrs Touchet had been a third wheel for so much of her life.

This was different. This was a desolate, an almost dizzying feeling of exclusion. She felt an acute awareness of every part of her face and body, as if her own person had suddenly become estranged from her, as if *she herself* were the exotic item, burst so suddenly onto the scene . . . Oh, but what nonsense! It was simply too hot, she was not as young as she once had been, her thoughts were confused. When young, she had never understood why old women dithered so. Why they led conversations down dead ends and almost always overstayed their welcome. She did not know then what it was to have no definition in the world, no role and no reason. To be no longer even decorative. All too easy to lose your footing, to misunderstand everything, get the wrong end of every stick. She was oppressing these two young people who only wanted to be alone, to talk amongst themselves, about things beyond her ken.

Obscurely humiliated, she was almost mute as they said their stiff, awkward goodbyes. She watched them walk away, towards Parliament, drawing the attention of all. To Mrs Touchet they no longer looked like noble sons and daughters of Africa – filled with the grace of suffering, illuminated by freedom – but simply like any other foolish boy and girl. She was unable to shake a sense of conspiracy between them, directed towards her own person. A conspiracy of laughter? Of pity? All the way home the idea pursued her like shame.

24.

An Earlier Bogle Mystery, 1840

'There's something very mysterious about our Mr Bogle,' remarked the new Mrs Doughty. 'He is never angry.'

'Oh, everybody is angry sometimes.'

'Yes, Edward, that is my point. Yet Bogle never is. Christmas is a taxing time: I hear Lily stamping her feet in the kitchen and Guilfoyle screaming at the stable boy. Nothing taxes Mr Bogle. It is mysterious. If he's angry, he never shows it – but then where exactly does his anger go? It must go somewhere. Sometimes I fear he is plotting against us.'

'Ha! You read too many novels, Kathryn. Ladies should stop reading novels – nothing good comes of it. If it were up to me, a petition to that effect would be taken to Parliament.'

Bogle himself, who had overheard this conversation, did not think of it again until one evening in the middle of August. He was bringing in the cheese, after dinner, and Sir Edward was reading aloud from a sheaf of papers in his hand:

' "*On the 15th of July, 1840, one hundred and ten negro houses and out offices were consumed with the furniture, clothing and other property of various inmates, many of whom only escaped with difficulty from the fury of the flames, with the mere clothing on their backs.*" This from the committee report. I used to *be* on that damned committee. Thank God I got out of that accursed business when I did!'

Mrs Doughty accepted a cheese plate from Bogle and agreed with her husband that it was a very queer business indeed, given how often things seemed to go up in flames.

'How many times, Bogle? How many times did we tell them not to ruinate pastures in July? One spark, one breath of wind and — *whoosh!* Nobody listened. Nobody on Hope knew a damn thing about estate management. It was me and Bogle against them all!'

The new Mrs Doughty agreed that this sounded very trying.

'I doubt Buckingham will survive it. What an old criminal he is! I shudder to think of the extent of his debts, at this point. Bogle, you can clear those glasses now and bring the ones for port. Ah, now look here: "*The committee also learnt that considerable sums of money, the property of the Negroes, was lost in notes and coins. Much silver was found melted and calcined with the earth of the jars in which it was kept.*" Mrs Doughty, you would not believe how many times I tried to tell that pig-headed Buckingham to let me get a spade and dig up the ground around those damned cottages. Who knows how many butter knives and candlesticks vanished from the Main House into the bowels of the earth! But nobody listened to me. And now look. My word, Bogle, whatever's happened to your hand?'

Bogle opened his shaking fist and watched the pretty little pieces of green glass tumble out onto the floor, red with blood, sparkling.

25.

'The great problem is at length solved', 1844

Despite the trouble over *Old St. Paul's*, Cruikshank had evidently forgiven William sufficiently to agree to illustrate *Saint James's or The Court of Queen Anne, An Historical Romance* – a book almost as dull as the reign of Queen Anne itself. At least he started coming to dinner again. So did Thackeray – more than anyone wanted him to – and even Dickens reappeared. Dickens who had so many other things to do. Could it be possible William hadn't guessed the reason why?

'Richard! But we didn't expect you! Will you stay for dinner?'

'May I?'

'Oh, we always have a "horn of plenty" for our Mr Horne. You're really very welcome.'

'William, in this lodge you keep a flaxen-haired beauty, a raven-haired beauty and an auburn beauty. That is plenty indeed. You should always expect me!'

Fanny was seventeen, Emily fifteen and Anne Blanche a year younger. They *were* beautiful. It surprised Mrs Touchet, who had never thought them attractive children. Nobody competed any longer to sit next to the cousin-housekeeper with the acid tongue. That honour now passed to Emily, whose black hair and porcelain skin were compared to Diana's so frequently you might have thought she had a quiver of arrows strapped to her back. Anne-Blanche favoured some distant Irish aunt of William's, and had single-handedly converted Dickens to the 'worship of redheads'. Fanny was the image of her mother. This resemblance caused Mrs Touchet pain. All that Fanny understood of it was that her father's queer cousin didn't seem to like her very much.

Mrs Touchet watched the literary men troop in and out of the house of a man they didn't respect, whose table was only passable, who frequently ran out of port. The base, transactional nature of it all! Was *this* what daughters were for? Even the girls themselves seemed only too aware of the conditional basis of their appearance at table, as if they had always known they owed men their beauty and now the time had come to pay that debt in full. The mutuality Mrs Touchet had always believed possible, an idealized table, around which men and women met as equals, employing only their wits – this was revealed to be a hopelessly naive vision. Beauty trumped all other considerations.

She felt a certain bitterness. But she knew that if she let bitterness overwhelm her, the 'pleasure of her company' would then not only be uncontested but actively avoided. Better to adopt a brittle, enforced optimism, with herself and everybody else. When William read his entry in *A Spirit of the Age*, she counselled strenuously against despair or revenge, and it worked: here was Mr Horne only a month later, welcome at dinner once more. When Thackeray attacked *Jack Sheppard* on the grounds of morality, she made a strong argument that his was only a case of envy, and Thackeray was soon pitied and forgiven. Still, there were limits to such mitigations. Sometimes we don't want to be chivvied out of our sadness or bitterness or anger. Sometimes all we want is consolation. Who would console Mrs Touchet?

'Look at this!'

Eliza sat down at the breakfast table and looked at the newspaper that had been thrown at her. Last night's carousing had left her with a bad head. Disguising this fact had been her only hope for this morning.

'The *New York Sun*. American?'

'Yes, Eliza, American. *Look* at it!'

SUN OFFICE
April 13, 1844
10 o'clock A.M.

ASTOUNDING
NEWS!
BY EXPRESS VIA NORFOLK:

THE
ATLANTIC CROSSED
IN
THREE DAYS!

SIGNAL TRIUMPH
OF
MR. MONCK MASON'S
FLYING
MACHINE!!!

Arrival at Sullivan's Island,
near Charlestown, S. C.,
Of Mr. Mason, Mr. Robert Holland,
Mr. Henson,
Mr. Harrison Ainsworth,
and four others

The great problem is at length solved. The air, as well as the earth and the ocean, has been subdued by science, and will become a common and convenient highway for mankind. The Atlantic has been actually crossed in a Balloon –

The pounding in Mrs Touchet's head was genuinely astounding.

'William, I'm sorry, I don't understand. This is a newspaper?'

'You can see that it is!'

'But – you have not been in any kind of balloon. Besides, a balloon could never make such a journey.'

'It's a fake, Eliza. A sort of "April Fool's".'

'Oh. How odd!'

'Mr Edgar Allan Poe is the true author of this particular article. It was written for the amusement of the public – although the greater part of them apparently believed it!'

'But – why? I still don't understand. *You* are in the basket? For what purpose?'

' "I" write a diary of this imaginary event. Which is excerpted below, in an imitation of my prose. I am the butt of the joke, Eliza. "I" in this case signifying a character that our American colleague has taken the liberty of inventing!'

William stood up and flicked several pages forward and pressed his finger violently to a paragraph:

The waters give up no voice to the heavens. The immense flaming ocean writhes and is tortured uncomplainingly. The mountainous surges suggest the idea of innumerable dumb gigantic fiends struggling in impotent agony.

Through the pounding, Mrs Touchet tried to think of something consoling to say. She thought she had never before seen her cousin's face so stricken, so desolate, so childlike in its need.

'Is he making fun of me, Lizzie? *Am* I a fraud?'

26.

Sink or Swim

Just before Christmas, she was presented, at table, with a little brown book with gilt edges, inscribed: *To Mrs. Touchet, From Charles Dickens, Seventeenth December 1843*. It sounded like a ghost story for the simpleminded. But she thanked him and put it on the shelf. Three years later she still hadn't read it, but like everyone else she was now almost as familiar with Scrooge and Marley, the ghosts, Tiny Tim — the whole Anglican confection — as she was with the nativity itself. Its success was even greater in America, apparently, if such a thing were possible. Charles had finally gone beyond mere sales to mesmerism.

It was all very hard on William. Never did he say a word on the topic, but she could see it in him, and in the books themselves, which became more frequent, their subjects bleaker. She guessed the subject of the next novel in the early spring, when books on the topic began arriving from Manchester: witchcraft. That autumn she made an attempt to read *The Lancashire Witches*:

Nance Redfern, it has to be said, was a very comely young woman; but neither her beauty, her youth, nor her sex, had any effect upon the ferocious crowd, who were too much accustomed to such brutal and debasing exhibitions, to feel anything but savage delight in the spectacle of a fellow-creature so scandalously treated and tormented, and the only excuse to be offered for their barbarity, is the firm belief that they are dealing with a witch.

A scene of witch-dunking. A situation well suited to William's interests and talents, such as they were. The straps around wrists. Wet fabric filling a mouth. The plunge into the depths. But thirty pages in and it was her cousin drowning. Always he had enjoyed writing scenes of torture and physical restraint, but now they were devoid of the usual romance and vicarious thrill. They were only sadistic. Purely blood, only misery. What she really didn't expect, though, was the moralizing:

> *And when even in our own day so many revolting scenes are enacted*
> *to gratify the brutal passions of the mob, while prize-fights are*
> *tolerated, and wretched animals goaded on to tear each other in*
> *pieces, it is not to be wondered at that, in times of less enlightenment*
> *and refinement, greater cruelties should be practised.*

Of all the things to steal from Charles, why choose the sermons?

27.

Offstage

I am managing decline. So thought Mrs Touchet as she mended her own clothes. Threadbare crêpe required re-lining, bombazine patching, stockings endless darning: it all took time. Why couldn't she wear the same black dress every day? Why couldn't she go about naked or in the many suits William had outgrown? Instead, she had to manage and maintain these last few shreds of beauty. Until old age arrived and released her once and for all from the tedious pantomime.

In the papers, she read about decline's opposite: revolution! In Italy, France, Germany, Denmark, Poland! She stuck her head out of her bedroom window each morning in an anticipatory fit. All she ever saw was the sleepy Harrow Road and its armies of sheep. Was England immune?

In September, Kensal Manor received an interesting letter from Crossley, addressed to them both:

September 14th, 1848

Dear William and Eliza,
    You may have heard that the so-called 'Greatest Debtor in the World', is finally and completely exploded, and all the contents of Stowe House are to be auctioned off. The man was born with seventy thousand pounds, married even more, inherited half of Jamaica — yet is up to his ears to the tune of a million. Much of which seems to have been spent on wallpaper. Well, it is a shameful business and a

notorious affair but I must admit that all that concerns me in it is THE BOOKS which are to be sold at Sotheby's, in January. At present my health does not permit me to leave Manchester. Nor do I foresee this situation improving in the coming months. And so I humbly beg you, for the love that you bear me: would one of you not consent to toddle off to Sotheby's with a paddle that says CROSSLEY upon it and kindly bid up to the sum of 40 pounds on the list of books enclosed within? I would be 'indebted' to whoever would consider it, though perhaps not to the extent of the poor Duke of Buckingham —

In January, William went to France for an extended stay. It was like him to go to a place just after something very interesting had happened there. Mrs Touchet, meanwhile, went to Sotheby's. She bought books about the 1745 rebellion, the South Sea Bubble, medieval folk practices, Guy Fawkes, Defoe on the plague, and many histories of London, in the full and guilty knowledge that she was more or less acting as middleman. Sure as the opium from the poppy fields reaches the addicts in the ports, so these histories would find their way back to William in the end, spawning novels, oh, so many novels . . .

1st July 1849

Dear Eliza,

Sad tidings from France. I was coming back over the Pyrenees with the hope of meeting our old friends Lady B and d'Orsay in Paris, but before I could reach them, the Lady died — leaving her debts to manage themselves. D'Orsay meanwhile is still wanted by the English police! The papers here had it that she died of un cœur éclaté, which is a very French way of saying her heart was enlarged and three times as big as it should have been. But of course we who loved her already knew that . . .

He would be back at Christmas. Then Easter. She sent a copy of *Jane Eyre* to a forwarded address in Vienna. In November, he wrote back with the news that he had started upon an autobiographical novel and would miss another Christmas. It took her a very long time to understand the obvious: there must be a woman – or women – on the Continent, and whoever she or they were, they could neither be respectably brought back to England nor completely relinquished.

28.

Theory

Mrs Touchet had a theory. England was not a real place at all. England was an elaborate alibi. Nothing real happened in England. Only dinner parties and boarding schools and bankruptcies. Everything else, everything the English really did and really wanted, everything they desired and took and used and discarded – all of that they did elsewhere.

29.

Infinity, 1851

The following March, Mrs Touchet saw her pet theory inverted, under a dome of crystal, in the middle of Hyde Park. Everything the British had ever done anywhere was now here, in London, and on display. She went with the girls. They were delighted by the combination of single gentlemen, wandering about in the wild, mechanical commodes for which one paid a penny, and so many exotic 'bays', each representing some aspect of the nation's global industry. Favourite sights of the morning:

The Noor diamond

Some dark-skinned, silky-haired, never-before-seen people hailing from New Zealand

A barometer employing leeches to predict tempests

Pause for lunch. Following the more salubrious element of the crowd, they found themselves on the second floor of Lady Blessington's old Gore House, recently converted into a restaurant by Alexis Soyer. There was no point explaining the poignancy of all this to the girls. Mrs Touchet ate her Dover Sole crowded in on all sides by the dead. Then it was back into the fray. Trailing the Ainsworths from spectacle to spectacle, Mrs Touchet watched the people and wondered about the sacred. Industry was sacred to the people, she could see that much, and the acquiring of land. The brotherhood of man and the strength of the pound were much the same thing in their minds, and peace on earth signified only the smooth flow of goods, from Liverpool to Bombay, from Melbourne to Manchester . . .

'It truly is a *great exhibition*.' Emily had inherited her father's habit of stating the obvious. 'The whole of the civilized world is here!'

'And the uncivilized . . .' Fanny pulled at Anne-Blanche's sleeve until this youngest Ainsworth was forced to submit to a protected position behind Mrs Touchet, although she was by now twenty-one, and often seemed to be the only real adult of the three. She was being shielded from the sight of a group of semi-naked Africans in the Dahomey enclosure. They were sitting on the ground outside a straw hut. They looked very bored. As the Ainsworths hurried by, Mrs Touchet could have sworn she heard one young tribesman say to another: *Where's Himself? I'm dying for a piss . . .*

But she was not particularly annoyed by the Great Exhibition of 1851 until she read Mr Dickens and Mr Horne's combined review of the event in *Household Words*:

> *We are moving in a right direction towards some superior condition of society – politically, morally, intellectually, and religiously.*

Did they really believe it? According to these two gentlemen, heaven was soon to arrive upon the earth. It was simply inevitable, given the progress everywhere. Only a few 'odd, barbarous, or eccentric' nations would be exempt from this Eden, and only because they were too stuck in their ways, perversely refusing to board the Scottish-built locomotives presently hurtling towards utopia. China and the Chinese were the favoured example.

> *It is very curious to have the Exhibition of a people who came to a dead stop – heaven knows how many hundred years ago – side by side with the Exhibition of the moving world. It points the moral in a surprising manner.*

The moral, according to Mr Dickens and Mr Horne, was progress. Forward. Ever forward. More and bigger. Humanity was to be 'advanced', agriculture perfected, efficiency made only more efficient.

Consider the greatness of the English results, and the extraordinary littleness of the Chinese. Go from the silk-weaving and cotton-spinning of us outer barbarians, to the laboriously-carved ivory balls of the flowery Empire, ball within ball and circle within circle, which have made no advance and been of no earthly use for thousands of years.

Yet these ivory balls, offering infinity in the palm of your hand, had been, for Mrs Touchet, the only moment of sublimity – the only touch of the sacred – to be found in the whole crystal warehouse.

30.

Fire Sale, 1852

Winter arrived again. Life contracted. Despite having spent the summer season making eyes at every bachelor in London, not one of the girls had managed to convince anybody that the dowry-less daughters of a drowning novelist were a good investment. With William still in France, Fanny begged Mrs Touchet to organize a dinner, but even if Mrs Touchet had been inclined to do such a brazen thing, reading Dickens on the subject of 'Bloomerism' set her heart against Charles in a permanent way. For it turned out he didn't like the idea of his wife – or any woman – speaking in public:

> *Personally, we admit that our mind would be disturbed if our own*
> *domestic well-spring were to consider it necessary to entrench herself*
> *behind a small table ornamented with a water bottle and tumbler,*
> *and from that fortified position to hold forth to the public.*

'Oh, why do you ever read that thing if it annoys you so!' Fanny wanted to know. 'You are ruining our prospects!'

A terrible sentence almost escaped Mrs Touchet: *You* have *no prospects!* Instead, the shield of the Targe raised. She put down the latest issue of *Household Words* and proceeded in silence to her room. Whenever William was gone for long periods, these silences opened up inside her. She sometimes wondered about the boundaries of them. How far might a silence stretch? She imagined herself ready for a nunnery. A life of silent contemplation didn't frighten her, no, not any more. What petrified her was the endless twittering chatter you heard everywhere you went.

January 3rd, 1852

My Dearest Eliza,

 In Madrid I met a bumptious, talkative American — is there any other kind? — who announced the following: 'Paris is the better dressed, Rome by far the more beautiful, Berlin exceeds us in intellect and you must believe me when I tell you New York is the most exciting place on earth. What, then, does London have to recommend it?' I thought of you, and replied with great confidence: 'The people. In London, Sir, the people are <u>uncommonly interesting</u>!'

Sometimes stating the obvious has a beauty of its own. *The people of London are <u>uncommonly interesting</u>.* But were they as interesting as they once had been? One of the complications of managing decline was nostalgia. Now those dinners of the '30s looked golden to her, and all the annoying young literary men transformed into people she felt almost lucky to have known — Dickens notwithstanding. Even people she had actively despised at the time she now found herself recalling with sentimental fondness . . .

 It was in this self-deceiving mood that she took the bus to Kensington one pretty May morning, alighting just outside Gore House. She was not alone: hundreds of people had had the same idea, although whether their motivations were nostalgia, curiosity, *Schadenfreude* or the simple desire for a good deal she could have no idea. She wandered from room to room, fingering the little yellow paper price tags tied to everything, from the curtains to the harp, from the bust of Napoleon to the bookshelves themselves. It was the last day of the Blessington Fire Sale: she heard a cockney rag merchant tell an old Jew that twenty thousand people had trooped in and out since last Thursday. There was not much left of worth, just things too large, or too expensive, or too ugly or impractical. Mrs Touchet bought a little German porcelain of two negro children, one whispering to the other, entitled: *A DARK SECRET.*

31.

The Brighton Years, 1853–67

William came back from Europe with a copy of *Uncle Tom's Cabin* and the news that a move was in the offing. Emily made the mistake of mentioning Charles' recent move from Doughty Street to even grander Tavistock Square, forcing William to be explicit: 'I'm afraid our move will be in the other direction. Kensal Manor is now beyond us.' The other direction was south. Not even Mrs Touchet could have guessed how far south things would go. But when Brighton was announced, she sensed some relief in the girls. London was the scene of their failure.

Fourteen years they passed in that tall, narrow, white stucco house facing the sea. Looking back, she found it hard to make a proper accounting of the time. In the winters, a cold wind came off the sea and rattled the windows, but those waves of internal heat that had once overwhelmed her and turned her cheeks scarlet and soaked her bodice were by then long finished: now she felt every draught. In the summer, the laughter and screams of children penetrated the glass and went straight through her spine. In other words, her spinsterhood extended itself there, and three once-young women, with varying degrees of resistance, joined her in it. William meanwhile wrote about a flitch of bacon, Charles II, the Lord Mayor of London, Cardinal Pole, the Tower, again, and himself. They saw almost no one but each other. Loath as Mrs Touchet was to admit it, there was a certain sweetness in it. When she was young, she had wanted to know everyone, touch everyone, be everyone, go everywhere! Now she thought that if you truly loved – and were truly loved by! – two people in your lifetime you had every right to think yourself a Midas. And when the girls were off in town, and she and William took to their small balcony to watch the sun dazzle the sea – she felt rich.

32.

Grand Unions

When Anne-Blanche turned thirty-one, she amazed everyone at 5 Arundel Terrace by announcing that she intended to marry a Captain Francis Swanson of the Royal Artillery. The Captain had spent a furlough in Brighton the previous spring. Fanny and Emily were speechless. William laughed and promised her a flitch of bacon. The couple were married in August, in a little medieval village in Buckinghamshire called Hardmead, home of the Captain, where William had to be manhandled out of the ancient churchyard and into the ceremony, there being a prospective novel lurking on every headstone. The service was sparsely attended; Fanny and Emily wept throughout. Mrs Touchet had planned ahead, surreptitiously tearing the American news from the front page of *The Times*. At the very moment of Anne-Blanche's victory over all other women in her family, Mrs Touchet was happily ensconced in her pew, the news hidden in her hymnal, internally praying for the swift defeat of the Confederacy.

Perhaps it was not so strange that when she thought back to 'The Brighton Years', the event that stuck in her mind was not that wedding but another, far more public union, held a year later, at beautiful St Nicholas' Church, which happened to be Mrs Touchet's favourite spot in all of Brighton. She was not invited, but read in the paper that the wedding party would process along the seafront, just below her window. At ten in the morning, she and William took up their places on the top balcony, relegating Fanny and Emily to the balcony below:

'I see them!' Fanny had the furthest view round the bend. 'It is like Hyde Park all over again!'

Emily gasped: 'Surely they are clothed?'

Mrs Touchet did her best to look past her wards to the Queen's ward, the 'African Princess', whom the Queen, in her wisdom, had now married off to a Captain, not unlike Anne-Blanche's Captain, only so very much richer, and also—

'—So black! I am almost frightened.'

William leaned over the balcony rail: 'Emily, don't be absurd.'

There were ten beautiful broughams, pulled by ten greys. Miss Sara Ann Forbes Bonetta astounded Mrs Touchet: so upright in her carriage, her head turned towards the sea. She looked like a queen herself, surveying her dominions. Even more astounding was the wedding party, which had apparently been designed with symmetry in mind, like a piece of wallpaper. Eight English bridesmaids rode with eight African grooms. Then, behind them, in counterpoint, came eight African bridesmaids with eight Englishmen. Fanny and Emily were scandalized. William more philosophical:

'Our blessed Victoria in her wisdom rescued this poor child from slavery and certain death. Now this prosperous African fellow will keep her in those fancy crinolines. I say it is a well-done business. The End.'

Mrs Touchet sighed, retired from the balcony and sat back down with her newspaper. Only children think one person can ever wholly save another. Only children think marriage means: 'The End'. And meanwhile, thought Mrs Touchet, the Confederacy makes gains in Kentucky.

33.

A Trip to Manchester, Pancake Day 1863

Forced to step over a beggar on the corner of his own King Street, William looked over beseechingly at his cousin: 'Perhaps we should not have come, Lizzy . . .'

She had forgotten how much poverty alarmed him. She was better prepared for the sight of it herself: with no novels to write, she avidly followed the news. On the train she had already calculated that if eighty per cent of the cotton for Manchester came from the southern states, and cotton goods accounted for forty per cent of all British exports – and an even greater proportion of Manchester's own wealth – well, then it was very likely indeed that they were about to alight upon a scene of utter—

'Eliza, that man's face was half eaten away. He should not be out of doors with a face like that. And every other child from here to the station has been in rags. This visit is a mistake. I regret letting you talk me out of the Olney pancake race!'

She knew he had a 1745 novel somewhere in mind, and had used this fact ruthlessly in her manoeuvres, remembering and sending for an old book she had once bought for Crossley. It was an eyewitness account – written by an Edinburgh schoolmaster – concerning Bonnie Prince Charlie's journey from the peaks of Holyrood, to high hopes in Manchester, disappointment in Derby, and finally retreat and disaster at Culloden. William was delighted by a description of 'the mob's' first glimpse of the young claimant:

*He was a tall, slender young Man, about five Feet ten Inches high,
of a ruddy Complexion, high nosed, large rolling brown Eyes, long
visage, red-haired, but at the Time wore a pale Periwig. He was in
Highland Habit, had a blue Sash, wrought with Gold, that came
over his shoulder.*

Far less delightful were the desperate mobs on the streets of William's home town. The closed factories, the rail-thin women lined up outside every church and workhouse. The starving, barefoot children everywhere! Yet for Mrs Touchet, all of this was a sight in which Manchester might take some cautious pride. In Liverpool, they were flying Confederate flags. She tried to explain herself:

'It is the consequence of the embargo. The South wishes to send cotton here again and could, given their current progress – but Manchester holds firm. There was a public vote in the Free Trade Hall, just after Christmas. The workers refused. They will not use slave cotton. They will continue Lincoln's blockade, in solidarity with him – no matter the cost.'

'But the cost is evidently too high. What on earth is the purpose of adding misery to misery?'

'William, that is like saying: "What is the purpose of paying a debt?" Paying a debt brings nobody joy. Still, it is owed.'

'Eliza, in this country we have abolished the trade, the practice, the business itself. Our debt to the African is surely paid in full.'

Eliza felt her face go very red.

'And who does that accounting, exactly?'

William was on his knees, examining the lower beams of one of the few Elizabethan buildings left in town. Awkwardly, he turned his head and looked up at her with a face of pure befuddlement:

'Who does *what*?'

'How, precisely, are such infernal books to be balanced? What if our accounting falls woefully short? It may *indeed be* that three hundred years of torture and murder and bondage has no earthly—'

'If you are about to start speaking to me again of *he that taketh away my cloak* – I beg you to desist. Besides, you have your own coat on as far as I can see – unlike that poor soul.'

Mrs Touchet did not speak again until the shivering young man had passed them by.

'I am entirely familiar with my own failings, William. I meant only to speak in praise of the working people of Manchester. And to suggest that, perhaps, from the perspective of a vision further and deeper than yours or mine or any on this earth, such sacrifices may prove to be the very *least* we can do.'

William sighed, stood up and made note of a different kind of measurement in his little journal. 'Eliza, you have always tended to go the "whole hog", as Charles puts it. In my view, there's never any need to go the "whole hog". These things have a way of working themselves out, by the grace of that very God whom you so like to invoke. As a young man, I wrote a pamphlet on the topic.'

On the journey home, Mrs Touchet cast her mind back to that pamphlet. It had been called something like *An Enquiry on How Best to Bring Immediate Relief to the Operative Classes in the Manufacturing Districts.* He was twenty-one. It was written for Mr Ebers, Frances' father, who at that point ran a little magazine called the *Literary Souvenir.* William had sent it to Eliza, for her approval, but she was then only twenty-six, and almost as politically naive as her cousin. She had considered it a sentimental indulgence, for example, to weep for a distant, heathen people, labouring in a warm climate, who were, by all accounts, well housed and well fed. Particularly when so many British peasants were being driven from their ancient lands, left hungry and cold outdoors, or forced into the city workhouses. That there might be any correlation between these two miserable states had not yet occurred to her. Yet even in this relatively innocent state of mind she had found his pamphlet oddly unsatisfying. Charity: that was essentially the conclusion of William's enquiry. Good Christians with money should start relief funds for good Christians without money, and in this way the good Christian poor would be relieved. But she had already begun to suspect that her young cousin's primary interest in the poor might be, in fact, their bodies, liberated as they so often were from all those frustrating stays and corsets, bustles and stockings. Aged twenty-one, he was an inveterate pincher of maids' bottoms, and already swooning over sturdy, middle-aged cooks. And though he had usually been the master in their private, cousinly games – and she often enough the 'maid' – she must have been, in his mind, a maid with revolutionary plans, for it was always the master who had to get on his knees.

34.

Kenealy Sums Up, December 1873

Kenealy's summing-up lasted the entire month of December, and half-way into January. His defence hinged on an endless repetition of the Wapping affair. Would a fraud ever have done anything as stupid, as monumentally incriminating, as *dare* to go to Wapping, to visit the Ortons? This logic Sarah considered unassailable. Kenealy furiously defended himself against ridicule on the point, abusing in the strongest terms anyone in the court who attempted to query it. His battles with Cockburn were now daily. As she transcribed, it became clear to Mrs Touchet that the tables had turned. Kenealy now considered *himself* both victim and defendant:

Kenealy: I have been treated as no other counsel has ever been treated in Westminster Hall.

Cockburn: Because, sir, you have brought it on yourself. Counsel cannot be allowed to violate all the ordinary rules of the administration of justice, and outrage all the rules of propriety without calling down upon himself the censure of the bench.

Kenealy: I would not complain, had the censure been conveyed in different terms, but Your Lordship has used to me the most bitterly offensive language that could have been selected.

The Claimant meanwhile continued his doodling, apparently unmoved by the drama unfolding before him and because of him. She had heard from Henry that he was living in a terraced house in Rochester Square, leased by his many supporters, and with only a beloved pug dog for company. His wife and children had long since been farmed out to South London. With an extra hundred a year, thought Mrs Touchet, such a life might be my own!

In mid-February, the Claimant was seen to weep, and to be comforted by his constant companion, the young mulatto. It was assumed he had finally comprehended the dreadful position he was in. In *The Times* the next day, Mrs Touchet read that his pug, Mabel, had died.

35.

No Questions

Compared to Kenealy's marathon, Hawkins' two-week summation for the prosecution was brief and to the point. He took the moral angle. A vote for the Claimant was a strike against the honour of Kathryn 'Kattie' Doughty, and of all ladies. Butchers could not be permitted to claim to have known, in 'the biblical sense', women of aristocratic birth. Anyone who supported the Claimant's claim was, *de facto*, aligning themselves with a scoundrel, and there could then be *no question* that they, too, were therefore scoundrels. Mrs Touchet scanned the courtroom. No one wished to be aligned with a scoundrel, nor to be mistaken for one. The prosecution rested.

When she got home that evening, she had the smut of the city on her fingers and William was nowhere to be found. The house was almost dark: only the hallway lights still burned. On the ottoman he had left her some post, and the finished manuscript of *The Manchester Rebels of the Fatal '45*. It was in only three volumes, which made her happy, but was dedicated to Disraeli *with every sentiment of respect and admiration*, which made her sad. When was the last time they'd seen Disraeli? Under the book there was a letter, addressed to her, in a scrawled hand she did not recognize. She sat on the stairs and opened it.

Misses Touchit, madam we get this adress from the man Atkinson and humblee hope it gets where it is tended. We are two yung girls hard used by life madam. we rite to say our mama was one what was

*daughter of Mistr James that was your husband now ded. He setled
a living on mama but her mind was fill up with devils from the
hardnes of her lif and one day long ago she went away. We was put
at the home they call it Barnardoes but wish to stay no more. we
must go. they give us our papers and the name that is yours madam
and was the name of he who was our grandfather. Only you can help
us we are outdors and we rite this best we can madam!*

    Truly,

        Lizzie + Grace

Mrs Touchet's hand was shaking. Out of the envelope dropped
another, single sheet:

Mrs Touchet,

    *To my great surprise and dismay, the beneficiaries of your
husband's will have been ill-advised by unknown parties and now
make their claim. It is imperative that this matter is dealt with
privately and quickly. I am informed by the bank that you never
came forward to withdraw your money. I hope you will see the
necessity now of staking your claim before it is too late. To that end,
it is in my view still within your power to refuse and repulse these
two claimants. They are both under the age of majority. In order
however for the bequest to revert to you, the rightful widow, they
must make what mark they can on a fresh contract, witnessed by us
both. I am sorry to ask this of you but I must ask if the worst is to be
avoided. Please come to my office, tomorrow at midday,*

    Your servant,

        R. L. Atkinson

Mrs Touchet had long believed there was something in coincidence.
She could not say what, exactly. Something. The mirroring of feeling
or gesture, the echo of one thing in another. Fortuitous crossroads of

time and place. The doubling of victories, and collisions of defeat. She glanced up from Atkinson's letter to find William before her, with the same look of utter bewilderment she wore upon her own long face.

'I walked all the way to Hampstead Road, Lizzie. Full of purpose. Opened the gate, went up the front steps . . . There sat the old devil in his front room. I could see him through his bay window. But – he was not *our* Cruikshank, Lizzy. It was nothing like our George. Such a sad, old, frail man was sitting there!'

She was silent for a moment, disoriented to find her cousin's story colliding with her own, as if he thought his was the only one. Then irritation overcame her:

'Oh, good God, William! What did you expect? Time to have stood still?'

She spoke too harshly. William recoiled like a kicked dog, crumpled, and sat down on the step beside her, right on top of her letters.

'I really can't tell if he saw me or not. I froze. Then he walked out of the front room – and was gone.'

'But what did *you* do?'

William put his head in his hands.

Why did she ask so many questions?

Why did he ask so few?

36.

A Dark Secret

The next morning, she claimed to have a midday appointment on Harley Street. 'Feminine Troubles' remained a demigod in the Ainsworth home and met with no opposition or questions of any kind, ever. Approaching Cordwainers' Hall, she wondered if she was lying to tell the truth, like a novelist. It was no exaggeration to say that if a thorough bleeding or an amputation had been truly what lay ahead of her, she could not have felt any more dread or fear.

'Mrs Touchet. I am so sorry it has come to this. I knew of their existence but I never imagined they would be so bold.'

She felt Atkinson's breath on her neck as he opened the door. Three years of not seeing this man had not succeeded in tempering her loathing of him, and of all men of his kind. There are lawyers who combine the qualities of leech, prude, and hypocrite. Forever guarding and profiting from the borders between things – between people.

'Don't be disturbed, Mrs Touchet. They are not here; I have placed them securely in my colleague's office, across the hall. I thought it wise. Of course, the shock for a woman of your keen sensibility must be – well, how can we put it? *Profound.*'

And how ridiculous it is, thought Mrs Touchet, that old women should be famed as gossips! The worst gossips she knew on this earth were all men. She decided to cut Atkinson off at the pass:

'I do not wish to speak of the past. I only want to do what is right in this moment, Mr Atkinson.'

Atkinson raised his eyebrows and held the door open.

'If you look to your left, Mrs Touchet – discreetly, there, through the glass – you will see the two unfortunates. Their mother we know was a mulatto, and quite pale, or so I have been led to understand. But their father is not known, and as you can see, we have to assume the worst.'

They sat close together on a bench. In the mind of Mrs Touchet, Barnardo's conjured images of waifs and little matchstick girls. But here was a pair of hearty-looking girls, big-boned, with hair that pro-truded so far up from their scalps it disappeared above the border of the window and ended who knew where. They still had James' eyes and James' brows. Somebody else's broad back, limbs, nose and skin. Were they wearing sacks? Mrs Touchet looked to the floor. Lawyer Atkinson sighed and closed the door.

'They must have the money,' she said quickly. 'Everything that has accrued and whatever is to come. I will sign whatever is needed or required.'

Atkinson was aghast: 'Mrs Touchet, I beg you to consider—'

'I have considered. That is my decision.'

'If I may first – there are some complexities that may influence—'

'That is my decision. These "unfortunates" as you call them are young women who must now make their own way in this world.'

The lawyer Atkinson sighed again and took a seat behind his desk.

'That is the complication, madam. Despite appearances, they are not grown women at all. The elder is thirteen. The younger, eleven. In my view it is better to have nothing to do with them whatsoever than to begin obligations which may then obligate one further . . .'

Mrs Touchet sat down in the nearest chair.

'These are your husband's grandchildren. They are of course no relation of yours – no *blood* relation. You have every right to deny them like Judas. Still, they are presently out of doors with no real family or connections. And having learned of their lineage they have, I am afraid, developed certain unreasonable . . . expectations. But as it is of course impossible to *imagine* them in your own home, as your wards—'

Mrs Touchet visibly bristled. The lawyer Atkinson paused, appearing puzzled.

'Unless, Mrs Touchet, you have some idea of—?'

Mrs Touchet sat back in her chair, defeated. Atkinson could not say he was surprised. It was as he had supposed: imagination had its limits. Even the imagination of a woman of such notably keen sensibility as Mrs Touchet.

'But they simply *must* have the money,' she said, again, quietly.

Atkinson did his best estimation of a smile: 'That is very charitable of you, Mrs Touchet, I am sure. But a hundred pounds a year is a vertiginous amount to settle upon two unlettered and unsupervised girls who may not—'

'It was never my husband's money! Much less mine! It is Samuel Touchet's money! I do not wish to touch money that was earned as his money was! I tell you they must have it!'

The lawyer Atkinson now looked away, out of the window. Had this peculiar woman not lived off Touchet money these past forty years? But it was always best to save the blushes of a flustered client caught in the trap of her own conscience:

'Mr Samuel Touchet is certainly remembered here, in the City, as a man of parts. He converted much base material to gold, and was a very acute businessman, in his time. Although of course, in the end, his reach somewhat exceeded his grasp . . .' Women have euphemisms for their bodies, noted Mrs Touchet, where men reserve such barbarisms for matters of money. 'A terrible end. Amazing, really, that any inheritance should survive him at all!'

'Are the girls to come in to sign now, Mr Atkinson?'

The lawyer Atkinson, sensing the unmovable obstruction before him, nodded, rose from his chair and left the room, coming back a moment later with Lizzie and Grace. Mrs Touchet tried her best to comprehend it. *Could* these be children?

'Which one is Lizzie?'

She had asked this of Atkinson, who was preparing the papers, but it was the taller girl who answered. She was almost as tall as Mrs Touchet.

'I am Lizzie Betts, ma'am. This is my sister, Grace.'

'I am pleased to meet you both. Eliza is also my name. Grace as it happens was my mother's name. But perhaps your mother knew that . . .'

The sisters looked perplexed.

'Our mother is gone,' said Grace, finally, and began to weep. 'Where, I just don't know!'

In reply to this explosion of sentiment, nobody could think of anything whatsoever to say.

The lawyer Atkinson stepped between them with a pen in his hand:

'Thankfully, both can mark their names in tolerable fashion. They learned that much in Barnardo's at least – and something of Jesus, we hope. Though I maintain that they were helped with that letter. Girls, sign your names here and here, and thank the lady for her great generosity. And comprehend, I beg of you, that all relation between you and the aforementioned Mrs Touchet ends here and at this moment. Is that understood? Her debt to you is paid.'

Mrs Touchet still wanted to know why they wore sacks – flour sacks – as if they were dresses, but Atkinson peered severely at her over his half-moons and when he passed her the pen, mutely she took it.

'A hundred pounds a year,' announced the lawyer Atkinson, in the tone of a vicar solemnizing a wedding, 'is a sum beyond the dreams of many men and women on this blessed island. It is by extraordinary luck that it has been bestowed upon two such unlikely specimens as you girls. May you use it well and thank God for it – and keep Mrs Touchet in your prayers, for she is your benefactor.'

They did thank her, in quiet voices. A few minutes later a mortified Mrs Touchet found herself out on the streets of London once again. She hung her head. To have fallen so far short of what was required of her in the judgement of the only power that mattered to her! Walking alone, she reminded herself of Atkinson's mollifications. She had done 'as much as anyone could have'. She had gone 'above and beyond the call of duty'. She had walked out of the terrible office of that terrible man certainly no richer, and yet — at least by the accounting of a man like Atkinson — no poorer, either.

37.

The End

Endings are hard. Two days after Mrs Touchet visited the lawyer Atkinson, Lord Chief Justice Cockburn began his summing-up. Mrs Touchet could tell it was going to be an eight-volume affair because after a week this valiant man had got no further than Wagga Wagga. Sarah had always disliked Cockburn but the iron entered her soul when he got around to 'Sir Roger's' marriage: 'We know from his own statement that his wife was a domestic servant, that she was perfectly illiterate, being unable to read or write, and that to the marriage register she affixed only her mark . . . I think it right you should consider how far it is likely that Roger Tichborne would have formed such a union . . .'

Sarah drew her lips all the way into her mouth: 'He *does not* know what he's about.'

Who does? thought Mrs Touchet. What was the name of my husband's lover? Where did he meet her? In whose scullery? Where did they copulate? For how long did it—?

'And now, I have done,' said Justice Cockburn, twenty-eight days later. 'I have tried to discharge my duty. For your part, the verdict which you shall render will assuredly be received by all persons – *who are not either fools or fanatics* – as the judgement of twelve men who have brought vigilant attention and marked and remarkable intelligence to the consideration of this case.'

The italics were Mrs Touchet's, but the triumph all Cockburn's. He knew how to tell a story. Mrs Touchet was somewhat awed. It is hard enough to tell the story of one's own little life. How to tell the saga of other people's? And Sir Roger's tale was so long and so winding, so hard to condense – even into a month's narrative. Yet Cockburn had skilfully managed it, weaving all the strands together, braiding it tightly, and roping it, finally, around poor Arthur Orton's neck. A tragicomedy of obscene length, the whole trial had lasted almost a year, longer than any in the history of British law. Now the jury left the room. Thirty-three minutes later they returned. In the anticipation of it all, Sarah gripped her housekeeper's hand, so passionately, with so much fellow feeling, that Mrs Touchet felt almost a little sorry there would be no more ladies' outings . . .

But in the end, it didn't matter what the new Mrs Ainsworth or Mrs Touchet thought. Even the truth didn't matter. It was Cockburn's novel and he had written it. The Claimant, upon hearing the verdict, asked to speak and was refused. He reached out his hand to Kenealy, who shook it shamelessly, in front of everybody: 'Goodbye, Sir Roger – I am sorry for you!'

When the end came, it was in the form of a single, unambiguous sentence: 'Arthur Orton is sentenced to fourteen years.'

38.

Fools & Fanatics

It is remarkable, thought Mrs Touchet, how quickly a man of flesh and blood can become mere symbol. The last time anyone had seen the Tichborne Claimant he was being led down to the cells. But it was as if his physical absence now allowed his name to circulate more freely. In fresh newspapers and petitions, in songs and plays, novelizations and epic poems, the Claimant was everywhere and nowhere. A dizzying body of societies and pressure groups and literature sprung up in his defence, and these in their turn grew peculiar arms and legs, one of which went by the name of the KENEALY NATIONAL TESTIMONIAL FUND.

'But why is it "Kenealy" if it is for Tichborne?' William wanted to know.

'Because, husband, he stands for all us "so-called" *fools and fanatics*, and we stand for him! We ain't so foolish nor so fanatical as not to notice that a poor man can't get a fair tug of the tail in this godforsaken country! Never mind that they dis-benched and dis-barred the poor bastard, so he don't have a pot to piss in himself any longer!'

'Help me, Eliza. The fund is to keep our poor Kenealy out of the poorhouse?'

Mrs Touchet looked up from her darning.

'The fund I believe funds his many efforts on behalf of Tichborne, Bogle, and the people generally. He has started another newspaper – the *Englishman* – and I believe a political group: The Magna Charta Association.'

'Aims?'

A conspiratorial look of amusement passed between the cousins.

'Ah, many, many. Banning all taxes, I believe, bringing back the bill of rights, an honest press, fair representation of the people, um . . . no smallpox vaccinations for children, the defence of the aforementioned fools and fanatics – and, well, much petitioning for the release of you-know-who! The last was two hundred thousand signatures, William, if you can believe it.'

'The only petition I believe I would sign,' said Emily, with a pious look on her face, 'is one that got poor Black Bogle back his annuity. But that is my trouble. I am too soft-hearted.'

'There is nothing wrong with a soft heart, Emily,' said Mrs Touchet, dutifully, 'but I fear it will take more than a petition to help our Mr Bogle.'

Her cousin opened his eyes very wide, spreading many wrinkles at their corners. 'Every man alive seems these days to be sending a petition to Parliament about one thing and another. Meanwhile I sit scribbling at my desk . . .'

'That you do,' said Sarah, sighing, 'that you do, for what good it does you! There is a Kenealy meeting called the Great Indignation Meeting planned for next week in Barking. But I will be at the dressmaker and Barking is too far for anyone to travel, naturally. Otherwise I would.'

In this new, expanding world of Tichbornism, there existed a strange struggle in which Mrs Touchet's continuing commitment to the cause had to be constantly compared to Sarah's and found wanting, even if, in truth, the enthusiasm was waning in them both. Sarah was otherwise preoccupied with the Queen's endless mourning. Meanwhile, Mrs Touchet could be heard nightly scribbling at her little desk, though to what purpose nobody knew.

'Do you think you might attend, Eliza?'

Before Mrs Touchet could answer this, Fanny bent over her father and kissed him fondly on the forehead.

'We are glad of your scribbling,' she whispered.

39.

The Great Indignation Meeting!

The lion of freedom has come from his den
We will rally around him again and again!

Mrs Touchet recognized the cry from the old Chartist days. On the dais sat Kenealy, Andrew Bogle, a man she didn't recognize, and Mr Onslow, who seemed, to Mrs Touchet, much reduced in style and spirit, sat off to one side to allow Kenealy the central spot. The cheers were for Kenealy: the cause had a new leader. All around her, people held up new and strange signs:

Fools and Fanatics for Kenealy!
BELIEVE BLACK BOGLE
No Vaccine For The Poor Man's Child
I MARRIED A SERVANT

Everyone in the crowd had been passed a copy of the *Englishman*, every column of which, as far as she could tell, had been written by Kenealy himself. Waiting for the speeches to begin, she read one on 'Newspaper Lying'. Was it not suspicious – the author wanted to know – that the British papers should report endlessly on the birth of wastrel princes and princesses, but never did you hear a word about the Kenealy–Tichborne manifestations taking place all over the country? In Leicester, in Manchester, in Poole? But this enjoyable piece of anti-monarchism was hard followed, in the next column, by an anti-Catholic rant. Mrs Touchet folded up the *Englishman* and put it in her longest pocket.

'It is John De Morgan,' said Henry, as the unknown man rose to speak. 'He is head of the Tichborne Propaganda Release Union. He took a Tichborne petition to Parliament himself. You should listen to him, Mrs Touchet. He believes the land belongs to the people. He is a great one for the people.'

A funny little man. Ringlets and a face like some nervous woodland creature. If Sarah were here she would have said he looked like a beaver. But he spoke boldly and with a cohesion Mrs Touchet had never heard from Kenealy. From the question of the disputed Tichborne lands he moved elegantly to the land question *in genere,* and the question of the commons in particular. Who had a right to it? What was to become of it? What rights came to a man because of it? Or because of the absence of it? He moved Mrs Touchet to tears, quoting John Ball. *When Adam delved and Eve span, who was then the gentleman?*

The crowd roared at this, and thus encouraged, De Morgan told them a little of his own story. He was an Irishman, and a radical since childhood. He had begun the Cork branch of Marx's International Working Men's Association and was forced to leave Ireland for this reason. Citizen De Morgan was his name now, but any fool or fanatic was welcome to call him John!

Mrs Touchet almost lost her footing in the surge of crowd enthusiasm; Henry steadied her. On the dais, she noticed Kenealy shifting in his seat, his fists balled up on his knees. *The notorious German is not one of* his *prophets,* thought Mrs Touchet. Aloud she said: 'I fear the stage is not common land enough for two Cork men.'

But you couldn't make Henry laugh, not about anything. He frowned throughout Kenealy's speech — *I was born to be a king of men! My spirit has pre-existed for millions of years! In the form of a palpable being it has played many parts! I am as well assured of this as I can be of anything!* – and hung his head when it was finally over: 'That man is not sane. My poor father.'

Mr Bogle, overhearing, put an arthritic hand to his son's cheek:

'We have come this far, Henry. We will go on.'

After his father had spoken and the crowd began to disperse, Henry was eager to stay and speak further to De Morgan, in the hope of a new, saner avenue of support. Mr Bogle smiled gamely and leaned against a wall. There are things beneath the ken of young people.

'I will take your father home. He is in pain, Henry.'

Mrs Touchet flagged down a cab and withstood the look of amusement on the face of the driver. They sat next to each other, facing forward.

'What do you make of it all, Mr Bogle? Will he be released, do you think?'

Mr Bogle turned to her, still smiling. Their knees touched.

'It will be good for me if he is. It will be bad if he isn't. It is already quite bad. There is no more money.'

It was her chance to ask him what he really believed. But something in his smile made this impossible.

'And what will you *do* now, Mr Bogle?'

'Oh, I suppose I will do whatever I must do, Mrs Touchet. I will survive by any means necessary. It is what my people have always done, if you understand me.'

The phrase 'my people' silenced her for a moment, as it always did. But she thought she did understand him. His methods were, by necessity, obscure and underhand. They were like her own.

'Will we soon cross the river, Mrs Touchet?'

'Oh, no Mr Bogle, we are already north and therefore on the right side. Now we only have to head west . . .'

Who was she, really? Who were her people? The Ladies of Llangollen? But then there had been, and always was, William. And now this queer feeling for Bogle. She had played the dominant Bloomer with Frances, the feminine muse for William, and perhaps, in some imagined utopia, she could be met on even, common ground with a clever soul like Bogle, who seemed to live as she had always wished to, that is, with no illusions. What would it be like to have a name for all these various people and urges within herself? But Mrs Touchet was her name! She leaned out of the window to instruct the driver to go by way of King's Cross, then sat back against the velvet to finger the rosary in her pocket, and chide herself for excess pride. All of our names are only temporary, she reminded herself. Only notations for something beyond imagining. They can give shape to matters too big to be seen, but never can they wholly describe the mystery.

'I will tell you something, Mrs Touchet. I will *never* understand this city.' Across the street a cabbie had come down off his box to scream blue murder at a barrow boy he had only barely avoided hitting. 'If you step on somebody's foot, it's them that will say sorry to *you*. But if a carriage comes out of nowhere and almost kills you? Always it's the driver who is vexed!'

Mrs Touchet laughed her loud, unfeminine laugh. In another life, this uncommonly interesting man would have suited her very well. But we only get one life.

40.

After Hackney Downs,
11th December 1875

Even now that she lived so far outside of it, Mrs Touchet's London remained a very circumscribed place. The North she knew, and the West, but it was where they combined that she felt most at home. Anything East was a perfect mystery to her. To find herself on Hackney Downs, in a crowd of thirty thousand, ringed all around by the constabulary! But she had decided to do — with whatever time was left to her in this life — whatever she had not dared do when young. She went alone, to Hackney Downs. She went with the conviction that the Downs did not belong to Lord William Tyssen-Amherst, or any man, no matter how many fences and stakes were driven into it. It was *Lammas land*, common land, the people's land! And if the people were not to be allowed to make a living off it any longer, at least a nice park might be established, where nice old ladies might walk, as had already been achieved on Camberwell Green. This afternoon, though, she was very determined *not* to be a nice old lady. But what if the police proved firm in their resistance? Would she then revert to niceness? The police stepped back. Mrs Touchet joined her fellow Londoners in protest. She was a stake puller — a stake burner! What a story to tell!

'Henry, I must tell you I have never had such a feeling in my life as when De Morgan stood in front of us all and said — wait a minute, I wrote it down somewhere — yes — *the fences which you see before you have been erected in defiance of popular feeling, and rights of way are being stopped which have existed from time immemorial. In these circumstances the only remedy that remains for the people – the only means of getting back their rights – is to remove the fences without delay.* And then the people began to pull up the stakes! And our hands were black from it, Henry, for the Lord Tyssen in his wisdom tarred all the fences expressly to stop them being pulled. But we looked like minstrels! I wish you could have seen it! I walked all around and spoke to people, and I realized – oh, so many things. But I'm soaked through. Shall we have some tea?'

There was no tea. The cupboards had been bare for some time. The sound of his father groaning in pain could be heard in the other room. But he let the old woman pace up and down the small space to warm herself, and listened politely as she continued to speak animatedly of her many realizations, her travels through the crowd, her impression of the various speakers. She did not appear to understand that grazing rights meant far more to a poor man than the space for a walk. Nor that a city park, once fenced all around, was a place where a city council could then prohibit any gatherings of poor or agitating men. But it was not her political ideas or the lack of them that were of interest to Henry. It was her freedom. Her freedom of movement. And it was as she prattled on about the slow and steady expansion of the franchise, that he suddenly lost all worldly patience with her:

'Why do you think it within your power?'

'I beg your pardon?'

'Where does it come from? This power? To bestow freedom. Every Englishman I meet seems to think he has it.'

Mrs Touchet was astonished.

'But I am quite lacking in that quantity, Henry. I have no power. I also beg you to remember I am a Scot – and a woman! However: I am a Briton, as you are yourself. The power invested in Parliament surely concerns us both . . .'

'Parliament hands down the laws that govern us, yes. It cannot bestow freedom itself.'

Mrs Touchet was confused: 'All I intended to say was that I feel confident that the arguments I heard today, on the Downs, although at the moment only concerned with the enfranchisement of working men, will surely, in time—'

'Time!' The noun itself appeared to disgust him. 'Why should I wait for what is mine by sacred right? Who can give to me what was never theirs to possess?'

'I really can't think what you mean.'

'Mrs Touchet, my freedom is as fully my inheritance as it is any man's. It has no time, I need not wait for it, it was mine from the moment of my birth. Does it surprise you to hear me say so?'

'Well, for one thing you speak as if *my* freedom is perfect.'

'I know it is not. And where freedom is concerned, Mrs Touchet, I would advise you not to wait for others to present a false gift of it to you. You will be waiting a long time. Better to "take up arms against a sea of troubles, and by opposing, end them". I have more of my grandmother than my father in me, I'm told, and I'm glad of it. I've read my Spence and my Wedderburn. I know the land is mine as much as it is anyone's. So said Mr Spence and so it says in Leviticus, if it should come to that. As for my person, it is eternally my own possession. I need not fight for that right nor beg for it. Yet this is exactly the position in which my poor father and I now find ourselves – so cruelly penned in on every side. I know you are a busy woman and I can see other matters occupy you at present – But did you know the Tichbornes pursue us still? They command my father to change his story. They will drive him to his grave!'

Mrs Touchet raised her eyebrows, like a teacher surprised by a bright student.

'Henry, do you know the very first thing your father told me about you? That you were a very fine as well as a very fierce young man. How right he was! You are eloquent. Your education does you proud.'

Henry kicked a patch of sawdust on the floor, under which, Mrs Touchet feared, something worse than sawdust was hidden.

'My education! What has that to do with it? Is freedom to be earned like a – like a *school prize*?'

'Of course not. I only—'

'My father is a patient man, Mrs Touchet. I am not. And no trick or bargain or exchange or fraud or meek Christian hope will win for me what is mine in God's sight and in my own. For it was ALWAYS MINE.'

Mrs Touchet, alarmed at the strident pitch of the conversation, lowered herself into the only chair and assumed a philosophic pose at the table while still clinging to her umbrella. Only to find herself babbling:

'I am still not sure I quite follow . . . That is, what you say may be true, in the realm of pure thought, and in the rarefied air of heaven, but in practice we are all, as you rightly say, "penned in" . . . And these are precisely the earthly binds right-thinking people attempt to loosen. Through argument, through public opinion, through revelation directed at the human heart – if it can be accessed – and finally through the law, without which—'

'But it is not the prisoner's right to open his cell that is in question, Mrs Touchet! It is *the gaoler's fraud in claiming to hold a man prisoner in the first place*. The first is self-evident. The second wholly criminal. By God, don't you see that what young men hunger for today is not "improvement" or "charity" or any of the watchwords of your Ladies' Societies. They hunger for truth! For truth itself! For justice!'

Mrs Touchet was very stung and, for a moment, lost for words. And then, beneath the sting, a disconcerting shadow moved.

'How dramatically you speak, Henry! You remind me that you are a young man, really very young. I spoke in similar tones when I was your age. But I hope that now, with the clearer view of maturity, I can claim at least some experience in these matters. I know this country well. Well enough to understand that justice takes time, and that the freedoms of a minority are rarely self-evident to the majority. What is perfectly self-evident to God is – unfortunately! – too often obscure or invisible to his flawed creations. The minds of men move peculiarly slowly. Those of Englishmen in particular. Parliament itself moves slowly! And if it were not for the patience and persistence of—'

'Justice has no time, Mrs Touchet! It is eternal, it is now, it is yesterday, it is tomorrow. Every man branded like cattle feels that pain infinitely: it echoes across all time and all space. Joan of Arc still burns. The poor soul bound hand and foot and thrown from the *Zong* still sinks to the bottom of the sea, along with five hundred more just like him, and they all drown eternally. I tell you that those who suffer *cannot wait*. No more can I. And I confess that I am not one of these people who believe it makes so great a difference if the gaoler speaks softly to his prisoner or throws a stone at him. What *really* matters—'

'Then God have pity on you! It makes all the difference in the world. We sin by degrees, as we do everything else. Otherwise, why ameliorate, why attempt anything at all? That would be the counsel of despair. Let us not make the perfect the enemy of the good. For in the meantime, our souls hang in the balance. And in the gap between the present moment and some future moral perfection surely all we have—'

But before she could finish the boy laughed! *Bitterly*, was the word that came into her mind, *the boy laughed bitterly*, and threw his head back, his eyes flashing *like lightning*, his wedge of hair horrible and huge in the candlelight, altogether reminiscent of one of William's more preposterous creations: a callous Duke, perhaps, or a Jacobite solider, or an amoral highwayman.

'As if it could possibly be the *state of my gaoler's soul* that is my proper concern! No, that cannot be my concern, Mrs Touchet. Only the cell concerns me. The illegitimate cell. And I say that any man or woman,' declaimed Henry Bogle, more like a seasoned speaker stumping from the balcony than a poor boy with a dirt floor beneath his feet, 'I say whoever sees and comprehends the truth of this illegitimacy MUST reveal it, it is essential that he does, that he make it his life's work, with every breath that he takes, and for every moment that he's alive, from now until Domesday. Such is the battle of life! Such is the daily war of all men who love justice and know the truth!'

As he loomed over her, Mrs Touchet was still able to note three things. Firstly, that there was no longer any 'she' in the coursing river of his speech, no more 'man or woman' – now there was only 'he'. Secondly: her face was wet, she was shaking. Thirdly, that this essential and daily battle of life he had described was one she could no more envisage living herself than she could imagine crossing the Atlantic Ocean in a hot air balloon.

41.

A Pauper's Burial, 1877

The first she knew of it was from Clara, but the message emerged garbled.

'Mrs Touchet, Mother says that a friend of yours has died. I am very sorry for you. She read it in the paper.'

Sarah was in Horsham, shopping. Clara could not say which paper it was, when it had arrived, or what kind of a friend it might have been. Mrs Touchet embarked on a process of elimination:

'Did he ever come here?'

'No one comes here.'

'A writer?'

'I don't know any writers except Papa.'

Mrs Touchet had to hang out of her garret window looking up and down the high street until she saw a clutch of too-yellow ringlets bouncing around on one side of the bus. She ran into the street, overturning Sarah's tower of packages.

'Why must you always go the whole hog, Mrs Touchet! Can't you wait till a woman's in her own home? It's Mr Bogle. Poor Mr Bogle over in King's Cross. And after all that, not a penny was raised for the poor bugger. He lies unmarked in the cold ground, God rest his soul.'

Mrs Touchet fell to her knees and wept.

42.

A Coincidence on a Train

He was always sympathetic and kind with young people. An instance, which happened about this same time, has been related to me by Miss Arabella Kenealy, the distinguished novelist. On one occasion, Miss Kenealy, when quite a young girl, was travelling on the railway near Brighton. An old lady and gentleman got into her carriage, and their talk concerned books, various works by Ainsworth being mentioned. Miss Kenealy, remembering certain criticisms she had heard on *Jack Sheppard*, felt constrained to join in the conversation, and remarked that she thought Ainsworth's books were of an injurious tendency and likely to have a bad influence on the young. Whereupon, 'the old gentleman' – to continue in Miss Kenealy's own words – 'smiled in a kind and amused fashion upon the young and eager person with ideas who ventured to express opinions upon so large a question. He said it was pleasing to meet one so young who had also intelligent views on something more than the mere story in a book, although the verdict was not favourable as to the tendency of certain works. He did not tell me who he was. It was his friend who – greatly to my horror – intimated his identity.' It was indeed the author of *Jack Sheppard* himself with whom Miss Kenealy had been conversing; but he bore his young critic no malice, talked much to her, and saw her into another train later in the journey. Miss Kenealy adds, 'On reaching home, I at once sought out Mr. Ainsworth's portrait and recognized it. He had, I think, too much kind tact to have revealed himself after I had committed myself to those opinions concerning his books.' Ainsworth never knew that the heroine of this amusing adventure was the daughter of his old friend and magazine coadjutor of thirty years before: Dr. E. V. Kenealy.

– From *William Harrison Ainsworth and his Friends*,
by S. M. Ellis, Volume II

43.

Up & Away

A loud thud came from downstairs. Later, in the memory, Eliza claimed to have known exactly what it was at the moment that she heard it. *But did you? Is that true?* A proud empiricist, she liked to ask herself such questions. Twenty years earlier she could have answered them. She had better understood, back then, how to separate body from mind, fact from desire, the truth from false memory. She had still believed it could be done.

Now she rose from her seat, hurried down the hall and the stairs to his study, and found her cousin there, collapsed on the floor. She might no longer be certain about truth, but she recognized Death. He had arrived somewhat awkwardly, curling William's legs up into his chest like a child, and throwing an arm over his eyes. She knew her cousin had never cared to think himself a figure in another man's story – much less a woman's – but in this moment it was unavoidable: she was his only witness and mourner. She knelt down and held his hand. More than thirty years had passed since she'd last held it, or held it down, so that with her other hand she might enter him, and hear that gratifying, boyish gasp. Now it was the hand of an old man. The double callouses – on the second and third fingers, where the pen had rested – were ugly and pronounced. All is change. All is loss. *Is he making fun of me, Lizzie?*

So much of life is delusion. Each attempt to make a crossing, every high-altitude ambition that any person might conceive of in this world – all of it falls eventually, inevitably, at His feet, and comes to nothing. But she couldn't help it: she had wanted to live! Although she had always known – ever since she was a very small girl – that this desire was not a properly feminine aspiration, nor perhaps even godly. She wanted to live. To make her own attempt at life, on her own terms, and to defend the attempts of others, be they ever so poor, forgotten, debased, despised! Some people live for love, or for work, or for their children. Eliza Touchet had lived for an idea: freedom. And when her own time came, yes, when she herself lay dead, very likely in this same room, she could at least leave this world safe in the knowledge that—

It was in the middle of this internal oration that Eliza remembered that the manuscript of *The Fraud* lay revealed on her dressing table upstairs, liberated from its usual hiding place: a stack of blotting paper. Her own name was on the title page. Vanity, but it had given her a little pleasure each night to look at it before going to bed. The list of potential pseudonyms was tucked in a posy of lavender, in the right-hand drawer.

Edward Trewes

Edmund Turner

Eliot Tavistock

Panicking for a moment, she dithered in a manner quite unlike herself: standing and kneeling and standing again. But why? William was gone. Her own dear William. The only person who had ever really known her, and therefore the only one from whom it had been worth keeping secrets. She knelt back down. She allowed herself to look one last time at that sweet mouth, still pink, cherubic, full of pleasure, though surrounded now by a goatish grey beard. An animal sound filled the room, like the scream of a fox. She put a fist deep in her mouth in an attempt to control it. *The only one who ever really knew her?* She could hear footsteps on the stair. She tried to staunch the tears with a handkerchief, sat back on her heels, laced her fingers together. Old tricks. They no longer worked. How could she have lived so long and thought so hard and yet have understood so little! What was this intolerable feeling? Love? She had been avoiding it for so long she had forgotten how painful it truly is.

Looking down, she saw she had soaked the collar of her own dress. Soon the door would open. She had only a few moments left in which to adopt the proper stance of the Targe: saddened by her dear cousin's death, of course, but already turning to practical matters, like the will. Whose house was this now? Who would inherit these books, this desk, these pens? Who would write in this study? She moved the arm that covered his eyes, and was horrified to find them wide open. *My William!* He seemed to be looking directly at this weeping woman bent over him, his forehead fixed in an expression of affectionate, puzzled interest, as if considering her for a character:

The mysteries of Mrs Touchet were, finally, unfathomable.

Afterword

William Harrison Ainsworth died in 1882, aged seventy-six, and was buried in All Souls Cemetery, Kensal Green, not far from several old friends, acquaintances and enemies – including George Cruikshank. In his lifetime he published forty-one novels, many of them wildly successful. (*Jack Sheppard* really did outsell *Oliver Twist*.) A hundred years later not a one remained in print.

The Claimant was released in 1884, having spent ten years in jail. He'd lost a considerable amount of weight by then, and almost all of the support of the British people. Eleven years later he took payment from a newspaper in exchange for admitting that he was indeed Arthur Orton – but soon retracted his confession. He died in 1898, destitute, and is buried in a pauper's grave, in Paddington Cemetery, just off Willesden Lane. Something in this strange man's death reignited a sentimental nostalgia in the public: five thousand people attended his funeral. The Tichbornes even allowed a name card to be laid atop the coffin, with *Sir Roger Charles Doughty Tichborne* inscribed upon it. The grave itself is unmarked.

Henry Bogle had eleven children with an Englishwoman, all of whom survived. England must therefore be dotted with Bogles, although few of them can be aware of the connection. We are lucky to have a little of Andrew Bogle's narrative genius preserved in the newspaper transcriptions of the two Tichborne trials. The small selection of them that I have reproduced are quoted *verbatim*.

Arabella Kenealy, daughter of Edward Kenealy, became a medic, a racial eugenicist, a prominent anti-feminist and novelist, writing over twenty novels, many of them about the importance of the sex difference. After a long career of radicalism, John De Morgan ended up in America writing dime-store African adventure novels for the teen market.

Mrs Touchet – a woman always partly phantasmagoric – extends herself far beyond her earthly span here: in reality, she died before her cousin, on the 4th of February 1869, just before William moved to Hurstpierpoint. She, too, is buried in All Souls, Kensal Green, although her grave is entirely obscured by a huge, impassable, spiky thicket of bramble. In 2009, her 1842 edition of *A Christmas Carol*, signed to 'Mrs Touchet', became the most expensive Dickens title ever sold at auction.

The second Mrs Ainsworth, hidden in life, continued her obscurity into death. Her daughter, Clara Rose, lived till eighty-three, ending up – as melancholy people often do – by the sea, in Torquay, where she died intestate in 1952. Ainsworth's only surviving child, she did not become his legally recognized daughter until the passing of the Legitimacy Act of 1926, when she was fifty-eight years old. On the 12th of April 1954, she makes a ghostly reappearance in Lancaster Chancery Court, where an enquiry was made as to the existence of any next of kin. Clara's estate was by then worth just over a thousand pounds. It is not known who, if anyone, inherited it.

Acknowledgements

This novel is loosely based on the life of William Harrison Ainsworth (1805–82). Few historians have considered his life worthy of consideration, but I am indebted to three literary scholars who did: S. M. Ellis, George J. Worth and Stephen Carver. Andrew Bogle was born on the Hope Estate, in Saint Andrew, Jamaica. *Hope Transformed: A Historical Sketch of the Hope Landscape 1660–1960*, by Veront M. Satchell, proved essential in the imagining of his life. As did Rohan McWilliam's *The Tichborne Claimant: A Victorian Sensation* and Robyn Kinnear's *The Man Who Lost Himself.* I am especially grateful to Dr Phyllis Weliver, a brilliant scholar of the Victorian period, and a great, close reader of *The Fraud*.